Romeo and Juliet

A Modern Day Sequel

James Edwards

Romeo Publishing Company

Author's Note:

This novel is a work of fiction. Names, characters, places, and incidents either are products of the imagination or are fictitious. Any resemblance to actual persons, living or dead, events, or locales is entirely coincidental. Trademarks belong to their respective holders.

First Edition: August 2007

ISBN: 978-0-6151-4730-7

Romeo Publishing Company
www.romeopublishing.com

Dedicated to star-crossed lovers everywhere.

Romeo Awakens

Why I descend into this bed of death,
Is partly to behold my lady's face.

- Romeo

Romeo Montague awoke curled in a vast cold desert with harsh gusting winds dancing around him — and all he loved was Juliet. The air was thin and cool, the ground a caked, muddy volcanic maze, stretching outwards into a vast mesa before him.

"I am a murderer," he muttered in a hoarse, dry voice. He stared at his bloody hands and remembered everything. His powerful, short-lived love affair with Juliet Capulet — Juliet, so young, beautiful, and confident, her hair marvelously smooth and long and how it glistened below the Mediterranean moonlight, which came down like a divine liquid, bathing them both and her parent's orchard in an otherworldly light.

He recalled his own tragic death and the terrible crime of murdering the good Count Paris. Mysteriously now, he felt no pain from his self-inflicted knife wound. His flight into death seemed to have happened just a few minutes ago, or maybe an hour at most. Yet for some reason, lying on this cold unfamiliar plateau felt comfortable to him. He wondered why Juliet wasn't at his side and felt that all too familiar lover's pain in his gut. Romeo felt something close to betrayal also.

"Isn't that what love is all about? When two lovers die together, don't they travel to some better place?" he asked a nonexistent audience, gazing up at the cloudy cold sky, half expecting an answer. After all, he was dead — wasn't anything possible?

Well, not in my case, he realized, as only silence answered him. Cold, indifferent winds ruffled his hair as they ran eternally across the silver blue sky pushing clouds briskly by — shifting images, like the memories of his life in Italy, racing fast but fading into the distance.

Romeo lay still. There was no sign of Juliet; worse yet, no sense of her in his mind's eye. He felt something had gone terribly wrong. *Why isn't she here with me in the afterlife?*

Another nagging mystery for Romeo was that he didn't feel dead. Apparently he had been granted a new life under these fast moving clouds. As to why his beloved wife hadn't joined him in death, he felt that question would be answered in time. His thoughts roamed back to Italy and their beautiful wedding night. Their plans for a new life, full of adventure, passion, and love had seemed so certain. *All cut off in death!* he lamented. He had been flung into a desperate land.

Young Romeo stood up and brushed the dark volcanic dust from his black wool suit. Drops of Paris' blood stained his clothing, but had dried in the strong wind. He leaned forward into the blowing gusts and began to walk.

He was at the base of a snowcapped peak of unimaginable height. *Maybe one of the Alps,* he reasoned a*nd beyond them is fair Verona, where Juliet lies — still in her family morgue.* Yet, a feeling radiated from the cold, snowy summit, which told him even if he could cross into Verona, somehow everything had changed. Verona felt like a dream and Juliet was dead. Who knew where she was in this vast creation?

"Well," he admitted to himself, "You got what you expected, a new life." He lifted his head to the sky and laughed. He had once been certain Juliet's love would transform him forever; instead, his own poison-tipped knife had been the agent of change in the dark morgue of the Capulet's. After finding Juliet there, lifeless, how could he have chosen any other fate? He had to follow his lovely wife into death.

Romeo felt watched now, as he strode forward, as if his love for Juliet was respected by the angels in heaven. They now looked over him, maybe with no more than mild curiosity or amusement, but they did watch and listen.

Maybe I am not dead, he speculated. *Maybe, I lie in some Apothecary, while a doctor tries to stay my self-inflicted knife wound. If that is true*, he deduced, *this current experience is a dream and this cold plateau, nothing more than the jumbled stuff between my ears.*

"If I am lying in some Apothecary, wake me. Hurry and heal me," he joked to the sky, laughing, shuffling forward against the wind.

Romeo imagined waking in Verona and suddenly the most unbearable emptiness hit him — he thought of life without Juliet. To survive his knife wound, knowing his angel had died for him, would be a pain too great to endure.

"Oh God no, I can't go back! That would be hell," he now pleaded into the wind.

A cold gust buffeted his body, as if in agreement. The wind soothed him, for there was no pain in it, no judgment, only the constant blowing sounds of eternity, roaring in the vast silent spaces he trod.

"Oh, dear God in heaven, keep me here," he prayed. "I couldn't go back without her!"

He scanned the horizon with his eyes and blinked, trying to make his current world more real. He was on a high plateau and breathing was hard. Having been to Mantua and then the Alps as a child, he knew how high he was. He noticed the edge of a vast pine forest in the distance and started for it.

As he hiked forward, he turned again and watched the fiery sun set against the snowcapped peak behind him. He walked faster now, atop his lengthening shadow, realizing he needed shelter; for if this wasn't a dream, his body would soon require warmth and nourishment.

As he moved closer to the forest's perimeter, a mist crawled on the black volcanic floor and surrounded him. He noticed more than pine trees in front of him. Huge ferns and flowers of unimaginable beauty began to dot the volcanic landscape. *How could these things grow in such a high place?* he marveled. *I am surely in another world.*

Suddenly, he heard a roaring sound above him and ducked instinctively. He looked up and saw a shiny object flying very high. It seemed more machine than bird. He thought of Juliet again. *What if she is trapped inside one of those things?* he wondered irrationally, ducking into the relative protection of the forest's dense canopy.

The rain forest was thick and maneuvering was difficult. Darkness had crept in between the ferns, as the sun set behind him. The sky became dark blue as he wandered deeper into the jungle's cool glades. Songbirds filled the air with a beautiful sunset symphony. Some of their calls Romeo recognized, birds that flew the world's trade winds, yet others were foreign to his ears. He was surely not in the Alps. *Maybe I am in Africa*, he pondered. A gentle mist began to fall.

His wool suit held up well against the moisture; yet Romeo knew it would soon be drenched. The chirping of crickets filled the jungle as darkness surrounded him. He could tell he was moving downward in elevation. The tall forest had effectively cut off the harsh winds of the barren plateau, but the temperature was falling fast. As night gathered, a cold rain began to fall.

Romeo struggled forward, frightened — not knowing where he was or even if there was even a civilization to find. He realized, with irony, he never expected to be fighting for his life after dying. Somehow, he knew he was. The thought made him feel more alive.

He stumbled into a huge fern. The wet plant seemed to grab him. He struggled to his feet, trying not to panic in the darkness. There was no moon to guide him, no beautiful full moon — like the one he and Juliet enjoyed less than a fortnight ago, when he had climbed her family's walls.

Not light, but darkness, a voice told him. Romeo realized he would injure himself soon if he continued further; so he stopped to rest, huddling at the base of a mighty tree to keep himself dry. It grew deathly cold and he grew very tired ... .

~

*E*ha I ka 'eha lima 'ole a ke aloha, a female voice echoed, far above the tall Ohia trees. Romeo was startled awake by the sound and began to shiver uncontrollably in the cold rain.

E hea I ke kanaka e komo maloko e hanai ai a hewa ka waha, another voice spoke in a deep, angry tone. The sound impossibly came from the tall branches of the large tree he was huddled under.

Haole Ki Kolea, the first voice spoke loudly, but from a different angle.

5

Ho'ona ke ola I ka hale o ke akua! the second voice shot back, closer to Romeo now.

He could tell they were arguing — maybe over him. *I am surely in hell,* he reasoned. *After all, I murdered Tybalt and Paris. These demons will probably rip me from limb to limb.* He shivered in the darkness, accepting his fate.

The rain quickly tapered off and everything became silent. Romeo convinced himself the etheric female sounds had only been a hallucination. He knew he had to stay awake so he pulled himself closer in his drenched wedding suit. Dozing off and imagining nonsensical babble in the trees had saved his life; although, he was still cold and hungry and dawn was nowhere in sight.

He sat up, leaning against the large trunk to stay awake. To his shock, before his eyes, was a glowing white hem of a gown, floating above the wet ground. It was dry and impeccably clean. He looked up at the impossible visage and beheld a tan woman with white shimming hair, reflecting against the rising moon.

Yes, Romeo surmised, *this is the afterlife. She is an angel taking me to my judgment. Maybe I can be with Juliet after all, even if in eternal hell. I wish ....*

"GET UP, HAOLE BOY!" the woman commanded impatiently, looking down at him with disdain. She appeared translucent, supernatural. Her alluring bronze skin and ancient white hair exuded a magnetic warmth.

"Get up," she uttered again, with a distant gaze. "Do not stare at me! I should stare at you. You are not from this land — I am!"

Romeo struggled to his feet. Even though it was growing colder, standing before this apparition warmed him.

"Don't look at me, haole! You're lucky my sister Pele' wants to keep you alive."

Romeo didn't know what to say. Aside from her strange accent, the angel did speak his language.

"I am lost," he began. "I woke in this world and am looking for a young woman named Juliet."

The goddess tilted her head back and laughed, a deep cackle that echoed throughout the dark jungle. Romeo noticed the clouds parting above him. Bright stars dotted the sky. The temperature continued to drop and he shivered.

"I think, haole boy, you are looking for my cabin, my fireplace," the woman remarked, with a distant smile.

"Please help me," Romeo pleaded. "I don't know why I am here."

Again, as if he was a comedian playing for a captive audience, the tall woman in white laughed loudly to the sky. A gentle wind lifted her long hair. Suddenly, she was silent again and looked piercingly at him.

"Oh Romeo, Oh Romeo, wherefore art thou? Do any of us know why we are on this world — I don't." She then paused and looked up, longingly, at the streaming Milky Way, as if her home was in the stars.

"How do you know my name?" Romeo asked, as politely as he could.

"Everyone knows your name, Romeo — and the name of your Juliet," the woman replied with a playful smile.

Romeo abruptly rose and moved toward her, almost threateningly. "Do you know where my wife is?" he desperately asked.

Again, the mysterious woman laughed to the sky. She then turned from him and began to walk downward through the dark thick jungle. "I don't care about you or your wife. But I do know of a warm fire I'd like to lead you to, haole boy — so you won't die."

Romeo sensed she was luring him somewhere, for something. He shivered and watched her bare feet as she walked, gliding above the uneven ground of the jungle. He realized he had no choice but to follow this magical woman. He wanted to live. He wanted to find his wife, Juliet Montague.

After a few miles of stumbling forward under the old moon, Romeo found himself facing a small wooden cottage set in a clearing of grass. He was breathing hard and had fallen many times, barely keeping up with the mysterious figure he chased. To his amazement, the woman in white walked through the cottage door without opening it.

"Oh my God, she is a ghost!" he exclaimed. He wanted to run. But before he could turn, the apparition opened the door from inside.

"Don't mind me. Come inside," she said in a surly voice. "It's winter in Hawai'i. You will not survive the night."

He coughed and shivered again. The shock of meeting this mesmerizing woman made him forget he was drenched, freezing to death. He bravely walked to the cottage door and entered her abode.

"You may call me Leheau," she remarked, stepping aside as he entered, motioning him toward a small chair by the fireplace. On the other side of the room was a scuffed wooden counter with carefully arranged rocks, feathers, and fruit.

"Let me take off your wet clothing," she reassured him, as he stood dripping and shaking. She was as tall as him and very beautiful, but in a distant, cold way. Leheau approached slowly and began to unbutton his drenched wool suit.

Romeo began to stutter, but could not speak. A warm fire had sprung up in the small fireplace. *When was that lit?* he dreamily wondered.

"I ... I ... I don't know what you are doing," he stammered, as Leheau's hands began to caress his shoulders and muscular chest. She was obviously aroused.

"You don't have to know anything, Romeo," the woman whispered, as she ran her smooth hands against his face. "I am seducing you. Normally I would kill you." She laughed, kissing him hard and deep. She then moved back, sensing his confusion, and poured him some hot tea that had been hanging by the fireplace.

"I am a guardian being," she explained as she handed him a smooth clay cup. "We guard the inter-dimensional doorways of this land, Hawai'i. You are on an island in your future. Sometimes humans try to leave this world from the high plateau you woke on." She tilted her head and gestured in the direction from where he had come. "But they have to get past me first," she added, with a cold smile.

"You have confounded us, Romeo. You came from the freedom of the void into this darkening world. You are like a man climbing prison walls to get *into* prison. We have never seen this before," she reflected.

"You must love this Juliet," she said softly, in a low, almost envious tone. She pressed her body against Romeo's. He felt her large breasts swell against his chest.

"I ... I ... can't," he weakly protested, becoming aroused.

"You like what you see, don't you?" Leheau asked with a cunning grin. She ripped off his shirt and pushed him onto a white fur-skin rug by the raging fire. Soon both were wrestling naked and he was inside of her, feeling that warmth he needed so, feeling alive again. Sparks flew out in every direction from the fireplace. Romeo felt one singe his black Italian hair as he moaned with wild satisfaction.

~

He awoke late the next morning curled up on Leheau's white rug as he had the day before on the cold volcanic plateau above him. The fireplace was empty, no ashes, no sign a fire had been lit at all. *Maybe it was a dream,* he wondered.

It wasn't a dream, Romeo had to admit. He suddenly felt a deep pain within his heart; he had betrayed Juliet once again. He had been with another woman on the very day they had died together for their love! *The gods are toying with me,* he realized. *So this is what a murderer faces after death.*

Romeo stood up naked, his stomach growling. He looked around and grabbed an apple on the counter. There was no sign of Leheau. He bit into the fruit, and paused, hearing the melodious call of songbirds outside the cottage. Peering out a small window, he beheld a perfect blue sky. Ferns and tall trees swayed happily in the morning sun. The same dark treacherous forest that had almost killed him last night was now a beautiful green paradise. The warm light of the morning gave him hope. He was reminded of Eden. The smell of the clear air and wet grass telling him, he was still on Earth.

But where on Earth? he asked. *And in what time?*

He noticed Leheau had left his clothes hanging neatly by the fireplace and ran his hand against the smooth dry wool. The warm, civilized feel of the fabric reminded him of Juliet. A tear came to his eye. He had killed himself to escape this pain — the hell of separation from his beloved angel. Now he understood how foolish suicide was, for the pain was still very real. He struggled to gain his composure as he dressed. *God, how I miss her already!* he lamented.

Romeo knew he had only so many hours of daylight to find his way through the endless jungle. He noticed a leather water bag, hanging from a wooden rafter of the cottage roof. It dripped cold beads of liquid onto the old wooden floor. Maybe Leheau had left it for him. He saw a large leaf attached to the strap of the flask. On it, he noticed beautiful white script that seemed burnt into the dark green matter:

Romeo, beware of Cousin Tybalt. He will strike when you least expect it … .

He was shocked. *How does this spirit know so much about me?* The ominous warning made sense though, he sadly realized. Maybe Tybalt had awoken a few days earlier on the same plateau. Yet something told him that Tybalt, Juliet, and all the old components of his life were very far away.

He walked outside and secured the leather canteen to his belt. *God this place is beautiful,* he marveled, as he stepped into the tall green grasses of Hawaii. The forest loomed high in every direction and beckoned him into its beautiful green matrix.

He searched for a trail and started down what looked like one. It was hardly a trail at all, and disappeared into the dense jungle. He needed to walk fast and cover many miles. If Leheau was right and he was on an island, his lungs told him he was still very high. *Civilization must be far below,* he reasoned. Romeo slung his coat over his shoulder and worked his way through the thick bush, hoping the barely discernible path would lead him somewhere and not peter out — like everything else had in his short life.

Romeo Becomes a Monk

Why rail'st thou on thy birth, the heaven, and earth?
Since birth, and heaven, and earth,
all three do meet in thee at once.

- Friar Laurence

Romeo hiked through the morning jungle, feeling pressed in by the thick foliage and still very lost. The trail was difficult to follow and cut downward like a green canyon through the lush walls of Stag ferns and Ohia trees. Tropical birds cawed at his approach and gossiped in the distance. The Hawaiian sun beat fiercely against his black wool suit and sweat poured from his brow as he made his way ever lower in elevation.

He took off his vest and neatly tucked it in his pocket. He heard the same distant roar that sounded last evening. Squinting toward the sky, he saw a silvery metallic shape glittering far above him. It moved quickly across the glaring horizon. The object appeared small — but being a natural at mathematics — Romeo knew it had to be large.

Maybe Leheau is telling the truth and this is the future, he reasoned. Perhaps far above him was a huge flying machine. He had always dreamed of becoming an inventor, so the idea didn't bother him.

If this is Earth's future, he pondered, *what future am I blindly walking into? Is Juliet in this world?*

What if she doesn't remember me? He pushed the unwelcome question from his head and walked more determinedly. Hours passed. Finally he was greeted by a cool welcoming breeze that brushed against his face and the refreshing sound of cascading water. He picked up his pace and heard the quick-running sound of a stream. Suddenly the trail broke through the jungle and to his right he saw a beautiful waterfall lazily cascading down a hard, rocky slope.

The rain forest parted and revealed to Romeo an endless blue ocean far below him. He inhaled the salty sea air, lifted high by the trade winds, then knelt by the fast moving stream, filled his leather water bag, and continued his march forward. The dense forest canopy covered him again, hiding his amazing vantage point.

"Hawai'i," he uttered the sound slowly. "I must be on an island," he exclaimed to the exotic birds around him, leaning back to taste a cool sip of water.

"Ahh … almost as good as the Alps," he commented and turned his attention back to the quickly descending trail.

He walked steadily for hours on end. The noon sun became the afternoon sun, as it fiercely tilted above him. He removed his shirt to let the warm rays bake his brown skin. As the trail wound downward, the beauty of the surroundings almost seemed too perfect. *Is this Heaven?* he wondered. *If so, how could a murderer like myself be sent to such a paradise? I surely have penance to do … .*

He finally grew tired as the steady sun finally sneaked behind the tall Ohia trees. He flexed his toes. His feet were beginning to stiffen and a few blisters had developed. The ground became moister, the ferns not as thick. From time to time he would pass beautiful mossy meadows. He did not stop to rest, though. Something told him he would not survive another night in this magical forest.

While deep in his thoughts, the trail suddenly broke open into an immense field encircled by mighty trees. A dirt road led to a small ranch house in the distance. The entire spacious property was surrounded by a white fence. Well-groomed horses trotted in the immaculately manicured grasses of the yard. A small black dog barked as Romeo approached cautiously. He heard the rhythmic sound of someone chopping wood.

Walking to the sound, Romeo saw a short, strong man holding an ax, concentrating intently on each graceful stroke. As he advanced, the small dog ran to him, barking and nipping at his ankles.

"Moses, come back here! We know him." A stern voice commanded. Moses ignored his master and continued to yelp, as if Romeo were a ghost.

The man stopped chopping wood and sighed, as if bored. He turned to Romeo and smiled. Romeo could tell he was older, a man from the Orient. His black robe seemed monkish, reminding Romeo of Friar Lawrence.

"Greetings, good sir," Romeo began, bowing slightly.

"Greetings to you!" the man replied heartily, grinning. He noticed Romeo's dirty face and laughed. It was a good laugh though, with no malice in it.

"I am Zen Master Lee, at your service," he formally began and bowed. "I have been waiting for you."

"Thank you sir, my name is Romeo. How did you know I was coming?" he asked, wondering if Master Lee was a spirit like Leheau.

"Romeo," Master Lee considered the name with a smile and bowed again. "We have never met before; so don't be alarmed. I am not a ghost," he said reassuringly, as if reading the young man's thoughts. "I simply felt during *zazen* this morning that I would meet someone today, someone who came from far away. So I stayed here, chopped wood and carried water. You already wasted most of my afternoon!" he finished gruffly, but winked at Romeo with a smile.

"What is zazen?" Romeo asked, curiously.

"Meditation, *Romeo!*" Master Lee shot back, emphasizing his name, as if it was funny or infamous to everyone.

"What is it about my name, sir?" Romeo politely asked.

"Everyone knows who Romeo is," Master Lee declared. "And I see that you are really him!" The Zen Master peered deeply into his eyes, grunted, then quickly turned and crossed his arms, in seeming disapproval.

"Master Lee, I know I am not alive, but I am hungry," he pleaded to the turned figure. "I know I am a murderer," he continued weakly and gulped, "but I am tired." He lowered his head, as Master Lee remained motionless.

"I have killed two people out of my own passion," Romeo confessed, as he would have done to Friar Lawrence. "I killed my beloved wife's own blood, Tybalt. I slay the good Count Paris in her family morgue. Please, if my love for Juliet has led me to hell, take me there now!"

"Ha! Ha!" Master Lee bellowed, and turned in merriment, as if Romeo had told them the funniest joke ever.

"Did you hear that one, Moses? He wants me to lead him to Hell!" Master Lee laughed again. Moses yapped loudly in merriment.

"Young man that was the best Zen joke I've heard in a while!" Master Lee remarked, as he carefully studied Romeo. A profound silence surrounded them.

"I know I am not alive!" he pleaded to the man in black before him.

Master Lee tilted his head to the sky and laughed harder. He remarked, "Now that, son, was a great koan!"

"I know I am not alive!" Master Lee repeated and giggled. He looked seriously at Romeo and frowned again. "You met Leheau up there, didn't you?" He motioned to the vast rain forest rising beyond his ranch.

"Yes I did," Romeo admitted.

"You're a fool. You're lucky she didn't kill you. Why did she send you to me?" he asked rudely, pondering his own question.

"I, I ..." Romeo stuttered, feeling a little insulted. "Sir ... Master Lee, I know I am dead! Why must you taunt me?"

"Huh?" Master Lee looked offended. He shocked Romeo by slapping him in the face.

"How dare you! I am a Zen Master," he started harshly. "I am beyond the wheel of birth and death. I have taught in Egypt, Tibet, Japan, and many other worlds. I taunt no one!"

The Zen Master began to glow and took on a supernatural visage. A golden light radiated from his head in a perfect circle, reminding Romeo of the saints. *He is an angel from heaven*, Romeo marveled, awestruck. Master Lee smiled as a great lightness and warmth radiated from him. It accepted Romeo Montague, murderer, adulterer, and the man who had caused the death of his wife, Juliet. Romeo, not knowing why, collapsed at the feet of the Zen Master and began to sob.

"Get up!" Master Lee commanded harshly, in a gruff accent. He continued to speak firmly to young Romeo. "You are too dramatic! You're so Hollywood! I remember this about you in every lifetime!"

"I need your help," Romeo muttered with his head hung low. "I also need to find my wife ... ."

"Ha!" Master Lee retorted sharply. "You need your wife — that's why you are a murderer! Your attachment has caused you suffering," he explained, factually.

"I know it has," Romeo sadly agreed. Master Lee had just articulated the sum of his feelings. "Please help me," he begged again.

Master Lee carefully studied the young man before him. "Humph," he muttered and turned abruptly away again, crossing his muscular arms. It felt to Romeo like the gods were deciding his fate and the Zen Master simply awaited their decision.

"Finish chopping the wood and stack it perfectly!" Master Lee commanded gruffly, as if disappointed by fate's choice to keep Romeo around.

"Yes, Master Lee," Romeo answered eagerly, feeling alive again. In this vast, mysterious creation, he had found a sense of belonging — of worth — even though his part in this modern world was only to chop wood for an evening meal, it was a start. Romeo had returned to his Earth.

~

Across the globe in England, a little girl in her father's garden imagined her prince from afar. He loved her endlessly and would someday come to protect her from all the bad things in the world. Of course, they would live happily ever after. The girl smiled — she could feel her prince out there now.

"Emilie, come in now. It's time for breakfast," her mother's voice called, breaking her out of her reverie.

"Yes, Mother. I am so happy. My prince has come to rescue me!"

"That's nice, darling."

~

After eating dinner, Romeo slept by the fireplace on the cold hardwood floor. The next morning he awoke to the sounds and smells of scrambled eggs, rice, and hot tea. Master Lee said very little, but was kind, treating Romeo like a lost child.

Romeo started to sit for breakfast. He was still hungry from his ordeal. "No!" Master Lee said sharply. Romeo stiffened. "Do not sit for a meal before bowing."

Romeo bowed.

"Good, sit down and eat. My monks will teach you the rest," Master Lee chuckled and continued to cook.

The next few days seemed like a pleasant dream to Romeo. Although he was no closer to finding Juliet, he felt a familiarity with Master Lee's ways and realized he needed this man to teach him about the modern world. Romeo, the murderer, had been granted a second chance and wanted to make the most of it. The Zen Master worked him hard. He chopped wood, carried old buckets of water from a well, and cleaned the stables of the small ranch that existed on the edge of the great rain forest.

Master Lee began to teach him martial arts. "Martial arts strengthen the mind," he explained and bowed. It was late afternoon and Romeo was dirty. He had worked hard all day and just been skillfully thrown by Master Lee near the woodpile where they had met.

"In a real fight, I would rather have a good rapier," Romeo asserted, rising wearily and brushing himself off.

"Oh really?" Master Lee asked playfully, challenging him. He motioned to a wooden sword resting against the house.

"Take it Romeo," Master Lee suggested.

Romeo picked up the sword. It looked more like cutlass to him, much wider than his father's swords. Suddenly, an image of his best friend Mercutio bleeding to death flashed through his mind. Mercutio had died because of Romeo and Juliet. Days later, Romeo had senselessly killed Count Paris, a kinsman of Mercutio. A shudder went through him and his hands froze. The blood of Paris had washed away with the first Hawaiian rains, but would stain him forever.

As if reading his mind, Master Lee barked, "Don't think of the past! It's all gone! There is only this moment. Now strike me!"

Romeo half-heartedly swung the sword in a graceful arc toward Master Lee's neck, vowing never to fight again.

"No!" Master Lee shouted, whirling forward at amazing speed. He snatched the sword from Romeo and pressed it painfully into the young man's neck. Master Lee let off the pressure and backed away.

"Never pull your punches," Master Lee advised and bowed. He proffered the sword to Romeo. "Either be peaceful — or fight to win. Take responsibility for your actions. You should have refused to hit me when I asked. Instead you wasted my time with your half-assed swing."

"Now hit me hard and fast with this *bokken* or I will kill you," Master Lee commanded in an ominous tone, bowing. The formalness of his threat made Romeo uneasy.

Romeo gripped the wooden sword. Less than a fortnight ago, he had been making love to Juliet, now he was a stranger in a strange land. Maybe he was in hell and Master Lee was a demon after all. He would find out. He would hit this old man, knock him out, or maybe even kill him; furious now, he didn't care which.

He wheeled fast, for he was fast, and swung the heavy sword at blinding speed toward Master Lee's neck. The Zen Master, instead of moving quickly, simply tilted ever so slightly. The blade brushed him gently as if he were a lover Romeo had caressed with a feather. In an instant, Master Lee slid in toward Romeo — somehow following the sword's blow backward. Without knowing how it happened, Romeo found himself on the hard ground looking up at the old teacher, who was smiling down at him.

"That was pretty good," Master Lee remarked, giggling like a little boy. "I've been trying to get someone to hit me that fast for a long time," he confessed and offered Romeo a hand.

"My students never swing that hard," he complained. "You wanted to kill me, didn't you?"

"I was angry ... but not at you, sir ... at my situation," Romeo confessed rising, embarrassed.

"Self-pity is not the way of Zen Buddhism," Master Lee said, studying Romeo's downcast eyes. "But since you tried to strike me with your best effort, it is my gesture to return the favor." Master Lee paused. "I am going to send you to New York City."

Romeo smiled. He had wanted to go into town for days. Master Lee was the only real person he had seen in this new world. "I would enjoy that very much, Master Lee. I would love to ride into this *New York* city with you." he exclaimed and smiled. "Shall I prepare your horses for our journey?" he asked formally.

The Zen Master laughed hard to the sky and Romeo didn't know why.

~

The warm fireplace sparked as Master Lee studied Romeo intently. They both sipped tea. A few days had passed since he had offered to send Romeo to New York City.

"Romeo, the world is not like you left it. New York City is going to frighten and overwhelm you," Master Lee began. "This is your last night in Hawaii. You are going to have to make it on your own and grow up — finally," he added cuttingly.

"I understand," Romeo said. "I will not be afraid of cars or airplanes, I assure you."

Master Lee laughed. "It will not be the cars and airplanes that will challenge you — it will be the people. There are so many more on earth and the pace of things is much faster than when you left."

"I promise to do well as a Zen student in New York City," Romeo declared and suddenly thought of Juliet again. *Maybe she is in New York City.*

"I know you are thinking of Juliet," Master Lee observed.

"How do you know?"

"Your eyes become sad whenever you do. You must love her very much," Master Lee remarked. He then became silent and looked away, maybe deep in his own memories of lost love.

"I do love her, Master Lee!" Romeo exclaimed, passionately.

"Juliet is dead," Master Lee bluntly informed him. The pale image of her, as she lay by Paris, flashed through Romeo's mind.

"But ... ."

"But nothing," Master Lee cut him off and continued. "At the moment

22

of death, she let go as one should. You clung to her and chased her through the void. Somehow your awareness wasn't shattered at death. You followed her outside of time and space and wound up here in an energy vortex in Hawaii."

Master Lee grinned at Romeo, playfully and continued. "It must have been those Egyptian lives." He smiled and winked. "You just slid between the worlds, didn't you? A Tibetan Yogi would have given anything for your chance," he remarked cryptically. "You could have attained enlightenment; but instead you chased a girl!" Master Lee sighed dramatically, feigning disappointment.

"I don't know ... Master Lee ... of these things you are talking about," Romeo stammered awkwardly, puzzled.

"Never mind. You're a young soul." Master Lee sighed and brushed off the topic with his hand. "Do you have any questions for me? Tomorrow you leave for New York City. You will be just another novice monk at a Zen Center. No one will understand you."

"I have two questions," Romeo replied.

"Well?"

"I don't know how to explain this, but I don't think I am speaking Italian," he confessed in the most reasonable voice he could muster.

Master Lee chuckled and sipped more tea. He slapped his thigh. "Yes, you are speaking English."

"English!" Romeo gasped, astonished. "That is a language of barbarians! How could I be?"

"I don't know. Maybe in a parallel universe you had a life here in Hawaii as an English speaking person. We have multiple selves and there are many worlds. Life is very big. In Zen, we really don't care about answers to questions like why we are here; we simply acknowledge anything is possible."

"What is your other question?" Master Lee asked seriously.

Romeo glanced toward the bookshelf in the hallway. The Zen Master gave him a knowing smile.

"Well," Romeo began shyly, "I haven't touched your book collection, of course, but I can't help but notice the title *Romeo and Juliet* among them."

"Oh, so you're getting a big ego because someone wrote about your pathetic love affair," Master Lee joked and patted Romeo on the shoulder.

"What's your question?"

"Should I read *Romeo and Juliet*?" he boldly asked.

Master Lee paused and considered. "No, you should not, not for many years, at least — not until it is time," he finished and closed his eyes in deep reflection.

"How will I know it is time?" Romeo asked

"You will not be afraid to read it."

The old Zen Master and the young Italian remained motionless, absorbed in their own thoughts as the fire flickered. Finally, Master Lee bowed and went to his room. Romeo slept on the bare wooden floor, for the last time in his life, within the tranquil safety of Master Lee's warm abode.

~

The next morning after breakfast, Romeo bravely stepped into a white metallic horseless carriage that had driven up to the ranch. He knew it was a car. This car shined more brightly than any manufactured object he had ever seen. He crouched into the vehicle and was greeted by a tall, beautiful woman with long sandy blonde hair. She was deeply tanned with emerald green eyes and shapely long legs. Master Lee told him she was a Zen monk. Romeo had never met a female monk before.

He figured out how to close his door and watched Master Lee bow ever so slightly as the automobile started. He watched amazed, as the woman operated the delicate controls of the machine, moving them backward then forward again, at great speed, onto a dirt road by the ranch.

"So your name's Romeo, right?" The woman asked and smiled, as if the name was funny.

"Yes it is. You are very beautiful. May I ask what is your name?" Romeo inquired, genuinely attracted to this woman.

"My name is Judy Grace," she answered. "And you can cut out the beautiful talk, *Romeo*. I'm engaged to the head of our Zen Center in New York, Roshi Jeff Garrity." She continued to smile at him.

"I am sorry, Judy. I meant no offense." he tried a Zen bow, but was awkwardly seated, which made bowing impossible.

"Romeo?" Judy asked, with a sarcastic smile, as Romeo bounced up and down to the rocky ride.

"Yes?" he inquired, gripping the side of his seat. He so wanted to be accepted in this new world and Judy was the first normal person he had met.

"Do you know how to use a seatbelt?" she asked.

"What is a seatbelt?"

Judy laughed kindly then slowed to a stop. Eventually, they both made it to New York City.

The Zen of Romeo

Call me but love, and I'll be new baptized;
Henceforth I never will be Romeo.

- Romeo

Zen Roshi Jeff Garrity thoughtfully looked over the group of students as they folded their bamboo mats and returned them to the corner of the immaculately clean zendo. *The sessin went well tonight,* he reflected, content with his meditation class. Amidst the pain and confusion of New York City, the Zen Center was a sanctuary for people who needed some measure of peace and solace in their lives. Jeff knew it wasn't Buddhist philosophy that usually attracted the forlorn faces to sit and listen to a dharma talk. No, it was simply that the Zendo was a temporary oasis from the hectic insanity of the big city.

Once in a while he would get a bright-eyed student who was actually interested in Zen. Jeff looked at one such individual now whose name was Romeo — of all names. Romeo was different from the other Zen students though; he seemed so out of place in New York. The young man had actually spent a week with Jeff's Zen Master at his private ranch in Hawaii. Jeff was almost jealous of that; still something about Romeo bespoke of tragedy; maybe it was the name.

Roshi Jeff recalled Master Lee's phone call last week, instructing him to

27

hire lawyers in the United States and Italy to create identification papers for this mysterious young Italian named *Romeo*. Jeff became uneasy when Master Lee had all but suggested Romeo would need false papers to stay in America.

"Roshi Jeff, I feel your concern," Master Lee had abruptly stated.

"Yes, Sensei" Jeff admitted, surprising himself, since he was not one to argue with a Zen Master.

"Sometimes it is the dharma to, shall we say, follow a higher law," Master Lee explained. "This young man needs our help, Roshi. You and Romeo were actually best friends in ancient Egypt," Master Lee revealed amicably, to win his senior instructor over.

"I will do what you say, Sensei," Jeff agreed and added, "I will help Romeo in any way I can. After all, we are friends," he joked.

"Good, Roshi," Master Lee said, delighted.

Jeff now watched Romeo stacking the chairs in the empty zendo. It was early evening and all the other students had left for whatever lives they led. He reasoned the kid couldn't be much older than eighteen, if that. He looked trim and fit, yet very lost.

"Romeo," Jeff began, in a kind but stern tone.

"Yes, Roshi," Romeo approached him and bowed. He had been at the Zen Center a week and had picked up the etiquette very fast. Jeff knew his young charge was eager to be accepted because he had nowhere else to go.

"You do not need to call me Roshi when the Zen *sessin* is over. Call me Jeff."

"Yes Jeff," Romeo answered, bowing again.

28

"Romeo," Jeff began, "would you like to have dinner with me and Judy tonight? Her cousin is in town, and Judy tells me she is very beautiful." To his surprise, Romeo lowered his head in sadness. "Did I say something wrong?" Jeff asked, hoping to learn more about the awkward young man.

"No Roshi ... I mean Jeff," Romeo answered, looking up slowly, using all his will to push out whatever emotion Jeff's invitation had triggered. "I will join you for dinner," he finally replied. "But Roshi, know this — I cannot fall in love with anyone."

Romeo's tragedy is love! Jeff realized. *Well, the name fits*, he joked to himself.

"Master Lee teaches that romantic love is an illusion. Did you know that?" Jeff inquired, hoping to comfort Romeo from whatever tragedy had befallen him.

"No I did not." Romeo perked up, genuinely interested.

"Well then, you have a lot of Buddhism to learn. Sweep the floor and be ready for dinner in one hour," Jeff instructed and turned toward his personal quarters.

"Yes Roshi ... I mean Jeff," Romeo replied, bowing. He liked the rituals of Zen, but everything else about it still seemed foreign.

"Roshi Jeff?" Romeo blurted out, almost unconsciously.

"Yes Romeo?" Jeff turned.

Romeo paused for a moment. "I hope romantic love is an illusion. I really do."

Jeff became speechless. For an instant, Romeo looked mythical to him. He felt he was face-to-face with Romeo Montague of Shakespeare's play — the young man whose love for Juliet was legendary. The stunned Roshi experienced vertigo and had to concentrate to regain his composure.

Romeo bowed his head in embarrassment and grabbed a broom by the wall. Without knowing what to say, Jeff watched the forlorn kid carefully sweep the zendo floor. *There is something very unique about Romeo,* he admitted. He could feel why Master Lee wanted to help the kid — and now resolved to do the same.

~

Seven years passed quickly for Romeo Montague. The students of the Zen Center taught him how to type and Jeff sent him to word-processing school. Soon he began to work as a temp in Manhattan. Jeff and Judy helped him rent his first apartment and taught him Zen and Buddhism.

The First Noble Truth of Buddhism is that all of life contains suffering. "Therefore," Roshi Jeff taught Romeo, "one should not indulge in self-pity."

The Second Noble Truth of Buddhism tells us that suffering is caused by attachment. This was Romeo's favorite truth. He lived that hell, still attached to his wife Juliet.

The Third Noble Truth of Buddhism describes a state beyond suffering, *nirvana*. This concept was difficult for Romeo to grasp at first. Yet, as he practiced zazen meditation he began to sense there was something else.

The Fourth Noble Truth of Buddhism consists of instructions on the right way of living and Romeo grew to love the simple Zen lifestyle. He was an exiled monk now, living a quiet life after his personal tragedy with Juliet. He volunteered for every possible job at the Zen Center, knowing he had penance to do.

He enrolled in night school so he could learn more about the modern world and get his diploma. He then attended computer school, as Master Lee suggested, since he was a whiz at math. As the years passed, he began to work with complex mathematical software on Wall Street. He even dated a few women. Jeff Garrity could see that Romeo had been a bit of a player before whatever tragedy had befallen him. He noticed Romeo's relationships never seemed to last though, and the quiet handsome Italian preferred to spend most of his time alone.

~

One thing Romeo did love was fencing. He met Jeff at the fencing club every week. Fencing was the only thing in the confusion of Manhattan that connected him to his old life in Italy.

"Romeo!" Jeff exclaimed across the lobby of the club.

Romeo was drinking from a cold metallic fountain after winning a small informal tournament. Jeff approached and patted him on the back.

"That was a brilliant win! Your style is so strange!"

"It's not strange to me. Your styles are strange," Romeo grinned and motioned with his hand to the large lobby. "They seem inefficient and largely for show," he remarked critically. "A good swordsman from my village could beat anyone here."

Suddenly, Romeo thought of Mercutio, his best friend. Mercutio had been a great sword fighter. He realized how much he missed his friend from Italy who was a lot like Jeff Garrity. Mercutio had died because of his foolish encounter with Juliet's cousin Tybalt.

A plague o' both your houses!

Roshi Jeff sensed Romeo's mood change. "Romeo, I didn't mean anything by that remark. Maybe 'strange' is not the word. Your style is deceptively simple, that's all," he reassured him.

"Yes ... Roshi," Romeo murmured. "You reminded me of an old friend."

"Was he a great fencer?" Jeff asked, hoping to find out something about Romeo's hidden past.

"Yes he was," Romeo replied, walking across the lobby with Jeff.

"What was his name?"

William Shakespeare suddenly popped into Romeo's mind. *Maybe dear Mercutio made it into the play*. Master Lee had admonished him never to tell anyone of his past. If he did, the Zen Master warned, Romeo might find himself locked up in a mental hospital.

"Jeff, that, I cannot tell you," Romeo explained, apologetically.

"That's fine," Jeff answered reassuringly, hoping to lighten the conversation. "After all, Zen Buddhism is about living in the moment and realizing the past does not exist."

"Yes Roshi, that is why I like it so," Romeo agreed, coming out of the lobby and onto the busy sidewalk traffic of Manhattan.

Enjoying the late afternoon sun, the two Zen monks strode briskly up Fifth Avenue to meet Jeff's wife Judy for dinner at the Avalon Bar and Grill. Executives were hurrying home with suit jackets slung over them like matador's capes; young couples were enjoying themselves, as taxis raced past the sidewalks, frantically stopping to pick up rush hour commuters.

"So," Jeff began, as they continued north, "What happened to that woman from Brooklyn you were dating?"

"Well," Romeo began, "She accused me of being distant and not loving her … ." His voice tapered off, as a loud bus halted beside them, screeching and belching smoke.

"Well, did you love her?" Jeff yelled over the sound, hoping to drive the Zen point home that all love was attachment — yet compassion is necessary in this world.

Romeo began seriously: "True love is powerful. I think if I loved this woman you would know. I can tell you love Judy, because you would die for her," he added cryptically, but with admiration.

Jeff was speechless. He had never thought of love in terms of death. For Roshi Jeff, love was something to make life better, to remedy the loneliness of the big city, or maybe the basis to start a family. Romeo's razor-sharp definition hit home because Jeff knew, if it came down to it, he would die for his wife Judy.

"Romeo, you never cease to amaze me," Jeff finally responded, as they stopped at a crowded intersection. "I never heard of love defined that way."

"I never heard of it either, Roshi," Romeo said with a touch of sadness. He lowered his head, perhaps he was about to say something more, maybe reveal to Jeff the story of his tragic past. But the light turned green and they continued their trek in silence.

~

"There she is!" Jeff exclaimed over the loud music. Inside the Avalon Bar and Grill, it was crowded and confused. Romeo finally spotted Judy sitting by herself at the far side of the room. He followed Jeff across the busy center of the restaurant. The beautiful people of New York City had all come out to party. The noise, the crowds, and confusion of the modern world were still a little too much for Romeo. He quickly made his way for a chair by the wall, directly across from Jeff and his wife.

"Hello darling, how was your day?" Jeff asked, kissing Judy on the cheek and sitting.

"Great," she answered, distracted, quickly glancing to her left at a shadowy table in the corner. "Darling," she whispered to her husband playfully, "That's Johnny Perfection over there!" Judy pointed.

Suddenly Romeo experienced déjà vu. At the far end of the restaurant he saw a brooding man, sitting all by his lonesome at a large table, downing a glass of Black Label whiskey. *It's the movie star Johnny Perfection*, he told himself .

Romeo Montague's hand instinctively went for his sword, as if he were again in Verona, confronting the enemy of his family — the Capulets. He felt an irrational loathing for this stranger. The actor's silhouette reminded him very much of cousin Tybalt, the man who had started the downfall of Romeo and Juliet.

"I think you are right darling; that's him." Jeff broke Romeo out of his trance.

Romeo sensed that his Roshi, on some level, was also threatened by the actor. Romeo enjoyed cinema very much. It was one of the few beautiful things of the modern age. Still, he never understood the obsession people had for movie stars. As he looked around the restaurant, he could see this madness everywhere.

Patrons shot glances of adulation at Johnny Perfection, as if he was their prince. The actor had a personal waiter behind him, probably hoping for a huge tip. Romeo was reminded of how the common people of Europe acted around nobility when they dined together (on rare occasions). He began to dislike this Johnny Perfection more.

"Romeo, don't stare! It's not polite," Judy scolded him playfully.

"What?" he asked blandly, still staring. He slowly turned toward Judy confused.

"I didn't think you would be the star-struck type," Jeff quipped, protectively holding his wife's hand, as if Johnny Perfection might requisition her for a night's pleasure.

Maybe I am star-struck, Romeo wondered, as he looked again at the man drinking in shadows. The famous actor had mysteriously transported him back almost eight hundred years — to all the bad memories that ultimately lead to this moment.

"Roshi Jeff," Romeo began formally. Judy was smiling at them. "I promise never to be star-struck again — it's silly." He looked down and opened his menu.

"I agree, Romeo," Jeff said.

Judy glanced at the actor one last time and then smiled at both men. "I agree with you guys too; but he is very handsome!"

Jeff and Judy laughed and kissed. *Yes, they are truly in love,* Romeo observed, wistfully. The waiter came and the three of them ordered a lavish meal.

~

Jeff's right arm was around Judy's waist, as the three of them huddled in front of the Zen Center. After their sumptuous meal they decided not to take a taxi, but instead strolled uptown through the windy autumn streets.

"Romeo?" Jeff began.

"Yes Roshi," Romeo replied. They had become best friends, but Romeo still liked calling him Roshi.

"Are you going to the Utah meditation retreat next week with Master Lee?" he asked, turning to unlock the front doors of the Zen Center.

"Yes I am."

"Well, Judy and I will not be going. Master Lee instructed us to stay here and keep the Center open," he announced, looking a little disappointed.

"I will tell you both what happened," Romeo promised and bowed slightly.

"Goodnight, Romeo," Jeff replied, unlocking the door of the Zendo. "And have a good trip if I don't see you before then."

"Yes, be safe," Judy added. Later, she wondered why she had said that.

~

"I'm taking you all to the end of time. My *chi* has opened up doorways in this desert," Master Lee announced. He stood fiercely in the dark, speaking to a semi-circle of Zen students who had driven far into a canyon then hiked deep down a gorge to meditate with their teacher under a full moon.

"The forces that protect this power spot are here with us. They will be here long after the human race is gone," Master Lee added. Romeo could see an immaculate golden aura around his teacher, filling the darkness of the desert with a heavenly glow.

"Romeo knows about places like this," Master Lee suddenly remarked. He looked down at Romeo, who sat cross-legged in the dark with the other Zen students.

"I found him wandering in a place just like this, looking for his Juliet," he joked to his captive audience.

Everyone laughed and Romeo smiled, embarrassed. He was not a senior monk and the Zen Master rarely engaged him as he did the older students. His teacher kicked a pebble and looked at Romeo again.

"So Romeo, are you still searching for Juliet?"

Romeo considered the question. "Not really," he answered truthfully. Everyone giggled.

"Not really," Master Lee echoed, playfully. He continued, "Well, you should search for her!"

The Zen Master scanned the group of monks seated before him. "You guys think love is an illusion, since the Buddha taught only enlightenment is worthwhile and this world is full of suffering and sadness."

Master Lee knelt in the sand and continued. "That is where you make your mistake. Enlightenment exists in relationships, in material success, in all the things of this world, as much as it exists out here in the wind, in the emptiness of this place — Samsara is Nirvana." Master Lee reminded everyone, leaning back, looking up at the stars.

"Running away from your desires only brings you closer to them," he remarked and glanced knowingly at Romeo. The Zen Master then rose to his feet again in one graceful motion.

"The world sees the play *Romeo and Juliet* as a tragedy," he stated. "From my point of view — it's beautiful. Their love for each other, consider its purity. Consider what they went through for each other. What happened in the physical world was illusion, but the love between them transcended time itself!" he glanced at Romeo and smiled approvingly.

"The tale of Romeo and Juliet is about the power of love. It is not a tragedy. Maybe it would have been a tragedy if they had ended up married with children — we would have had to watch their love fade." Master Lee let everyone silently absorb his words. A warm wind swirled around the sitting monks, as if in agreement with his thoughts.

"In Zen Buddhism," Master Lee broke the silence, "we feel this surface life is meaningless without compassion and love. Buddhists name the source of love, Nirvana. Yet for Romeo — it is Juliet. What's in a name anyways," he joked. Everyone laughed.

"Well I didn't come up here to talk about Shakespeare," he declared sarcastically to his audience.

"At dawn you guys are going up the trail — back to your cars and lives — I am staying here. I am leaving this world. Your time to roam this mystical desert is over."

Gasps went through the crowd of sitting monks.

~

"I'm incredulous, Romeo!" Roshi Jeff protested, pacing in his small office above the Zendo. "I can't believe none of you called the authorities!'

"But Jeff," Romeo pleaded, "I was not in charge. I am not one of the senior monks."

"Don't bullshit me! You're my friend and I feel you know what happened." Jeff pointed an accusing finger at Romeo.

"Why do you say that?"

"The other students," Jeff explained. "He talked about you right before he announced his departure, didn't he?"

"Yes, I was shocked. He usually ignores me."

"Where did you come from before Master Lee met you in Hawaii?" Jeff interrogated.

"Roshi Jeff, I cannot tell you that," Romeo replied with regret and lowered his head.

Jeff sighed. "OK, can you tell me where Master Lee went?" he asked.

"Roshi Jeff," Romeo smiled, "I think Master Lee went into the void."

Jeff excused Romeo from his office and sat down again, examining the papers sent to him by his Zen Master's estate. He still couldn't believe it. If Master Lee didn't return soon, he would be the head of the oldest Zen center in New York City. The hard working Roshi slowly looked up at the picture of his teacher hanging in the office. The respected Zen patriarch of his order seemed to smile back at him, mischievously.

"Why didn't you let me come with you?" he finally asked the silent image. Of course, they never found any trace of Master Lee.

~

Seven more years passed after Master Lee's dramatic exit. Romeo discovered he could sell mathematical software from anywhere in the world, so he moved back to Hawaii, the place of his origin, his rebirth. He bought a small home overlooking the ocean along the Hamaku Coast of the Big Island. As the years passed, he began to meditate more deeply and started to feel the presence of Juliet, somewhere in the modern world.

He knew he could not search for his beloved in a society of billions, but his heart whispered to him that someday fate would lead him to her. And late one afternoon everything did change for him, as he lazily swayed in his white cotton hammock. It was a mild winter day and the trade winds had brought with them a warm air from the south.

He had just received a frantic call from a client who desperately needed him to run a complex algorithm before the opening bell on Wall Street. Romeo swung to his feet, walked inside, and powered on his server. As he waited for the results, he mindlessly clicked on his Yahoo Chat icon. He had downloaded their software a few months ago and found speaking with faceless strangers mildly entertaining. He never expected to fall in love online. He simply wanted someone to talk with, maybe a new friend — and that is exactly what he found also.

Johnny and Emilie

How if, when I am laid into the tomb,
I wake before the time that Romeo
Come to redeem me? There's a fearful point!

- Juliet

Johnny Perfection, Hollywood superstar, arose from his musty, wrinkled bed sheets and stretched lazily. His mistress, the beautiful young actress Emma Gallant, lay asleep by his side, curled gently like a lotus leaf floating in a pond. John loved fucking her, but Emilie was one of those high-maintenance starlets. He sleepily rubbed his eyes. Yes, she was a great conquest — but the price of empire was always high.

She looked so innocent lying there next to him. John had been her first lover. She was amazingly beautiful and less than half his age, only eighteen. He was over forty, married with children. *What is there not to love about this?* he asked himself, smiled, and slid out of bed.

He slapped his growing belly and shuffled in his cool arrogant manner to the bathroom mirror. Outside the bedroom window the sounds of Manhattan were already roaring but he didn't hear them; John was at the mirror and the mirror was actually how he and Emilie made their living.

"Mirror, mirror on the wall, who's the handsomest asshole of them all?" he muttered and then quickly gargled some Listerine.

Being on all the top ten lists of the beautiful people didn't mean shit to John this morning. He had gotten roaring drunk last night, staggering through the Chelsea district with his driver, bodyguard, and a few friends. He felt just as ugly as all the other middle-aged men in Manhattan waking up with their Saturday hangovers and girl Fridays.

"Fuck, that was good beer. I don't feel that fucked up," he muttered optimistically.

He scowled into the mirror, willing back that Johnny Perfection look the Hollywood execs loved so — that brash silhouette which landed him the lucrative role where he met the charming young actress Emma Gallant.

"It made me a killing, and now I'm fucking a goddess," he announced while turning on the hot water. "Thank god I got away from my wife this month," he added, patting down his cheeks with shaving cream. It wasn't going to be a bad hair day after all. He had missed Christmas with his family in Malibu, to party in New York and spend time with Emilie.

In the mirror's reflection, he saw Emilie stirring in their bed, her hips perfectly curved to the rays of the morning sun, her curly light brown hair cascading delicately across smooth regal shoulders, tracing a perfect "S" along her back. *It's as if she is already made up on a set,* he marveled. She was truly a natural beauty and that made John proud.

Unfortunately, he knew how this movie would end. He had told her, from the first day he tried to fuck her, that they were just friends. He explained they must keep their affair secret or the paparazzi would eat them alive, not to mention his wife's lawyers.

"I've fucking done everything right with this girl," he defended himself to the mirror and began to carefully shave. John pictured himself an upfront guy and he truly admired Emilie. Whatever you could say about her she wasn't an airhead like many Hollywood bimbos he had bedded.

"Damn, she's going to be big someday," he absentmindedly muttered, still looking at her beautiful form.

Although perfect for Hollywood in his own rebellious way, John had only begun to break into the mainstream. Emma Gallant was the angel of the big screen from across the sea. She had the fresh look execs wanted in their top roles. Furthermore, unlike John, she had a wholesome image — an image the industry sorely needed to counter the political railings against the growing immorality of liberal Hollywood.

John knew the kingmakers would abandon him in a second over her if their voracious affair ever became public. He knew he couldn't damage *their* merchandise without feeling the heat. He had to be careful with Emilie.

"I know how this is going to fucking end," he predicted tiredly, stepping into the shower. The warm water refreshed him, as he washed the smell of beer from his pale skin. John indeed knew how this would end. Emilie was nothing more than another teenager with a crush on him. *How could she not love me?* he argued rhetorically, soaping himself under the steaming water. After all, he was smarter than most of the other assholes within the golden walls of Hollywood. More importantly, John was her first and most women tend to fall in love with the man who holds that distinction.

He stepped out of the shower, wiped himself off, and began to comb his multi-million dollar hair, as he leaned into the steamy mirror. *Emilie has become so needy lately, so moody,* he reflected. Obviously she dreamed of marrying him, *like a little girl would*, he realized and smirked.

John already had his fun, popped her cherry. He wanted to fuck other women — women less needy and less in love with him than Emilie was. He felt a wild rush whenever he imagined dumping her cold and breaking her heart. Something about crushing such a beautiful flower was irresistible.

Fuck, I wish she had been a slut when I met her. Then she wouldn't cling to me so, his thoughts flashed uncomfortably, as he muffed his hair with jell. He glanced at the reflection of Emilie's peaceful form and dabbed some aftershave lotion on his neck. He had never wanted to trade his current wife in for another, yet that was exactly what was happening.

"John dear," Emilie's voice startled him with its articulate Cambridge accent. It was as if she had felt him thinking of her. "Aren't you going to make love to me?" she asked smiling, as he walked toward her with a towel wrapped around him.

He could tell Emilie was totally in love with him, from her first conscious thought in the morning. John almost felt like her incestuous father now. He had tried to impress upon her they were just friends, as most Hollywood lovers claim to be; obviously, his plan wasn't working.

"I'm going to meet with my agent about a new script," he replied calmly, as he gazed into her doe-like sapphire eyes. He could sense a potential argument brewing. He leered appreciatively as Emilie raised herself, arched her back, and shuffled on her knees to the foot of his bed.

She wanted him to say something now, he knew it. She slowly untied her hair and continued to admire him with her gorgeous deep eyes. "I will make love with you tonight, my dear," John finally promised and started to dress.

"Well I hope you do!" Emilie replied cheerfully, combing her long smooth hair. She reminded him of a child sometimes. "I hope you make love with me tonight John — before you start drinking," she added in a kind but maternal way.

God, she's so immature! She doesn't even know how annoying she is, John angrily thought. She made him feel like he was with is wife, or maybe even his mother. *It's cute though*, he admitted.

"Let's both have some wine tonight. I'll buy a French Bordeaux for us," John offered, gazing into her steady obsidian eyes, hoping to stun his prey. He grinned and added, "I promise to stay in and have only a few glasses, my angel."

"OK dear," she agreed. Her thoughtful brow wrinkled. She smiled and rose to kiss him.

"What are you doing today?" John wondered as he put his arm around her thin waist. Not that it mattered. She was a very introverted girl. He didn't have to worry much about her running around.

"I'm going to workout this morning then to acting class," she informed him with a smile and rested her hands on his shoulders. John ground his body against hers and gave Emilie one of his million-dollar kisses to let her know there was a lot of hard sex coming tonight.

"I love you, John," Emilie declared softly, breathing deeply now.

"I love you also, girl," John brusquely replied and twirled away from her, toward the dining area. The mention of love always angered him. *Doesn't she realize we are just friends?* he asked himself, as she dutifully followed him down the hallway. He was relieved his agent had scheduled a meeting on Saturday — John didn't feel like fucking his friend this morning.

~

When evening came, things had changed considerably for Emma Gallant and Johnny Perfection. John had reluctantly agreed to have dinner with his agent and some industry execs. A few uptown models had joined them and the champagne began to flow. He would join Emilie soon ... after a few more drinks. John shot a glance at the jazz band and then at the snowflakes falling outside the large dark windows of the Rainbow Room.

Suddenly a twelve-year-old girl with braces bumped into his arm. He decided to notice her. "Can I have your autograph Johnny Perfection? My mother loves you."

John obliged. "Her mother loves me," he repeated sarcastically to his agent Richard Glass, who was dressed in an impeccable white suit and a faggoty peach tie. Richard snickered with a big fake smile and gave John a pat on his back.

"Johnny, this new generation of girls doesn't like you as much," he joked. "You're losing your touch."

What an asshole, John thought. At that moment he wanted to turn and punch Dick in the mouth.

"Well some younger girls do like me, as you know Richard," John retorted in a deep, calm, cold manner.

His agent smiled blankly and froze. John knew the look. He had seen it in Hollywood for years. Richard Glass looked weakly away, as he always did whenever confronted with anything uncomfortable. He knew all about John and Emilie — and became even more a Hollywood phony whenever John mentioned the affair.

Both John's Star Agency and Emilie's Capulet Agency had agreed to keep the affair quiet. Emilie was simply too innocent and pretty to be linked to an alleged reformed married cad like Johnny Perfection — who had been selling himself as "Mr. Family Values" of late. If news of their passionate tryst leaked, it would be very inconvenient.

John glared at Richard, as the blushing girl sprinted off clutching the autograph. *He is such a pussy with his fake hair plugs,* he angrily observed. Richard simply pretended the affair with Emilie didn't exist. If word ever got out, John knew, his agent would shamelessly milk another one of his failed romances for free publicity,

"Et tu, Brutus?" he asked Richard, who was turned to an executive in a starched suit. John was angry about the whole thing now. The music was too loud for Richard to hear his brilliant sarcasm. He glanced at the tall, sexy model sitting to his left, smiling stupidly, nervous.

God, I could fuck the bitch in the coatroom and forget about it the next morning! What a concept, he cynically realized, as he leered at her tan, long legs. *I can't do that with Emilie. No, she is too special for that!*

John knew he would probably have to dump Emilie soon. In reality he was a married man with a family and Emilie was merely another conquest — the latest in a parade of beautiful actresses he had dated then emotionally trashed and drained throughout his checkered career in Hollywood.

He had vowed not to do that to Emilie though — to hurt her. He always reminded her they were just friends, *friends with benefits,* as young Emilie liked to put it. Yet, in the end, romance had won out. Even he was developing feelings for her.

"Dammed if you do, dammed if you don't," he muttered and took a vigorous shot of tequila to complement the champagne.

~

When ten o'clock hit the cold winter streets of New York City, Emilie was far above them still waiting for John. She was crying, lying face down atop the same bed she had shared with him this morning. Alone in a strange apartment, she missed her home in England; worse yet, Emilie was beginning to feel like a sucker.

She had always wanted her first lover to *love* her, not refer to her as a *friend* as John did. She spent her teenage years reading romance novels between her hectic filming schedules and flights around the world. She always joked that Danielle Steele was her literary vice. And now like a fool, she had fallen in love with a legendary Hollywood bad-boy, one of the most handsome men alive. Yet for her, John had become just another painful part of life.

"A painful adolescent part," she corrected herself aloud.

How pathetic, she scolded herself. *A married man is my first lover, and he doesn't love me back.* She buried her head in the pillow and sobbed. *Why hasn't he at least called?* she lamented for the thousandth time. He was hours late.

Emilie was smart and knew life had lessons to teach her. She wiped the tears from her eyes, laughing painfully at her situation. She then lifted herself off the bed, walked slowly toward the dining area, and sat down by her laptop, as if it was a crystal ball that would solve all her problems.

She glanced at her cell on the dining table and thought of calling Mum. They hadn't spoken since before Christmas. Her mother was still furious over her affair with John, acting as if Emilie's relationship was a high crime, forgetting her daughter was grown up and did not need a chaperone anymore.

It had been mum who launched Emilie's career in Hollywood and set her daughter up with the powerful Capulet Agency. Mum had been a stage actress herself, unlike father, who was a professor of Egyptology at Cambridge. As Emilie grew older and more successful, her mother kept her on a relatively tight leash. Traveling from location to location with her stunning daughter — mum made Emilie feel like a powerless child and not the breathtaking beauty the world was beginning to adore.

"How could she!" Emilie complained and buried her head in her hands. She recalled her mother's tantrum with the Capulet Agency when she first found out that none other than Johnny Perfection, the Hollywood bad-boy, had deflowered her so intelligent, churchgoing daughter.

Ultimately though, Emilie knew mum had valid concerns. She was the secret lover of a married man. There was a growing realization within her that she would have to live with this fact for the rest of her life. How could she tell her future children about her first lover? How could she one day expect her own husband to be faithful? These thoughts had plagued young Emilie's mind of late.

It had all started so logically. John assured her his wife knew he had affairs. Emilie's affections were indirectly helping his wife. She would be keeping him happy during their long separations. He almost made Emilie feel it was her artistic duty to give herself to him. John had coached her in acting and wanted to coach her in fucking as well. They were just friends, so he would do the friendly thing, make love with her, be her first and teach her all about sex. His wife wouldn't mind — Emilie was simply keeping her husband safely occupied during their long separations.

Emilie now realized the truth was drastically different from what John had sold her on. His wife might tolerate an occasional one night stand with a groupie, but Emilie knew she would feel threatened by her husband's affair with a successful starlet.

Is this film already over? she sadly asked herself. Her eyes filled with tears as she recalled an argument from a few days ago. John had actually encouraged her to date other men! *How could he be so cruel?* she painfully wondered. He meant it as an insult and a challenge for her to breakup with him.

It can't be a good sign when your lover encourages you to date, she sadly realized. John had made her feel like a whore with that suggestion, indicating her services were no longer required. A wave of anger rushed through her. She gazed blankly at the computer screen. She needed someone to talk with. She always felt so lonely in her lover's dark apartment. It did not feel like a home but more a hideout — somewhere John stored her away like an exquisite jewel, as he ran off doing God knows what.

She stared at her laptop's sleek black keys and decided to explore the Yahoo chat rooms. It was relaxing being anonymous and not *Emma Gallant* all the time. The Internet leveled everything and made ordinary people accessible to her, people she never would meet in her sheltered world of bodyguards, private jets, and red carpet events.

The chat occupants all fascinated Emilie, talking about *her* films, religion, politics — chat rooms full of horny teenage boys and men. They reminded her of John in many ways, all so full of themselves, so kinky, as they bragged to her of their exploits. She felt a sexy vulnerability talking to these strangers. A few times, she even traded photographs with them. They all thought she was beautiful, of course; yet none of them had recognized her.

"What losers," she remarked, a little jealous of John. Her star was rising, but his was at high noon.

She clicked on her Yahoo icon and wiped the wetness from her eyes. Leaning forward, she typed with concentration. At least she was doing something to kill time as she waited for John. He was more than five hours late.

"God, why hasn't he called?" she bemoaned again, slumping into her seat and feeling that lover's pang in her gut. She straightened herself and mindlessly entered a romance chat room. As she sat there, upset with John, a few men messaged her and drooled over her head and shoulder image, which she traded for their meager pictures.

"What in God's name am I doing here?" she whispered to herself. *You aren't doing anything Emilie; this is John's doing*, her mind shot back in defense.

Yes, John had discarded her again. He had traded her in for the mistress of alcohol and whatever else he found attractive about the dark bars of Manhattan. She was in exile now and wandered lost like Romeo did when he first awoke in this age. Yet her wanderings were the electronic desert of Internet, searching for love, searching for rescue.

Emma Gallant had a projected future worth over two hundred million dollars, according to the bean counters within the Capulet agency and was insured for twice that. She was a corporation unto herself. Lawyers, accountants, and artists, all depended upon her to support their families and lavish lifestyles. And tonight, their young star was giving out private pictures of herself, albeit tame ones, to strangers on the Internet.

Romeo and Emilie

But, soft! What light through yonder window breaks?
It is the east, and Juliet is the sun.

- Romeo

As midnight approached New York City, five thousand miles to the west, Romeo like a bored Gilligan, also roamed Yahoo. Of course, his mental machinations were not as bleak as Emilie's that evening. A beautiful band of dark blue still lingered on the ocean's horizon beyond his office window. He entered a romance chat room and noticed the screen name *JohnsAngel*.

"Hi 32/m/hawaii/pic," he instant messaged *JohnsAngel*. He hoped she wasn't a robot and waited for a response.

Emilie studied the pop-up window displaying the stranger's text. *Hawaii,* she thought, somewhat intrigued. "Hawaii," she uttered the word aloud, surprising herself with the sound of it.

"18/f/nyc/pic," she responded.

"Would you like to trade pics?" the man from Hawaii asked.

"Sure." *A little pushy,* she thought; *but at least he isn't a phony.* She loaded up her picture for Mr. Hawaii to see and then clicked to unveil his photograph. Emilie saw a tan man standing on a sandy beach, and behind him, a glistening blue wave frozen in time. The beach lured her as much as the man did. The image was poor, she thought disdainfully, *but he does look vaguely handsome. I bet he is really stupid though*, she reasoned with her one hundred sixty IQ.

"You are very beautiful," the man from Hawaii finally typed back.

How boring, she thought, *of course I am. Beauty is what got me into this current mess with John in the first place.*

~

Far to the west, things changed considerably for Romeo Montague. As soon as he saw the image of Emma Gallant and stared into those beautiful two hundred million dollar eyes — he fell in love. He was not completely aware of this, yet his heart told him this woman was special.

If I ever was to met her, I would fall in love, he did admit to himself, as he gazed at her soft, kind smile and appreciated her shimmering brown curls as they fell gently against a smooth delicate shoulder and swelling bosom.

"What's your name? I'm Romeo," he introduced himself.

"lol," Emilie responded. She giggled and put her hand over her mouth. *This man must be hiding his real name*, she reasoned. *He is probably married ... like John.*

"My friends call me Emilie," she answered.

"Beautiful name," he replied. "Surely, you would be the key to any man's heart," he mindlessly typed, still mesmerized by her photograph.

"Thank you," she responded, flattered now and more interested in this *Romeo.*

"I hope you don't think I am lying, Emilie. My name really is Romeo."

She paused. It was as if he had read her mind. Of course, she thought he was lying. Yet this man felt kind and honest to her. She suddenly felt a little guilty for laughing at his name.

"No, Romeo," she smiled and continued to type, "It's a beautiful name."

"Well you seem charming yourself, Emilie. I'm flattered," he responded.

"Thank you. I try never to do anything unladylike," she typed, not knowing why. Her problems seemed farther away now. It felt a part of her was already friends with this man from Hawaii. A mysterious and wonderful feeling stirred within her, something new. It gave her hope — an emotion she forgot existed only an hour ago.

"That's a beautiful photograph," he remarked.

"My friend John took it," she wanted him know she was seeing someone.

"Do you mind our age difference, Emilie?" Romeo asked, already feeling protective toward this beautiful stranger.

"Not at all," she bragged. "John is over forty."

"So what do you do in NYC, work or go to school?" he inquired, trying not to feel jealous.

"Work," she replied factually.

"Really, what do you do?"

Emilie paused. She didn't want to reveal to this stranger that she was a movie star and not only because she wanted a private life — something else had insinuated itself — she had always dreamed of meeting a man who loved her for who she was and not because she was *Emma Gallant*.

"I guess you could say that I am in the entertainment industry," she replied truthfully.

"Are you a stripper?" Romeo asked boldly. He didn't think she was, but her coy answer sounded seductive.

"No, my parents would never approve of that," she cleverly replied and then laughed in her empty suite.

"Are you a model?" he guessed again.

"I've done some of that," she replied with a touch of disdain. Modeling was so beneath her, yet endless publicity shots were part of her job.

"Well then, you must be a beautiful Shakespearean actress," Romeo deduced. For what else could she be? She had the most stunning intelligent face he had seen in his life. She was even more beautiful to him than his fading memory of Juliet. Finally, he might love again in this new world.

"Thank you," Emilie typed. "It's ironic, but I'm reading *Romeo and Juliet* now. I figure, just because I'm beautiful ... why be stupid?"

Romeo became worried. *What if she talks about the play?*

"So what do you do for a living, Romeo?" Emilie asked, thankfully changing the subject.

"I write mathematical software, darling."

Interesting, she thought. *This man is intelligent, after all.* She didn't mind him calling her darling either. Oddly enough, it felt like the most natural thing in the world.

"I'm thinking of going to college next year," she typed. Of course, that was the last thing her agency wanted her to do.

"You should; I can tell you are a very articulate and intelligent."

"Thank you." she smiled.

"You must be a great lover," he typed longingly, staring at her picture and throwing caution to the wind.

"You would have to ask John about that. He's the only man I've ever been with," she bragged.

"John is very lucky to be your friend."

"I have many friends."

"I would love to be one of them."

~

A s if to compassionately balance the universe as a whole, Johnny Perfection, at the very moment his mistress Emma Gallant was straying online with a stranger, was himself leaning against the rails of an elevator. The beautiful blonde model whom he had dined with was now giving him a rousing hummer. John's black leather trousers were halfway down his legs. He concentrated more on not throwing up and keeping his balance, than on the stirring oral dissertation the young woman was reciting to his attentive member.

"God I'm going to have a headache tomorrow," he muttered drunkenly, to a golden bobbing stream of hair. He smiled at the pun and realized the bimbo was oblivious to it. He stroked her beautiful braids with his right hand, grasping an almost empty bottle of champagne with his left.

Finally John came. "OK girl, I need to go home."

"Sure, Johnny," the kneeling woman replied sheepishly in her high voice, as if she was a bad girl for daring to stay with someone so famous, even a minute after the orgasm had been consecrated.

How pathetic, he thought. *I should fire Richard for dragging along these women.*

"You know I'm married," he said, looking into her eyes. The blowjob had put him in a good mood. He would let her down easy. Obviously, he wasn't going to give this bimbo his number.

"I know," the blonde began dutifully, in her soft voice. "Your wife Renee lives in Malibu with your children. I've read all about you in People magazine," she added, kneeling and smiling up at him, as if in recital to a living God.

A wave of anger swept through John. An average Joe getting a blowjob from a stranger wouldn't have to hear about his family. *How dare this bitch talk about my private life!* his thoughts flashed angrily. *Fuck her!*

The elevator door opened and he briskly walked into lobby, muttering "bye" to the star-struck model who was still kneeling. He had wanted to slap the stupid bitch in payback for her comment about his wife; but of course, he couldn't do that. An average Joe could, but he didn't have that kind of freedom — word would get out.

"IF I FUCKING DO ANYTHING WRONG," he yelled to the sky while pushing open the glass doors of the NBC building, "EVERYONE FUCKING KNOWS ABOUT IT! I HAVE TO BE LIKE FUCKING JESUS!"

A few late-night couples looked at him wearily, as his voice echoed against the masonry of Rockefeller Center. He quickly ducked his head and disappeared around the plaza's golden terraces and onto 5th Avenue to catch a taxi. After a quick jaunt downtown, he departed from the yellow cab and stepped onto the cold, steamy street below. The midnight air was dry and the salt on the ground felt like the sand of a barren desert. The freezing cold gusts made his brow clammy. He needed to deal with Emilie now, who lay behind his door, probably very angry.

~

Inside his warm apartment, Emilie was startled when she heard John juggle and drop his keys. She quickly said goodbye her new friend and logged off. As John opened the door, it seemed like an intrusion. Not because he had stood her up again, but because she had been so happy chatting with Romeo — and now she had crash-landed back into her complicated life.

"Hi baby," John cautiously greeted her with his million dollar Bogart impression. He expected an argument and wished he had called her earlier — even though they were *just friends*.

"John!" Emilie remarked, startled. She ran to kiss him.

He could tell she was embarrassed, as if hiding something, *like a little girl caught reading someone else's diary*. He wondered why she wasn't upset with him. After all, he had stood her up most of the night. He grabbed her slim waist and kissed her back deeply.

"I'm sorry for not calling baby," he apologized.

"Have you taken another lover?" she asked concerned.

"Not unless you think Richard and I are lovers."

"You act like it sometimes, John," she said resigned, finally acknowledging that he had missed dinner with her.

John glanced at the laptop where she had been sitting. "What were you doing when I came in babe?" he asked, with mild suspicion. He studied her up and down and added, "You looked busy."

"I was talking to a man on the Internet from Hawaii," she bragged.

He grinned. "Really, did you have cybersex?"

"No darling, I just don't jump into bed with anyone," she joked seductively, twirling her hair. She leaned in and kissed her lover tenderly, lifted off his glasses, and pushed him onto their couch. John had been forgiven for the botched romantic dinner and Emilie had an excess energy she wanted to spend on him.

Far to the west, Romeo soon logged off. He had no desire to chat with anyone after meeting such an alluring and intelligent person like Emilie. He couldn't get her out of his mind and wanted to fly her west, to Hawaii, far away from the noise of NYC he had escaped. He felt a deep familiarity with this young woman, as if they were connecting on hundreds of levels. It dawned on him, as he climbed into his shower — he had not felt this way since Verona, Italy.

Tempting Extremities

Come, night;
come, Romeo;
come, thou day in night;

- Juliet

Emilie pleasantly awoke to the sun's rays lying next to John, who was fast asleep. For some reason, she found herself wanting to be alone, wanting him to leave their bed. Although they had great sex last night, meeting Romeo had triggered something deep within her, something private.

Her first thought of the morning had been of the man from Hawaii. She lay still next to John and blinked. He seemed almost alien to her. Somehow, Romeo felt closer. John felt like the stranger, the one-night stand, or at best, *just a friend* — as he loved to remind her.

She quickly rolled out of bed and tied her nightgown at the waist. She decided to use this newfound detachment to her advantage. Today the thrill of being with Johnny Perfection didn't blind her. She had grown to resent that star-struck rush whenever it hit her. It made her feel stupid, weak, and nothing more than a groupie.

As she walked toward the kitchen, Emilie wondered if she was any better than a groupie. John had been the forbidden fruit and like a Hollywood Eve, she had bitten with gusto into that apple. Being with him made her feel special, not only special, but somehow destined for success herself.

Her torrid affair with a married superstar had given Emilie a naughty feeling of power. One word from her to the right people and a feeding frenzy would hit the rumor mill! Just one word from her and their affair would be plastered over the entertainment magazines of the world! This made Emilie feel important, in playful way, for she was now a *player* in Hollywood.

Yet this morning, as the sun streamed through the kitchen window, her limited power was only of passing interest. She began to fill the coffee machine with Brazilian beans. She concentrated not to spill any on the white linoleum floor, wrinkling her cute intelligent brow, imagining what it would be like making coffee for Romeo.

How foolish! her mind flashed. She didn't want to get obsessed over a man she met over the Internet! Still, Romeo was magnetic and intelligent. She had met the top directors, actors, and writers of the industry and Romeo exuded a power like they did. He was very interesting. Yet, for all she knew, he had kids and was very married.

Emilie sadly smiled and turned on the coffee machine with her long graceful fingers. A married Romeo would be no different from her current situation. Suddenly, as if in agreement with her thoughts, John's hands were on her. She jumped, startled — so deep in her own reflections, she had not heard him crawl out of bed.

"Ah! John!" she exclaimed.

"Baby Emilie," he replied in a seductive growl and grabbed her small waist tighter with his strong hands. She didn't turn to kiss him; instead her body stiffened. A part of her didn't want him anymore.

"John," she began like a stern schoolteacher admonishing a rambunctious student. "I'm making coffee, darling … can't you wait?" she girlishly asked, turning to face him. She noticed how confused he looked. Had she never seen this basic confusion in his face before? He was handsome though, very handsome.

John grabbed her and kissed her hard. Their tongues swirled together in a seductive, yet empty dance. Kissing him felt like an amusement park ride, full of twists and turns, but leading nowhere really. She backed away from his embrace, as he grabbed her firm behind, and moved quickly back to the growling coffee machine.

"What's wrong, baby? Let's hop back in bed." he motioned with a comical smile toward the bedroom.

She looked at him and wondered, *what kind of smile is that, the smile of a man who loves me or only wants me at his convenience?*

"John," she started, and feigned a giggle.

"What is it, babe?" he rubbed her shoulders.

She became aroused, but still, she didn't want to be close to him this morning. She turned and told a white lie: "I have a publicity shoot. I have to get ready." Actually, her appointment wasn't until noon. She looked at him with her clear, soft eyes and noticed mild disappointment in his.

"OK baby," John agreed, pleasantly. "I'm going to take a shower." Looking a little hurt and forlorn, he quickly retreated toward the bathroom.

How cute, she thought. She considered going to him now, holding him and making love to him in the shower. *God I love him! Of course I love him*, she thought. John had been her first and he was special. *Millions of women all over the world would sell their soul to be in my position,* she reminded herself. Yet now, Emilie was fascinated at how the dynamic of their relationship had changed overnight. She felt in control for the first time. He was the needy one today — the one that could be hurt.

She heard him close the bathroom door and listened as he started the shower. She imagined how it would feel if Romeo had kissed her by the coffee machine this morning. *What would it be like now?* she asked herself. *What would it be like, knowing Romeo was behind that door taking a shower?*

Suddenly, she was aroused. Thoughts of making love to Romeo were spinning in her head. She mindlessly took a sip of coffee and cautiously walked to the sound of John's shower. Resting her hand on the warm brass doorknob, she turned it and entered the steamy cloud of his morning. For now at least, he was still her Romeo ... and she let him know it.

~

As morning became noon under the faint pale sky of New York's winter, the young star Emma Gallant could be seen walking briskly up Madison Avenue. She was casually swinging a shopping bag holding a Valentino dress. Like all successful actors, she was constantly being sent clothing from the top designers of the world. Simply the act of her wearing a particular outfit to an opening could change the fate of a whole line of apparel forever. Regardless, like most girls her age, she loved to shop — receiving dresses through her agency just wasn't the same thing.

She swung her bag gaily and almost hit a slowly shuffling pout-faced woman wearing a heavy black coat. The woman gave her a dirty look. Emilie smiled back playfully and continued her healthy gait uptown, enjoying the meager sun that temporarily banished the winter chill from her bones. She was free today, truly a woman. Her mother and her agency had tried to keep her a child as long as possible. Now, thanks to John, the idea of anyone protecting her was ludicrous.

By turning eighteen, and letting Johnny Perfection take her, she had freed herself in one brilliant stroke — untied the Gordian knot her mother had wound so tightly around her. Sadly though, the double Victorian faux pas of losing her virginity, and to an older married man, had so shocked her strict church-going parents, she had not spoken to them since before Christmas.

Emilie had confessed to mum in mid-December that she was not simply filming in New York and staying in every night, as mum knew her precious daughter would. She casually informed mum she was staying in every night with Johnny Perfection. Her mother had gone ballistic then hysterical. She acted like Emilie had wandered into a radioactive waste site with only days to live:

"HOW CAN YOU DO THIS TO US?" she screamed into the phone, crying. "Oh my God, what has he told you?" she lamented, in shock, as if her daughter had joined a religious cult.

Emilie hung up after a few minutes of listening to her mother rant and rave with the phone safely away from her ear. The memory was almost comical now. It was as if John had become the devil to her mother. Wasn't it a few years earlier that mum had met Johnny Perfection at a dinner, star-struck, tongue-tied herself?

Her family and John's had eaten at an elegant jazz club in London. During dinner, Emilie noticed her mother eying John. A few months later, she saw it again on a movie set. Mum was having some fantasies of her own as she traveled the world's hotels with her daughter. *Well why not,* she reasoned as the light turned green, *they are practically the same age.*

Deep down though, Emilie didn't like to see her mother suffer. She had missed Christmas with her family. Never had she imagined that would happen. Everything had exploded after she told them about John. Her affair had also crushed the young man from England she had dated a few times, Paris Beauregard. When she told Paris of John, his eyes welled up in tears. Yet Paris and Emilie rarely saw each other — she traveled the world and he was a student at Cambridge.

The Hollywood tabloids all placed Emma Gallant with the wealthy heir, Paris Beauregard — that's the line the towers of Hollywood sold Emilie's wholesome fans. The Capulet Agency went to great pains to hide the truth and young Paris had become the perfect beard.

John shamelessly told Larry King on national television, only a few weeks ago, that being a husband and father had morally grounded the Hollywood bad-boy. Emilie had been thankful she hadn't watched that. Luckily at the time, she had been filming. She felt uncomfortable her lover had lied through his teeth to millions of people. The hypocrisy of it all was a little too much for her. *Am I a part of that hypocrisy?* she asked herself, as she crossed 63rd street and over the red carpet of the Pierre Hotel.

A sweet voice snapped her out of her reflections. She noticed a cute petite teenager with blonde braids smiling up at her. "Excuse me, are you Emma Gallant?" the girl asked in a shy, cheerful way. The wind whipped up. It was getting colder. Emilie turned to the girl, flattered.

"Why yes I am," Emilie confessed. She was always kind to her fans. Mum had taught her that much. She loved children and wanted to encourage them to go into acting as she had done. She dreamed of one day having her own beautiful daughter, maybe like the girl in front of her now.

"Oh God!" the young fan exclaimed, in a high-pitched squeaky voice. "You're my favorite actress! You're so talented … I'm into acting myself … I'd love to have your autograph," the girl pined, with a large winning smile that was almost devotional.

"Why of course," Emilie offered cordially. She knew the look. The girl would talk about this moment for years to come with her friends. She asked the girl for her name.

"Stacy." Stacy nervously fumbled for her school notebook and handed Emilie a pen. "Oh God, thank you!" she moaned, as Emilie took the notebook and pressed pen to page. The freezing wind made her delicate hands stiffen, as she struggled to brace the notebook against her knee.

"What was it like working with Johnny Perfection?" Stacy blurted out. "It must have been so great. He is so hot. He must be such a cool guy!"

The question hit Emilie like a bucket of cold water. The girl beamed even more reverentially at her. She paused, flustered from hearing the name of the man she had just shared a shower with. A shy embarrassed smile formed on her lips. Emilie finished signing her name and handed the notebook back.

"Well, he is a talented actor — and a good friend of mine. I will tell him you said that," she remarked.

Of course, she would never tell John. John hated Hollywood fans, but she wanted to make Stacy feel special. She knew what it was like being on the outside and then meeting someone big. That had happened last year when she had met Johnny Perfection in preparation for her biggest film yet.

"Thank you," the girl blushed awestruck, as if Emma Gallant was a canonized saint.

Emilie smiled curtly then briskly walked into the cold Manhattan wind. The sun ducked behind roiling clouds and the temperature dropped further. She now resented the girl mentioning her lover John.

Am I jealous of his fans? she asked herself. Or was she upset because she saw herself in the girl? *Am I also star struck?* she challenged herself. *Am I sleeping with a married man only because he is Johnny Perfection?*

"Of course not," she reassured herself. Emilie only wanted to be mature and reasonable. John was simply a dear friend and great lover. *He is also a great actor and very intelligent. He is a great catch,* she reminded herself.

She was lucky. John had not lied to her, simply loved her, maybe just as a friend; but John wanted to make her first time special and he had. He made Emilie feel adult, sexy, and free. Sexuality was not some terrible thing, as it was with mum — for John it was another reasonable, healthy part of life that could be negotiated like anything else.

She opened the glass doorway on 65th Street and walked through, flashing a guard her ID, thankful she had not taken a limousine. A blizzard had kept her from her workout sessions last week and she needed the exercise. She began to worry about her million-dollar figure and entered the elevator. She had gained a few pounds in the last month, and her skin was pale white. Pushing these thoughts out of her head, being the professional she was, she pushed the button for the top floor.

She stared at the glowing amber elevator lights. Everything was good between her and John. She needed to keep her cool about the whole thing.

After all, she thought, *I am a mature intelligent woman; it's not such a bloody big deal! If they would just let us alone, everything would be OK.* Yet when she arrived on the 34th floor, she still hadn't figured out who *they* were.

~

"Darling, I'm going to read over some scripts after dinner," John informed Emilie in a serious tone, slouching against the couch, eating pizza. He wore spectacles as if he were a French philosopher about to critique bourgeois Hollywood. Emilie loved his intellectual look. He had come home tonight and not gone out drinking.

She looked at John with her exquisite glistening eyes, then out his large living room window at the snowflakes, gracefully falling toward the yellow taxis that negotiated the slush below. It was a beautiful, romantic moment.

To her chagrin though, John never even glanced at her; instead, he insisted on reading a trade magazine as they sat in silence. After a few minutes, she tearfully realized — they were actually just friends. All the love and passion she felt when she had first given herself to this man had disappeared. He continued to read his magazine, making her feel like an actor during a lunch break in a low budget movie.

Emilie thought of Romeo as she watched John stare at his magazine and chew diligently on his pepperoni pizza. Hadn't Romeo told her if they were to meet, he would constantly admire her beauty? *What would it be like*, she asked herself, *to have dinner with a man who loved me deeply, who wanted to make me his wife? Isn't that what I always wanted, my first love to be my true love?* She began to resent John's indifference as they continued their silent meal.

John finished, quietly clearing off their table, probably sensing her anger. Emilie silently stacked the dishes in the dishwasher. For some reason, she didn't want to be near him now. He muttered something, kissed her shoulder and retreated to the bedroom.

Emilie started the dishwasher, and without anything else to do, wandered to the door of his bedroom. Although open, it felt invisibly closed to her. She watched John peer intently at a script — obviously trying to ignore her.

Of course, he knows I am here, she thought, a little angry and hurt. His glasses were intelligently tilted downward. She loved that look and he knew it. A wave of anger swept through her. *Has he manipulated me?* She wondered. *Does he see me as simply another girl he seduced?*

"I'm going to be at the computer … if you need me," she finally snapped, interrupting his concentration. Her voice almost cracked. *Thank God, it didn't,* she thought. She couldn't let him know how much he was hurting her.

"OK dear," John replied, lazily. He didn't look up. She turned sharply in a perfect ballerina pivot, now very angry, so angry, even he could feel it.

"I'm sorry darling," he added, as she stormed away. "If you need anything, just holler."

John was beginning to feel trapped, slouching in his comfortable bed. He had simply wanted to enjoy pizza with his girlfriend and then review a few independent film scripts. Now it was beginning to feel like home in Malibu with his wife and kids. Emilie wanted romance, love, and to be the center of attention.

He had tried to impress upon her all he wanted was a good time. She was pushing it now. She wanted him to say he loved her; he knew the look. She wanted him to say he would leave his family; he knew the look — he had seen it so many times before.

He listened carefully and could hear her typing on the laptop. *She is chatting online*, he realized. He felt flattered; she was trying to make him jealous. He looked down again at the screenplay on his bed, smiled, and eagerly grabbed a nearby glass of wine.

In the dining area, Emilie logged into Yahoo and immediately saw Romeo's name bolded on her buddy list. Relief washed over her, a quiet joy. *What if Romeo doesn't remember me?* she worried. But then he instantly messaged her, filling her with shy excitement:

"Aloha beautiful," he greeted her.

"Hello" she quickly typed.

"Darling, how was your day?"

"Good, thank you. How was yours?"

"Excellent. I went for a hike in the jungle," he answered. "I thought of us walking together, hand in hand, through a beautiful rain forest. I hope you don't mind."

"Of course not, I'm flattered," she replied and smiled, for she had been thinking of him too.

~

In Hawaii, it was five in the afternoon, when Emilie informed Romeo of how flattered she was. The sun cast a golden glow on Hakalau Bay below his house. The open window invited in a gentle wind through his study. Romeo was wearing a bright aloha shirt, his hair still wet from the shower.

"Well, Emilie," he typed, "I can't imagine anyone not being mesmerized by your beauty and charm."

He had hiked deep into the jungle earlier, the same forest that ultimately lead to the place he had entered this world. During the hike, he couldn't get Emilie out of his mind. She seemed sensitive and kind, a woman capable of loving and being loved. Her heart felt eclipsed, though. Romeo was not willing to believe a woman this beautiful, this intelligent, was happy with an older man who had pounded into her head that they were *just friends*. It was contradictory to everything he felt about her. She was simply the most romantic and unique woman he had met since Juliet.

"I wish I could hold your hand darling", he typed. "You must have the softest hands in the world."

"Thank you," she responded. "I wish we could walk hand in hand on that beach in your photograph, Romeo. It would be wonderful."

"I would love that, darling," he agreed. "I would write you love poems if you were to visit me. I hope that wouldn't bore you."

"No, not at all, I admire an intelligent man. I would adore it," she typed. She was becoming more intrigued with this romantic man by the minute. He made her feel safe and cared for — the way she dreamt of as a young girl, when a prince from afar would rescue her and bring magic into her life. He made her realize how lonely she had been, lonely, even though she shared a bed with one of the most desirable men on earth.

"You are the most beautiful and intelligent woman I have ever met. You're so pure," he declared, gazing into her soft, wise eyes, mesmerized by the photograph she had sent him.

"I'm hardly pure," she typed back, correcting him, wanting him to know she was a mature woman. A wave of regret swept through her, wishing Romeo had been her first.

"I didn't mean pure in a Judeo-Christian sense darling," he explained. "It's your energy, your aura; it feels so beautiful." He paused and added, "I meditate and can see that in you."

"Thank you," she replied, smiling and blushing. She had magically forgotten her problems now and was holding hands with Romeo on a windswept Hawaiian beach.

"So darling, that's amazing you're an actress," he commented, changing the subject. "I am sure you are skilled at your art."

"Why do you think that?" she inquired.

"Because when I look at you, you remind me of an Egyptian Princess."

"I've dreamed of ancient Egypt since I was a little girl," she confessed, excited.

"Ancient Egypt was last civilization women had equal access to the mystical and spiritual arts as men, and you do seem very evolved Emilie," Romeo observed.

"Thank you. I'm sorry for logging off so quickly last night," she added.

"Love is never having to say you're sorry, dear," Romeo joked. A few weeks before he had seen the movie *Love Story*, now the famous line came out naturally.

For Romeo, Emilie was a rare wondrous bird trapped in a golden cage. He sensed she led a sheltered life. She was wealthy and destined for fame, or so he guessed. She seemed alone though, singing beautiful songs, songs no one else could hear in this dark world — at least, no one but Romeo.

Like a solitary bird from far away, he had landed beside her golden cage, perhaps by chance. He sensed her spirit craved true love and knew he had to open the doors of her gilded life carefully. He didn't want to startle his shy and vulnerable friend. One day she would take his hand and they would soar together free — forever in love.

She broke him out of his revere by clicking on a background of tropical fish, filling their chat window. "Darling, it feels like we are swimming in Hawaii together," he remarked.

"I'm glad you like it. I wish we were together now," she confessed, as she stared at Romeo's photograph and the bright blue wave behind him. She wanted to show this wonderful man her romantic side, her deepest self. She was so comfortable with him. *It is as if we have known each other for years*, she marveled happily.

"Hopefully someday I can hold you in the Hawaiian waters," Romeo mused.

"I would love that," she replied. "I can almost feel you holding me now."

"Well Emilie you can visit me whenever you want," he offered. "I live alone and I would love to have you as a guest."

"That sounds wonderful, Romeo. I am going to England soon, but I will ask my assistant Lauren about Hawaii," she eagerly typed.

Romeo smiled. Emilie already had an assistant. She was more successful than he had suspected. But it didn't matter to him if she was a poor mill worker or a princess, for he was falling in love and knew she was too.

~

A week passed as they chatted every night and even played chess once. It had been a long day of filming when Emilie finally sunk into her dining room chair and eagerly turned on her laptop to speak with Romeo.

She noticed her online conversations were beginning to make John jealous — yet that wasn't really what kept her talking to this intelligent, kind man. Emilie knew what love was, and for some strange reason, she was falling in love with someone she had never met ... or so she thought.

Tonight John was watching a black and white French film in his bedroom. *Maybe that is fitting,* she reflected, as the bleak existential soundtrack droned on. John felt black and white to her now, cold, like the frigid winter New York was having, that she was having, in a strange city, with a strange man, far from home.

Her mind turned to Romeo and blue Hawaii as her notebook finished its login sequence. She opened his photograph and felt the warmth of the beach he was standing on. Unlike John, Romeo was in the land of eternal summers and bright colors. She logged into Yahoo and found her Romeo waiting.

"Aloha beautiful," Romeo greeted her, relaxing in his office. The cooling trade winds moved through the open windows, caressing his white shirt. He had returned from a swim in the cool ocean and just showered.

"Hello Romeo," Emilie typed and smiled.

"Darling, how was your day?"

"It was good," she replied, flattered he cared about her.

"I thought of you today, darling. I'm sorry I beat you at chess last night, my love."

"That's OK. I enjoyed the game," she assured him. "I'm sorry if I wasn't much of a challenge." Romeo had beaten her in three moves. This had impressed her, not because she cared about Romeo's chess playing ability, but because he had tried his hardest to win — and that felt so refreshingly honest to the Hollywood actress.

"Love is never having to say you're sorry … darling," he reminded her, playfully, as he had a few times since they met.

She smiled. Romeo had caught her apologizing again. She was beginning to love that line from the movie. Why was she apologizing so much? *Why do I want to make such a good impression on him? Am I falling in love with this man?* she wondered.

"You're already falling in love with me, aren't you?" she daringly asked, already helplessly in the spell of their magical affection.

To the west, Romeo was surprised when he read her question. This wonderful woman impressed him again, by boldly daring him to state his feelings. "I admit I am falling in love with you, Emilie," he typed truthfully. "But I think two people have to spend time in person to fall in love totally." He had been telling himself this for days now. He knew it was strange to have such strong feelings for a woman he had met on the Internet and wanted to appear reasonable. After all, she was the shy bird in his vision. He had to reach gently and slowly into her gilded cage, so as not to startle her.

"I agree Romeo," she answered, impressed and flattered by his answer.

"But darling," he returned to the keyboard, "can you deny that you don't have the same feelings for me?"

"Of course, I can't," she admitted, dramatically and truthfully, surprising herself.

Far away in Hawaii, Romeo smiled. He was flattered and relieved that she had confirmed what he already knew — both were falling in love. Yet, he was not on a high balcony overlooking a moonlit orchid as he had been with Juliet. He could not look into his beloved's eyes to know her feelings,

76

as lovers can do. Yet despite that, both were victims to the maelstrom of affection that spun wildly in their hearts.

Their growing feelings for each other were a force neither could control. It lifted them like a silent wind above timeless depths, through amazing and vast spaces. As Emilie and Romeo continued to chat, they soared over images and feelings that neither really understood. They talked about their lives, their favorite movies — trivial things. As they did, both traveled to a wonderful world that neither had dared journey to in ages — not since one fateful night in Verona, nearly eight hundred years ago.

With Extreme Sweet

What satisfaction canst thou have tonight?

- Juliet

Johnny Perfection finished showering and carefully combing his hair. He reached for the light by his nightstand. From the living room, Emilie smiled when his room darkened, not wanting him to know she was going online tonight. Ironically, it would be convenient if he had gone out drinking. But no, he was tucked away in bed, resting for an early morning shoot.

She quietly closed the magazine she was flipping through, as if John had superhuman powers and could hear the rustle of pages. She walked slowly and delicately, wearing loose slacks and a green blouse. to the dining area and sat, carefully straightening her beautiful long hair while waiting for her laptop to start. She leaned toward the screen like a praying mantis, eager. She wanted Romeo now — she wanted him bad.

She had dreamt of him last night. He was tan, handsome, and broad-shouldered. He smiled to her on a windy Hawaiian beach. She could feel his energy rush into her when they held hands. They had made love on the warm sand; it was delightful, erotic beyond words. The dream awakened a sweet passionate energy that had lingered all day.

Her smooth hands touched the glossy black keyboard. God, she wanted to visit Romeo in Hawaii! She hoped he was online. To her chagrin, his name was not bolded. A panic hit her. *What if he is on a date in Hawaii? What if he decided Internet chat is foolish?*

She slowly rose from her chair with her eyes still fixed on his screen name and moved to the refrigerator to get a Pepsi. She reached out absentmindedly for the cool drink and didn't bother to get a glass — instead, she sat again and took a dainty swig.

What am I doing here? she asked herself.

Yes, it was absurd that Emma Gallant, voted as one of the most beautiful women on earth, was pining for a man on the Internet named Romeo. *But isn't it equally absurd that I share a bed with Johnny Perfection?* she countered.

Suddenly, his name bolded in the upper-right corner of her screen! It was as if the gods had sent him to dispel her sadness. She could feel his presence thousands of miles away — Romeo, smart, brash, and unpredictable. He kept her on her mental toes. No one had ever done that before. He was probably the most intelligent man she had ever met.

"Aloha Beautiful," she read.

He always greeted her this way and she loved it. Everyday she dreamed of going to Hawaii now. She had already talked to her assistant Lauren about traveling there. Lauren had giggled when Emilie admitted she had met a man from the Internet.

"Romeo!" she typed happily, pretending to be surprised.

"How was your day darling?"

"Great, and yours my prince?" she asked, smiling.

"Excellent, my angel, aside from the fact I wasn't with the most beautiful and intelligent woman in the world, today."

"lol," she typed, flattered.

"I wish I could hold you in my arms and kiss you, my love. I dream of the day when you will come west to Hawaii," he declared.

Emilie could almost feel Romeo holding her. Yes, this is what she had wanted, true love, not what John had sold her on, a life of casual sex, as one of the elite movie stars traveling the world — enjoying the fruits of her labor and playing by a different set of rules. No, John's world didn't appeal to her and Romeo's did. He was unmarried and the most romantic man she had ever met.

"Romeo," she typed, almost cunningly.

"Yes my sexy angel?"

"Have you ever had cybersex?" she asked, innocently.

"Once," he admitted, "recently, with a forty year old divorced punk rocker."

"Oh, do you still talk to her?" she asked, jealous.

"No darling, it was a one night stand," he joked. "I only spoke to her a few times after that."

"So what is cybersex?" she inquired, relieved Romeo still wasn't talking to this woman. Emilie certainly wasn't the punk rock type!

"Well," he explained, "It's not that great, simply two people imagining having sex while masturbating." He was blunt. She pondered his explanation.

Romeo hadn't enjoyed cybersex the one time he tried it, for he was still from another age and sex on the computer seemed alienating and strange.

Yet Emilie's curiosity meant she wanted to try cybersex with him and he was so enamored with her — the temptation was too great. He knew she would be too proper to ask first.

"Darling," he formally inquired, "would you like to have cybersex with me?"

"I've never done it before. I'm afraid I wouldn't be any good," she replied with a coy innocence. She had wanted to have cybersex with Romeo for days now.

"Don't worry darling, I am sure you are a natural," he reassured her and smiled. Romeo was being reasonable, just as John had been when he had first taken her.

"Imagine us together, darling," he instructed her. "Imagine a scene for us."

"I don't think I can," she typed, embarrassed.

"Would you like me to think of a backdrop?" he offered.

"Yes I would Romeo, very much."

Romeo thought for a moment. "OK, my love, we are back from our first date, a romantic dinner in Hawaii. I take you for a stroll across a moonlit beach. Do you like the opening, Emilie?"

"Yes, it's beautiful," she immediately agreed.

Romeo:	"Emilie, let's sit down on the warm sand, my love."
Emilie:	"Of course, darling."
Emilie:	I put my arms around you and we kiss.
Romeo:	I move against you, as we continue to kiss harder. You feel the soft sand as my body presses into you.
Emilie:	I slide under you and return your kiss, my prince.

Romeo:	"Oh darling, you are such a good kisser."
Romeo:	I feel your beautiful body moving under me. I can tell you want to seduce me. I Hold you tighter and kiss you again.
Emilie:	I kiss you back deeply.

"It's working, isn't it?" she asked, out of character, afraid she wasn't any good at cybersex.

"Very much so, I almost feel us together," he replied truthfully and continued to type:

Romeo:	My hand gently strokes your back, as we make out.
Emilie:	I'm kissing you as warm waves touch our feet.
Romeo:	"Oh God Emilie … I've never been kissed like that."
Romeo:	I kiss your neck then your shoulders.
Romeo:	"You're more beautiful than I imagined."
Romeo:	I begin to massage your shoulders.
Romeo:	"I want to make love to you," I say, gazing into your eyes.
Emilie:	"Then what's stopping you darling?" I playfully ask, as I unbutton your shirt.
Romeo:	"Oh Emilie, you're hands are so soft."
Romeo:	Wildly, we rip each others clothing off, eager in the moonlight.
Emilie:	I wrap my leg around your waist.
Romeo:	I press you into the warm sand and fill you with me.
Emilie:	"Oh Romeo!!!"

Romeo:	My chest presses against your breasts. I push deeper, staring into your beautiful eyes, pressing you against the soft warm sand.
Romeo:	"God, I love you."

"You do?" Emilie asked. But she wasn't in the fantasy anymore. She wanted to know if Romeo really did love her, because she was falling in love with him.

"Yes I do, Emilie," he informed her, noticing her strong reaction to his declaration of love. "Can you look into my eyes and tell me you don't feel the same thing?" he boldly asked, as before.

"Of course not, dear," she typed, at that moment loving Romeo and wanting to be with him forever.

"We are both prisoners of love," he informed her. Indeed, the magic of romance was raging around them like a storm — a little too quickly for Emilie. So, she decided to retreat back into her role:

Emilie:	I kiss you hard and deep.
Romeo:	I push you deeper into the warm sand, staring into your eyes. I gently kiss your breasts as you arch your back. My size rocks into you faster.
Romeo:	"Hold me tighter, love."
Emilie:	I wrap my arms and legs around you like a vice.
Romeo:	I move faster, harder, pushing, kissing your forehead and penetrating deeper.
Emilie:	"Oh my God, Romeo ... Yes!!!"
Romeo:	My arms grab you and I stroke your back as I lift you and fill you again.

Emilie:	I begin screaming loudly.
Romeo:	I thrust with passion, crazy, and wanting to drive you crazy. I penetrate deeper as we bounce together.
Romeo:	"Wrap your legs around me tighter dear."
Emilie:	I kiss you deeply ... Oh Romeo!
Romeo:	We stare at each other as I grow inside of you. I tremble. My cheek is against yours.
Romeo:	"Oh Emilie, I love you ... ."
Romeo:	"I'M CUMMING, DARLING!!!"
Emilie:	"I LOVE YOU, ROMEO!!!!"
Romeo:	Ahh ... .
Romeo:	I feel my seed gushing into you. My forehead gently touches yours. I bend to kiss your neck, then suck your beautiful hard nipples.
Emilie:	So hard, they hurt.
Romeo:	Oh God ... .
Emilie:	Mmm ... .
Romeo:	"I love you Emilie, forever dear."
Romeo:	I kiss you lovingly, still inside you. I feel your soft face flushed against my cheek, as you orgasm wildly.
Emilie:	Oh, Romeo ... .

~

Emilie was spent. Her orgasm had been amazing and she was sure Romeo's had been also — evidenced by his lack of typing. "When we came together, I felt something very special," he finally remarked.

"I did too, Romeo," she agreed smiling, zipping up her loose slacks. God she had enjoyed that! Her body was tingling. Their love was exciting and magical, yet simple and natural. She had finally found someone who loved her for who she was. She hoped it would all work out.

After Romeo logged off, Emilie sat in her warm chair, grinning. Her shirt and other parts of her were now ruffled. *I actually had cybersex with Romeo*, she proudly thought. *And he was so kind*. He had been her teacher, just as John had been. But unlike John, Romeo seemed to love her endlessly.

Romeo and Perfection

I will withdraw: but this intrusion shall
Now seeming sweet convert to bitter gall.

- Cousin Tybalt

"**A**loha beautiful," Romeo typed the next morning.

"This is John."

Romeo was intrigued, but decided to keep his cool, not plunge into an indulgent drama like he had foolishly done with Juliet's cousin so long ago. He was chatting with Emilie's mysterious *friend* — the man who was slowly breaking her heart.

"Oh sorry, have fun," Romeo shot back with a touch of sarcasm. He closed his chat window and moved his mouse to his business mail folder. To his surprise, another message popped-up.

"Do you want to speak to Emilie?" John daringly offered, curious about this *Romeo* character and wanting to show Emilie he was not jealous of this guy — he actually wanted her to date other men.

Meanwhile, Romeo sensed the nastiness within this man's selfless question. By inviting, almost encouraging him to chat with Emilie, John was letting Emilie know he didn't really care about her at all.

"Sure," Romeo answered cheerfully and hit the enter key.

There was a tense pause. He waited.

"Romeo!" Emilie exclaimed. "It's so good to talk to you."

"Hello beautiful, how is your day going. Did I interrupt something?" he asked.

"No, John was just looking for directions to a restaurant," she explained, feeling the primitive excitement of two men fighting over her. John and Romeo felt like matter and anti-matter, and their small explosion flustered her. She felt almost giddy after their uneventful clash.

In Hawaii, Romeo realized how deeply this man was hurting her. Her *John* obviously wanted someone to take Emilie off his hands, and was letting both of them know it. Emilie's *friend* was finished using her, done draining her aura — as Master Lee taught men often did with women. Now it was convenient for Emilie to cling to someone else, someone who would clean up whatever mess this man had made within that wonderful, trusting, yet naive mind that Romeo cherished so.

Romeo and Emilie began to chatter about meaningless things for a few minutes. He could tell Emilie was surprised, worse yet, insulted by her lover's daring move of handing her off to another.

~

Johnny Perfection angrily paced in the dining room as he watched Emilie voraciously chat. Everything had backfired. He had seen this guy online and wanted to show her he wasn't jealous. Somehow, in the short encounter, he had lost the advantage. This *Romeo* had called his bluff, deadpan, as if they were both playing high stakes poker for a woman.

He shot angry glances at Emilie as he buttoned his shirt. She was crouched by her computer, totally enthralled. *Like a little girl talking to her prince charming doll*, he observed disdainfully. She seemed to jump into a childish, romantic world with her online friend that he could not, or would not, follow.

Surely, this man is fucking with Emilie. He is trying to lure her to Hawaii, he speculated. *He is dangerous.*

"Darling," he spoke up, trying to remain calm. The tone sounded too needy. He was now the jealous one! He tried to suppress the emotion and became even more enraged that Johnny Perfection could be jealous of anyone, let alone an Internet pervert!

"Emilie, let's go to lunch now," he insisted, almost like a disapproving father. "I thought you were coming," he added weakly.

She was hunched over the computer, still mesmerized. Suddenly, John wanted to get away from this Romeo character as fast as possible. More importantly, he wanted to get Emilie away from him as well.

"I thought we were going to lunch later, darling," she finally remarked distracted, in a tone that subtly mocked him.

"No, I want to go *now*," he insisted, visibly angry.

~

John's anger hit Emilie like a scorching fire as she chatted happily away with her *friend* from Hawaii. Romeo seemed to have a maddening effect on John that Paris or other men did not. *He shouldn't have embarrassed me like that*, she reasoned, feeling justified.

"Romeo," she typed.

"Yes my love?"

"I have to go now. Is that OK? I'm sorry."

"Love is never having to say you're sorry, dear."

"lol"

"Have a great day, my love."

"Goodbye Romeo." She logged out of Yahoo.

"If you don't want to come, I'm going now," John complained, moving for the door.

"No darling, I just said goodbye," she replied casually. After all, John could have a monogamous relationship with her if he wanted. He could put a stop to her online romance by leaving his wife and whatever other girlfriends he had. *Maybe Romeo will make him see how much he loves me,* she hoped to herself, grabbing her black coat. She joined him by the apartment entrance, noticing his forlorn face, realizing she had just hurt him.

Why does Romeo make him so jealous? she wondered, as John opened the door. *Maybe he senses my feelings toward him.* She walked past John in her tight jeans and held her head high as he leered at her. She had caught him in his own contradiction. John had heartlessly encouraged her to date other men — but now he was jealous of a man she hadn't even met!

Are all relationships this way, people playing games with each other, maneuvering? she wondered, as she rode down in the elevator. When the dented metallic doors opened, John quickly exited and angrily crossed the lobby, flung the glass doors open, and silently hailed a taxi. Emilie followed reluctantly.

~

"I'm going to Swifts. Do you want to come?" John asked in a bored tone, hoping she would say no. He was still pissed off from his short encounter with Romeo. It was evening now and he wanted to get roaring drunk.

"That's OK darling," she answered, distracted, from the dining area.

A few weeks ago, he reflected, *she would have started an argument over my drinking and staying out late.* Emilie might have even have joined him, to keep an eye on him, worrying about all the other women that constantly threw themselves at Johnny Perfection. At least she had paid attention to him then. *But no*, he sarcastically realized with disdain, *not now … Emilie has found her Romeo.* John wasn't angry at this Romeo character; instead, he felt a growing contempt toward Emma Gallant, a beautiful actress reduced to having a cyber-romance.

Pathetic! he thought bitterly, reaching for his hat. *She has some psychological issues.*

For an instant, he felt a twinge of guilt. *Did I cause this?* he wondered, as he grabbed his thick grey overcoat and opened the apartment door. Through the corner of his eye, he saw Emilie's delicate shape hunched by her laptop. She didn't seem to be typing though. He could tell she was waiting — waiting for her Romeo.

He rode down in the small elevator with an older bald rabbi who lived above him. The Rabbi nodded to him with slight embarrassment. John smiled back politely. He thought of Emilie and looked up at the dirty tin ceiling, hoping to see her in his mind's eye.

God, he thought, *she is like a lonely child with an imaginary friend. Since they can't fuck each other, I guess they have to bullshit each other.* He glanced over at the rabbi who was uncomfortably waiting for the elevator doors to open.

But still, he protested to himself, *Emilie is beautiful and famous. How could she be doing this?* John felt she was betraying the Hollywood mystique itself; for what is the glamour of Hollywood when a beautiful young actress, adored by millions, gives herself to perverts on the Internet?

Romeo was a cursed name to him now. "Fuck Romeo," he muttered, as he exited the lobby and took a breathe of the freezing Manhattan air. *Obviously, that isn't his fucking name,* he deduced. *How could Emilie be so fucking stupid to believe him? If his name isn't Romeo, he must be lying about everything else.*

He hailed a yellow cab and stepped in. A tall driver wearing a turban smiled at him, in a manner a little too cheerful for his glum mood. "Take me to Swifts on 4th and Bowery," he commanded, angrily.

"Yes sir," the taxi driver perkily replied, in a thick Indian accent.

"Cool man," John muttered, happy he was moving quickly away from Emilie and Romeo. He was going to drink his ass off tonight. *God, I miss Los Angeles,* he realized. He even missed his wife, Renee. *She wouldn't make a fool of me by going online to meet perverts,* he reflected. *Renee is an adult, a mother. She wouldn't fuck with me in this way!*

Emilie is still a child ... and I have to look out for her! he bemoaned, as his taxi headed south.

~

"Well Emilie, I'm going to log off now and get some sleep," Romeo typed. Many hours had passed since John had left to get drunk. It was midnight in Hawaii and five AM in New York City.

"Romeo, stay with me. I'm alone," Emilie suddenly pleaded with her fingers. "John is out drinking," she confessed. "I don't know why he drinks so much. It doesn't seem to make him happy."

"Of course I will stay with you, my angel," he assured her. "What do you want to talk about?"

"Oh anything, Romeo, I love your company," she turned and stared out the cold dark dining room window.

"Well, I feel you are destined to win three Oscars," he declared, gazing at her beautiful picture. He hadn't expected to say that, but he was tired now, typing whatever came to mind.

She snapped up in her chair, surprised at his prediction. She had almost dozed off. "Why do you say that?" she asked. *Maybe he knows I am Emma Gallant.*

"Because I meditate, dear," he explained. "Your aura is so strong and you are far more beautiful and intelligent than any actress I have seen."

"Thank you, Romeo. You're so kind to me," she remarked, with a tired smile. "I have an audition Tuesday," she added. It normally wasn't like her to talk about auditions.

"That's wonderful Emilie."

"Well, I'm nervous. It's been snowing here and I haven't been able to workout," she confessed.

"Don't worry," he reassured her. "I will pray to my Zen Master for you to get the role."

"Thank you," she replied tiredly. Emilie then heard the rattle of John's keys and said goodbye to Romeo. A few weeks later— she did get the role.

~

John juggled his keys, dropped them, cursed, picked them up, fumbled with them, caught them, shuffled through them blurry-eyed, and finally recognized his door key. When he stumbled inside, he was surprised to see Emilie motionless by the refrigerator, probably upset he had stayed out until dawn.

"So how is Romeo doing?" he asked, sarcastically, hoping to seize the moral high ground.

"Why do you ask that, John?" she wheeled to face him, dramatically. After all, she was an actress.

"Because I love you baby," he staggered forward to kiss her. She felt cold and distant.

"If you loved me, you wouldn't be going to Malibu to fuck your wife tomorrow!" Emilie spat out. John was leaving for the coast in the afternoon.

"Oh, now suddenly my marriage is a problem!"

Emilie quickly retreated to the sink. *Please, let there be a dish I can wash,* she pleaded desperately. To her chagrin, the sink was spotless. She mindlessly rubbed some lotion from the counter onto her trembling hands and turned on the water. She hadn't expected him to yell.

John noticed his loud voice had frightened Emilie. He walked unsteadily toward her, totally shit-faced, trying to balance himself while reaching for her shoulders. The moment he touched them, Emilie shivered and began to cry. This startled him, allowing her to duck under his arms quickly and move to the refrigerator.

"Well, if that's the way you feel, I'll be in bed darling," he mumbled, too tired to argue or feel guilty. Tomorrow he could travel back to California, to his family — and he had never thought that a relief until now. He turned and wobbled toward his bedroom, like a sailor on a stormy sea.

Am I being a total bitch? Emilie's head was down by the sink. *No, I can't think that way! John is married. I have to be strong!*

She wiped her tears with the back of her hand. She couldn't live in a world without love. She turned to the window and saw the reflected glow of Manhattan below. The holiday colors were beautiful, swirling red circles above cold streets. The dancing light on the window pane reminded her of being a little girl, snug by the fireplace in Cambridge. She had felt so much love then and she wondered why the same feeling was so elusive now.

~

Johnny Perfection angrily swung his glossy black 1968 Mustang around a sharp curve. The orange glow of the California sun bathed the landscape. He had been in Malibu a few days and had just escaped his screaming wife — who was throwing dishes at him! She had found out about his affair with Emma Gallant and John was in deep shit.

"Fuck, why did this have to happen now?" he complained angrily as he screeched to a stop, waiting to cross the Pacific Coast Highway. He slammed his fist on the chrome-chained steering wheel of his favorite car.

"Fuck, why did Renee have to yell at her. That bitch!" John growled, furious with his wife. She had fucking screamed at Emilie on his cell and now he had to calm the situation down! The light turned green and he swerved into a mini-mall. He had to talk to Emilie, get her on the same page. He lunged to a stop in front of an old phone booth with faded red trim.

"Fuck, I don't have any fucking quarters!" he swore. He knew, back in New York, Emilie was freaking out. Hell, he was freaking out. Renee was threatening a divorce! *And over what?* he wondered. She knew he fucked around!

He stormed out of his car and slammed his door shut. Emilie had been so fucking stupid for sending him a text message to his cell phone. But then, he angrily realized, wrestling open the creaky door of the phone booth, he had been a fucking moron to leave the cell by his wife's bed.

"What do you fucking mean you don't accept VISA?" John screamed into the receiver.

"Sir, I am only an operator, and if you continue to use that language, I will have to hang up."

"Well, fuck, what am I supposed to do?" he yelled.

"Sir I can connect you with MCI or Sprint, but please stop that language," the operator chastised him.

"OK," he agreed, sounding defeated.

~

Emilie had been crying for hours. *Why hasn't he called?* she lamented, sprawled out on her bed in agony. *Oh God, his wife called me a whore! I am so afraid. What if she tells everyone? That doesn't matter,* she wildly realized. *I love John so!* Yet deep down, she wasn't sure if that was true. Maybe she was just trying to save face.

Suddenly, in accordance with her thoughts, her cell rang. She quickly flipped it open:

"Baby, I'm sorry," her lover's deep voice begin from the other end.

"Oh God John, what happened? I'm so afraid for us!" she exclaimed, hoping desperately that he still wanted her.

"Nothing baby, my wife just found your message." John seemed cold and detached. She grew nervous.

"Are you still coming to New York next week, John?" she asked, panicked.

"No baby, Renee is crazy now. We have to cool it for a while," he informed her.

"What are you saying?" she began to cry.

"Look baby, I don't want to get a divorce over this and she is freaking out over you for some reason," he explained. "Maybe you can see Paris for a while, hon," he added — hurtfully.

"John, what are you saying?" she cried weakly. "I thought we were a couple!"

"Baby," he began awkwardly. *I wish Emilie would stop her fucking crying.* "Baby ... you know I want you also, but things just got fucked up."

"John!" she exclaimed, "When will we be together? I want to be with you. Don't leave me alone!" she pleaded hysterically.

"Look Emilie," he began awkwardly. "I'm at a phone booth. Things are just too hot now — maybe in a few months. I'll call you soon."

"John, speak to me! Why can't we meet sooner?" she demanded, as tears generously flowed down her cheeks.

"Emilie I can't ... look, I told Renee I was going to get cigarettes. I have to go." He hung up.

"John ... John ... Oh God he hung up on me!" A shudder went through her and she sobbed harder — but also shook with indignation. John had been so cold and heartless. He had enjoyed dumping her. *Maybe his wife's tantrum had only been the perfect excuse,* she sadly realized.

~

Hours passed, Emilie's room was almost pitch black. A meager light shone through the thick curtains of her uptown Capulet Agency penthouse. She struggled up from the bed. She had cried for what seemed forever and then prayed.

She sat down at her desk and turned her laptop on. Romeo's name was bolded on her buddy list. She waited for him to message her. A few minutes passed and she nervously began to pace. It was as if John's wife had also called Romeo! An hour later, he was still online but not speaking with her.

Why is he ignoring me? she asked herself. She felt tears welling up in her eyes. She suddenly hated John even more. He had forced her to meet this online Romeo to make him jealous. John had manipulated her and discarded her — now Romeo seemed to be doing the same thing.

"Calm down, Emilie," she admonished herself, as she sat still by the laptop. *Simply because Romeo isn't by his computer, doesn't mean that he has betrayed me. That's silly,* she told herself, sniffling.

Maybe Romeo is at the beach, she wondered, as she turned again to the clock. *It's still early there.* She smiled and imagined being on a Hawaiian beach with him. *I'm just being silly,* she told herself. *I should message him.*

She began to cry and thought of John again. How pathetic she had been to fall in love with a married man! She wondered if there was anyone out there who would love her for who she was and not leave her, as Romeo and John were doing now.

Maybe she was imagining things and Romeo would message her again; but it didn't feel that way. He was like a magical bird that had flown into her life, suddenly appearing and singing mysterious, beautiful songs, only to fly off without a goodbye. *Maybe the encounter with John frightened him away,* she reasoned.

After about an hour of watching Romeo online, Emilie turned off her laptop and stood in her nightgown by the windows overlooking Central Park. The moonlight cast a beautiful glow through the glass and illumined her streaming hair and graceful silhouette, which now looked so utterly alone.

The Resolute Ascension

O gentle Romeo,
If thou dost love, pronounce it faithfully.

- Juliet

Romeo mindfully steeped the green teabag in boiling water. It was raining and on rainy days his home became cold. Like most dwellings on the Big Island of Hawaii, the new but modest wooden house had no central heating. It was late afternoon and he had returned from a swim in the chilly Pacific. The rain began to fall harder against his roof, the sound making him feel very alone.

How nice it would be, he mused, as he tested his mug of hot tea, *to have a lover of my own.* Suddenly, he felt a pang in his heart and remembered Emilie. He had not seen her online for over a week.

He wandered into his study and turned on his computer to the sound of rain whipping against office windows. In the distance, huge grey waves rolled in, pounding mightily against the volcanic cliffs below. Romeo sat by his computer and clicked on his chat icon, bored. He noticed his buddy list was disabled and recalled the computer upgrade last week. His heart sank. Emilie could have logged in many times and assumed he was ignoring her!

"Oh Shit!" he swore and began to reset his buddy list options.

At that moment, Emilie was sitting alone in her Capulet Agency suite on Park Avenue. She never liked the oppressive silence of the large, impersonal penthouse. She had been crying tonight, recalling how she and John would watch black and white films together; even that she missed now; for the sounds of her penthouse were silent.

Emilie hated John, but loved him also — or wanted to love him. She missed him. She missed her dreams of marrying him and being on the cover of People and Time magazine. Silly dreams, but they had been hers and now they were gone forever.

John had made a fool of her, she realized. Her parents and friends had known all along how it was going to end. Of course, she had seen the ending herself and tried to stave off the inevitable for so long. She was furious with John for proving her mother and everyone else right! She recalled how people looked at her, when she dared accompany him to private parties in Manhattan. Everyone treated her as if she was just another naive actress, too star-struck to realize she was simply another placeholder, for another married alcoholic actor, having another midlife crisis.

At least her filming project was over in New York. She could leave this empty suite forever and return to England. She knew she would return humiliated though. Her mother and everyone else would say: *I told you so.*

Her mind turned to Paris, the young man she dated before John had swept her off her feet. Paris had been so polite, so *gallant* about things. When they broke up, he vowed to remain her friend. Emilie had lost respect for Paris though. He had rolled over too easily when John snatched her from under his nose. He had acted like a king; while Paris and her behaved no better than serfs.

Paris though, she acknowledged, had done the strategic thing by simply waiting patiently for her disastrous relationship with John to self-destruct. How could she even face him now? He would have that same: *I told you so,* look on his face.

She gazed at her laptop and thought of Romeo. Unfortunately, he had proven unreliable like John. He had hurt her feelings by ignoring her for over a week now. She had seen him online a few times, but decided not to message him first. He clearly had better things to do than chat with her! He had seemed so trustworthy at first. She had been sure he was falling in love with her and that felt so flattering in contrast to John's indifference. But Romeo disappeared after having cybersex once. He had treated her like a conquest, just as John had done.

Are all men like John and Romeo? she asked and turned her laptop on. She decided to surf the Hollywood websites and her fan sites. It was her job to keep up with the industry. Reading about movies, movie stars, and even herself, might cheer her up. When she logged into Yahoo, she saw Romeo's name bolded. He was still ignoring her — most likely having cybersex with another unsuspecting female.

~

Once Romeo changed his buddy list settings, almost to his chagrin, he noticed Emilie's name bolded.

"Aloha Darling, how have you been? I've missed talking to you," he started. There was a long pause. He could feel something was wrong. He could feel Emilie was in pain — sensing it was because her *friendship* with John was over.

"You don't have to talk to me if you don't want to," she haughtily shot back.

Romeo was shocked. Emilie had never spoken rudely to him before. He could feel her condescending tone and it hurt. Yet he wanted to clear things up, for he felt this sensitive woman needed someone — now more than ever.

It's so simple, he told himself, *all I have to do is get her to see the love that is already between us.*

"But I do want to talk to you, far more than any other woman on the Internet or in real life. You are so beautiful and intelligent," he told her and waited ... no response.

She must think I've been ignoring her, he realized. "My buddy list hasn't been working, darling," he explained. "I didn't see you online. I have missed you, Emilie."

He sat patiently. Something deep within him felt he might lose this exceptional woman forever. They would just become two more lonely souls, too blind to recognize true love, too foolish to follow their hearts. He had to tell her this in his own way, even if she didn't want to hear it.

"I want to bring out your magical side, Emilie. I think we have known each other in past lives," he revealed.

He waited in silence, feeling her reluctantly reading his words. That's all he could ask for. He had never spilled his heart out to a woman he could not see. For a moment, he recalled courting Juliet in the Capulet's orchard — so long ago:

She speaks, yet she says nothing; what of that? Her eye discourses; I will answer it.

"You are the most amazing woman I have ever met. I care for you deeply Emilie. I can see beyond your physical beauty. You have a beautiful soul and I don't want anyone to destroy that beauty."

Still no response, yet he felt a tension, a presence. There was a breathtakingly gorgeous young woman at the other end of the world, a stunning actress who could win the heart of any man she wanted, wondering if she should trust a stranger. She was the solitary bird in Romeo's vision — he had to act fast before the golden latches of Hollywood snapped shut forever.

He decided to tell her what he saw in his heart, the more successful she became, the more danger she would encounter — danger, not in the sense of physical danger, but the danger of losing that unique magic of hers that he cherished so.

"I want to protect you from the negative energies of Hollywood," he proclaimed.

Romeo waited for her to say something. He could tell he was getting nowhere. He didn't want to make a fool of himself. He was already breaching Internet etiquette by his continued unanswered messages. He had put his cards down. If she left him now, she would do so with open eyes.

"You are too beautiful and evolved for this dark world. I want to protect the magic I see within you darling," he continued. Pausing, his heart sank. She logged off.

At least she read my words, he told himself. *If our love is real, she will return. If not, then I have said goodbye.* He logged off himself, content.

~

"You don't have to talk to me if you don't want to," Emilie typed flustered, insulted that Romeo would casually message her after ignoring her for over a week. Like John, he felt he could just waltz into her life at his convenience! She found herself wishing he knew she was a movie star.

Maybe then he wouldn't treat me like second best, she complained. Her laptop chimed:

"But I do want to talk to you Emilie, far more than any other woman on the Internet or in real life. You are so beautiful and intelligent."

She suspected he would say something like that. A part of her wanted to hurt him now. *If I am so beautiful and intelligent, why have you been ignoring me?* she rhetorically asked, reminding herself of all the handsome actors and artists who wanted to date her. She certainly didn't need this Internet Romeo!

"My buddy list hasn't been working darling. I didn't see you online. I have missed you, Emilie," he implored

She closed his message window again. Maybe she would talk to him later, but why? The magic between them was gone, well almost gone. Her computer chimed — prodding her. *Can't he see I don't want to talk to him now?* she asked, frustrated, as she rubbed her cried-out eyes drier. She looked around the large empty bedroom and decided nothing else was going on, so she opened her chat window:

"I want to bring out your magical side, Emilie," she read. "I think we have known each other in past lives."

She adored Romeo when he spoke that way. But words weren't enough. John had wooed her with beautiful words too. A chill went through her, as her laptop rang to his declarations:

"You are the most amazing woman I have ever met. I care for you deeply Emilie. I see can beyond your physical beauty. You have a beautiful soul and I don't want anyone to destroy that beauty."

She began to feel him in her heart again, as she had before. She smiled sadly in her high solitary suite. *There is something interesting about him*, she admitted. *Maybe I have known him in other lives.* Still, she didn't want to talk to anyone now. Yet Romeo evidently did, for he continued to type:

"I want to protect you from the negative energies of Hollywood," she read.

Her heart stirred. as she smiled weakly at his remark, understanding only too well, thanks to John, the negative side of Hollywood. *Is Romeo my prince charming, come to deliver me from my charmed life?* she cleverly asked herself. She considered messaging him now. Tears welled up in her eyes, as the tips of her fingers touched the sleek keyboard. She wasn't sure if she could trust anyone at this point.

"You are too beautiful and evolved for this dark world. I want to protect the magic I see within you darling," he declared.

Emilie had to admit his words were poetic and strong. He was articulating feelings she had felt since childhood. He spoke to her in lyrical ways she always dreamed her prince would — a prince who would know her heart and simply love her for who she was.

Yet she was too tired to speak to anyone now and didn't know what to say. Besides, she had cried over John all day. She wanted to sleep and then return to England. Maybe if things didn't click with Paris she would chat with this unique man again.

She logged off and slowly walked to the well-appointed bedroom she used to share with John sometimes. Romeo spoke wonderful words tonight — words she probably needed to hear. She perched on the side of her bed, carefully combing her sleek, long, hair. Tomorrow a jet from the studio would take her back to England, far from New York and all her bad memories.

Yes, she admitted, as she crawled under the satin sheets of her king-sized bed, *I want to speak to Romeo again*. She curled up, imagining herself in Hawaii by his side. He had touched her heart tonight, something no one else had done in such a long time. People only wanted to see the surface, the irresistible movie star, the sensation, the millionaire Emma Gallant.

She sighed and rolled on her back, imagining Romeo's strong arms around her. In his embrace, she would be safe. In Hawaii, she would be far away from her problems and all the people who wanted a piece of her. Romeo only wanted Emilie to be herself. *I want to meet him,* she finally admitted as she fell asleep, *so I can find out who I really am.*

~

Hours after Emilie drifted into a comfortable sleep, Romeo undressed and turned on the hot water above his bath. He had made a fool of himself tonight. He smiled boyishly and walked into the powerful stream of water. As he slid the door shut, he realized there was a good chance he would never speak with Emilie again.

Romeo dried off and sat down at his meditation table cross-legged, wearing a black Zen robe with a red dragon on it. He chanted a Buddhist mantra and focused on the heart center, for it was the heart that had been the topic of the evening. As he meditated, he pushed away thoughts as they entered his awareness — many were of Emilie.

He bowed to close his meditation and crawled into bed. Relaxing and stretching his legs, he stared at the wooden ceiling, wondering if the universe would give him another chance at love; although, a Zen monk now, Romeo reminded himself that in a different time he had murdered, and then killed himself — all for the love of a woman.

Is Emilie a chance at redemption? he wondered.

Suddenly — Romeo sensed her presence and turned. Impossibly, next to him, he beheld the glowing energy body of Emma Gallant. But the form was not the Emilie he knew. She looked younger, curious, a precocious child. Her luminous figure smiled and marveled at him as she lay by his side, resting her head on a hand. She was spellbound with him, joyous, as if she knew wonderful secrets about them both.

He felt such unconditional love radiating from her astral visage. Her eyes sparkled and adored him with pure acceptance and adoration. The child Emilie peered wide-eyed into his aura, viewing images of their past and future lives he could not. He turned the other way. It was no use; he could still feel her by his side. He rolled over again and marveled at her brilliant form of light.

His Zen Master had taught that people traveled in the astral dimensions when they dreamt. *Yet, this is so visual and real*, he marveled. *Emilie is indeed a powerful and evolved soul. She must have fallen asleep considering my words*, he realized. *She loves me very much, deep inside.* Images of young Emilie, playing in her father's garden, raced through his mind.

Is she Juliet, reincarnated? he finally wondered. His eyes grew heavy, as he lay by her shining form. He felt their energies merging as he drifted into a peaceful sleep, into her dreams — where she smiled at her prince from afar and offered him a hand.

Hollywood and Juliet

Hollywood is a place where they'll pay you a thousand dollars for a kiss and fifty cents for your soul.

- Marilyn Monroe

The Gulf Stream jet landed tentatively, almost seductively, on the long Los Angeles runway. The early spring air was silver-grey above the airport. Emilie watched the late morning fog eagerly caress the plane's sleek wings. She felt a strange freedom as the wheels touched down and began their long taxi on the runway. The breakup with John seemed farther away and her mother was not accompanying her on this trip. She was free in Los Angeles — in Hollywood itself, the source of those huge contracts that made her and the Capulet agency rich.

Exiting the chartered jet and stepping out onto the loud tarmac made Emilie feel like a woman, an artist even. She had landed the part of *Estella* in Dickens' *Great Expectations*. Her actions would help determine the fate of the film. Working hard would redeem her and give her strength — the strength she needed to mend a broken heart.

She had been depressed in Cambridge after her time in New York. Although she had agreed to see Paris, the few times they had gone out, he had failed to remove that empty feeling in her gut. She still missed John. A part of her still loved him.

111

Is it because he was my first lover? she wondered, as a glossy white limousine streaked toward her luggage. An old dashing chauffeur with sculptured grey hair stepped around the vehicle and opened one of the large doors for her, smiling in the bright Los Angeles sun.

"Do you have any more suitcases, Ms. Gallant?"

"No, thank you. I will carry my own handbag," she answered, ducking into the plush interior. Her driver finished loading the luggage and merged into the busy traffic of Sepulveda Blvd.

As cars hurried around her, she watched the endless grey expanse of tract homes, smog, and roaring traffic parade by her window. The side rails of La Cienega Boulevard rattled as her limo climbed Baldwin Hills toward the city of lights. To her right, ancient pumps laboriously coaxed oil out of brown dusty ground. The view contrasted with her spotless white outfit and the immaculately clean limousine. She smiled, thankful to be sheltered from the snarled, hot confusion of Los Angeles.

As her driver descended the other side of Baldwin Hills, she was overwhelmed by the endless valley of cement and roaring traffic that disappeared into the hazy morning. Being alone in this vast city made it intensely more real for her. She suddenly thought of something Romeo said a few weeks ago:

You are too beautiful and evolved for this dark world. I want to protect the magic I see within you.

Frantic cars and trucks sped by, as she crossed Pico Boulevard reflecting on the words Romeo had typed. She was now a stranger in a huge raging city. In line with her thoughts, an overweight prostitute in a dirty blue skirt appeared by her window, jutting out her thumb for business.

Maybe I am too beautiful for this world. Maybe I do need someone to protect me. She looked down embarrassed and folded her hands.

~

 inally the bellman finished carrying up her luggage and she was alone in her hotel suite at the Beverly Regent. It was early afternoon. The spacious room relaxed her. She could feel her own mind again. She walked to the large bed and sat on its soft white embroidered cover. Resting on her night table, a fruit basket and card from the studio.

Emilie's suitcases surrounded her at the foot of the bed. She was too tired to unpack. She noticed a beautiful mahogany desk by the window and recalled the concierge mentioning Internet access. Thinking of Romeo she looked out her window, west toward Hawaii.

She lay down on her back and studied the intricate patterns of the white ornamental ceiling. She didn't want to fall asleep. *Better to stay up now,* she reminded herself. *Maybe there is something on the tele. I'll check that in a few minutes. I just need to rest my head for a moment. Perhaps I should connect my laptop to the Internet ... I want to speak with Romeo again ... I wonder if that is really his name ... .*

~

 he ringer blared loudly. Emilie awoke startled. Someone had forgotten to turn the bloody volume down on the dainty Victorian phone by her bed. She reached for the elegant handle and pressed it to her ear.

"Darling," It was her publicist Beth, speaking sharply with her Brooklyn accent.

"Yes ... Beth ... I am ... I just dozed off."

"I know hon, jet lag," Beth retorted quickly. "I just wanted to give you a wakeup call for your *Entertainment Tonight* piece."

She looked at the clock. *Damn, it's bloody four in the afternoon!* She had slept almost three hours and was supposed to be live, on the air, in two!

"Are you there, Emilie?" Beth checked.

"Beth," Emilie began, tired, "let me shower. I will be ready in thirty minutes," she promised.

"Yes darling," Beth replied. "So how was your flight?"

"Long ... ."

"I'm sorry we had to schedule the interview tonight, hun."

"I know."

"Well, bye darling," Beth said and hung up.

Emilie wiped the sleep from her eyes. *At least I got some rest*, she told herself. Unfortunately, she had slept in her clothes, without pulling her hair up and had only thirty minutes to get ready, before millions of people would see her on television. She glanced out the sliding doors of the suite. The sun already hung low over the California coast, tilting far to the west against an endless silver ocean in the distance, reminding her of Romeo's words:

I want to protect you from the negative energies of Hollywood.

She undressed and strode naked into the large sumptuous bathroom. After tested the water of her shower, she stepped into the pulsating spray and lathered herself with soap. She thought of her agency, the Capulet Agency, then Paris and Romeo. As she carefully massaged Aveda shampoo into her hair, it dawned on her that many of the names in her life seemed to revolve around Shakespeare's play. *Is God trying to tell me something?* she wondered.

Even Johnny Perfection's real name, she knew, was John Tybalt. His hippy parents had changed their names to *Paramiti* when he was ten, which translates from Sanskrit to perfection. When the young John had first told his agent the story, a star was born — *Johnny Perfection.*

She added conditioner to her hair and relaxed to the warm shower's caresses, delicately untangling her beautiful braids in the exact way the top hair stylists of the world had instructed. As the cascading water woke her up, she wondered if she might have been Juliet in another life. Romeo had spoken of reincarnation many times.

"Romeo and Juliet," she recited aloud, and rinsed off her conditioner to the comfortable streams of water.

~

An hour later, Emma Gallant's beautiful white slipper inched out of a shiny black limousine and touched a dirty grey curb. A small crowd, consisting mostly of young girls, gathered around the entrance of the studio. Scattered amongst her cheering fans were paparazzi, waiting like vultures, hoping to get that one great shot of Emma Gallant.

"Look, that's Emma!" a shrill voice exclaimed as she stepped out of the car.

"Oh my God! She's so beautiful!" a second girl squealed, as lights flashed eagerly around Ms. Gallant.

Another gasp, as Emilie walked elegantly up the curb in a peach skirt. The crowd beheld her in awe, as if she was Joan of Arc and could inspire nations. Instead, she smiled shyly amidst a few camera flashes, waved, then ducked behind the glass doors of the building.

"Emma I love you!" she heard a girl shriek from behind her.

"EMMA PLEASE SIGN THIS!" another scream.

"OH GOD, IT'S HER!"

"GOD DAMN, SHE IS FINE," a deep male voice exclaimed in a southern drawl. Her publicist Beth snapped orders for a guard to shut the doors. The small crowd was unexpected. She wondered why the studio hadn't taken her through a side entrance. *Maybe they encourage the fans*, she realized. *After all, this is Hollywood.*

"Hey you!" Emilie turned to the sound. Beth had motioned to an elderly security guard across the lobby, her voice echoing in the large marble space. Emilie watched the old man slowly close his newspaper then tiredly shuffle toward them, while fans still screeched behind thick glass doors.

"You," Beth pointed to the old guard, as if he was guilty for walking too slow. "Escort Miss Gallant to her dressing room!" she commanded.

"Yes Ma'am," the guard replied tiredly, and made a call on his walkie-talkie.

Suddenly Emilie felt a tap on her shoulder, turned, and found herself face-to-face with a thin, tall and awkwardly handsome young man looming uncertainly over her. He was a few years older than her, she guessed. Dark black hair fell to his brow and he wore spectacles. She suddenly felt a rush of sexual energy between them.

"Excuse me," he began nervously. "I am from the L.A. Weekly ... ."

Beth suddenly stepped between her and the awkward young journalist. "Who let you in here?" she demanded accusingly, pointing at his chest.

"I ... I ... I ... Our offices are in this building," the young man stuttered and froze. He had dark blue eyes and wore a faded aqua shirt. He intrigued Emilie, maybe because he was the first authentic looking person she had met since landing in Los Angeles.

Her publicist moved in for the kill, sensing the stuttering man's fear. "Do you know who this is, young man?" Beth asked, accusingly. "Emma Gallant doesn't have time for interviews." The boyish journalist apologetically retreated.

"Who is your editor?" Beth interrogated, now on the offensive.

Emilie found herself hoping the young writer would defend himself against Beth's onslaughts, but before she could wait to hear her potential champion's stuttering response, the old guard motioned to her.

"Ms. Gallant, this way please."

She listened to Beth berating the guards and the shy journalist as the elevator doors closed.

~

Emilie lay exhausted again on her bed at the Beverly Regent. The hotel had made up the sheets perfectly and a box of mints lay on her pillow. She reminded herself to tip well at the end of the stay. God, she was tired. Worse yet, the *Entertainment Tonight* piece had not gone as smoothly as she had hoped.

"I looked so terrible!" she bemoaned, as she gazed across the room at a large mirror. She had lost her great tan from last summer and the cold winter had caused her to gain weight.

Yet she knew the real reason why she had lost that vibrant glow — it was because of John. He had broken her heart and humiliated her. Crying over him made her face puffy too, she suspected. She touched her eyelids and soft cheeks with the tips of her fingers and thought of something Romeo had once said:

Your aura is so strong and you are far more beautiful and intelligent than any actress I have seen.

He had typed that during a cold winter night, while she had foolishly waited up for John to return from a drinking binge. Romeo had surprised her that evening, by declaring she was destined to win three Oscars.

"Three Oscars! God, I would be happy with one," Emilie informed the empty room.

She tiredly moved to the bathroom and quickly showered, dried off, and slipped under the silk covers of her bed. She wondered if her relationship with John had drained her aura. She gently touched her face and turned to the mirror by the nightstand, peering at the tired young woman looking back at her. She so wanted to fall in love again. She wanted to feel beautiful again. She rolled over on her back, comfortably. She was in California now — the land of the stars, and she was one of them. She smiled softly, flicked off the lamp, and fell asleep.

~

After a long shower the next morning, Emilie put on a robe and headed to the hotel phone to check messages. Paris had left one during the night and so had mum, both congratulating her on her interview. This only upset her, since she knew the interview had essentially sucked.

She decided to get her laptop connected. She was supposed to email Rick Carter, director of *Great Expectations*, when she arrived in town. She hoped he hadn't seen the *Entertainment Tonight* piece, but of course he had. She reminded herself to look especially beautiful when she met the cast for lunch Thursday.

She dreamily looked past the shiny wooden desk out the clear window. The day was sunny and warm. She had not even unpacked her luggage, but for some reason, wanted to login to the Internet. Emilie wasn't kidding herself either; she wanted to chat with Romeo. With John out of the picture and predictable Paris far away, Romeo weighed heavy on her mind and everyone else seemed to fade. The beautiful things he said to her during her last night in New York City had rekindled her feelings for him.

She plugged in her laptop but was confused as to how to get Internet access working. She reached for the phone on her desk and asked for the bellman.

"Yes Ms. Gallant, what can I do for you?"

"I seem to be having trouble with my Internet connection," she replied in a proper British tone, feeling a little naughty about her online affair.

"Don't worry, Ms. Gallant. I will be right over," the bellman assured her.

Before she could dress, she heard a knock on her door. *God, I'm still in my bloody robe!* her thoughts flashed angrily. She didn't want to answer her door in a robe! People might see her.

Emilie raised her voice, "Come in."

The bellman inserted his card key and entered. Emilie pushed away from the desk still seated. *He thinks I am a lonely actress, starving for sex,* she worried and realized she was exactly that.

As the bellman fumbled with the cable like an eager monkey, she reflected upon what she was doing. Of course, she was going to need to communicate with the cast of her new movie and for various other interviews; yet the real reason why the bellman was crouched behind her desk was Romeo.

"Ma'am, I have your Internet access working. As you can see, I have a Google search window displayed for you."

"Thank you," she replied, hoping the bellman would leave quickly. She wanted to see if Romeo was online. He usually was, since he had his own computer business in Hawaii.

"Is there anything else I can get you?" he asked.

"No ... thank you."

Picking up on her mood, the bellman left for the door. He smiled and gently closed it — as if he had just tended to the Virgin Mary in her manger. Emilie eagerly scooted her chair back to the desk and clicked on her chat icon, hoping Romeo was online. *He is!* she noticed. *I hope he doesn't ignore me again!*

~

In Hawaii, Romeo was taking his first morning sip of Darjeeling tea. He had finished his meditation and was about to check his business email. It had been weeks since he last spoke to Emilie. Yet, the beautiful things he said to her, followed by his amazing astral vision, gave him hope they would speak again.

So he wasn't surprised when he saw her name bolded. The last time she had ignored him. If his words went unanswered now, he would gallantly leave this exquisite woman forever.

"Aloha Emilie," he typed, cautiously.

"Romeo!" she replied happily. "It's so good to talk to you again."

"How are you doing my angel?"

"I'm fine darling, how are you?"

"Great, my beautiful friend," he answered. "I'm sorry if what I said to you last time was too weird … I got a little carried away."

"No, not at all," she reassured him, smiling.

"So how have you been. I've missed you?" he asked. Her return proved her interest. He felt their destinies merging again.

I'm in Los Angeles now!" she typed excited.

"That's amazing, darling. What do you think of it?"

Emilie surprised him. "It's the most superficial place I've ever been to."

"I totally agree, Emilie. My Zen Master once said the exact thing about Los Angeles. You are so wise."

"Thank you, Romeo."

"So what are you doing there?" he asked, curious.

"I got the role in the movie we talked about!" she happily exclaimed. Romeo recalled praying to Master Lee for her to get the role. "It's a lead role," she added boldly, apprehensive because he would probably ask all kinds of questions. But to her surprise, he only typed:

"Congratulations. I am sure you are a great actress."

"Thank you, Romeo. You're so kind."

"You're welcome, darling."

"So my angel, what is the movie about?" he inquired.

"It takes place, long ago, in England," she answered.

"Really, is the story derived from a book?" he asked, genuinely interested.

Emilie became apprehensive. She wanted to tell Romeo she was a film star, but doing that was already becoming more complicated than she had thought. The studio had not officially announced Emma Gallant as *Estella*. Until then, she was under contract not to speak to anyone about her role.

"Romeo," she typed cautiously, "I can't talk about the movie; I am under contract. I'm so sorry."

"I understand Emilie. It's the artist within me that's curious," he assured her and smiled. "Besides, darling, love is never having to say you're sorry."

"I am the same way with new movie scripts, dear," she typed to assure him. "I get too curious myself. Please understand."

"I understand my angel. I would never want to interfere with your dreams."

As they continued to chat, Romeo realized Emilie's affair with John was over. Her feelings for him seemed unfettered. He could tell his presence made her smile. He sensed she was searching for someone who would love her endlessly and now vowed to be that man.

About an hour into their conversation, Emilie's cell rang:

"Emilie, this is Beth."

"Beth," Emilie awkwardly replied, shooting a glance at her watch. Beth had scheduled lunch with a magazine editor at noon!

Why did I agree to all these meetings? she asked herself, exasperated. She wished her publicist wasn't in Los Angeles. *But where else would she be?* she realized.

"Romeo, I have to go now. I loved talking to you again," she typed hurriedly.

"I love your company also, dear. I can't wait for us to speak further."

"Me too," Emilie agreed and reluctantly logged off.

Romeo and Narcissus

You kiss by the book.

-Juliet

The Hawaiian sun was already high in the sky when Romeo finished his morning meditation and turned on his computer. He had been speaking with Emilie for a few evenings since she had come to Los Angeles and could feel the magic between them growing, even faster than when they had first met.

His roof creaked to the heat of the tropical morning, as the air in his house became warmer. It was going to be a hot day. He decided to head for Punalu'u beach in a few hours, a beautiful black sand bay to the south of his house. He took a sip of orange juice and logged into his Yahoo account to check email.

To his surprise, Emilie's name was bolded on his buddy list. It was rare to find her online in the morning. She obviously had the day off from whatever work she was doing to prepare for her upcoming role. His heart sped up a little.

"Hi there, angel," he typed.

"Darling, it's so good see you," she greeted him.

"Ditto," he agreed, "I love when you call me darling."

123

"Good," she typed confidently.

"So how is your day going? Are you getting ready for the limelight?" he asked kindly, with a touch of sarcasm.

"I'm actually having a nice day and it just got better about a minute ago," she informed him, with a flattering coyness.

"Why thank you, dear," he typed. Emilie was such a charming woman.

"You're very welcome."

"You already know you are the key to my heart," he declared. "I think if we met I would fall hopelessly in love with you, like a schoolboy."

"lol," Emilie replied, blushing.

"But of course there would also be a healthy level of lust," he assured her.

"I like the thought of that," she eagerly commented.

Romeo sensed Emilie wanted something more than simple chat this morning. A sweet sexual energy had begun to arise between them. He could almost feel her hunger — her appetite.

"I hope someday to make love with you. I would want to bring you so much pleasure," he assured her of his lust.

"I'm sure you would succeed," she predicted with a knowing grin.

"Simply kissing you would drive me wild," he confessed. "You are so alluring dear."

"Let's explore something like that, shall we?"

"Sure, do you mean now, seriously, or both?" Romeo asked. He wanted to make sure Emilie still wanted to meet, not wanting to harbor such strong feelings for a woman he could never hold in his arms.

"Both," she answered confidently. "Choose a really wild setting, something that you normally wouldn't do, or somewhere you wouldn't have yourself," she urged him.

"Sounds fun," he remarked and added, "I can see the influence of Los Angeles in your request." He felt a little taken aback, almost prudish. Emilie had never expressed interest in a kinky fantasy before.

She ignored his cryptic remark and asked, "Can you give me a few minutes?" she wanted to change out of her stylish black dress. She rose and grabbed a white cotton robe, for her Romeo.

"I will await your return with baited breath," he joked.

"It will give you time to think," she replied.

As Romeo sipped his morning tea, he scrolled upwards, reading her response about meeting for real. Meeting her was a long way off, he realized. He needed to win her trust again and allow her time to see what he already knew — the two of them were soulmates, falling hopelessly in love with the other.

"I'm back," she announced in her bathrobe.

"Great, the new and improved Emilie! Darling, no ideas have come to mind for our fantasy," he confessed.

"Don't worry dear — I've thought of one."

Emilie:	You're hiking in the mountains in Hawaii, and you hear a plane overhead. The engine is sputtering and the plane is wobbling, smoking terribly. You watch as it crashes into the hillside next to you. You run to see it and find me, laying a short way away from the wreckage, with a large cut on my upper arm, black eyes, and lying unconscious.

Romeo: I like that Emilie. You are so creative.

Romeo: I run toward you, bend down, and notice how beautiful you are. My hands shake your shoulders gently.

Romeo: "Are you all right?"

Emilie: I open my eyes, wincing in pain.

Romeo: "Don't worry." I hold your hand. "You were just in a plane wreck. Do you remember anything?"

Emilie: "No ... I don't ... where am I?"

Romeo: "You are in the countryside of Hawaii and my name is Romeo." I look into your beautiful eyes.

Emilie: "Nice to meet you, Romeo ... My name is ... I ... uh, can't remember."

Romeo: "You seem not too badly hurt." I admire your beautiful hair. "Can you walk or should I lift you?"

Emilie: "I think I can walk ... ."

Emilie: I try to get up, but fall again, realizing my leg is broken.

Romeo: "Oh God, I think your leg is hurt!"

Emilie: "I think you may be right."

Romeo: "Let me lay you down on my blanket."

Romeo: My strong arms move you above my blanket. Our eyes meet.

Emilie: I relax, wincing slightly

Romeo: "Your blouse is torn dear." I stroke your soft hair.

Romeo: "Let me remove your blouse. Your arm, it's cut."

Romeo:	I look into your gorgeous eyes.
Emilie:	I pull my arm out of my shirt.
Romeo:	I slowly unbutton your blouse and notice your supple breasts and shapely hips.
Romeo:	"I wish I knew your name. You're irresistible."
Emilie:	"So do I." I smile at you.
Romeo:	I stroke your hair.
Romeo:	"Well at least for now, I am the only man you remember." I kiss your forehead.
Romeo:	"Please rest my angel." I hold your hand, aroused.
Emilie:	I fall unconscious again.
Romeo:	I shake you gently and feel your soft skin.
Romeo:	I whisper in your ear: "Wake up dear," and kiss you tenderly.
Emilie:	I open my eyes again.
Romeo:	"Oh! You didn't mind me kissing you, did you?"
Emilie:	"No, not at all."
Romeo:	"I felt you would awaken like a sleeping beauty. I know this sounds strange, but you are the most beautiful woman I have ever seen."
Emilie:	"Thank you."
Romeo:	I look at your eyes again and suddenly kiss you deeply with my tongue.
Romeo:	"You are like an angel fallen out of the sky."
Emilie:	I kiss you back, the deepest kiss you've ever

experienced.

Romeo: My hands caress your bare shoulders. I kiss your neck now. You feel my eager manhood rubbing against you through my jeans.

Romeo: "God you're beautiful!" I kiss your breasts gently.

Emilie: *Moaning lightly*

Romeo: I put my cheek against yours and passionately kiss your shoulder. My hands cup your breasts.

Emilie: "Oh God, Romeo!"

Romeo: "Oh God, you are so beautiful! I love your voice dear."

Romeo: I kiss you again and look into your eyes.

Emilie: I nibble on your lips.

Romeo: "God, you are like a beautiful young deer."

Romeo: I kiss back with passion and then become upright as I unzip my pants.

Emilie: My eyes grow big at the sight of your size.

Romeo: "I want you more than anything dear."

Romeo: I look at your swelling breasts and beautiful neck and then rub my manhood against your belly.

Emilie: I spread my unbroken leg far from the other.

Romeo: I bend and grab your thin waist, look into your eyes and pull off your dress.

Emilie: "Make me yours!"

Romeo: I press my talent against your softness, guiding it inside you.

Emilie:	*Moaning loudly*
Romeo:	I thrust myself in harder, pushing you down into the soft grass and pining your cute hands under mine.
Romeo:	"Oh, Emilie, you feel so good."
Emilie:	"More darling, give me more Romeo!"
Emilie:	Arching against you.
Romeo:	I pump harder.
Romeo:	"Wrap your legs around me darling!"
Romeo:	I hold you tight, rocking you, pushing your body into the grass.
Emilie:	"OH YES ROMEO!"
Romeo:	I stroke deeper and deeper, slamming myself against your body. I suck your nipples and kiss your neck, holding you like a wild animal.
Emilie:	"Oh God, Romeo!!!"
Romeo:	I look into your eyes as I move furiously inside you, vibrating your whole body and pounding my hips against your supple form.
Romeo:	... .
Romeo:	"Darling, I'm cumming!"
Romeo:	I push into you, faster and faster.
Emilie:	Fill me with it, darling.
Romeo:	You feel me growing inside you.
Romeo:	I bite your shoulder as my body shivers.
Emilie:	YES!!!

Romeo:	... .
Romeo:	AHHHH, I shoot my seed deep inside your body.
Romeo:	I push harder and harder.
Romeo:	You can feel my balls pulsating, as I hold you shivering.
Emilie:	I climax, screaming and clawing at your back.
Romeo:	I lift you in my lap in one barbaric motion, bury my head your breasts, and pump upwards, shooting my last drops into you. I now hold you tight with my strong arms.
Romeo:	"Oh God, I don't know who you are, but I love this."
Emilie:	"Oh Romeo!"
Emilie:	I kiss you back deeply.
Romeo:	"I hope you never remember anything dear."

~

Emilie, now flustered, tied her warm cotton robe together at the waist. Romeo forcefully zipped up his pants and began to type:

"So was that good for you?" he inquired.

"Yes," she answered dreamily, still breathing hard.

"I came hard, darling," he informed her.

"Goof ... I mean good," Emilie typed back. Her hands were moist and slippery. "I wish I could see," she added hungrily.

Romeo began to type, wanting the same thing. "I love our passionate time together, Emilie."

"Me too dear, I adore it," she agreed, more than satisfied by her climax with Romeo. She was supercharged with energy and loved this stranger more than she ever thought possible. He was her prince, husband, and the man of her dreams. She wanted to have his children and be with him forever.

"I want your children."

Romeo was surprised. She had jumped ahead of him, seeing a possible future he hadn't dared dream of — maybe because of his tragic past. Yet as Romeo considered her words, making this sensitive young woman his wife felt like the most natural thing in the world.

"I would let you have my children, dear. Our children would be beautiful, and probably too smart for their own good," he joked.

She giggled and blushed.

"I'm glad you like me, Emilie"

"I do ... very much," she assured him.

He remembered something he had wanted to ask her. Since she was alone in Los Angeles, he felt he should offer to visit her first. "I could meet you in Los Angeles sometime if you want."

Emilie was a little taken aback. She always dreamt of vacationing in Hawaii to meet Romeo. Now the thought of him entering her complex world seemed absurd. Not wanting to discourage him though, she politely typed:

"I'd rather come there, I think."

"That's fine," he assured her. Romeo didn't want to rush things. "I'd rather meet in Hawaii myself, darling. It is far more romantic. I feel something very special between us," he added.

"I want to give you my soul, Romeo," Emilie assured him, touched that he felt the same way she did.

"I want to give you mine also. I feel so natural with you. I feel so united with you."

"Romeo, I love you with all my heart."

Narcissus and Juliet

My love is deep; the more I give to thee,
The more I have, for both are infinite.

-Juliet

"Hello beautiful," he typed. Emilie had been waiting online for him. Romeo was minutes out of the shower, wearing his black silk robe after a trip to the beach. He had swum for hours in the chilly Hawaiian waters to cool off from the hot cybersex of the morning.

I hope she doesn't think I've been ignoring her, he worried. His computer had been on while he was showering.

He typed again. "I just got out of the shower. I want you so bad."

Thousands of miles to the east, in a hotel suite above Beverly Hills, Emma Gallant smiled. Romeo had not been ignoring her after all, but was only away from his computer. She had been online just a few minutes herself, back from a boring champagne reception at the studio.

"Kissing you deeply, I've missed you so bad," she confessed.

"Holding you tight," Romeo replied, imagining just that. "I thought of you all day."

"I thought of you too," she assured him.

"I thought of you as I swam in the ocean and how I wanted to make

133

love to you," he declared, wondering if she was in the mood for sex or conversation tonight.

"I felt so lonely without you," she confessed. Emilie was falling in love with this handsome, caring man. Being alone in Los Angeles, surrounded by all of its fast-moving glitter, made her want him more. L.A. was a barren, superficial desert — and England a soap opera, a tea party. Nothing compared to Romeo now.

On the other end of the connection, Romeo, although flattered by her words, didn't want her to feel lonely, not with him in her life. "You don't have to ever feel lonely with me. I want to hold you and protect you. I want us to connect on many levels," he assured his beloved.

"As do I," Emilie agreed. Her love for Romeo was now unfolding like a rose with endless petals. She felt so much affection for this mysterious, wonderful man who lived across the blue Pacific.

"I want to know everything about you, not just verbally but inwardly," he told his beloved.

"Stroking your cheek softly," she imagined, wanting to be with her Romeo forever. Life was incomplete without him.

"I imagine holding you on my couch," he continued to type. "I love you Emilie — I will never leave you," he added, knowing her *friend* John had loved her and left her.

"I love you, Romeo," she declared.

"I won't betray your love," he assured her, "but make it grow ... to passionate levels."

"I feel your heart against my cheek," she replied dreamily to her Romeo.

"How sweet," he typed, not knowing what else to say, overwhelmed by their mutual emotions. Romeo hadn't dared dream such an irresistible woman would fall in love with him so fast.

"I stroke your hair to make sure it's perfect," he imagined.

"It's yours ... of course it's perfect," she countered, rather vainly. She stroked her soft lustrous hair to make sure it was perfect — It was. She wanted to surrender everything in her life to this man. Romeo deserved the best, and she vowed to be that for him.

"I kiss your forehead and look into your eyes," he returned. "I feel our love exploding. Your beauty makes me such a happy man. I love you deeply Emilie. I want to always hold you as my angel."

"And so you shall. I'm yours," she pledged herself to her beloved, surrendering her heart to him — and it seemed the most natural thing in the world to do.

"I gladly accept you," he answered. "I want us both to become drunk with love." Romeo knew he loved this woman — he would give his life for her.

"Snuggling against you," she intoned, feeling safe and secure for the first time in years.

"I cradle your head gently, kissing you," he fantasized. "I look into your eyes and see a beautiful Egyptian princess, skilled in the arts of lovemaking."

"You know, darling," she began thoughtfully. "The pharaohs of the past used to identify their lovers in such a way that if another man so much as touched them, the pharaoh would know."

"Really dear, in an occult sense?" Romeo asked. "Lovemaking in Egypt and India were ways of reaching higher consciousness, tantric sex, my angel." Emilie's thirst for knowledge was intoxicating to him. She starved for wisdom amidst the idiot lights of Hollywood.

"No," she politely corrected him. "The pharaoh would usually identify them with a small marking of *henna,* or *kohl* which would be smeared. If any man other than pharaoh touched her, the pharaoh knew."

"Really? I love your wisdom. I've studied more of the mystical side of Egypt. Your intelligence makes me so much more attracted to you," he typed, more enchanted with this brilliant woman as the minutes passed.

"Smiling softly," she reported, flattered like she had never been before. She had finally found a man who appreciated her mind, not only her piercing beauty.

"I enjoy sex with you and hanging out," he typed. Of course, he meant cybersex. Romeo had never touched Emilie in his life, heard her voice, let alone "hung out" with her.

"I enjoy anything with you," she agreed, now drunk with love for this kind man, enraptured in his wonderful calmness amidst her frantic existence.

"I'm glad you feel the same way I do about you, Emilie," Romeo happily agreed. The powerful energy between them was finally being articulated — and with such grace. For an instant, he recalled the night he declared his love to Juliet so long ago — the memory felt vague and far away.

"I want us to be lovers so badly, dear," he continued longingly. Romeo could finally shed his past and love again. "We have so much to teach each other. You are wise for your years. I want to unlock your sexual passion; but don't worry I am a kind man; I won't smother you."

"I've never had a problem thinking that, darling," she assured him.

"I love when you call me darling," he replied, intoxicated like a poet. "I'm glad you see the potential between us." He knew their love was only a potential, since they had never met.

"When I fall in love, I do so deeply," he confessed.

"You and I," she sadly agreed, recalling her love for John. How foolish she had been to open her heart to such a cold man. Romeo now shone like a warm star to Emilie, his light revealing the banal shadows of her past.

"What's on your mind my angel?" he asked.

"I'm sorry if I was too voracious earlier today," she remarked, wanting Romeo to know her feelings were far beyond sexual.

"I desire you just as much; trust me," he assured her. "I understand your refinement, beauty, and the many sides of you. You are my dakini and spiritual sexual consort."

"I do like the sound of that," she agreed, blushing. Emilie was learning so much from this man in their short time together and suspected she had only touched the surface of his knowledge. It felt so flattering to know he respected her intellect too. John had used their mutual intelligence to only impress or ensnare her in his morbid, cynical thoughts. Romeo only wanted to expose her to new and exciting ideas. No man had ever encouraged that side of her.

"You are a dakini from heaven sent to practice tantric sex with me and bring me to enlightenment," Romeo declared.

"You are the most enlightened man, I believe, I've ever met," she informed him, truthfully.

"Thank you," he replied and added, "I actually did study with an enlightened Zen Master once. Not many women can even comprehend that side of me."

"Be honest, most don't try," she firmly replied, with a dashing touch of drama.

"That's true," he agreed. "Can you imagine the superficial women I have met in this modern age? That is why I love you so." Emilie was staying in Los Angeles, a place that manufactured the superficial. Romeo felt she was destined to become a famous star and knew the energies and distractions of Hollywood were strong, so he continued to type:

"I want to protect you and heal you from the negative energies of the world. I don't want the world to steal your magic. I want to increase your magic — to make you even more amazing, even though we are all people."

"Snuggling against you," Emilie imagined, smiling with tranquility. His words were enchanting. She didn't know what else to say. Her eyes were watery. Romeo had tenderly washed away the pain in her life with his love. She was safe in his arms. He was the light in her heart and not the darkness of her past.

"Holding you to keep you warm," Romeo imagined Emilie in his arms. "I love you Emilie. I'm sure your voice is even more beautiful in person," he added, knowing the next step in the relationship was phone contact.

"I would love to whisper into your ear as I held you," he continued to type tenderly. "I don't want you ever to feel lonely, my dear."

Emilie smiled, her love for Romeo seemed infinite. "When I'm with you, I'm happy, safe, and fulfilled," she proclaimed to her soulmate.

"I hold you tighter, remembering our wild morning," he imagined. "I am so glad you are such an intelligent and complex woman," he declared to her. "I also know I must surrender my heart to your magic. You are my muse."

"I've never been a muse before," she remarked happily. A shiver went through her as she read his beautiful words.

"May I write you a love poem?"

"Of course you can, darling."

Romeo typed a poem for his muse now. It flowed easily:

> *To hold you in my arms,*
> *Is to hold all the forests of the earth,*
> *And that mysterious fire behind us.*

"That's beautiful," she exclaimed, her heart opened a little further. No man had written her poetry before. She was flattered and impressed. *He is so talented*, she realized, *an artist like me.*

"Thank you. I'm glad you have good taste," he replied jokingly, knowing he was a natural poet and hopeless romantic. He decided to compose another short poem:

> *Emilie, I love you endlessly.*
> *I want to overwhelm your past*
> *And drive you into the bright mornings*
> *Of this dying civilization.*

Emilie was overwhelmed by his words, his ideas. As she read his lyrical poem, her current life seemed a stage play and before the curtain had opened, she had known Romeo in other times, in other lives.

"I want to journey back to my origins with you as my prince," she declared cryptically, surprising both of them, yearning to understand their mysterious relationship and explore Romeo's mystical world.

"Really ... well, our origins are Egypt," he replied casually. "We must learn the mysterious tantric sex rituals. I must teach you to meditate and gain power," Romeo, the Zen monk, informed her. "I think we have been together in past lives."

"I think you're right," she agreed. Emilie was far beyond her worries now. This man had the ability to lift her into other worlds. Like Hollywood transporting audiences to epic pasts, Romeo wielded the same power, but without movie sets, lights, cameras, actors, directors, or screenplays. He intrigued her so.

"I feel we are very similar deep down," she happily read. "The deeper we go the more amazing things we will find."

"I hope you didn't mind the line about the dying civilization?" Romeo asked.

"No," she replied. His mind was so fast. She loved when he switched topics quickly. He had once told her it was a Zen thing.

"I couldn't resist," he added, with a touch of bravado. "I'm saddened by all the war and terrorism in this modern world."

"As am I," she sadly agreed. "I don't approve of the sacrifice of precious life for the sake of battles that have been raging for thousands of years, and will not stop."

"Yes," he added, "and when I think of us, darling — it seems worse. Our love is so good; yet a part of this world is hell."

Romeo felt another poem arising out of him. The beautiful energy between them, the light of their love shining in such a dark world, made a great dialectic for verse. He began to compose:

Far from the wars, my love,
I will hold you in my arms.
I will enfold you in these western jungles
And we will hold together and witness
The end of this age.

"You are my muse. Do you like my pretentious poems?" he asked.

"They're not pretentious darling," she typed. She was thrilled by the beauty and skill of his words.

"Well, I don't want you to think of me as a show off, even though I was as a boy in Italy," he confessed endearingly.

"So what's on your mind my love? I love you."

"I love you also," she intoned, wanting to be with him forever. Everything in her life would change again, hopefully for the better.

"I want to kiss you," Romeo declared, longingly.

"Kiss me darling."

"I would learn how to kiss you perfectly."

"You already do."

"Different kisses for different occasions."

"Like what?" she asked, curious as a child.

"Well, deep tongue kisses for passion, soft kisses to enjoy your lips, Eskimo kisses to let you know I love you. How do you want me to kiss you now, my dearest?"

"Anyway that I may taste your lips, darling," she answered poetically, yearning for a taste of Romeo Montague.

"I would kiss you and you would know how deeply I love you," he imagined.

"Come with me, darling," she beckoned him again, "back to the place of my origin, to my father's palace." She was dizzy with happiness. A magical energy seemed to arise from their love. She wanted to explore their mystical past forever.

"Really dear in Egypt, beside the Nile and the temple of Isis and Ra?"

Romeo asked dramatically, setting the scene for his magical lover.

"Yes."

He wondered who his beautiful and regal friend had been in Egypt. "Is your father Pharaoh?" he asked.

"Yes."

Romeo gulped, almost frightened by the answer. Emilie probably had been an Egyptian princess and now was destined to become a famous star. Not to be upstaged though, he described himself:

"I am from the mystery schools darling — a handsome young occult adept who studies with the High Priest in the underground caverns below the pyramids. What are you wearing? I am dressed in blue silk and hold a staff; there is a diamond in my third eye."

Emilie then recited a childhood vision she once had of herself, an image Romeo would never forget:

"A gauzy dress of white draped around my body, the princess collar that extends from shoulder to shoulder, a golden band around my arm, golden sandals, and a small crown seated on my hair."

Romeo had never been led to such a place by Emilie in their fantasies. Ancient Egypt was the realm of his eclectic Zen Master. Yet today, he walked the Nile with a young woman he had met on the Internet:

Romeo:	I stand before you.
Romeo:	"Princess, thank you for granting me this audience."
Emilie:	I smile at you.
Emilie:	"Might I offer you food or drink?"
Romeo:	"Why thank you princess."
Romeo:	"Your beauty is stunning."

Emilie:	I wave my hand. Bearers with trays piled with food and pitchers of wine appear instantly.
Romeo:	I ignore them according to etiquette and bite into a mango.
Emilie:	I select a bunch of grapes from one of the trays, and eat them slowly.
Emilie:	"Please ... be seated."
Romeo:	I sit, resting my mystical staff against the chair. I notice your supple breasts bursting out of your dress; and your face, it's so beautiful. I know I could lose myself in it.
Romeo:	"So princess, I assume you know why I am here?"
Emilie:	"No ... I have no idea and I certainly hope it's worth my time."
Romeo:	"It is, but you may not like the news."
Romeo:	"Your father has decided not to marry you to the king of Sumeria."
Emilie:	"What?"
Romeo:	"And my occult master, the High Priest, agrees."
Emilie:	"Why in the name of Horus would he do something like that?"
Romeo:	"Your father finds you far too beautiful and intelligent to give to a barbarian."
Romeo:	"Your other sister will suffice. You are to learn the mystical arts of Isis and Ra with me instead. Since I am a prince, there would be no shame."
Emilie:	A coy smile forms on my lips.

Romeo: "I can see you have read of our mystery schools and of our sexual tantras."

Emilie: "As I might remind you, I am the daughter of Isis. I'm quite aware of her ways and blessings."

Romeo: "I am sorry princess, forgive me."

Romeo: I lower my eyes. "May I speak freely?"

Emilie: "You may."

Romeo: "The priests have chosen me as your teacher."

Romeo: "I have known you since you were a child and have always felt something between us."

Emilie: "They've chosen you for me?"

Romeo: "Well yes, but as your occult teacher, your father would have to approve anything beyond that, although he wants you trained in the skills of lovemaking."

Romeo: I look into your eyes and smile.

Emilie: I nod.

Romeo: "I must remind you princess, I have studied the occult arts and have seen you watching me during those dinners. There is something powerful between us. Astrologically, we would make vigorous lovers."

Emilie: I lean back in my chair.

Romeo: I stand and offer you my hand.

Emilie: "I think my bodyguards may have different ideas about that."

Romeo: "Shall we take a stroll then, out of their way?"

Emilie: Taking your hand to stand.

Romeo: I look into your eyes.

Romeo: "Princess your power is strong. Can you feel the electricity when we hold hands?"

Emilie: My maidservants follow us closely.

Romeo: "Please, don't see me as a man who wants only a night with you. To become tantric lovers in the sacred fertility rights of Isis is something of great power."

Emilie: "My father will be most displeased if we do not continue his family line."

Romeo: "Yes and he would rather have you marry a prince of the mystery schools than a King from the east. Your foolish sister can marry him."

Emilie: "I'm to marry you? I thought I was only to study with you."

Romeo: "Well your father wants you to study with me. I have not asked him for your hand in marriage yet. In the mystery schools we take wedding vows very seriously, and know this: I have loved you since you were a child."

Emilie: "You have?"

Romeo: I hold your hand as we look out over the Nile.

Romeo: "Yes I have, my princess. Please forgive me."

Emilie: "Forgive you? Why would forgiveness be required?"

Romeo: "Because as a priest of the temple of Ra, I should control my passion."

Emilie:	"You have not acted on that passion yet."
Romeo:	"Well darling I have, by becoming your new tutor in the tantric arts."
Romeo:	I gently twirl one of your braids
Romeo:	"You will learn that action can sometimes be hidden."

"Romeo?" Emilie broke in.

"Yes darling? Do you like our fantasy?"

"It's beautiful. But I'm getting tired. I'm sorry," she apologized. Her eyes were heavy, eager to dream of her prince from the Nile.

"Don't worry, my dear. Love is never having to say you're sorry," he reminded her.

She smiled. "Goodnight Romeo. I love you."

~

And so another week passed and the two online lovers met faithfully online every evening. Some nights they would fantasize about sex, other evenings, ancient Egypt or Hawaii. Yet they did not talk about Romeo's life as a Zen Buddhist or Emilie's life as an actress. Both facts were only incidental to their love.

During the day, Emilie remained busy rehearsing for her upcoming role and doing publicity shots for her upcoming film, *Mary Queen of Scots*. Through all the hustle of Los Angeles, she focused on Romeo, the man she now loved. Once she had free time, she would fly west to Hawaii and be with her prince forever.

Romeo and Hollywood

Some consequence yet hanging in the stars,
shall bitterly begin his fearful date.

- Romeo

Emma Gallant exited the Beverly Regent with a confident stride. Santa Ana winds playfully teased her exquisite white Roberto Cavalli dress. Winter was banished by the uncontrollable love that beat within her heart. As her chic outfit hugged her tight waist, she walked with a power, grace and confidence she hadn't felt in a long time. The Jimmy Choo high heels she wore and her beige Louis Vuitton purse, made her look both successful and stunning.

She ducked into a white Capulet limousine amidst the musical sounds of swaying palm trees, dancing below a windy blue sky. *Today I'm happy,* she proclaimed and smiled gently. She had landed the role of a lifetime as Charles Dickens' *Estella* and now had a naughty torrid online romance with a man from Hawaii. *A secret lover, of sorts,* she smiled knowingly, adjusting her sunglasses. The limousine moved forward.

A *wonderful man who won't tie me down.* Romeo had done what no other man could — help her forget about Johnny Perfection. The inevitable heartache she suspected would follow when John discarded her had been magically swept away by Romeo's affections — a man she had never met.

Her limousine made its way north to the Cajun Bistro on Sunset Boulevard. Emilie's publicist, Beth, was joining her for lunch to go over her schedule. This was to be their only private meeting, before Emilie left for England to film.

Beth Penhard was a stunning woman herself of about forty who always dressed impeccably. Originally from Brooklyn, the Capulet Agency hired her straight out of college. In the ensuing years, her aggressive gung-ho attitude helped transform the Capulet Agency into one of the richest money-making partnerships in Hollywood.

Beth fascinated Emilie, from the day they had met for dinner years ago. Unlike Emilie, Beth seemed to thrive on confrontation. Emilie recalled meeting Beth in a noisy London restaurant, listening with her mother, as Beth rattled on about all the battles within Hollywood. Beth was definitely a power player and Emilie was glad she was on her side.

Beth had been furious when she found out about John from Emilie's screaming mother. Although Beth had suspected the affair herself, the prospect of the rumor spreading sent the powerful publicist into a panic. She quickly flew to New York to have lunch with Emilie and urged her not to tell a soul about the affair:

"Look kid, I understand love," Beth had remarked in her thick Brooklyn accent, "and don't think I'm not jealous. I'd probably go to bed with Johnny too ... but I'd kick him out the next morning ... the louse!

"I'm not going to tell you what to do," she declared, "but the Capulet Agency doesn't want this to get out and, personally, I think John is a worm ... OK, I've said my piece."

Emilie was furious with her mother at the time for telling Beth. Her publicist proceeded to faithfully plant the media story that Paris Beauregard was Emilie's beau. The Capulet Agency also paid off a few paparazzi that were lucky enough to photograph Emilie and John together in the city.

Now, months later in the cheerful Los Angeles sun, that chapter of her life seemed like a bad dream. Everyone who knew Emilie saw how miserable John had made her. She was willing to concede that point if it came up at lunch, and she made a mental note not to mention Romeo.

When Emilie arrived at the restaurant, Beth was on her cell hovering over a white round table with flowers. A waiter was hastily clearing it off from the last customer. Obviously, she had pushed her way into the busy café demanding a seat. Beth said goodbye and flipped off the cell as she watched her client, Emma Gallant, approach. She hurriedly shuffled a large bundle of contracts into her leather handbag and sat.

"Emilie, you look stunning today," Beth remarked endearingly. She sounded nervous for some reason.

"Well, why shouldn't I? Isn't that why you like me so much?" Emilie quipped and took a seat.

Beth studied her. "You look great. I was worried when I heard about your breakup with John. Los Angeles seems to agree with you."

"Let's not talk about that," Emilie said, lowering her head, surprised at how fast Beth had mentioned the affair.

"OK, Emilie whatever you say," Beth agreed and looked down at her menu. "Look, let's order; I'm starving." Beth said distracted, tense. *Does she have bad news for me?* Emilie wondered.

Beth continued, "So how have you enjoyed your visit?"

Emilie didn't tell her what she had told Romeo. Los Angeles felt superficial and intimidating. "It's a wonderful city and a beautiful day," she remarked and smiled.

The two proceeded to talk about family and friends. When their waiter came, they both ordered salads and iced tea. Beth also ordered a tall cappuccino. She was obviously planning another high-powered after-noon, Emilie noted.

"Emilie, I don't know how to tell you this," Beth awkwardly began, "but Lauren told me you are talking with a man on the Internet and ... you plan on visiting him in Hawaii!"

Emilie was shocked. Her face turned red, as she realized in distress that she had mentioned Romeo to her assistant a few times. "I can't believe she would tell you that!" Emilie protested, like the rebellious teenager she was.

"Look," Beth said, as if she had caught Emilie performing an unnatural act, "I totally understand and so does the Capulet Agency."

"It's really none of your business, Beth!" Emilie retorted angrily. She couldn't get over the fact that Lauren had told her about Romeo. But when she looked into her agent's penetrating eyes, she realized Lauren never stood a chance at keeping anything secret from her willful publicist.

"Emilie," Beth gasped as if she was scolding a child. "*You* are our business!"

"OK, Lauren is right," she confessed, shyly. "I did meet a man on the Internet."

"Oh my God, I knew it!" Beth burst out. "That rat! John, that rat! I knew he would break your heart!" Beth grabbed her hand in a dramatic, sympathetic gesture. As Emilie felt her publicist's cold palm, she realized Beth didn't care at all about her. To Beth, Emilie was no more than a doll, an expensive commodity she was charged to keep watch over.

"That mother-loving rat," Beth continued, hoping to deflect the awkwardness of the moment. "He broke your heart," she lamented insincerely. "I couldn't believe it when Lauren mentioned you were falling for a man on the Internet, but now I understand … That rat John broke your heart … Oh God Emilie, I'm so sorry."

Emilie withdrew her hand from Beth's phony grasp. "So what's your point?" she asked and shot a disdainful glance at Beth while rubbing her hand. "I've dated Paris a few times; doesn't that make you happy?" she remarked sarcastically, becoming angrier by the moment.

Beth immediately responded, as if she was rehearsing a script: "My point is that John did this to you and I don't blame you for what you did … going on the Internet and all. By the way, what did you tell this man? Does he know who you are?" she questioned Emilie in a whisper.

"No … I haven't told him who I am," Emilie slowly replied, looking down and feeling a little guilty — maybe because she hadn't told Romeo she was a star.

"Oh, thank God!" Beth exclaimed and put her right hand against her chest in relief.

Both Beth and John desperately do not want Romeo to know who I am, Emilie realized. *They both feel the same way. Something about Romeo threatens them … or is it something about me?* she speculated.

"Emilie," Beth began in her best business tone, "please don't do that again!"

"Do what again, Beth?" Emilie asked indignant and alarmed.

"Talk to someone like that … on the Internet," Beth answered tentatively, sensing her star's anger.

"How dare you! I am allowed to talk to anyone I want!" Emilie blurted out. "I can't believe Lauren told you this!" she repeated.

Beth sneaked her hand atop Emilie's again. "Look, Lauren didn't spy on you. She thought it was romantic and told me, that's all … we are only looking out for you dear." Beth grinned, witch-like, at that moment.

Emilie snatched her hand back from Beth's phony grasp, rubbed it again, and spoke quietly: "I can't believe you are prying into my personal life. You somehow think because of what happened with John, I'm not responsible enough to make my own decisions. Don't you?" Emilie challenged her, albeit through sunglasses.

Beth was worried now. The young woman before her was worth many times more to the Capulet Agency than she was. It wouldn't pay to get her top star angrier. She hadn't anticipated this, as Emilie was usually so charming and agreeable.

"Darling," Beth sighed, hoping to gain sympathy. "I'm just concerned for you. Besides, things like this are forbidden in your contracts." She dropped the last sentence like a nuclear warhead.

"What do you mean?" Emilie snapped back incredulously. No one was going to tell her falling in love was against a contract!

"Well Emilie," Beth began, feigning sadness, "there are clauses in your contracts about moral and safe behavior. People have been thrown off productions for doing drugs and alcohol, as you know … ." her voice trailed off to let the last point sink in — everyone knew Johnny Perfection had been thrown off movie sets for doing just that.

Emilie was furious and did something neither expected. Thinking back on it later, playing the part of the Egyptian princess with Romeo might have given her the strength to do what she did next.

"Beth," Emilie commanded coldly, "have the attendant bring my limousine forward. I suddenly don't feel well."

"Emilie, you're not being reasonable!" Beth was shocked. Her young star had just given her an order! She decided to drop another brick. "I've spoken with Peter Segal about this. The Capulet Agency frowns on what you are doing!" Beth chastised, hoping the name of her boss would compel Emilie to acquiesce.

"Beth," Emilie snapped, summoning up all her strength. "Get my limousine. I will not have this ridiculous conversation with you anymore!" She was livid. Something instinctual within her wanted to fight. She was compelled to defend, not only herself, but the man she loved, Romeo. The urge was primal, deep, and powerful. Emilie was ready to explode.

Beth paused, sensing her peril, as Emilie glared at her through her sunglasses. Beth had forgotten she did work for a Hollywood star. The fortune that flowed into the Capulet Agency was now sitting across from her in the form of a furious teenager. Emilie was radiant today, but that radiance which the world loved so, was now focused, full force, against her publicist.

As for Emilie, she knew her day was totally ruined. Romeo had been a secret, a wonderful secret. She wasn't sure if, or even when, they would meet, or exactly how much she loved him. All she knew was their love seemed in peril — and that felt like the most terrible thing in the universe.

"OK, Emilie," Beth finally said in defeat, with the tone of a disappointed mother, "I will get your limousine."

Emilie sat motionless, shocked. She now felt like a Hollywood slave, chattel, a prostitute that could only fuck men sanctioned by her agency and the large studios. She lowered her head as indignant tears formed.

"Waiter! Waiter!" Beth angrily yelled. She had failed in the task that her boss, Peter Segal, sent her on.

"Yes ma'am," the waiter approached with an eager smile.

"Please bring this young woman's limousine forward!"

"Emilie, give this man your ticket!" Beth snapped, disappointed, as if Emilie was a child who had been bad. This only enraged Emilie further. She fumbled in her purse and slammed the valet ticket down on the table and then handed a hundred dollar bill to the waiter. Later she wasn't sure why she had done that — aside from the fact that her publicist had made her feel like a whore.

~

Emilie sat in the white leather interior of her limo, shaking. *Oh God what have I done? Beth is going to tell Peter Segal!* She did not want a call from the head of her agency. Whenever Peter Segal smiled, it seemed cold to her, as if she was only an ATM machine to him.

God, I was happy and in love with Romeo only a few hours ago! she lamented. But maybe Beth was right and she did have responsibilities regarding her image. *No!* her heart cried out. *Romeo is right for me and I am right for him!*

When she returned to her cool suite, she sat on the bed and began to cry. Everything in her life had gone wrong since she met John. She had been happy last year, finally an adult, knowing she could date any man she wanted; but John had turned romance into a dark midnight chore. *Did John cause the Romeo thing? After all, I never would have gone online for romance if he had treated me well. Maybe Romeo is a replacement for John,* she speculated.

It was early afternoon. She considered ordering some food but realized she wouldn't be able to eat, not after her encounter with Beth. *God, things are dangerous now*, she realized. She lay on her bed and tiredly rolled on her side, staring at a Monet print hanging on the opposite wall. The green grass reminded her of Romeo and Hawaii. She turned toward the phone and decided to call her best friend, Sarah, for advice.

"Sarah, it's Emilie."

"Emilie!" Sarah answered surprised. "I haven't heard from you in ages. How are you?" she could tell Emilie was not her usual happy self.

"Well I'm in Los Angeles now," Emilie answered slowly.

"I heard. How do you like it?"

"It's OK," Emilie remarked, bored by the small talk. "Sarah, I need your advice on something. That's why I called," she began excitedly.

"Really, did you meet someone in Los Angeles?" Sarah asked, curious. She knew Johnny Perfection had broken her best friend's heart.

"Well no," Emilie replied awkwardly, "but do you remember that man I met on the Internet?"

"Yes, I remember. You told me how jealous he made John," Sarah recalled with a mischievous smile.

"Well, I'm still talking with him," Emilie informed her tentatively.

"Really?" Sarah asked in a peculiar tone.

"Yes," Emilie continued casually, "and … I think we are falling in love," she announced, as if planning a wedding, but knowing she was dropping a bomb.

"Emilie!" Sarah exclaimed, with tired amusement. It was night in Cambridge and she was exhausted from her long day of studies.

"What?" Emilie retorted, upset. She could tell Sarah wasn't going to approve of Romeo either.

On the other end of the phone, Sarah didn't know quite what to say. She had known Emilie since they were six. Now everything moved so fast for her friend, the Hollywood star. Admittedly, Sarah would have given anything to sleep with Johnny Perfection — yet watching a married man slowly break your best friend's heart is a vastly different experience. John had hurt Emilie in a way Sarah had not thought possible for her strong, vivacious friend.

"Emilie," Sarah began softly. "You don't even know this man. And even if he is a nice guy, who cares? Are you ready to fall in love again?"

"I didn't expect you to be against my falling in love!" Emilie protested.

"I'm not against that," Sarah said sincerely. "But I can't believe you are seriously considering meeting a man from the Internet. That's dangerous!"

"Well, I am falling in love and I plan to visit him in Hawaii," Emilie informed her matter-of-factly.

"I thought you were seeing Paris again. This is crazy, dear!"

"Paris and I are not a couple yet," Emilie informed her.

"But Paris thinks you're his bird! I ran into him last week at the pub," Sarah recalled, more confused than ever.

They both paused until Sarah decided to break the silence. "Emilie, I know you are upset about John." She could feel her friend ready to explode and continued gently, "Meeting a man from the Internet is not a solution. You're a movie star. What if the whole world finds out? What if Romeo is ugly?"

"I can't believe you would say that, Sarah! I see nothing wrong with visiting Hawaii to meet someone. It's not like I would sleep with him right off," Emilie exclaimed, knowing she was lying on that point.

"But Emilie, this is crazy! You're successful, beautiful, and smart. You could date any man you wanted. Why go for someone over the Internet?"

"Sarah, I can't believe what I am hearing from you. You're not so innocent yourself. You've taken risks with men. I simply wish to meet a man and you attack me," she accused.

"I'm not attacking you. I just want you to be careful," Sarah explained in the kindest tone she could summon. "Please don't do anything until we talk more about it. Will you promise me that?"

Emilie was furious. She had called Sarah to commiserate over her lunch with Beth, but Sarah had essentially taken Beth's side before she could even mention what happened. *How can my best friend think this way?* she lamented. Everyone wanted to keep her locked away, like a little bird, caged up and safe — far away from her Romeo.

"I have to go now Sarah, goodbye," Emilie said coldly.

"Emilie ... ." Sarah began apologetically.

Emilie slammed down the phone, frustrated, then rested her head against a pillow. The world seemed pitted against her and Romeo. It was becoming more and more like Shakespeare's play, she realized, closing her eyes to relax.

~

The chime of Emilie's cell was pleasantly soothing. *I must have fallen asleep,* she thought wearily. Her eyes opened to the long shadows of the afternoon sun. She reached for her phone before it could ring a third time.

"Hello," Emilie answered in her best actress voice. After all, she didn't want the top directors or producers of the world to hear her tired or depressed.

"Darling, it's me!" the eager voice of Paris Beauregard echoed in her ear.

"Oh … Paris," Emilie sighed and stopped pretending she wasn't tired.

"Emilie, you don't seem happy to hear from me … I've missed you," Paris remarked in a sweet but needy tone.

"Well I've been very busy," Emilie explained, with a bit of haughtiness. "Besides I'm not your girl yet," she added cuttingly.

"What do you mean, dear? I thought we were dating again. I want to be there for you," he reassured her nervously. "Have you found someone else?"

Emilie paused. She had not really "found" Romeo yet.

"No Paris," she began sternly, "but I don't appreciate you assuming I am exclusively yours simply because of a few dates!" she could tell Paris was hurting, so she continued. "I want to take things slow."

"Emilie, I haven't heard from you in days. What's wrong?" he asked.

"Nothing, I'm just busy."

Mercifully, the call-waiting tone cut in. She decided to seize the opportunity. "I have a call Paris, goodbye dear."

"Hello," Emilie greeted the caller, in a most elegant tone. After all, she didn't want the top directors and producers of the world to hear her flustered or angry.

"Emilie, it's your mother," the serious voice informed her. It was the last voice she wanted to hear and she knew the tone. *God, I hope this isn't about Romeo!* she thought, wishing she hadn't hung up on Paris.

"I just got off the phone with Beth," her mother continued somberly, as if reading a guilty verdict. Emilie's heart sank.

"It seems you met a gentleman on the Internet," her mother added and waited for an answer.

"Mother, I'm tired!" Emilie replied exasperated. "Beth has blown everything out of proportion."

"Well, she told me you are planning to meet this man in Hawaii and that he calls himself *Romeo!* Darling, how can you be so naive?" her mother asked, exasperated.

"Mum, I simply chatted with a man … I don't think it's any of your business whom I meet!"

"None of my business! Darling, I'm your mother!"

"I can't believe Beth would call you!" Emilie shot back, furious with her publicist, since mum was simply being predictable.

"Well, I forbid you to meet anyone from the Internet!" her mother hissed. "You could get raped or killed, darling. What on earth has come over you?" Her mum continued in a more tender tone. "I know this is because of John, dear. I thought you were planning to see Paris when you got back."

"Mum, why do you have to constantly pry into my life?" Emilie complained, exasperated. "This is not about John," she continued. "I can't believe how everyone is acting. I am simply talking to someone. Don't I have any freedom?"

"Emilie!" her mother exclaimed. "What you are doing is dangerous!

Would you like this Internet affair of yours to be plastered all over the cover of the National Enquirer?"

"Mum stop this. Nothing has happened!" her mother was articulating her own deepest fears regarding Romeo.

"Well, what should I tell Beth?" mum asked in a disappointed tone. "She knows you're angry with her."

"I don't care what you tell her!" Emilie exclaimed, embarrassed.

"We will discuss this later young lady, with your father, when you return to England!" her mother retorted, firmly.

"I will not discuss this, mother! And I don't care what you tell father!" Emilie hung up the phone, angrier, and started pacing.

Oh God, how she hated Lauren! If her assistant had not blabbed to Beth about Romeo, none of this would be happening. She knelt down and began to fold her clothes for the long journey back to England, crying softly. Thankfully, no one else called. She then ordered her last supper at the Regent.

~

Evening came and the Los Angeles sky beyond her window blazed with a pinkish-red glow. Emilie rang the front desk to have her elegant Brikenbag suitcases taken down for tomorrow's flight. She had been in Los Angeles for more than two weeks and packing had taken time. The last thing she left out was her laptop.

At least she wasn't crying anymore. She was tired and wanted to get back to England. But she needed to speak with Romeo one last time before she left. Everyone had attacked *them* and Emilie had to decide what to do about him, so she logged in.

"Aloha, beautiful," he greeted her immediately.

"Hello, Romeo," she typed cautiously. A part of her wanted to tell him about the problems *they* had today; but that would mean telling him everything, so she decided to wait.

"Hello, my love. How was your day?" he asked.

She paused. "It was OK. I don't have much time tonight darling. I'm sorry, but I need to wakeup early."

"Love is never having to say you're sorry," he reminded her. She smiled sadly. Both paused.

"Well, what should we talk about tonight?" he asked, breaking the silence. "We can talk about anything, my beautiful princess."

Emilie's heart was heavy. For some strange reason, something deep within her whispered she might never speak with Romeo again. It felt as if the high walls of Hollywood were about to shut this man out forever.

"I want to be with you in Hawaii," she typed longingly, fighting her dread. "I want to be at your house, Romeo."

A few days before, she had received pictures of his house by the ocean. Those blue and green images had become part of her dream, a simple dream really, just an overworked actress vacationing to meet a man in Hawaii. *Is this the closest I will get to him?* she asked, staring west out her window. *I'm going to be working hard soon*, she admitted.

Romeo: (Starting the fantasy).

I am wearing Levi's and a tan shirt. We are in my backyard.

A tear formed in Emilie's eye. It felt like she was saying goodbye to this man forever. Yes, she planned to message him again when she returned home. Nevertheless, a poignant emotion hit her and made her shiver.

Emilie:	(Wanting to make Romeo her husband)
	I am wearing a white gown with flowers in my hair.
Romeo:	(Feeling something is wrong)
	I lead you to a meadow behind my house.
Emilie:	(Crying, not typing)
Romeo:	(Wondering if he should be sexual)
	"I love you. Kiss me." I kiss you as we sit in the tall green grass.
Emilie:	(Crying, typing, and in love)
	"Romeo, will you stay with me forever?"
Romeo:	(Worried, sensing his beloved is crying)
	"Of course I will. Emilie my angel, lay your head down on my chest, dear.
Emilie:	(Empowering Romeo to rescue her)
	"Romeo, you are my prince, my love."
Romeo:	(Flattered, yet for some reason, worried too)
	"Emilie, I will always be your prince. Let me protect you."
Emilie:	(Wiping away her tears, now resolved)
	"Romeo, I want to live with you in Hawaii."
Romeo:	(Serious, but sarcastic, hoping to lighten things up)
	"Yes darling, we can live together and you can fly to the coast to shoot your movies."

Suddenly she became disconnected.

Romeo's heart sank. *Did my remark about the coast upset her? No*, he realized, *something was wrong throughout the conversation*. He knew she began filming in England soon. *Maybe she knows she can't be with me*, the terrible thought entered his mind uninvited — terrible because his love for her made it unbearable.

~

"**R**omeo I want to live with you in Hawaii," she declared to him, resolved, ready to castoff her stifled life in England and the cold hypocritical world of Hollywood. Then suddenly, the connection went dead. She had used her modem tonight because high-speed access hadn't been working. The phone by her laptop blared now, jarring her back into her current life. She picked up the receiver, hoping it wasn't Beth.

"Emilie ... John," she heard that deep, familiar, ominous voice that used to thrill her.

"John!" she gasped, surprised, feeling a little guilty out of habit, as she had on those cold nights after chatting with Romeo when John returned home drunk.

"How did you get my room number?" she inquired, feeling a tad violated.

"I know a few people at the Regent," he bragged. "Your cell is off."

"John, I'm busy," she informed him, wanting to login again and speak to Romeo. She glanced longingly toward her laptop.

John didn't like the way she sounded. It was as if he had caught her in bed with another man. He angrily remembered Romeo and the stupid online romance she had used to get him jealous. He decided to tell her the good news anyway.

"Baby, I'm going to be filming in Wales this summer, so we can see each other ... and baby," he added sympathetically, "I'm sorry about what happened with my wife."

"That's nice John," she said, distracted. "Can we talk about this some other time?"

"So what are you doing?" he asked with a nervous laugh, "talking to Romeo again?"

"As a matter of fact John, before you disconnected me, I was," Emilie spoke in a calm but sharp tone. John had hurt her, and she enjoyed sticking the knife back into him now. He had treated her like a piece of property, in the same way Beth had done today.

"Oh God, Emilie, you're so fucked up," John ominously remarked and took a gulp from his bottle.

"Excuse me?" she asked, offended.

"You're crazy, baby, talking to this guy. I bet he is a paparazzi or something ... trying to get nude pics of you," he desperately blurted out, feeling threatened and extremely jealous.

"Well John," she informed him cuttingly. "I plan on visiting Romeo in Hawaii this summer — if it's all right with you," she added with cruel sarcasm.

"Oh ... bitch," John moaned deeply. He burped and continued. "If you're that stupid, I will fucking tell the world about your sick cybersex addiction and about us."

"How dare you threaten me?" she admonished, shocked.

"Shut up," he ordered her. "Don't you dare fuck us over by meeting this sick fuck in Hawaii!"

Emilie was too afraid to say anything. John, sensing her fear, put on his concerned fatherly voice — after all, he still wanted to fuck his friend. "What if he rapes you or kills you baby? They'll blame me for not stopping you," he explained soothingly. God, he was too drunk to want to articulate the obvious.

Tears welled up in Emilie's eyes. John was threatening her. "I can't believe I am hearing this from you, John. Goodbye!" she slammed down the receiver.

Emilie was trembling and taking short breaths. John had reacted to Romeo in the same way Beth had at lunch. Her last day in Los Angeles couldn't have been worse. She knelt to the ground and looked at her laptop, shiny and sleek — it was her obelisk. Behind it, she could feel a man named Romeo who wanted to be part of her life, while everyone around her conspired to push him out.

She looked at the clock. It was almost nine. She wiped the tears from her eyes, trying not to shake. The phone angrily rang again; it was probably John. She leaned over and pulled the jack out of the desk.

Why did I have to fall in love with a man on the Internet? she lamented. *Would John tell everyone about us, only because he hates Romeo?* she nervously wondered.

She prepared for bed with the loose fitting white gown she had imagined wearing in Romeo's backyard. As she set the alarm, she realized how difficult it was going to be to visit him. She began to think of Shakespeare's play. *Maybe I was Juliet in another life,* she pondered, as she looked up toward the regal ceiling. The idea frightened her because the forces now aligned against Romeo reminded her, far too much, of the classic tragedy.

Filming would soon begin in England. She could bury herself in her work then decide how to proceed. God, she resented this! She was a successful, hard-working woman. Why did everyone oppose her desire for adventure, her desire to meet a romantic, intelligent man in Hawaii? Yet, in her heart, she knew why. She was Emma Gallant, a far too valuable commodity to risk on a stranger from the Internet.

She thought of Romeo again and imagined his arms around her as she turned on her side. Her sleep was fitful, as her troubled mind tried to find a solution to the Romeo problem and when she awoke exhausted before dawn — there was none to be found.

Romeo and Tybalt

Romeo, the love I bear thee can afford
No better term than this: thou art a villain.

- Cousin Tybalt

As with Emilie, Johnny Perfection did not sleep well that night either. *Things have gone so fucking wrong,* he muttered repeatedly, tossing in drunken frustration. He recalled his childhood, living in a trailer home in Pennsylvania with his hippy parents. His father, obsessed with new-age religion, had trouble keeping food on the table and debtors away from the door.

John Tybalt had not had Hollywood's silver spoon rammed up his ass as a teenager like Emma Gallant. Instead he had worked hard to climb the ladder of the stars. He knew what it was like to be poor, unknown, and just another jealous actor, waiting tables and dreaming of making it big, like a penniless kid peering through the window of a candy store.

Tonight though, his success seemed to be slipping away. He couldn't get Emilie and that asshole Romeo out of his mind. He couldn't stand Romeo's name! Worse yet, there was a gnawing feeling that this Internet pervert threatened to take away everything he had worked for. He grabbed the bottle of Southern Comfort by his nightstand and took a vigorous swig. It was getting light outside and the sounds of Manhattan were growing steadily louder. He turned on his stereo, blasting a punk station.

Things have gone so fucking wrong, he angrily realized. God he was furious! But he was nervous also. That bitch Emilie was going crazy on him. He was really beginning to hate her. She seemed to know exactly how to piss him off. *Maybe that means I love her*, he wondered drunkenly and took another sip from his bottle — as if that would give him the answer.

"I can't believe that bitch is still talking to him! Fuck Romeo!" he yelled over the loud music and burped.

Unlike Emilie's fitful sleep though, John's night had yielded a solution to the Romeo problem. He knew what he had to do. *She actually wants to meet this pervert in Hawaii!* he marveled. What made him angrier was that Johnny Perfection was jealous — jealous over a nobody, a loser on the Internet! *How could things get so fucked up?* he wondered again.

"FUCK HER!" he roared over the loud music. "I have to be her fucking babysitter," he complained tiredly, taking another shot of whiskey, more determined than ever now.

He knew what he had to do. It felt right. God, if Emilie went to Hawaii to meet this pervert, if something happened, everyone would blame him. For he had deflowered *their* property, and although that was actually encouraged within the decadent walls of Hollywood, the one golden rule still applied: *Don't damage the goods.*

"Fucking Emilie is so fucking damaged," he muttered in a raspy voice, as he chased down more whiskey. *God I shouldn't be drinking this early*, the alcoholic thought to himself.

"BUT SHE FUCKING STARTED THIS SHIT!" he yelled in his defense.

168

Furious, he hurled his almost empty bottle toward the bedroom wall. It didn't break, but simply rattled against the corner of his room and then lay perfectly still. He watched, as the last rich brown drops of whiskey trickled onto his rug.

He knew what he had to do and knew he had to act quickly. *I hope that stupid bitch didn't give him her phone number*, he pensively thought. Things were still manageable if she hadn't. He had to act now, as Emilie's parents would. She was so fucking immature and naive. But John was a nice guy. He was going to do this favor for *her*, stick *his* neck out, call in *his* favors. Maybe he'd tell her in the future (when she grew up) and she'd thank him. He grinned.

He was more certain than ever he was doing the right thing, the compassionate thing. He was protecting one of his own. He couldn't let Emilie fall in love with this man. *They haven't even fucking met. How could she be falling in love with him?* he wondered again. Yet deep down John was threatened by something else. He and Emilie were the new nobility, the Hollywood elite. If a sorry-assed pervert on the Internet could steal a famous starlet from him, the order of things would be upset forever.

It was all bullshit though, and he knew what he had to do. He had the power and the right to do it. The idea had always been in the back of his head really, at least since Emilie had started bragging about Romeo. He had to protect her and the prestige of Hollywood itself. *She is just too fucking immature to see the truth of it.*

John turned down the blaring music, lay still in his bed, contemplating what he was about to do next. He grabbed his cell phone, breathed his thick whiskey breathe to it, and began to punch the keys.

~

S am Hall sat in his stinky West Hollywood one-bedroom studio with dirty boxer shorts around his ankles. Life was good. He was masturbating, after cracking another password to a great porn site. He watched a black woman fuck a white woman with a dildo and almost came. Then the phone rang.

"Shit!" Sam hissed. He could already feel his insipid hard-on getting smaller. He stretched for the phone to scream at whoever had called this late and fucked with his groove. It was fucking past three am in Los Angeles.

"Sam, Johnny Perfection," the deep familiar voice began, business-like, in that low serious tone that frightened Sam sometimes. As if John was omniscient, he gasped like a little girl and struggled to pull his boxers around his 350-pound frame. Fat Sam was a computer graphics person by day and had met John during the animation phase of a movie.

Over the years, Sam had done little favors for John and other Hollywood types. Fat Sam was considered an expert hacker within the dark walls of Hollywood. He had once remotely broken into a paparazzi computer for John, finding child porn on it. After one threatening phone call, compromising pictures of John and a drunken hooker in Burbank never surfaced.

"Johnny," Sam exclaimed nervously, faking a laugh. He couldn't wait to brag to his friends that Johnny Perfection had called. "How are you doing, big guy?"

"Cut the crap asshole. I'm out of whiskey," John said, trying to be funny, since Sam annoyed the fuck out of him. He lit a cigarette. "I don't have time for your ass kissing, Sammy boy," John explained and exhaled a puff.

"What's up, Johnny? Are you OK, man?" Sam stuttered. "Need any favors?" He grabbed a cold slice of pizza and took a hearty bite. Although John's tone made him nervous, he sensed John needed his help, which gave him leverage.

"Of course I need a fucking favor, asshole! Why else would I call you?" John angrily replied.

Sam, sensing John was upset, put on his best face. "OK John, calm down. What do you need man?"

"I need a favor … ."

So, Johnny Perfection, Hollywood superstar, explained to Fat Sam that a female friend of his had gotten involved with an Internet stalker. John's friend was also an actress, so something needed to be done, quickly and discretely.

"Man, I totally understand," Sam assured John in a maternal voice; for he had stalked a few women himself. "Johnny Baby, this is easy, man," Sam calmed him down. "You're lucky they met on Yahoo. I can probably hack both their accounts, since they are free. I can also flood your friend's account with Spam … so no one can email her …" he droned on.

"OK," John interrupted, already getting a headache from Sam's techno-babble. "Just do it!"

"What's this asshole's account name? Let me bring it up now," Sam asked excitedly, giggling, as his pudgy hands went for the keyboard.

"Romeo in Hawaii," John replied. *How could I forget such a stupid fucking screen name*, he thought and smiled. Things were going to be OK now.

"Man that is weak," Sam chuckled, as he typed fast to bring up Romeo's profile and picture. "John, this guy is such a poser. What an asshole! Consider it done."

"Good, I assume you want my friend's email address also."

"Of course, John, if we don't hack her account, this Romeo freak will just message her from another account," Fat Sam explained.

John hesitated. "The name is *JohnsAngel* … one word," he answered embarrassed and glanced at the whiskey bottle on the carpet, wishing it wasn't empty.

"Fuck!" Sam gasped as he brought up the second profile. "This is Emma Fucking Gallant!" he began to drool over Emilie's photo as it loaded. "Is she your bitch … I mean woman?" he asked.

"None of your fucking business!" John answered harshly. "And if you tell anyone about this, I will kill you."

Silence on the other end.

"Do you get that, you fat fuck? And if you do pull this off Sam, I won't forget it." John smiled.

"Sure … Johnny," Sam giggled nervously. *John is crazy over this woman … Emma Fucking Gallant!* he realized.

"OK … Samuel," John concluded, with mock formality. "I'm counting on you. Call my answering service in New York when you're done and tell me everything is cool."

"For sure, John," Sam nodded, obediently. He heard the line click dead on the other end. He suddenly became afraid, but couldn't imagine why, since this was going to be an easy hack. Still there was something strange about the whole thing, strange about Johnny's mood.

Fat Sam pushed these unpleasant thoughts out of his head. He had work to do. *Emma Fucking Gallant and some online pervert,* he marveled and smirked. He had to be careful with this one and hide his trail with proxy servers or he might find himself under a microscope, like the fat careless bug he knew he was.

~

Romeo Montague awoke curled not in a volcanic desert, but comfortable in his bed. His life was about to change. He and Emilie were falling in love. Although she was working in England, a time would come when she would fly west and they would see if their affections were real and lasting. Romeo had always dreamed of experiencing a love that would last for years, since he had only loved Juliet a few precious days.

He showered, meditated, then slowly drank some orange juice as he booted his computer. Birdcalls filled the perfect blue sky. He couldn't wait to show Emilie the beauty of Hawaii. She had acted strange last night, though; it had worried him a little.

When his computer booted, he noticed an error with his chat Icon. It had failed to login. He looked at the message:

Invalid Login

Romeo was worried and tried logging in again and failed again. His hands began to tremble. He tried using his browser to login into his email account. Nothing worked.

"Oh God!" he exclaimed. His heart sank. His account had been hacked into! He felt a force out of Los Angeles and in his gut knew it was all about Emilie. Something awful had occurred. An alternate future was exploding into reality, one in which he would be lost forever without his beloved. Romeo felt banished again — as he had in Verona.

Don't panic, he admonished himself, breathing harder. *How do you know this is because of Emilie?* he argued to his feelings.

He began frantically working the password help screens. They asked for personal information he had entered years ago. He tried different combinations of birthdays and zip codes, but alas, he could not remember — If he had given his real birth year, 1228 AD, no computer in the world would have accepted it.

His whole body shuddered. *Why do I feel this is because of Emilie?* his mind suddenly went back to a conversation he had with her last winter:

"Romeo it's so wonderful chatting online. We can talk to each other whenever we want!," she had happily exclaimed.

Her words triggered a vision of an exquisite, yet fragile crystal of light, which was their love. Romeo had wanted to tell Emilie that a love as beautiful as theirs was usually crushed or opposed in this world. He had learned this from bitter experience in Verona. Yet Emilie's wonderful optimism had stopped him from typing such strong words. He decided instead to follow her lead and focus on the goodness of life.

He sat sadly stunned in his office, realizing this was his fault also. He had never pressed Emilie for her phone number. They had discussed getting microphones and video just last week, but he had not pushed these issues since she would be unavailable to visit him while filming anyway.

He dialed Yahoo from his office and waited patiently for a customer service representative. Yahoo accounts were free. They had no credit card information of his and Romeo didn't remember what birthday or zip code he had registered with. After a few minutes with a friendly operator, he realized they couldn't help him.

Romeo was now in a state of low-level panic and dread. It wasn't the account that bothered him. It was the terrible feeling inside that he had lost Emilie forever. The feeling was irrational because he could simply message her from a new account — unless her account had been hacked into also — and this was his deepest fear.

Why do I sense all of this? Why do I feel Emilie's account has been tampered with? Why am I so nervous? he wondered. He smiled and told himself he was being irrational. He created a new Yahoo account and sent Emilie an invitation. When she logged in tonight, she would have to accept or deny it.

As the days passed, she didn't login. Romeo watched his empty buddy list as he worked in the day and sat torn apart at night. He would awake with tears each morning. Life without Emilie was unbearable. He felt unnaturally torn from her. He sent her an email, on the slim chance she was checking mail and not chatting:

Dear Emilie:

I hope you have been having a great time in your new endeavor. I miss you and think of you often. I am using this new email account. Thanks to Yahoo, I lost my old account. I am not even sure if you will get this. But if you do, I hope you read it in happiness.

I dream of us strolling that beautiful sandy Hawaiian beach by my house. I hope this dream, in particular, comes true.

Love,

Romeo

To confirm his worst fears, a moment later his letter bounced back:

Mail Account Invalid or Full

With dread, he realized his intuition had been correct. Someone had separated them. Someone had skillfully found the weak point in their relationship and pressed ever so slightly. Hollywood's high walls had separated Romeo from his beloved forever.

He staggered out of his house in confused pain and roamed the beaches crying into the soothing trade winds. He knew the beauty around him was a lie, it was like a movie set; for he had been cast out, once again, into a cruel hateful world, a world without love, a world where he and his beloved could not be together. As the days turned into weeks, a more dreadful question crept into his consciousness:

What if Emilie is Juliet reincarnated ... and I failed to see that?

I should have guarded our love, he bitterly chastised himself a thousand times over. *I should have known a love so strong is hated by this world. I should have remembered Verona. I will find Emilie — that I vow — with all my power!* Romeo was resolved, yet lost, blind, and staggering — far from his beloved soulmate in his false paradise of Hawaii.

Emilie and Estella

I do remember where I should be.
And thee I am. Where is my Romeo?

- Juliet

Oh God, I'm about to cry. That is not going to happen! She told herself sternly and gazed forward with determination, yet Emilie's confident dark eyes did become a little wet. They glistened delicately, while two assistants and numerous lights focused in on the star at the obtuse hour of four am. She was on an outdoor set north of London.

As her hair was bound back by a short redhead stylist named Silvia, the effeminate French wardrobe manager Serge fluffed the ruffles of her beautiful 19th century dress. The crew was a little tired, but the excitement of the first day of filming was evident. One could almost feel the oceans of future audiences who would one day be entertained by the difficult work now going on.

Emilie had arrived in England just yesterday. She wished, more than ever, that jet lag was her only problem because she he was hurting inside. God she was confused! She had fallen in love with a man on the Internet and was now being swept away in the deluge of her real life. Her heart ached and her intuition told her something very wrong had occurred between Romeo and her. She missed him, yet almost felt abandoned. She knew that wasn't fair. She wasn't sure what happened. She felt betrayed and upset, but she wasn't sure by whom, or at whom.

Yesterday, she had tried to chat with Romeo. She was sleepy after her long flight, but wanted to tell him she was in England, wanted to let him know she was busy, but still thinking of blue Hawaii, his tan body, and their love from afar. Yet when Emilie clicked on Yahoo, she had received a password error. She subsequently tried a few things with her browser and then climbed into bed. Her short nap was broken and fitful. She felt as if she had been shut off from Romeo. A hateful burning energy had torn them apart. She couldn't quite place it.

God, why did I have to fall in love with him? she lamented, angry at herself, yet unable to deny that something profound and wonderful had occurred between them. Her rationalizations were not working to push out the hurt she was feeling.

"Darling you seem sad," Serge the wardrobe manger noticed, breaking her out of her tired thoughts. "I'll bet it's man troubles. I know the look. I've seen it in the mirror so many times," he joked playfully, flipping his wrist and gracefully shuffling backwards to tighten her dress at the waist.

"I have a good man now," he bragged as he fastened a pin in her hair. "But when I was your age, I knew nothing about love."

She gently smiled to deflect his statement, but appreciated the remark. It seemed no on cared about her feelings regarding romance, regarding Romeo — no one had understood.

Obviously, she had never told Paris about Romeo. Why insult him? Paris had suffered enough regarding John himself. Why make waves? Paris might be better for her anyways, she reasoned. Romeo's location and mysterious ways made him less accessible.

Only a few days ago she had wanted to be with him forever. Now, amidst the huge tower of lights where she sat, she didn't know what she wanted. Worse yet, she was still thinking of him and not her lines for the upcoming scene.

A Bullhorn screeched: "OK, everyone. I want to start the first shot in 15 minutes. Serge, why aren't you ready with Emma?" the director's voice blared.

Serge went to the makeshift intercom and pressed the button. "Rick, I have to make her perfect. You're going to love the dress!"

The quiet redheaded assistant hurriedly administered the final dabs of makeup to the star. Serge returned to Emilie and pranced around her, neurotically, picking off imaginary lint as he fluffed out her dress. Emilie quickly got up when the makeup girl finished. Serge and Silvia seemed to crowd her. *I wish I could be alone to think, not on a movie set!* she lamented, then scolded herself: *Emilie, you are being paid a fortune for the role of a lifetime. Get a hold of yourself!*

"Thank you Serge, I think I should talk to Rick," she replied in a low voice, like a teapot ready to boil. Somehow, she had been separated from Romeo. Emilie was angry.

Serge, unperturbed, followed behind her, annoyingly adjusting the sleeves of her long lacy dress. When she got to the green director's chair, she felt dizzy. For a second, she imagined herself in a rain forest with Romeo — as if in some parallel universe, she had run away with him and never returned to England.

"Emilie," Rick Carter the director began. "You know, I was thinking last night of doing a lower camera angle when Estella first runs to the window. I'd like you to glance down further when you notice Pip. We are going to mark the spot for you to look at."

Emilie nodded blankly. She didn't want to seem like a Hollywood bimbo so she replied, "I understand. Thank you, Rick." *What would Estella do in my situation?* she wondered.

"Probably go crazy," she muttered softly.

"Did you say something darling?" The large woman to her right inquired, hugging a massive script, as if she was clutching the Talmud.

"No, Martha, just going over my lines," Emilie replied softly.

She thought of a photograph she had seen of Romeo's house just a few days ago. She wished she could be with him now on his sunny green lawn overlooking the sea. She felt sexual and flushed, yet alone and rejected.

Oh God, she thought, *the last thing I need is this*. She was being paid ten million upfront for the role of a lifetime. *What is wrong with me? More importantly, what happened to my Yahoo account?* she asked, frustrated. *This is John's fault!* she angrily decided. *If he had treated me well, I never would have fallen for Romeo.* For some reason she wanted to blame John for everything.

She forced a smile and raised the plastic sheet that contained her lines and stage positions and began to concentrate. As she did, she was lifted far above her problems, like the child she once was in her father's garden, playing with imaginary friends in the cool summer breeze of morning, dreaming of her prince from afar ... .

~

"What's wrong, dear? Why aren't you eating?" mum's concerned voice broke Emilie out of her thoughts. She sat quietly at the family table, set with a lovely white cloth and flowers to celebrate her return home. It was Friday now.

She was picking at her food, which consisted of russets and roast beef. At the end of the table was her father Stephen Gallant, Professor Gallant to everyone at Cambridge. Stephen was tall, thin, and sported streaks of dignified grey hair. He wore gold-framed reading spectacles and was an agreeable sort of chap, always pondering something. Tonight he had sneaked in a translation of an obscure Egyptian scroll to dinner and was glancing at it as he sipped wine.

"Stephen!" Emilie's mum started harshly to her husband. "Emilie's not eating and you're reading at the table."

"Yes, darling," he said, poking his head up from the manuscript like a confused ostrich. He turned to Emilie. She was gripping her fork in one hand and knife in the other, like she used to do as a small child when she wanted something she couldn't have. He was reminded how much he had missed his exceptional daughter.

"Stephen, you aren't listening to me! You know I hate it when you read at dinner," his wife complained.

"Yes dear," he said, reluctantly folding the manuscript. He studied his plate and dug his fork into a potato.

"Emilie," her mother began again, "Why aren't you hungry, dear?"

"I don't know … ." her voice trailed off. She had tried to login to Yahoo before dinner. It still didn't work for her. Why did she feel so awful, though? Yes, she loved Romeo, but already her real life in England had come crashing back, making their love seem like a childish dream.

Her father broke the silence at the table. "I think I'm going to write Will Sanders at Harvard regarding this intriguing manuscript. It was written by an individual named Thuth and it's about moving pyramids," he explained dreamily, glancing back at the ancient translation. "It's very mathematical," he muttered.

"It's a pity, Stephen. Your daughter won't eat and all you can think about is work!" his wife lamented.

"I'm sorry, dear. I'm sure she is tired."

"Well, don't you think she needs nourishment?" mum asked. "She is already too thin as it is!"

Stephen turned to his daughter again, as if he had forgotten something. She did look a little sad. *It must be that louse Johnny Perfection*, he surmised. He was proud of her though. Even his own students at Cambridge treated him with more respect because he was father to a film star.

He decided to defend his successful, overwhelmed daughter. "Mum," he began politely, "Emilie's tired." He knew his wife had been too hard on Emilie after finding out about John. He looked over at his daughter's forlorn expression again.

"Emilie dear, you're fine, aren't you?" he put his hand on hers.

"Yes father, I'm sorry. I know it's our first dinner together. I'm just tired, that's all."

Stephen took his hand off Emilie's and had another sip of wine.

"Well then," mum said rebuffed, "If you two don't want to eat anymore. I will clear off the table!"

"Thank you … dear," Stephen said. He looked at Emilie. "I am sure our daughter, the great success, will regain her appetite in time."

Emilie blushed. "Dad … ."

"Dad nothing dear, I am proud of you," he announced, while his wife retreated into the kitchen with a pitcher of water. They heard her turn on the sink.

"Thank you, Dad." Emilie smiled. She had always assumed her father looked down on acting, since she so admired his knowledge of ancient Egypt. She suddenly thought of Romeo, her lover from Egypt — a feeling of intense loss hit her.

"Darling, I know your mother went ballistic over John," Stephen began gently, sensing his daughter's pain.

"Dad ... ." Emilie began embarrassed, trying to cut him off. It was awkward. He had never brought up her affair with John in person. More importantly, she was hurting over another man, Romeo.

"Dad nothing," her father said again. "I just want to say how much we have missed you, Emilie." He shot a glance toward the kitchen to make sure his wife was out of earshot, then put his hand on hers and spoke quietly.

"Dear, we both know this nonsense with John probably hurt mum more than you. But I'm proud of how you handled it and it doesn't lower my opinion of you one bit. I will always love you, my princess from Egypt." He touched her cheek, playfully. He used to call her that when she was a child.

"Thank you father," Emilie smiled, blushing. She sadly realized that only her dad and Romeo shared her dreams of Egypt. *God I miss him*, she thought. *Something went wrong. What happened to my account!*

"Oh cheer up," her father encouraged her, breaking her out of her consternation.

"I will. I promise. I'm going to my room now."

"OK, darling, if you find yourself hungry, come into the study and have some chips with me," he offered. Emilie rose and pecked him on the cheek. She noticed that his distinguished grey hair had grown a little whiter. The world was moving fast around her indeed, as she labored in the timeless bubbles of Hollywood.

She plunked down by her laptop and tried to figure out how to email Romeo. She couldn't use her agency account, so she created a new Yahoo account. *What is his email address?* she wondered. She hoped it was the same as his screen name. In the months they had known each other, he had never sent her an email — they only chatted. She almost resented that now.

Dear Romeo:

I have missed you so much. Something happened to my old Yahoo account. Please write me back on this new one when you have the time, darling. I want you so, my prince.

Love,

Emilie.

Her letter did arrive — but it was dead on arrival — and like one of Bartleby's dead letters so long ago, it would sit anonymous on computer disks forever unseen, forever unable to change the fate of two star-crossed lovers.

~

Rick Carter was standing with Emilie on a picturesque green hill west of Rochester, England. A photogenic mist hugged the lawns of the beautiful spring fields below them. He had taken Emilie aside, away from the bustling stage crew, to have a word with her. Something was wrong with his star. Something he had to correct, before the critics ate them both alive.

"Emilie, something's wrong. You're not concentrating," Rick began. "When I look at the dailies, you're just going through the motions," he complained, as pleasantly as he could. He knew from personal experience young actresses were often moody — he had married a few.

"Yes, Rick ... I'm sorry," Emilie replied embarrassed, knowing all too well she wasn't doing her best work.

"You're the pivotal character, and don't get me wrong, I'm satisfied with your work. But we can do better. You look distracted. What's wrong?" he asked, looking into her eyes. He wanted to make sure his star was OK. Just these few minutes to correct her was costing the studio thousands of dollars.

"Nothing, Rick, I will concentrate harder ... I promise," she replied, looking shyly at her hands.

"Well, we can shoot around you today — if you want," he offered.

Emilie was shocked but managed to hold her smile. No one had ever suggested rescheduling a scene on behalf of her bad performance! *Oh God, this whole Romeo craziness has got to stop!* she chastised herself. For some reason she couldn't get this man out of her mind! In Los Angeles she had thought she loved him. Now it was becoming a silly and dangerous fantasy.

"Rick, I'd like to shoot my scene today. I'm very sorry," she answered, firmly.

"Emilie, don't be sorry." Rick put his hand on her shoulder. "This is art. Things don't always come together as planned. Take fifteen minutes. Calm down — put some water on your face and push out whatever is bothering you. Just push it out!" he emphasized his last statement with a clenched fist.

"I've been through three divorces on movie sets, but you know what?" He paused dramatically, hoping to cheer his star up.

"What?" she asked, with a slight grin.

"I just say 'fuck it' the moment I hit the set." He grinned. "For me, my work becomes the only thing in the world. I just say to myself: 'Rick your wife is going to get all your money anyway, so work harder to make it back and forget about her!'"

Emilie giggled.

"OK Emilie, be back in fifteen minutes and *be* Estella!" Rick said with encouragement. He quickly turned and yelled, "I want more lights on that ground mist!"

Emilie walked back to her trailer with her head hung low. She opened the door and closed it quickly. Her long flowing dress became stuck against the small refrigerator stand. She cursed and untangled it.

Oh my God, I have to push this bloody Romeo thing out of my head! she chastised herself and turned to her laptop. *I already checked my mail this morning*, she reminded herself. Romeo had not responded to her letter. *He must have other girls in Hawaii ... He is handsome*, she admitted. *Maybe he is married ... like John.* She realized how foolish she had been. She had let a silly, immature online romance interfere with the most important project of her life.

The whole Romeo thing had begun as a desperate attempt to find a replacement for John. But even if he could have been that man, the cyber-romance had been childish. They had been like kids playing dress-up, pretending they were husband and wife — now she had to grow up.

More importantly, she had to forget about John. He was the one that had actually broken her heart and started this whole mess. She bitterly recalled all the dark lonely nights that she had waited up for him. The whole Romeo thing was John's fault. Emilie ruffled her lustrous hair by the mirror and smiled. Neither John nor Romeo would get in the way of her career now. Thousands of people were depending on her and in a year, millions would see her on the big screen.

She shuddered at that cold assessment, knowing she still loved Romeo in her heart, knowing she trusted him more than anyone. That is why his lack of response to her letter was so puzzling. But they never had met. She had to push out these feelings out of her, as they were interfering with her work. Both John and Romeo had hurt her. Emilie looked in the mirror and thought of her character Estella.

Estella wouldn't let these men ruin an opportunity like this, she told herself. She stepped out of her trailer smiling. After all, her character Estella had made difficult choices, so would she.

~

"Emilie, darling," Paris Beauregard hesitated, then approached her in her father's garden.

It was a mild night and she had run out of the dining room after another comment, by her mother, about what a perfect a couple she and Paris were. *Ever since John, mum has been trying to force him on me!* she bitterly thought.

Emilie turned toward Paris. She had been pushing him away since her trip to Los Angeles, and the primary reason had been her online romance with Romeo. She couldn't believe how immature she had been. Maybe in Los Angeles she had needed a *Romeo* — now, that dream seemed distant and out of reach. Beside her, was standing a real-life caring man. Paris had only been good to her.

"Emilie," Paris repeated, as he came up to her. He put his hands on her bare soft shoulders and gently asked, "What's wrong?"

She bowed her head. He was obviously referring to her heartache over John in his usual, polite way. John and Romeo now blended into one confusing and painful memory. John was with his wife in Malibu and Romeo was on the other side of the world — a man she had never met and evidently, never would.

She now regretted how she had treated Paris. His warm hands on her shoulders felt comforting. She needed someone to be with. Paris was here. John and Romeo were far away — only girlish dreams, girlish mistakes, merely shadows.

"Paris," she turned to him, stunning him with her gorgeous eyes.

"Yes, darling?"

"Kiss me," she commanded. He kissed her tentatively. She could feel how much he wanted her.

"I am sorry for the way I have been. Make me yours tonight," she whispered and moved into his arms, kissing him back deeply. Her old dreams felt confused and distant; she wanted them washed away. Paris would help her finish the film happily. They kissed harder and she let him take her while the evening was still young.

First Remembrance: Egypt

I have lost myself. I am not here;
This is not Romeo, he's some other where.

- Romeo

The weeks passed for both Emilie and Romeo and she was the luckier of the two. Emilie could finally love a man who loved her back, a man not married, famous, drunk, or halfway around the world on a tropical island. Paris was real and banished the darkness of her long winter. He satisfied Emilie both physically and emotionally. She could love him safely — for he only loved her. Her love for him grew steadily, not like a raging fire as it had with Romeo.

As for Romeo, it was his karma to suffer greatly. He had finally found love, finally shaken off his haunting memories of Italy — thanks to a beautiful heart. Now that future had been crushed before it could ever blossom, before he could ever feel Emilie in his arms. He was more conscious than she was of what happened. He sensed interference from forces within Hollywood, forces around her, which had so skillfully crushed their fragile connection.

Each morning he awoke with a raging emptiness, a longing for a love lost that his heart feared would never return. What pained him most was that his deep connection with Emilie was fading fast. He was torn in two.

Romeo was only half of himself because he loved Emilie as his better half — just as he had loved Juliet ages ago.

He could sense she was with another man now, probably falling in love. He couldn't blame her though, knowing she needed someone, knowing she was afraid of being alone. His pain made him realize another thing — he had to find her, even if it took years.

Because he knew Emilie was an actress from England, Romeo went online and searched for British actresses. Maybe he could write her somehow. He came across so many Emma's, Emmy's, Emily's, etc. ... it was confusing. He always assumed she wasn't that famous, just another beautiful young woman trying to break into films. He also realized he couldn't be sure what her real name was. For all Romeo knew, Emilie could be her middle name, or perhaps a nickname. She had only told him: *My friends call me Emilie.*

When Romeo stumbled on Emma Gallant's photo, he hesitated. He had never heard the name, yet it was obvious this young woman was already famous and successful. He looked at her image on a fan website but, as luck would have it, it was for her upcoming film, *Mary Queen of Scots*. Not only was Emilie's hair red, but her eyes were a deep sea green.

If he was to write Emma Gallant, Romeo realized he would have to write other actresses who looked like Emilie as well. He clicked his mouse through more pictures of the young star. He couldn't be sure if this was the woman he loved and none of the Hollywood stills reminded him of his intelligent and shy friend. Instead, they felt empty and artificial. Later, of course, he would marvel at his own stupidity.

Confused by all the glittery images of Hollywood and the names of so many stars, Romeo decided to explore his only other clue, ancient Egypt.

Both had been certain they knew each other then. Their mutual memories were overwhelming and must contain some truth, he reasoned.

So one bright clear spring morning he packed water and hiked deep into the desert side of Hawaii, climbing to the top of what some people claim are ancient pyramids from Lemuria. There, he meditated for hours, burning under the glaring white-hot tropical sky, sweating, patiently sitting. Finally, as the powerful sun became orange and set against the Kona coast, a light wind hit his face and a vivid vision began of his life in Egypt so long ago.

Romeo's name had been Thuth ... and Thuth was a cold man.

~

D eep in meditation, Romeo felt the early spring wind blow gently against Thuth's face, as his former self walked alongside the river Nile thousands of years ago. The soothing sounds of migrating songbirds filled the air above the shimmering marble docks of West Luxor. Thuth was a sorcerer of the Egyptian mystery schools and had wandered in from his hermitage, deep in the desert, to prepare for the occult task of moving a pyramid.

Thuth strode north in his perfectly fitted sandals and long blue robe. His cap of pure gold signified mastery of the occult arts. Thuth had studied sorcery and mysticism for almost two hundred years, yet was considered only middle-aged by his peers.

He walked indifferently across the grassy park by the river. Today was a holiday, the day of fertility to celebrate Isis and the spring planting. Laughing children played energetically in the immaculately trimmed gardens by the docks, their voices melodious. Yet Thuth hardly noticed them, as his long strides traced their way through the crowded lawns.

People made way for him as he moved through the holiday crowds. He wore the insignia of *linesman* and carried an occult staff of polished wood with the head of a golden serpent. Thuth was in a strange mood today. He hadn't been as repulsed by the children and the parents as he usually was when he strolled through the park on holidays. *Thank Horus, families are not allowed here other days*, he thought. *They ruin its solitary energy.*

He stepped past the smooth sculptured green hedges of the park's border and soon the hot Sahara sands hugged his ankles. Focusing on his mystical third eye, he saw the desert floor as a glowing grid of energy lines, lines that went out to infinite worlds. He moved his body onto one of the power lines and slid up a huge dune.

Thuth maneuvered around the top of the sandy ridge, squinting as the punishing sun moved lower in the western sky. He looked toward the Nile River. Yachts of the rich rolled lazily north while Cargo vessels laden with fruits and grains from deepest Africa wound their way through the holiday boats, carrying their vital stores, the lifeblood and fertility of mother Egypt. Beyond them, towered the golden city of Luxor and the great palace of the Pharaoh.

He descended the sandy ridge to a flat area where the younger acolytes of the mystery schools ate their evening meal. He found the initiates mildly amusing. Of course, he would never let them know this. Yet maybe the real reason he tolerated their company, was that they reminded him of when he was young.

~

"Here he comes!" exclaimed the young student through a mouthful of wrapped hummus.

Sintar, his teacher looked up and saw Thuth cresting a tall dune. Sintar had studied as long as Thuth in the mystery schools, but Thuth had long since surpassed him. Thuth was one of the few linesmen in all of Egypt — priests that moved pyramids with their minds.

"Don't worry Élan. Thuth isn't concerned with us."

"Yes, but he's so cold; it's frightening sometimes," Élan responded.

"Human emotion is inefficient," Sintar explained to his student. "Thuth can stop thought at will and move through worlds of power. I admire him."

"Well then why does the High Priest tease him about his somber moods?" Élan asked, smirking.

"Silence initiate!" Sintar slapped his student on the head half playfully. "Eat your dinner and learn to move pyramids yourself one day!"

"Yes, teacher, I will."

Sintar watched Thuth gracefully slide down the dune and noted that he kicked up no sand. *Walking on an energy line to show the students a thing or two,* he observed. *Whatever people say about him, Thuth isn't egotistical. He genuinely doesn't care about anything.* Thuth felt cold and technical to him, like iron, and instructed the initiates with the same emotion one would have watering a houseplant.

Thuth hadn't always been like that, Sintar knew. He had been a dashing young prince of minor royal blood from the Sudan. In their youthful days, they had been best of friends. They would sneak out of the initiate's dorm at night into the town of Luxor to meet lovers. Thuth had once courted a ravishing merchant's daughter named Lola.

And then, something happened. His friend suddenly stopped crossing the Nile to see Lola. He still sneaked out of the dormitory at night, disappearing into the desert to meet a woman from the palace of Luxor. Whatever Thuth had been doing, something had gone terribly wrong. The High Priest had abruptly sent him hundreds of miles west into the scorching Sahara for safety ... or so it had been rumored.

As the years passed, the problem, whatever it was, apparently disappeared. Thuth returned, but didn't seem the same to Sintar. He immersed himself obsessively in the occult arts. He never crossed the Nile again or set foot in Luxor. It felt to Sintar as if his friend was burying himself in his studies to escape some unspoken tragedy.

A hundred and eighty years have passed, and what have I accomplished? he asked himself. *Thuth moves pyramids. Whatever his personal tragedy was, he overcame it.*

Thuth approached Sintar, who rose to greet him. His students also stood, according to etiquette.

"Linesman," Sintar bowed in greeting. "I have not seen you for many moons. I look forward to the movement of the great pyramid."

"Why do you desire that?" Thuth asked vaguely, as he gazed beyond Sintar into the distance. Thuth's golden skullcap glittered against the setting sun.

"Well Thuth, is it not a great occult feat to move a pyramid?" Sintar nervously asked his distant friend.

"No different than ants moving grains of sand," Thuth muttered, distractedly. Sintar's training told him Thuth was deep in meditation and merging with the energies of the sunset. *He must actually feel that way,* Sintar realized as he gazed at his old friend's silhouette. *Moving pyramids must be boring for him — as it is for the slaves who build them.*

Sintar could see the energy lines of the sands tighten around Thuth's mystical staff. Thuth was opening a doorway in the desert as the initiates stood, and whether they knew it or not, they were being imbued with power.

"I would rather see one sunset than a thousand pyramids move," Thuth finally remarked in a whisper. The wind began to blow harder from the west. It seemed to race through his perfectly still silhouette.

"Thuth, I am your friend; that is why I like to watch you move pyramids," Sintar explained nervously. He was trying to reach his roommate from so long ago. The wind howled and Thuth walked a few steps forward, hesitated, and then finally turned halfway to Sintar.

"My ... friend," Thuth murmured, as if uttering a dead language that hadn't been spoken for thousands of years. He continued, "I suppose you are that." The linesman bowed slightly, according to etiquette, and slowly walked up the next ridge. The young initiates around Sintar quickly sat again to eat.

Thuth shuffled down the dune, out of sight of the dining students. The sun was a fiery dome against the horizon. A chill went through him. Sintar's remark about their friendship reminded him of his youthful days in Luxor, days when he had been such a fool, such a child, *such a lustful animal*, he recalled with disdain.

Another shudder went through him and a tear, probably the first in over a hundred years, came from his eye and touched the hot desert sand. Thuth remembered what it was like to love. He had not really been an animal after all... .

~

He was only twenty-three when he had met her. Ironically, he was already falling in love with an alluring, erotic woman named Lola. Thuth, a tall dark-skinned student of the mystery schools had swept the beautiful young Lola off her feet. Their lovemaking had been vigorous. Her father, a powerful merchant in Luxor, had disapproved of Thuth, knowing that students of the mystery schools rarely marry.

Everything changed one night. Thuth had been mysteriously drawn out of his dorm. The moon was full and something beckoned him. He crawled out the window of the room he shared with Sintar, not knowing where he was going or for what reason. Even now, the older Thuth remembered exactly how the warm sand felt against his sandals as he dropped to the ground from that balcony so many years ago.

He asked himself at the time: *What is drawing me out here?* There was something beautiful in the warm wind, as if it was whispering of a wonderful destiny that was his. Maybe his destiny was only a moonlit stroll through the ancient Field of Obelisks that lay beyond his sleeping quarters. Aside from the docks, there was nowhere else to go. All other directions led into the deep desert and sudden death if one became lost.

Thuth strolled casually toward the Nile. The obelisks of the mystery school honoring the gods of Egypt cast huge shadows against the desert sand. Young Thuth could feel the power of the night oozing through every pore of his being. The moonlight streamed down as a clear liquid, reflecting off the ancient marble with an otherworldly light. He breasted the last hill before the river and beheld the bright torches of Luxor.

He turned north, away from the docks, feeling the cool mud of the Nile delta hug the sides of his feet. After about a mile, as the melodious river rippled by, he heard the sound of a rope, a rope from a sail whipping against the side of a boat. He climbed the next hill to avoid the marshes and beheld a beautiful pleasure craft with golden and red yards that marked the house of the pharaoh. Two female servants sat at perfect attention, gazing impassively at the shore. Each wore flowing purple silk robes and rested a large oar in their lap.

Thuth hurried to the base of the small hill, curious as to why a royal pleasure craft would visit the sacred shores of the mystery school. For a common person to dock here might mean death; but the real deterrent was fear. The people of Luxor knew the Field of Obelisks was full of spirits from Egypt's distant past, so they avoided it like the plague.

As he approached the water's edge, he heard a beautiful sound, as if sung by a songbird. Thuth beheld a woman in white praying, chanting, and crying softly. At first, he thought the sound must be in his own mind, since it was so perfect. He looked at the crouched figure. He had never seen a more beautiful visage in his life. The woman appeared translucent as she knelt below the moonlight. Her black hair seemed as soft and gentle as the desert wind, which lifted her intricate, soft braids over regal, delicate shoulders.

She has to be a spirit, a goddess, a daughter of Isis — that is why the gods drew me out here! he surmised proudly. *Oh Horus, she is so beautiful!*

As he cautiously approached the alluring woman, Thuth realized she was not an apparition or goddess. No, she was not much more than a girl really, sobbing and crying quietly — her voice inexplicably familiar to his ears.

He looked over at the two slaves docked by the reeds. The strong rowers tensed as he walked up to the kneeling woman. He nodded to them and they bowed reluctantly back. *They must be superstitious,* he

197

realized. *They think I am a sorcerer. They don't recognize the initiate insignia on my robe.*

"Excuse me, lady?" he delicately inquired, from a safe distance.

"Oh!" the woman exclaimed, startled, and whirled toward him, resting a hand on her chest in fright. As their eyes met, Thuth became lost in her gaze. At that moment, he felt he could love this woman forever and saw that she could love him too.

"I didn't mean to startle you," he broke the awkward silence, as they stared at each other.

The woman finally looked down at his robes, sizing him up with her beautiful brown eyes. She blushed, as if the sight of him was pleasant, wrinkling her intelligent brow, probably wondering how to respond.

"I will go now," he said, still awestruck by her beauty. "I am sorry to disturb you." He didn't know what else to say.

The young woman looked away from him and began to weep. It was as if their magical meeting had upset her more. He glanced at the two burly women on the boat eying him suspiciously as he moved closer, standing over the weeping woman.

"Is there something wrong? Is there any way I can help you?" he inquired.

"No thank you," she replied and looked up sheepishly. Their eyes locked again. *Trust me*, his eyes said to hers. *Maybe I do*, her eyes spoke back gently. Thuth noticed an ugly bruise on her right arm.

"Are you hurt?" he inquired.

She turned away from him, quickly, perhaps in embarrassment. He wanted to put his hand on her shoulder and comfort her. It felt as if she was already an old friend. He glanced again at the two servants in the boat. They stared back impassively, but for some reason were willing to let him hover over a woman of Pharaoh's palace. *She probably is a concubine in the royal harem*, the young Thuth reasoned.

"May I touch your shoulder? It looks bruised."

"You may not," her sweet voice retorted in a dignified tone.

"Then may I sit beside you, lady, and keep you company?"

"I am not formally a lady yet," she answered softly. "I am unmarried. If you knew anything about royal insignia you would have known the yellow band on my gown represents maidenhood." The lovely girl spoke quickly and intelligently. One could tell she was lonely and craved real conversation.

Thuth smiled and boldly sat beside her, "Well then, I will be seated, since I have already failed your test on royal etiquette," he remarked playfully.

"I never gave you permission to sit!" the young woman shot back to Thuth, in a dignified but girlish way. "I know by the markings of your robe that you are no more than an initiate," she accused. "My foolish servants think you are a priest. Look how afraid they are!" she laughed weakly.

"What is your name?" he asked.

"I would never tell a stranger my name. But since I understand insignia better than you do, I can tell by your ring you are a prince from one of the southern tribes loyal to Egypt. I can't tell which one though."

"I am from Amara, far to the south," he explained, "and although the people in my village consider me a prince, I am only the youngest son of a poor beer exporting family." Thuth modestly grinned. "My name is

Thuth."

"Well since you are of minor royal blood, I will tell you that my name is Keisha," she said haughtily.

"Thank you, Keisha," he slid closer to her. He wanted to hold her hand. He glanced longingly at its smooth regal shape.

"Why did you move closer to me?" she demanded.

"Why are you crying?" he retorted.

"I asked you first."

Thuth looked at her smooth shoulders and so wanted to caress them. "I moved closer because I find you beautiful," he confessed and continued tenderly, "I don't want you to cry."

She folded her hands and blushed.

"Why are you crying?" Thuth asked her again.

"Why do you care?"

"I asked you first," he replied playfully and watched a small smile form on her lips.

She looked into his eyes again. Whenever their eyes locked, time stood still. Her exquisite hair glowed in the moonlight. Thuth knew he would do anything for this woman and felt an overpowering need to protect her.

Keisha finally spoke. "I am crying because my father wants me to marry a cruel man, a Sumerian."

Suddenly, sadness crept between them, not only sorrow for what she had told him, but an even more absurd feeling insinuated itself — Thuth wanted to marry this beautiful stranger himself, and could feel she was thinking the same about him. He never planned on taking a wife; yet now, being with Keisha felt like the most natural thing in the world. He was speechless.

"Well, I answered your question," she said, almost bitterly, as she turned from him again. "Why don't you leave?"

"I want to make sure you are all right," he replied. He had no intention of leaving yet.

"Well, I am all right."

"Why did you come out here to the Field of Obelisks? This is a forbidden place."

"I am of the royal house. We can go anywhere."

"But it is dangerous here. There are bandits to the north." He made a sweeping gesture with his hand so he could smell her enchanting perfume as he spoke. He so wanted to kiss her. "And these fields are full of ghosts," he whispered into her ear, leaning closer.

"Why are you leaning toward me? Do you want to kiss me?" she asked suddenly, still turned from him. Although she tried to sound harsh, her voice softened with the question.

"I do want to kiss you," he admitted. It came out of his mouth before he could think.

"Well then, I will tell you Thuth, that although I am a maiden, I have lost my maidenhood to the man who will be my husband." Her voice cracked at the word husband.

"I don't think your maidenhood would matter to any man," Thuth proclaimed. He so wanted to comfort her. "I can tell your heart is good and you seem very intelligent to me."

She whirled quickly toward him, stunning him with her irresistible brown eyes. "Thank you, initiate priest, but my maidenhood mattered to me. Please leave now." She looked down again.

Thuth yearned to put his arm around her, but resisted the temptation. *She must be a royal concubine, promised in marriage as part of the peace settlement with Sumeria*, he reasoned. He knew it was common for Pharaoh to placate his enemies through strategic marriages. He now understood why this magical woman wanted to be alone. Soon she would be leaving civilized Egypt forever, as a defenseless wife in a barbaric land.

"I will take leave of you now, Keisha," he stood and bowed, sensing she needed to be alone with her thoughts.

"Thank you, Thuth," she said softly. The edge of a smile formed on her lips as she spoke his name.

"Thank you, Keisha," Thuth replied and gave a slight bow. He boldly asked: "Will you be coming here again?"

"Why do you ask?"

"I ... I want to get to know you," he replied, embarrassed.

Her silhouette froze; but she considered his words and did not answer. He turned and slowly began to walk toward the dunes, realizing he would remember this stunning, regal woman forever. Suddenly, she replied from behind.

"I would like that also, Thuth. I may return."

~

The next night Thuth left his dormitory and found Keisha sitting in the same place with her head hung low. She didn't seem to be crying though; instead, she was *waiting*. He realized she was waiting for him. He also hoped she was falling in love with him, for he already loved her.

"I thought you would come," she said coyly, as he approached. The smile on her lips was now unmistakable.

At first, the two talked about everything. He asked her about her family. She was the youngest of three daughters. She seemed to have very strict parents. Of course, she was nobility of some sort but that subject was never brought up; nor did Thuth discuss his studies in the mystery schools.

A week passed as they met every night. They would lie together and look up at the stars, or quietly hold hands. He never tried to kiss her, sensing she wanted him to wait. One evening Keisha brushed off a dusty golden plaque on the marble slab they were lying on, her eyes glistening curiously like a child. She tried to decipher the ancient script embedded at the marble base of the obelisk.

"Thuth what does this plaque represent, darling? I can't read the ancient writing," she asked eagerly like a curious child.

He glanced at it, more intent on holding her now than reading an old relic. He recognized the script. "Oh … It's a name — Hollen Cel Nar," he answered, disinterested. "He brought mathematics from the Atlantean cataclysm to Egypt. I think a local chieftain cut out his heart and ate it," he finished, dramatically. They both laughed.

"There are twelve plaques at the base of this obelisk, darling, honoring the twelve Atlanteans who landed here after the great flood. Much of our knowledge derives from them."

"You're so intelligent dear," Keisha remarked lovingly, admiring him with her sparkling eyes. He finally kissed her, ever so gently.

"I love you, Thuth," she admitted.

"I love you Keisha and have from the moment we met," he admitted.

"I know."

They kissed again. He rolled on top of her gently, kissing her more sensuously.

"Thuth?" she asked, as he backed away from a kiss.

"Yes darling?"

"Is it forbidden for students of the mystery school to take a wife?"

"No my love, although it does take the approval of the High Priest. Why do you ask?"

"I don't know ... I so wish I wasn't promised to another!" she lamented and stroked his cheek with her delicate hand. She added boldly, "I wish I was to marry you."

"I wish that also, my love, and think about it all the time," he confessed and tenderly kissed her.

"I know, dear. I could feel you wishing that the first night, when I told you I was spoken for." She kissed him back affectionately as the old, cold moon rose in the dark sky.

~

"Father?"

"Yes, Keisha?" Pharaoh Neferkasokar of Egypt looked down at his youngest daughter from his marble throne, lovingly, but with pity. He held a staff of gold and wore red silk and cashmere. He was flanked by beautiful serving girls who fanned him with palm fronds. Ministers and warriors stood in the corners of his court ready to move at the slightest gesture from Pharaoh. Fountains rippled perfectly around the base of his dais and birds danced in the waters behind him.

She continued, "If I loved a man of noble blood, would you let me marry him?"

Pharaoh sadly considered the question. His daughter was so naive, he realized. *Doesn't she understand the peace of Egypt hinges upon her marriage?* He looked down at his favorite child from his throne. *She is beautiful and so special*, he thought. *I never wanted this for her. But she will make our ancestors proud.*

"I would love to, Keisha," her father finally spoke and paused. His daughter bowed her head, already knowing what the answer would be.

"But I can't. The peace of Egypt depends on your marriage. You are a daughter of Isis! You are Pharaoh's daughter."

She began to cry softly, as her Pharaoh continued tenderly from the throne, "Sometimes common people believe we do nothing to enjoy our great wealth and power. Yet there is a price, Keisha." He looked away from her and proudly continued, "As a royal daughter, you have enjoyed riches few on this earth have. It is time to repay your people. Your sacrifice will be for the good of Egypt. I too, despise the man you must marry."

Neferkasokar watched his daughter cry harder now. He knew she loved him and would never challenge Pharaoh. Of course, she understood what her duty was. She was his smartest child and her sacrifice would save thousands from death in a useless war with Sumeria.

After a few moments, Keisha bowed and turned to leave. As Pharaoh watched his daughter walk away, it felt like he was making a terrible mistake. Yet for the life of him, he couldn't figure out what it was. Her marriage was going to solve everything.

~

When evening came, Thuth breasted the last hill and saw Keisha by the obelisk. She was crying as she had the night they met. He hurried down to comfort her.

"What's wrong dear?" he asked, sitting beside her and putting his arm around the woman he loved. She said nothing. He gently turned her toward him with his strong arms, and kissed her smooth lips.

"Why are you crying?"

"Oh dear Thuth, I asked my father if I could marry a man like you," she paused, turned from him, and continued. "He said I cannot."

She began to weep harder. Thuth held her tightly until her trembling stopped. He was flattered, since he had not formally asked for her hand in marriage. *How wonderfully naive she must be*, he realized. *To think personal preferences would have anything to do with a royal marriage. She must have known the answer before she asked.*

He kissed her again and held her hands. "I love you so, Keisha. I love you for even asking, my dear."

"I want to marry you Thuth!" she wildly proclaimed, between his passionate kisses. "I know I have been your wife in other lives."

"Darling, I feel the same. Let's run away together," he suggested boldly. "Let's escape Luxor and go south, deep into the African continent where no one will find us." He drew her beautiful form toward him and moved her passionately against the marble base of the obelisk.

"Thuth, I want to be yours forever. Take the coldness from my heart." she commanded, stroking his cheek and pushing her gorgeous body into his.

He was more than aroused and instinctively ripped open her gown, kissing her breasts and shoulders, then pressing her cute hands against

206

the marble. He kissed her firmly and entered her. The two forms moaned as they merged, grappling with tender, rhythmic abandon below the Milky Way, star-crossed stars — hanging over them like a scythe.

~

"Thuth?" Sintar, his roommate, inquired. "You have been sneaking out every night. Tell me of your female conquest."

"I have no conquest, Sintar." Thuth grinned as he bent to tie his sandals. "I have fallen in love and don't worry — she is not of the mystery schools. She is from the palace of Luxor itself."

"I'm surprised. What about Lola?"

Thuth considered Lola for a moment. He had written her a farewell, only last week. "Lola doesn't need me Sintar. There are a thousand men in Luxor who would marry her today. Yet the woman I love does need me. Besides, Lola's father doesn't approve of us." He smiled tranquilly at Sintar and bound his hair back in a ponytail. He then turned away and calmly splashed water on his face from a plain white ceramic bowl by his bed.

Sintar was surprised. He had been certain Thuth was meeting a female student of the mystery schools in the desert. An affair with a woman from the palace of Luxor could be dangerous. *What is my friend getting himself into?* he wondered, as he watched Thuth climb out the dormitory window.

"Good luck," he called out. "Your affair sounds dangerous, the best kind," Sintar added, although not very sincerely.

"Don't worry," Thuth replied, landing on the sand. "It's not dangerous, only complicated. Have a good night with your studies."

Sintar bent back to his ancient book of hieroglyphics, wishing he was as smart as Thuth. He had to study twice as hard just to keep up. Thuth's words echoed in his mind: *She is from the palace of Luxor.*

Sintar recalled hearing last week that Pharaoh Neferkasokar would announce peace with Sumeria, a peace through the giving of lands, wealth, and the marriage of his youngest daughter to the prince of Sumeria.

"No, he couldn't be seeing the princess," Sintar assured himself and chuckled. He opened his scroll and began to study the ancient mathematics of Hollen Cel Nar. Sintar loved math. It was reasonable and safe. The odds Thuth was seeing Pharaoh's daughter were infinitesimal, he rationalized.

As he began to write down geometric equations on his papyrus sheet, he couldn't shake a vague feeling of dread regarding his friend's mysterious affair. For whomever Thuth's lover was, if she was from the royal palace, she was someone else's property — and if they were ever exposed, that someone was going to be very angry.

~

Thuth's heart sank when he crested the ridge above the small bay where they met every night. Keisha's pleasure craft was not to be seen; furthermore, Keisha who always waited by the Atlantean obelisk was not there. Instead, he noticed a small canoe floating by the reeds. He recognized the burly woman inside the craft as one of Keisha's rowers.

He quickly approached the woman. "Is there something wrong?" he asked.

The woman thrust out a small scroll of rolled papyrus. "I have been commanded by my lord to deliver this message. Please do not ask me more." Thuth stepped into the muddy marsh and took the note from her hand as his feet sank into the silt.

"Is she all right?" he asked.

But before he could even expect an answer, the woman quickly turned her canoe and rowed away. He considered yelling after her, but why? He already had Keisha's note.

My Dearest Prince:

We must be star-crossed lovers, darling. My marriage date has been moved up. Meet me here tomorrow evening. I want to run away with you. I want us to be together, forever, my only love Thuth ... be safe.

Your wife,

~K

He rolled the papyrus sheet quickly. He too felt the danger Sintar had earlier — a danger he sensed Keisha was already in.

The next day was a blur for Thuth. Sintar helped him arrange for a quick sailing vessel to be placed by the docks of the mystery schools while Thuth made repeated trips across the river, traveling on a passenger barge in the stifling heat to purchase provisions for his flight south. Once they reached his father's village, the two lovers would be married secretly and then disappear into the heart of Africa forever.

~

Jonas, prince and sole heir of Sumeria, wheeled quickly. His strong arm buried the jade-handled knife into the female servant's chest. The startled woman died, choking on her own blood with bewildered eyes. Jonas grabbed her head and shoved the bloody slave to the floor.

"That will teach their servants how Sumerians treat liars!" he growled and spat on the bloody face of the now dead servant to Keisha.

"She talked easily," observed Jonas' old, frail first minister who had tortured her. "Maybe the Egyptians are weak after all. Your father should have declared war on them."

"I know," Jonas growled bitterly. "But now I am arranged for marriage as if I were a girl myself!" he roared and hurled his bloody knife skillfully into the wall of the guest quarters, sinking it deep into the finely polished cedar.

"I am going to kill Keisha myself now! How dare that Egyptian whore disgrace me?" he muttered with clinched fists.

"I would have suggested taking this insult to the Pharaoh himself had you not already raped his daughter," the first minister began with a grin. "I advise ... ."

"SHUT UP, I TOOK WHAT WAS MINE!" Jonas interrupted with a roar. He pulled out a long dagger from his side and lifted the minister by the collar. "Foolish minister, had I waited for marriage before I took her, I would have been a henpecked husband. Now she knows who is master. Do not speak of this again!" he hurled the old man backwards. The minister staggered painfully against a marble drinking fountain.

"OH, HOW I WISH I COULD KILL THIS WHORE NOW!" Jonas roared to the ceiling of the Pharaoh's guest villa in Luxor. He hated this town of marble and gold and would soon take his foolish bride and, more importantly, her wealth home with him. Jonas knew his old father would murder him if he failed to bring Keisha and her dowry to the palace of Sumeria. *That bitch is the key to my becoming king*, he bitterly realized. *And she almost got away ... whore!*

"Did the servant tell you where they planned to meet?" Jonas asked, turning to his minister with a sinister smile.

"Yes, Jonas." The first minister picked himself up and grinned, recalling how he had slowly pulled the servant's nails out. He so loved effective torture!

"Then let us meet the lover of my bride tonight," Jonas declared and smiled cruelly. "Ready a warship at the docks at sundown!"

"Yes, my lord," Jonas' minister bowed and hurriedly left to make preparations.

Jonas chuckled and imagined presenting this man's head to Keisha. It would be his wedding gift to her. Maybe he would place it in her bed tonight. But that wasn't a good idea, he sadly realized. The Egyptians were far too civilized to have any real fun with the ladies. Jonas laughed, took another swig of wine, and left his quarters to tell his bride the good news.

~

Keisha shuddered as the large shadow of Jonas, prince of Sumeria, loomed over her. He was as tall as Thuth and twice as wide. She saw blood on his leather vest and feared for her life. *Why does he have blood on him? Why is he smiling so?* her mind asked, over and over again.

"Darling bride," he began, gloating. "This bloody hem is from your servant." he held up a blood-soaked piece of cloth and chuckled.

She shuddered. *Please Isis, don't make this be about Thuth*, she prayed. Suddenly, he grabbed her hair and pulled her toward him. She cried out in pain. Now she only wanted to die quickly. It was about Thuth — they had been caught.

"Don't sob my bride, I have good news for you," he growled and pulled her hair tighter. "Your servant delivered your love letter yesterday. My father told me to spy on you. He told me all daughters of Egypt are whores!" he smiled cruelly, breathing fiercely into her face, which now streamed with tears. Jonas's first minister appeared at the door, coldly studying her.

"When I tortured your servant she told me you two were friends since childhood," Jonas' minister gleefully informed her, sporting a wide grin and rotting death. He ravenously looked her over, as if she was to be his evening meal. Keisha knew the old minister was a foremost expert in Sumerian torture techniques.

Poor Amaranth, my chambermaid ... Oh Horus, I have murdered her! she lamented amidst the excruciating pain from Jonas' hair pulling. *Oh gods of Egypt, he is strong! Let him kill me quickly!*

As if granting her wish, Jonas flung the princess onto her bed like a rag doll. He leaned into her and pressed his fists into her face. "OH CROM, HOW I WOULD LOVE TO POUND YOUR FACE IN!" he screamed, practically foaming at the mouth.

"Kill me quickly, Jonas. I don't want to marry you," she spoke plainly in a defiant tone.

"No, Keisha." Jonas was breathing hard.

"GET UP!!!" he commanded

Keisha trembled and lifted herself off the bed. She stood inches from Jonas' huge armored chest. She had never been this frightened in her life. Jonas exuded raw strength, he exuded quick death. She thought of Thuth and straightened herself. Thuth's love had given her dignity again. Although she would never see her lover in this life, she wanted to die in a way that would make him proud. She regretted not telling him she was a princess of Egypt.

And so the youngest daughter of the most powerful man on earth stood face-to-face with one of the fiercest warriors of Sumeria. She was a daughter of Isis and through her beautiful clear eyes, Isis glared back at the figure of a man that towered over her.

Nothing will cause the house of Egypt to fall, a tender voice echoed in her mind. She felt the power of her ancestors flow through her. Jonas was no more than an insubstantial shadow. Her shaking subsided.

"Ah!" Jonas gasped, recoiling, startled by the glare of the Pharaoh's youngest daughter. *Maybe I knocked something loose inside her skull*, he wondered. Yet for some reason, his whore bride had just terrified him.

He looked away from her terrible gaze. *A witch she is also!* he angrily realized. *Probably some Egyptian magic ... break out of it man!* Why had his father forced this marriage upon him? he angrily roared to the roof.

"AHHHHH!"

The scream collected all his energy into one raging emotion. He clinched his fist, reared back, and punched his insolent bride as hard as he could in the gut. She crumbled to the floor, gasping for breath like a fish out of water. She began to cough violently and spit up blood. His blow had been a good one. He smiled.

"Jonas, remember what we discussed. Let us not mark her before the wedding," his minister's voice started tentatively in the background.

"I know," he growled. At that moment, he wanted to turn and hit his first minister with the same punch. Sadly though, his old minister was probably even weaker than Keisha, he realized with disdain.

The look of total fear and subservience was again on Keisha's face.

Whatever weak magic she had used, a good punch in the gut had put her in her place. He kicked her shoulder roughly and then pinned her cheek against the floor with his huge muddy boot as if she was a dog.

"Well, whore, I must go now and visit your lover across this cursed river. What was his name?" he yelled back to his minister with his boot still firmly planted on Keisha's muddy cheek.

"Thuth," the first minister answered cautiously, knowing his prince was furious. It would not be wise to agitate him further.

"What a stupid fucking name!" Jonas bellowed, lifting his boot off Keisha's cheek. He leaned into her and spat on her face.

"We shall mount Thuth's head above our dining room, my wife!" Jonas exclaimed gleefully, looking into her eyes with crazed delight.

Keisha gasped for air, harder. She had wanted to cry out, upon hearing her beloved's name. But Jonas's huge fist had knocked the wind out of her. All she could do was curl into a ball and groan. *Thuth, my love, I cannot even scream pity for you*, she lamented.

Jonas turned to leave. When he reached the door, he looked down at his gasping bride-to-be. *She is so pitiful*, he realized. He noticed she had finally gotten enough air in her lungs to sob, probably over her soon-to-be dead lover.

"Darling," he began with encouragement, "you took that punch well. I once killed a man with the same blow. You will give me strong children and they will see Thuth's head mounted in our dining hall while we eat!" he laughed cruelly for the effect. After all, Jonas wasn't a total barbarian. He loved theater and thousands of years hence would incarnate as Johnny Perfection, the actor.

Jonas bowed dramatically, giving her one final mischievous grin. He then strode majestically down the hallway with his Sumerian guards, his deep laughter echoing against the cold marble chambers of Luxor. He had a date to keep with a man named Thuth. Jonas was giddy.

Keisha struggled upward, bracing herself with her hands. Blood was dripping out of her mouth. She trembled and coughed as she leaned against her night table for balance. She tried to stand against it but it crashed with her to the floor.

Oh Isis, I wish to die now, she prayed. She glanced up at a small clear vial on the shelf above her bed. It was a deadly extract of black passion flower provided to all of royal birth. Since childhood, she knew she might be commanded to drink the potion and join her Pharaoh in the afterlife. She had tried to escape her duty once and probably killed the only man she would ever love by her defiance. To end her life now, to escape her fate, would betray Egypt once again. Her father wanted peace with Sumeria, terrible Sumeria, and she was the awful price he had paid.

Oh Thuth, be careful now! I will always love you, she prayed for his safety and cried harder. An hour later, when the sun set by her window, she was still on the floor crying — knowing that within her heart — the sun would never rise again.

~

Again, Thuth was surprised when he breasted the final sandy bluff above their rendezvous point. Instead of seeing Keisha's royal sailboat, a huge rectangular warship lay docked in the bay. Over a hundred imperial guards armored in gold and bronze stood at attention. Something was wrong. His heart sank, realizing his beloved was in danger.

Thuth, being a stealthy lad, could have easily turned at that moment and walked away. But the warship somehow involved Keisha, he sensed. So he carefully shuffled down the sandy dune, keeping in plain sight of the vessel so as not to startle any of its archers. He realized there was a good chance he would die tonight.

It was the seasoned river captain who first noticed Thuth rambling down the sandy ridge. The captain's eyes had been trained by a century of war. He recognized the figure's robe — nothing more than an acolyte of the High Priest, attracted by the peculiar event of a warship docked by the Field of Obelisks.

The river captain couldn't figure out why this white-skinned barbarian, Jonas, had demanded they put anchor in this magical place. The silence of the cove was unnerving. Jonas had only informed him they were search-ing for a man who had dishonored him, nothing more.

"THERE HE IS!" Jonas bellowed, mounting the seat of the captain's chair where he sat.

The river captain watched mud from Jonas' boot grind into his finely polished cedar chair. The captain was under command by Pharaoh himself to protect the barbarian prince with his life, and in the last month he indeed had. The crazy prince offended almost everyone in the royal court and fought nightly in the seediest bars of Luxor.

"YOU IDIOT," Jonas yelled, jumping off the chair. "DIDN'T YOU HEAR ME? THIS MAN TRIED TO STEAL MY WIFE! YOU FOOL, KILL HIM!"

Jonas's hot spittle hit the captain's face. Worse yet, something felt terri-bly wrong. The war captain had not felt this way since he had been a new recruit, just a boy. Then, nomads had ambushed his regiment deep in the Tarfa canyons by the Red Sea. He always would remember the eerie

216

silence right before the deadly attack. On that day most of his companions had died.

And now the silence of this place, the Field of Obelisks, felt like the silence of the ambush so long ago. *Why on earth has this mad barbarian dragged us here?* the captain wondered. He knew he had to speak fast or Jonas would hit him.

"Prince, there is no one here but an initiate of the mystery schools. Surely this man is not the one you seek."

Jonas slapped him hard. The strong captain's head rung to the tune of his vibrating helmet. The captain struggled to remain motionless. He wasn't going to give this Sumerian bastard the satisfaction of knocking him over.

"YOU EGYPTIAN FOOL. THE MAN I AM LOOKING FOR IS RIGHT THERE! I DON'T CARE WHO HE IS!" Jonas commanded and pointed to the motionless figure by the shore.

The captain said nothing. Jonas, exasperated by his empty stare, turned to the crew and barked, "Arm your bows, kill this man! Bring me his head!"

The Egyptian soldiers looked bewilderedly at Jonas, as if he was a performer who had just told a bad joke. *Doesn't he know we cannot dock here?* the captain wondered. *This land belongs to the priesthood. Most of my men would not set foot on these shores if I ordered them.*

"YOU FOOLS, I COMMAND YOU TO KILL THIS MAN!" Jonas roared at the puzzled soldiers. These were the greatest warriors of Egypt, the personal guard of pharaoh, handpicked by Neferkasokar himself, winners of the many games he loved so. Yet they all stood frozen, helpless, not about to the break the taboo of this sacred land for a barbarian prince. The river captain realized he would have to diffuse the situation, and fast — it was beginning to feel more and more like the ambush at Tarfa Canyon.

"Prince, we cannot kill this man here, nor may we even step foot on the shore." He spoke firmly to Jonas, who was turned from him.

Jonas wheeled around. "What? I will kill you myself! What are you saying to me?"

"My lord, this land is sacred to the Temple of Isis and Ra and does not belong to Pharaoh's house."

Jonas considered hitting the river captain again, but was uneasy now. *Why won't these soldiers follow my simple order?* He decided to use sugar, not salt, and stood up on the captain's chair to address the crew:

"Men, I am not asking you to take this land," Jonas began, as he looked over the palace guards. They stood impassive like statues. He put on a winning grin and continued. "I am simply asking that you kill that man by the shore! I want his head! I will offer a sack of gold to the man who brings it to me."

Silence, nothing but the lapping of the relentless Nile against the war vessel.

"Well then, don't kill him. Apprehend him for me!" Jonas protested. "This man has insulted the honor of Sumeria!" he explained, looking over the soldiers — still no movement. In fact, to add insult to injury, some of the warriors were now turning to the river captain for orders.

Jonas looked at the man by the shore. He was no more than thirty yards from the ship. Something within him stirred as he glared at the motionless Egyptian, a deep hatred. Both men were young and both were fighting over a woman. There was no mystery here.

"SO YOU ARE THUTH? ANSWER ME!" he commanded.

"I am," Thuth replied softly. Jonas realized there had been no reason to yell. Everything had taken on an eerie silence, as if the rocks and waves themselves were curious about what the two men would say next.

"My army here ... ha!" he motioned derisively back to the guards. "They tell me they will not kill you or take you in for me." Jonas laughed nervously.

"Where is Keisha?" Thuth demanded.

"WHAT? HOW DARE YOU SPEAK HER NAME TO ME!" Jonas yelled. Thuth was making him uncomfortable with his stare. It felt like the same stare Keisha had used on him earlier today.

"DON'T YOU KNOW WHO KEISHA IS, YOU FOOL?" Jonas screamed. The figure by the shore wavered.

"KEISHA IS THE DAUGHTER OF YOUR PHAROH AND I AM THE PRINCE OF SUMERIA AND YOU ARE DEAD! I SHALL COME ASHORE AND KILL YOU MSYELF!" Jonas bellowed and began to climb over the side of the ship.

"I think not," a simple voice uttered quietly behind Thuth. He turned and looming over him was the High Priest of Egypt, an incarnation of Ra, who was over eight hundred years old and stood almost seven feet tall. Thuth noticed four female archers at his side, covered in war paint, fierce and bred for battle by desert tribes, the personal guards of the High Priest. Their poisoned arrows were now aimed toward the warship.

Prince Jonas heard a shuffling noise on the deck and snapped his head back. The crew of the ship was prostrated head down — even the war captain crouched like a frightened girl. *How I hate Egypt*, he lamented. *My father was wrong. We should have fought these superstitious weaklings to the*

219

death.

Yet what now demanded Jonas' immediate attention were the five freaks by the beach that had sneaked behind Thuth so skillfully. He was at a distinct disadvantage, as he straddled the side of the warship like a whore riding a lover. He noticed the female warriors' bows were trained on his exposed figure.

"Who are you, old man?" Jonas bellowed, looking sideways at the priest by the shore. "Tell your wenches to put down their toys; I am the prince of Sumeria." He noticed the female archers tense and stretch their bows tighter at the word "wenches." Evidently these women were not as emotionless as the useless guards that cowered on the deck of the warship.

"I know who you are," the High Priest responded in a detached, deep, ancient voice that made Jonas feel like a child.

Jonas used his will to ignore the High Priest's affect on him and continued. "Old man, go back with your circus freaks where you came from. I have come to restore Sumeria's honor!"

Jonas hurled himself overboard and splashed gracefully into the shallow water, unsheathing his cutlass in one motion. He would take this arrogant Thuth's head himself and tell his future children the whole glorious story!

"I think not," the High Priest said again, plainly, now staring directly at Jonas. He nodded to one of the female archers. She glared at Jonas with disdain and with inhuman speed an arrow split his feathered war cap.

"Huh?" Jonas remarked and comically took off his helmet to inspect the damage. He looked like an angry child now, dressed up as a pirate, wanting to play a game no one else did.

Prince Jonas realized the precariousness of his situation. He was without a helmet, facing four very good archers. Their eyes seemed to burn into him. They pulled their bows tighter, *wanting* to strike him. He now wished he had not called them wenches. Obviously these people on the shore, Thuth included, were insane. His future wife had fucked a crazy person; he smiled at the idea.

Jonas put on his charm. "Look, I don't want to break up your circus old man. But he dishonored my bride!" Jonas accused, pointing at Thuth. "Let my captain take him into custody. I am reasonable." Jonas glared at Thuth. He had no intention of taking him to the Pharaoh's court and would kill him on the war vessel.

"I think not," the High Priest remarked, impassively again.

Jonas looked into the eyes of the old tall priest. He felt like a little boy, facing an angry father. He glanced back to the warship for support, but it appeared empty, the occupants still prostrated on the deck. He turned again to the ancient figure by the shore, staring at him with fierce eyes. For the first time in his life, Jonas was too afraid to speak.

"Is there a captain of this vessel?" The High Priest's voice boomed dismissively over Jonas.

The weathered river captain stood trembling. He had never thought he would get this close to the High Priest of Egypt! A bad night had turned disastrous. The river captain realized that whatever happened, he would probably be put to death.

The High Priest peered into the river captain's eyes and began to speak, "Stop trembling, warrior, and get thee out of my lands. Take this pale-skinned Sumerian with you or I shall fill him with poison arrows and feed him to a fifty-thousand-year old spider that lives in the desert."

The river captain was afraid he was going to ask that — to forcefully remove the prince of Sumeria and return him to Luxor. Yet, to disobey the High Priest of Egypt would have consequences beyond his now probable death, he realized. The captain motioned to his guards, who were still crouched on the deck.

"Oarsmen, prepare to leave. Sergeant, fetch the prince!" It felt good to say that. The captain smiled for an instant. Years to come, he would fancy only the High Priest had noticed that smile.

"WHAT?" Jonas yelled incredulously back to the captain. Six men jumped into the water, and to the barbarian's astonishment, surrounded him. Jonas whirled abruptly and glared at the High Priest.

"How can you do this old man?" he asked and pointed to Thuth. "HE FUCKED THE PHAROH'S DAUGHTER!"

Jonas turned to the soldiers surrounding him in the water. "Why are you brave warriors following the orders of crazy people?" he pleaded and then angrily glared at Thuth. In that moment, Jonas hated him more than he had ever hated anyone.

Thuth spoke to Jonas first. "No one is protecting me. You are right, good prince. I have dishonored you and will fight you, if you wish. Fetch me a sword"

A smile began to form on Jonas' lips; but it was cut off.

"I think not," the voice behind Thuth intoned again.

Thuth turned in protest to the High Priest. He wanted to fight. The thought of Keisha spending her life with this violent barbarian was unacceptable. He looked up at the great occult master who towered over him like a terrible statue.

"I have never met you before, initiate, nor do I think I want to. You will

222

not fight Prince Jonas!" the High Priest commanded and looked beyond him toward Jonas.

"And you will not fight either, Prince Jonas," the High Priest declared. "For although you are a great warrior and would most likely kill my foolish initiate — there is a very, very small chance you wouldn't."

Jonas, for some reason, chuckled uncontrollably at this and smiled at Thuth like a prideful bully. He then caught himself and grew angry again.

The priest raised his voice to address the guards on the warship: "If Jonas were to die in this foolish fight, then war would break out with Sumeria."

The High Priest looked up at the stars that were coming out above them. "I don't care about your wars," he dreamily began. "But if war breaks out now, the trade routes to the East will be closed.

"Egypt will not last forever. Our priesthood has seen this for many centuries. We will be transporting the knowledge of enlightenment to the East and we cannot do this while there is war with Sumeria. Therefore Jonas, you must marry the princess of Egypt," the priest concluded, studying Jonas with a steady gaze.

Everyone understood, everyone but one. And that one, Jonas, laughed nervously in the cold shallow water, surrounded by guards of the Pharaoh. *What a foolish fantasy*, he thought. *Is Egyptian foreign policy run by fairy tales?*

"Old man, your story would have put me to sleep as a child," Jonas exclaimed. The High Priest smiled The smile encouraged Jonas. He continued, "Whoever you are old man, what if I refuse to marry Keisha until I have Thuth's head on a platter?" Jonas eyed Thuth and laughed. Maybe calling this old man's bluff and playing into his fairy tale would win him Thuth's head after all. The priest peered deeply into Jonas' eyes. It seemed the old man was considering his bluff.

"I think not," the High Priest finally answered — and before Jonas realized he had lost, the priest motioned to Thuth and both began to walk up the dune.

"NOOOO!!!!" Jonas screamed.

The female archers tensed. Jonas looked around at the imperial guards surrounding him in the shallow water. *They all look frightened, but not of me,* he observed angrily. *They all want to leave this place.* He glanced at the archers by the shore pointing their quick death toward him. His comment about their being wenches had not served him well — he saw in their eyes how they yearned to kill him.

"YOU WILL ALL DIE," he declared angrily to the High Priest and Thuth, as they crested the first dune of the desert. "I WILL COME BACK HERE WITH AN ARMY! I WILL TELL YOUR PHAROAH OF THIS INSULT AND MY FATHER!"

~

And now, nearly two hundred years later, it was dark and cold. The brilliant stars of Egypt shone above the desert floor. The sun had set long ago. Thuth had been crouched in the sand for hours, deep in remembrance. It had been so long since he had thought of her, his beloved Keisha. He never saw her again. She married the prince of Sumeria and traveled north, away from Egypt.

Something inside him stirred, he shuddered involuntarily and then looked toward the Nile and the lights of Luxor. *That was long ago,* he reminded himself. He had been so primitive then — so human. He reached out with his mind and felt the great city across the river. *Unevolved souls seeing through their senses and chasing their animal urges, rutting like pigs,* he observed disdainfully. *Thank the gods I am beyond that.*

The next day Thuth rose before dawn and walked miles to the base of the great pyramid. It was sunrise. Two hundred initiates and teachers from the mystery schools had formed a perfect rectangle to watch the event when he arrived. He and the other two linesmen of Egypt maneuvered to each point of the pyramid's western base. The wind blew hard. Thuth could feel it was a powerful day. Moving the pyramid would be easy.

Suddenly, to his surprise, horns blew and the great Pharaoh of Egypt was borne by slaves on a dais over a dune and carefully set down to witness the event. This had never happened before. Thuth gazed at the Pharaoh's golden robes fluttering in the wind. *He looks older and tired,* he noted. *He is her father... .*

Thuth pushed the last thought out of his head. One stray emotional impression as the pyramid shot across the desert, might cause a flaw in the energy lines and certain disaster. It was the linesman's job to stretch and lift the great power lines of the desert plain. They stretched them tight with their minds, right before a pyramid was moved. Then, when the High Priest folded space, the pyramid would slide above the desert floor, like an ice cube, snapping to its new location in space and time.

After a few minutes, the High Priest Ra, who had saved Thuth's life centuries ago, strode calmly to the base of the great pyramid. The great priest ignored even the Pharaoh, for he was deep in a trance. Thuth focused on the energy lines of the desert that he was to pull tighter. He could feel occult power from the High Priest filling the current space of the pyramid and emptying a new space twenty miles away — the pyramid would soon be compelled to its new location in the universe.

Thuth gazed intently on the luminous astral fibers of the desert, pulling them tighter with his third eye. His staff vibrated violently against the power lines that stretched into the West. Suddenly, a force pulled at his gut, as the lines buckled to the mass of the great pyramid. Thuth held them with his will and saw the pyramid shoot into the distance as a glowing matrix of lights.

A gentle wind caressed him now, as he relaxed in the tense silence. Finally, horns echoed faintly in the distance, signaling that that the great pyramid had arrived at its new location in one piece. He watched the High Priest open his eyes. His own staff glowed with energy and was hot to the touch. *Yes — it is a powerful day*, he observed.

~

At sunset, he found himself on a sandy ridge overlooking the Nile. He decided to visit the young initiates having dinner, as he had the previous evening. Thuth moved gracefully east over a dune, glowing as he paced above the hot sands.

He reached the summit of a tall orange ridge and saw the acolytes below enjoying their meal. *They are like animals feeding at an oasis*, he observed with disgust. Across the Nile, he glanced at decadent Luxor, bathing in the last rays of the sun.

"I am going to the Indus River to die," a deep voice suddenly boomed behind him. Startled, he recognized the High Priest's voice and turned to bow. His teacher looked frailer now, his huge frame diminished after such a long life. He appeared ethereal, like a spirit that was barely in this world, glowing brightly to Thuth's well-trained eyes.

"I am leaving Egypt forever with the next moon. And you will not be coming with me," his teacher coldly informed him.

"But I would, Ra, if you required me," Thuth sadly replied, feeling rejected.

The High Priest motioned and they sat. "I received your application to study in the advanced schools of enlightenment last week." There was a touch of sadness in his tone. "I cannot accept your application."

"I have applied one hundred eighty times, once per year, Lord Ra," Thuth answered respectfully, his voice cracking.

"I know Thuth, but you've never told me a joke," his teacher replied cryptically.

Thuth considered the strange remark. "I have tried to go beyond human emotion, beyond the human form. I don't see how jokes are important," he answered.

"You're still not over her, are you?" the High Priest abruptly asked.

Thuth was shocked and angry. Usually his emotional control was perfect. "I am over ... her. I find human sexuality to be repulsive and animal-like."

"Who said anything about sex?" the High Priest questioned him.

"I consider tantric sex the most inefficient pathway to the other worlds," Thuth explained, feeling violated that the High Priest had read his deepest thoughts.

"You're slow, Thuth; that's what I like about you," the High Priest said, not offended by the tone of his senior priest. Instead he smiled and continued, "I don't care if you can move pyramids, but I'm glad you haven't lost your stupid side!" the old priest laughed heartily and coughed.

"I meant you no disrespect," Thuth lowered his head. "Please explain to me why I am too stupid to study enlightenment."

"Thuth, you are too intelligent to study enlightenment!" his teacher exclaimed. "That's why I like your stupid side, it gives me hope!"

"Lord Ra, if you command it, I shall enter the orgies in the Temple of Hathor right now," Thuth offered.

His teacher laughed harder and coughed again. "Thuth you are stupid! You haven't told a joke yet; but you certainly have made me laugh!"

"Master," Thuth pleaded, "then accept my application to study enlightenment!"

"I cannot," the High Priest answered firmly, "Because you are stupid. I was speaking of love earlier, not animal instincts — your love for Princess Neferkasokar. You have shut out the wonder of life because of a pathetic broken heart!" the High Priest's voice was harsh as he drove the point home. "How dare you even apply to study enlightenment with me, while you are still pining over a girl?"

"I am over her, I assure you," Thuth answered as calmly as he could.

"Yes, Thuth, *you* are over her. But the man I see in front of me has hardened his heart and suppressed his own humanity to accomplish that feat." Ra stood and loomed over Thuth's stunned figure. "You disgrace me Thuth, a linesman of Egypt, too afraid to attend ceremonies in Luxor because he is frightened of bumping into a woman!"

The High Priest ruthlessly continued his critique. "You are just another heartless sorcerer doing tricks with pyramids to feed your fat face. Who is the animal, Thuth? Keisha has children today. Is she a Nile river rat? Shall I summon her to the Field of Obelisks so you can tell her she is an animal?"

Thuth shuddered. *Keisha has children*. She had left for Sumeria so long ago. *Maybe she is visiting Luxor*, the idea shook him like a lightening bolt.

Ra softened his tone, perhaps reading Thuth's thoughts. "Maybe it was my fault," he speculated, resigned, lowering his head. Both became silent as the wind whipped around them. Finally his teacher spoke again:

"Maybe I expected too much of you. Maybe I should have treated you like a kid with a broken heart." Suddenly a strong gust blew sand in Thuth's face and when he looked over, the High Priest of Egypt had vanished — he did that sometimes.

Alone in the silent desert, Thuth wearily rose, ashamed. In his heart, he knew Lord Ra was correct. He would not be going with his master to the Indus River but would continue as a linesman in the hot deserts of Egypt. He began to walk dejectedly toward the novices enjoying their evening meals.

When he crested the ridge and was spotted, the dining students immediately stood and bowed perfectly. He wondered why they had jumped more quickly today than usual and realized they had just witnessed him move a pyramid. He nodded to them slightly and they all sat in unison, returning eagerly to their meals.

If they only knew what the High Priest just said to me! he lamented, wandering dejectedly among the seated novices. As they ate quietly, Thuth sadly realized they were all afraid — of him. He noticed there was no teacher present to supervise these kids. Therefore, protocol demanded he wait for a fully ordained priest to arrive.

Normally, having to babysit initiates would have angered Thuth. Yet as the sun touched the western horizon, he simply watched the kids eat happily and chatter away. He realized he was no better than they were, and, more importantly, they were happy. Yes, they were only animals eating food, but he was just an unhappy animal holding a mystical staff. His heart opened a little. He realized how profoundly he had failed in teaching the younger generation of his order.

"You," he pointed to the novice who seemed to get along well with Sintar, his old friend.

The novice quickly sprung to his feet and bowed. "Yes, Linesman?"

"Where is Sintar?" Thuth asked the young man.

"He will be here soon, Linesman. He is late today. Sintar is now tutoring at the palace of Luxor."

Thuth quickly put his thumb on the young novice's third eye and empowered him with an energy that would last for weeks. *Funny*, he thought, *I've never done this before. Why haven't I ever given the younger members of the order my energy?* After a few moments, he mindlessly motioned for the boy to sit down.

He turned from the students and looked in the direction of Luxor. The High Priest had been correct. It was because of *her* that he had never crossed the Nile in almost two hundred years. As Thuth stood motionless considering this, he overheard the boys and girls speaking as they ate:

"Élan, how does Sintar like tutoring the princes of Egypt?" one boy asked.

"He is not tutoring the princes of Egypt," Élan corrected him. "He is tutoring the princes of Sumeria."

Thuth's heart jumped.

"Is Jonas now King of Sumeria?" A female acolyte asked.

"Technically, yes. His father finally died." Élan paused and grinned dramatically. "But the military revolted the day he took the throne. So he fled with his wife back to Egypt."

"Coward!" exclaimed another initiate sharply, laughing.

The other boys and girls giggled at the remark. Thuth remained motionless, helpless, as all of the pain and love from his past flooded him. The High Priest had known it all along, he had been suppressing his heart, his heartache for Keisha, by becoming cold, logical, and oh so good at moving pyramids.

"Does Sintar like his job as a royal tutor?" the young female acolyte asked.

"No," Élan answered, "Sintar tells me Jonas beats the princess of Egypt everyday. Her cries can be heard throughout the palace."

Gasps went up among the young novices. To strike a daughter of Isis, one Pharaoh's daughters, was inconceivable to these young students because they had been taught since childhood that Pharaoh, himself, was God.

~

Thuth did not hear their gasps though. He was in a rage. A cold fury possessed him and he forgot where he was. All that mattered was Keisha. She needed him and was across the river. He smiled slowly now, realizing what the High Priest had been trying to tell him. He had lost his heart, but today it beat like a thousand suns. He was alive again.

He strode quickly toward the river, forgetting the acolytes. He imagined Jonas beating the woman he had never stopped loving and realized he was not ready for the schools of enlightenment — for he was about to break all of its vows. Thuth walked faster, confidently toward the docks. He felt his power coming together. His staff bent and coiled like a serpent, anticipating battle.

He opened his third eye with his awareness and could feel her now across the Nile — indeed, Keisha was in great pain and darkness. He had not dared to touch her mind in ages, knowing he would only find sadness there. Yet now, when he felt his beloved, even the sadness was beautiful to him.

When he reached the docks, two awkward boys bowed to him, terrified of his dusty blue robe and golden skullcap. Everyone knew the great pyramid had been moved today and Thuth was a linesman.

"Take me to the royal house of Luxor," he demanded coldly, ready to kill anything that got in his way.

"Yes, Priest!" The boys bowed and scurried toward the ropes of their small craft. One of them surprised Thuth and carefully laid a white silk cloth on the passenger bench. *White, the color of funerals, today will be mine, most likely*, he reflected and awkwardly stepped into the boat as it rocked gently. He had not stepped into one in almost two hundred years.

Thuth sat and watched the boys hurry their oars and launch the craft into the dark swirling currents of the Nile. Soon they were carried swiftly north and the western bank of the great river faded fast. To his left, he saw the Field of Obelisks where he had met Keisha years before.

He turned to the east, for the western desert was his past. The great palace of Neferkasokar was inching closer, ever so slowly; its black marble spires and golden trim loomed high in the sky. Beyond them, he gazed at the shining city of Luxor glittering in the sunset — for the last time in his life.

As the royal docks grew closer, Thuth realized he would have to start killing people soon. The jewel in his third eye was glowing and his staff was shifting, the great coiled serpent inside coming alive. His own body's power was surging — for a body knows when it is about to die.

Thuth looked down at the mysterious swirling currents by his side, they reminded him of the magical love he had for Keisha. Their short time together had been like the river, natural, effortless, and so unique, every moment beautiful, poignant. He understood why the High Priest had been correct. Moving a pyramid was nothing compared to the power of love.

The small boat now angled toward the private docks of the Pharaoh's palace. Tall guards eyed the shabby craft as it approached the outer moorings. One of the boys adroitly jumped out and pulled a rope around a golden moor. The water lapped gently against the immaculate pier, shimmering against the setting sun.

Thuth absentmindedly stepped out of the vessel and found himself standing face to face with a huge palace guard. He positioned his staff to kill the man, but the guard simply bowed.

"Linesman of Egypt, what is your business at the palace of Luxor?"

Thuth looked at him coldly and uttered the two words he had been afraid to say for so long: "Keisha Neferkasokar."

Pharaoh's guards actually led Thuth to the palace wing where Keisha was housed with Jonas' clan and then returned to their posts. Thuth calmly entered the rich gardens that lined the guest palace. The sun had disappeared beyond the horizon and it was already becoming cold. He could also felt an inner coldness around the empty grounds. Sadness and shame seemed to cover the beautiful lawns like a heavy cloak of darkness.

He was now resolved to rip that dark garment apart.

He heard voices and music beyond the palace walls. It sounded like a great celebration. He entered a large open marble patio and walked dreamily down a long hallway with cedar arches. Thuth's body suddenly became tense. The battle had finally arrived.

Two gigantic guards blocked the mighty polished wooden doors where the raucous sounds were coming from. *This must be the main court of Jonas. I feel her beyond these doors*, his instincts told him.

"Priest, what is your business here?" One of the guards asked him warily. Thuth's sandy dust covered robe looked totally out of place in the guest palace of Pharaoh. He focused on his third eye and his awareness shifted. The guards and the walls beyond became moving energy, not objects. The power he had summoned this morning to move the great pyramid was stronger than ever.

"I am here to kill people," Thuth replied matter-of-factly. The warriors were stunned and looked at each other. Thuth thrust his staff between them, creating a powerful wave of energy. Both men were slammed into marble walls by an invisible force, usually reserved to support a hundred million ton pyramid. Their bodies splattered.

Thuth, determined, smashed his staff against the huge wooden doors. It sparked wildly and the heavy bronze lock snapped. He could feel Keisha now. She was close and needed him. She needed him to kill.

When the doors splintered open, Thuth expected gasps, cries for help, and quick fighting. But instead his senses were bombarded by music and wild cries of pleasure. Sumerian soldiers were on the floor copulating with slave girls, musicians played strange music from the north, and Egyptian guards lazily loitered by gigantic marble columns smoking hash. No one was paying any particular attention to him — yet.

As he walked forward into the noisy majestic space, he noticed the center of the room was set lower than the front. There he saw Jonas lounging on comfortable pillows surrounded by naked women feeding him slices of banana and waving huge palm fronds to keep their "King" cool. Jonas laughed and giggled with them, enjoying a large bottle of swill. He was still far from Thuth in the huge space.

"You, what is your business here?" an Egyptian guard near him spoke in alarm and pointed. Thuth blandly stared at the soldiers as they stiffened. One of the musicians playing a flute stopped in mid-note and dropped his instrument, noticing Thuth's staff coil and fight against his grip.

Thuth clinically watched his fellow Egyptian guards go for their weapons. The Sumerians were still oblivious, half-naked, wrestling in slow motion on the marble floor with their pleasure girls. He gazed at the massive circular column by the guard who had noticed him. Then he motioned his staff carefully forward and twisted an energy line only he could see.

The column began to crumble. Thuth heard the screams of women, as he motioned his staff again, slamming another wave of energy with such violence, that musicians, naked women, and palace guards were hurled all directions. People smashed into walls like bugs. Huge clouds of dust rose from the crumbling marble and the roof cracked audibly as he strode to where Jonas lay, awestruck.

Thuth's mind was working at uncanny speed and sensed a long spear darting toward him. His mystical staff sprang like a snake, elongated in his grip, and crushed the fast moving object like a twig. Guards to his right stormed him. He waved his staff casually and released another huge charge of energy, hurling the stunned men thirty feet backwards to their deaths against cracking walls.

He continued forward cautiously. An eerie silence filled the space. While women could be heard sobbing and men groaning in death agony, it seemed strangely silent. The moans could have been drunks in an audience waiting for him to speak. Everyone was watching him — every-one that was still alive, that is.

Thuth approached the marble descent in the center of the room where Jonas sat stunned. He almost felt pity for the disgusting barbarian. Beyond Jonas, he beheld Keisha for the first time in ages; their eyes locked.

"YOU!" Jonas roared and began to stand. Thuth broke away from Keisha's stare, pleading with him, as if she was afraid for his life. He turned to Jonas with a cold glare.

"I have been waiting for this, Thuth," Jonas growled with recognition and smirked. He angrily threw his wine bottle against one of the broken columns behind him. But before he could draw his sword, Thuth slid on an energy line only he could see and was against Jonas with uncanny speed. He smashed his huge staff against the barbarian's head in great fury.

With that one blow, which would have killed most men, Jonas went insane. He was inundated with a great volume of raw mystical power, amplified by Thuth's intense anger. Jonas staggered backward, foaming at the mouth and fell to the floor squirming and gargling.

As Jonas swallowed his tongue and twisted on the floor by Thuth's sandals, Thuth noticed an Egyptian warrior by his side. It was the old river captain from the Field of Obelisks. Thuth could feel his mind, he was about to reach for his spear.

"Don't," Thuth advised, glaring into the old captain's eyes. He didn't want to kill this man; but then he was distracted again.

"Thuth! Oh Thuth!" Keisha exclaimed sadly, from the far side of the room. She had a bruise over one eye and a puffed lip. He noticed her maidservants standing loyally and protectively beside her, shaking with terror. They also had marks of beatings from Jonas, who was squirming at Thuth's feet, choking on his tongue and dying.

Thuth looked into Keisha's eyes again. Nothing else mattered now. He approached her. In her timeless gaze, he saw the light of Isis, the love he had shut out for all those years in the hot deserts of Egypt. The High Priest had been right, how could he study enlightenment without under-standing love first?

"Oh, Thuth," Keisha lamented. "Why did you do this?" Tears filled her eyes. He only smiled back at her gently, calmly, as if they were casually meeting, as they had years ago.

He lifted her delicate hands. They had a few wrinkles on them, yet still felt so soft to his calloused touch. He found himself wishing the wrinkles on her hands were from the years of their love. Their eyes met again and she smiled. Both had not smiled in such a long time. He would escape with her now. *Maybe we can go to the Indus River … .*

Suddenly, he felt a great pain shoot through him and clinically noticed the bloody tip of a spear jutting out from his chest. The old river captain had thrown it.

How fitting, Thuth mused. He looked at Keisha for one last time, almost apologetically. He could not speak; a warm salty liquid came out of his mouth. He had wanted to tell her how much he loved her.

"I will always love you!" Keisha cried out. Thuth then collapsed at her feet and died.

~

"And so Pharaoh, we have an understanding," the High Priest spoke, as he sat on a golden dais next to the royal throne.

"Yes, Ra, there will be no recriminations against Thuth's family. And you are free to leave for the Indus River," the old Pharaoh spoke, wheezing. He was sick and dying.

"Have you executed everyone that witnessed the event?" the High Priest asked.

"Yes," the Pharaoh answered coldly, "everyone, except my daughter, of course."

"Of course," the High Priest stood and bowed. "You were correct in doing so. There must be no memory of how a fully ordained priest, a linesman of Egypt, attacked your house. Egypt would fall within two centuries. It is my disgrace. I ask your permission to take leave and prepare for my journey east."

"Goodbye, Priest," Pharaoh Neferkasokar answered and motioned with his hand, tiredly but proudly. When the High Priest Ra reached the doors of the imperial court, the old Pharaoh spoke up again, loudly, surprising everyone present in the vast chamber:

"This Thuth ... I would have liked to have met him. A father knows when his daughter is in love. Was he a good man?"

Lord Ra paused ever so slightly. "Yes, he was," he replied with a touch of sadness. He then lowered his head and walked out of the court of

Egypt forever.

~

Pharaoh Neferkasokar dozed comfortably on huge silk pillows. He felt the air from palm fronds caress him. The royal court was silent. He listened to the birds in the fountains singing. There was a simple happiness in the palace again, a happiness he had not felt in such a long time.

Just yesterday, he had strolled with his daughter Keisha in the royal gardens. She looked radiant, like the beautiful and intelligent child he remembered. He was proud of her. His youngest daughter had passed through the Khet Hells, according to her blood duty, and now the gods had rewarded her with riches beyond belief.

Pharaoh's favorite daughter was beyond the reach of men now. She could not be given away as chattel, as he had mistakenly done years ago. There was even talk in Sumeria of making her queen — apparently, the generals who usurped Jonas couldn't get along amongst themselves.

Neferkasokar smiled knowingly. He was tired. Breathing was hard. His daughter was heir to the throne of Sumeria and peace reigned throughout the lands. The trade routes to the East were open. But more importantly, happiness had returned to his child's heart and the royal house itself, maybe not in the way anyone had expected, but it had returned — in the form of a secret lover named Thuth.

Pharaoh recalled his dream of last night. He had been running through a wet field of grass, grasping an oblong leather ball and skillfully avoiding other men who were trying to tackle him, huge warriors, wearing shiny round helmets. It was nighttime. He was sprinting toward the center of a massive stadium with glaring lights all around him. A crowd of magnificent size broke into a frenzied roar. Just a few minutes ago he had asked the High Priest what the dream had meant. The ancient sorcerer had only told him it was a vision of one of his future lives — nothing more.

The dying Pharaoh slipped into a deep sleep for the last time. His breathing finally stopped and Thuth, the man who might have been his son by marriage in a more perfect world, smiled to him from the beyond and led him past the *Sekhet-Hetepet* underworlds, to the *Fields of Aaru*, the realms of paradise, and away from Egypt forever.

~

The vision of Egypt faded into a golden light as Romeo meditated silently in Hawaii. It was dark and windy now. He opened his eyes. There were tears in them, reflecting a pain he could not endure. His whole body shook — and it was not because he and Emilie had been lovers in Egypt that tore him apart so — he cried because of whom she resembled in his vision. She had looked exactly like Juliet!

Emilie was Juliet and Romeo had been too blind to see!

Romeo and Ed Sullivan

Plainly know my heart's dear love is set,
On the fair daughter of rich Capulet.

- Romeo

He leaned in and kissed her tentatively on his new white couch. He had bought it a few months ago, hoping he could one day kiss Emilie on it when she visited. But spring had turned to summer and Romeo had not spoken to his beloved soulmate in months. He was still in great pain. For he had found out, only too late, that the woman he had met online had been his wife Juliet from Italy.

He felt Melanie's smooth, thick black hair fall against his strong hands as he stroked her shoulders. He knew he needed to lose himself in the caresses of another woman if he ever was to heal. He needed to get his own power up, and maybe then, could solve the riddle of Juliet, the woman Emilie he loved so.

He had met Melanie at one of his neighbor's, Uncle Ukali's, famous Luaus. She was an island girl and her shapely strong hips pressed up against Romeo as she returned his kisses. Suddenly, she pulled away.

"What's wrong?" he asked.

"Well ... I think we should stop here," Melanie informed him.

"Is it something I said or did?" he politely inquired.

"No, Romeo," Melanie paused and smiled, wistfully. "It's just the way you spoke of that woman you met on the Internet during our drive back from the beach. I could see in your eyes that you still cared for her very much." She abruptly stood up.

"I was only trying to be honest. I just wanted to let you know I've had my heart broken," he defended himself, apologetically.

"I know and appreciate that," she remarked and pecked him on the cheek. "Most men would never do that. It's so sweet."

Melanie paused and continued, "I just don't like being number two with any man. And when you spoke of her, I knew I could never be like she was for you." She lowered her eyes. Romeo averted her gaze also; a shiver went through him.

"Look, I'd love to spend the night with you, but I'm afraid I would fall in love," she explained gently.

"I'm sorry," he muttered, embarrassed, lowering his head again.

"Don't worry about it." Melanie waved her sleek jet-black hair to compose herself. After all, Romeo wasn't the only handsome man on the island and the night had not been wasted; he was a great kisser.

"So you really liked this girl?" Melanie asked.

"Yes," Romeo said, sensing something new.

"Well let me look at her picture. I'm curious to see if she is more beautiful than me," Melanie quipped and flashed Romeo a sarcastic smile, reminiscent of Judy Garrity. Romeo led her to his office and displayed his only picture of Emilie. To his surprise, Melanie giggled.

"Why that's Emma Gallant. She's one of the hottest young actresses in

Hollywood," Melanie remarked smiling, unwilling to believe that Romeo had spoken to such a famous star.

The moment Romeo heard the name Emma Gallant, a mystical light from above hit him. Melanie's words struck him down, wonderfully, on his road to Damascus. *Emilie is famous. I need to keep this a secret,* he realized. Melanie studied him and waited for a response.

"Well she must have given me a fake picture. I suspected as much," he finally replied with a false display of resignation.

"Oh really?" she asked, still curious and maybe a little skeptical.

"Yes, I lost contact with her soon after she sent the pic," he lied. "Maybe she left because she had not been truthful with me." He lowered his head in mock sadness.

"Well, I'm sorry. Maybe one day you will find out who she really is," Melanie comforted him.

Romeo secretly smiled, as a new power surged through him. His purpose for being in this world was to find Juliet and he had succeeded! He drove Melanie home in silence, pondering what to do next.

~

The next morning, his meditation was agitated. He was so excited. Yet, as in Italy long ago, Romeo could already feel that portent of tragedy hanging in the air. After all, in this life, Juliet was a famous movie star. This was going to complicate things, he realized.

How could I have been such a fool? How could I have not recognized my own wife sooner? he bowed, ending his zazen session. You aren't supposed to think during meditation, but that is exactly what he had been doing: *Emma Gallant, Emilie, a movie star ... my Juliet.*

He skipped his morning tea and impatiently waited for his computer to boot. He needed to confirm that Emilie, Juliet, was indeed the actress Emma Gallant. He didn't even bother checking his business mail and went directly to his browser, Googling the name "Emma Gallant" and was overwhelmed.

Yes, this is Emilie, he admitted, barraged by images from hundreds of fan sites, pictures of the woman he had once loved as Juliet Capulet. The world seemed to adore her as much as he did.

Emma Gallant Voted the Most Beautiful Woman in the World!

The colors spun wildly and made his head dizzy. He saw endless articles, news releases, and video clips of his beloved. That quiet, intelligent girl from Verona was now amplified by multinational corporations, raging fans, and the mystique of Hollywood that goes all the way back to ancient Egypt.

Hollywood Sensation Emma Gallant Speaks to Jay Leno About Her Latest Film!

He browsed faster. He had chased Juliet through death, into this world, and now she was right in front of him — the darling starlet of Hollywood. He happened upon a fan site:

www.emmagallant.com

He clicked on the link and saw endless images of his wife. They all seemed artificial and made him feel farther away from her, not closer. The pictures mocked him, laughed at the absurdity, the hopelessness of his situation — a nobody, in love with a famous star.

As he read on about his wife's current life, he realized she had been traveling like a business executive for years. Romeo had done some consulting on Wall Street himself and knew how hard a life of travel was.

But of course, Hollywood wasn't telling you any of that stuff, he bitterly observed. They sold their actors as narcissistic gods that led charmed lives of perfect happiness — gods that would sell tickets to the mediocre formula films their pulp mills churned out.

He happened upon a web page that had the movie sensation Emma Gallant's schedule plastered all over it, as if she was the Pope touring Christendom. She was doing Leno, King and Letterman. So this week, from the media's point of view, she was bigger than the Pope. He noticed her new movie *Mary Queen of Scots* was actually opening tonight in London.

"London," he uttered the word aloud. It sounded so far away. But his wife from old Italy was already far from him — in a social sense — far above him, looking down from the dark towers of Hollywood, in the same way she had as a princess in Egypt.

London, he mused, *it must be evening there … .*

~

The hammering drums and bass echoed loudly in the Islington district. It was opening night of what the studio exec's hoped would be a great summer blockbuster. A light drizzle had respectfully stopped and the sun had set. The London crowd was eager with anticipation. Cold, bright stars poked through fast breaking clouds that raced eastwards.

A white limousine was noticed pulling up to the base of the red carpet walkway. A door opened and an elegant black slipper, exclusive from Vera Wang, touched the damp grey curb. Above the shoe, a trim shapely ankle hugged perfectly in close-knit Donna Koran stockings inched out, followed by a beautiful shapely leg and a perfect black hem that rose with the graceful hips of Emma Gallant. She confidently walked onto the curb. The star had arrived and the crowd went wild!

Thousands of screaming fans, taking advantage of the free food and live music, struggled to catch a glimpse of the beautiful young starlet Emma Gallant. The studio had paid a fortune for this massive block party to help boost the world premier of *Mary Queen of Scots*. The star strode proudly and confidently down the red carpet, elegantly oblivious to the rambunctious crowd and the pounding sound of the techno-trance band that had been hired for the event.

This is the hardest part of acting, Emilie reminded herself. *I am going to do this perfectly*. She corrected her posture, and became even more regal, raising her head proudly. She smiled and waved to the crowd as hundreds of bright flashes went off near her. Her fans, safely beyond police barriers, roared their approval and screamed whenever she glanced in their direction.

Old men and women lined the walkway admiring at her with proud saintly smiles as if she were their successful granddaughter. Husbands held their wives' hands and stared longingly at Emma Gallant, wishing they were holding her hand, or perhaps her checkbook. Young girls and boys screamed behind red silk ropes and jumped when her eyes caught theirs, as if she was their Egyptian princess, a daughter of Isis, come down to earth to bless them.

Deep inside herself, Emilie knew she had done this before, in other lives. She could feel the electric power of the crowd flow into her; it gave her a charge and a purpose. She thought of her childhood fantasy of being an Egyptian princess — and now she was one again.

She turned and waved to her right, smiling every so slightly. The mass of humanity near the gesture went wild. The band continued to generate its trance beat impossibly fast, the rhythm seemed to feed on the energy of the fans. She ignored their cheering and made her way toward the podium at the far end of the plaza.

~

Meanwhile in the tranquil Hawaiian morning, Romeo continued his online research. He read about Emilie's current boyfriend, the wealthy heir, Paris Beauregard. *Count Paris!* he marveled. Paris even looked the same as he had in Verona.

He had sensed that Emilie was with another man now. The fact that it was the good Count Paris did not upset him as did the image of Johnny Perfection. He saw a picture of John and Emilie together on a movie set, understanding everything when he read the name:

JOHN TYBALT

"Cousin Tybalt," he uttered in a low menacing voice. "We meet again." He recalled the Hawaiian goddess Leheau had cryptically warned him about Juliet's cuz years ago. He realized, it had been Tybalt that had destroyed their Internet accounts, separating them.

For now though, he decided to stop tormenting his mind with images of his loves and hates. Instead, he sat still and quietly reflected. He didn't want to be rash, to make the same mistakes he had in Italy. *After all*, he reminded himself, *I am a Zen monk now.*

He had failed to recognize Emilie as Juliet in the time they had known each other and knew it would take her much longer, if ever, to remember she had been Juliet Capulet in a previous life. Unlike Romeo, she was womb-born of this world and could not recall her short life in Italy as he

could. He knew if he went to her now, it would be considered inappropri-
ate and he would be considered just another Hollywood/Internet stalker.

In a few days, Emilie would be in New York City and on the Letterman
Show. But Romeo could not meet her there. Emilie was part of the new
nobility, the Hollywood elite, and probably well guarded. He would be
treated just as the Capulets had treated him — and if he told anyone the
truth about his wife, he might be locked up in a mental hospital. Yes,
Master Lee's monks had taught Romeo well; it was a hard world. The first
noble truth of Buddhism simply states: *All of life contains suffering.*

The memory of Paris' murder, even Tybalt's, weighed heavy on his
mind. He recalled the sight of Paris' blood when he first awoke in this
world. The fact that he was with Emilie almost seemed just. He realized
his chances of stealing her away were small, to say the least — after all,
she and Romeo had never met.

~

Safely to the east of Romeo, above an agitated sea of excited faces,
Emilie carefully made her way up the red-carpeted steps leading to
the makeshift stage. The mayor of London and his wife stood and cheered
her on. It was an election year. The mayor clapped vigorously, sporting a
fake smile.

He is envious of me, she realized, as she turned toward the ecstatic
crowd. *He is afraid of my power.*

The Hollywood elite must have once held the power of the earth and
had lost it, somehow, she reasoned. Now she had to acknowledge his
power. Emilie was no longer a princess of Egypt. She tilted her head to the
mayor, ever so slightly. The crowd noticed the gesture and roared louder.
The mayor smiled and some of the envy seemed to seep out of his phony

grin as he moved toward the microphone.

"Good Evening, London!" their mayor started enthusiastically, as the crowed cheered.

"How's everyone tonight?" he asked in a playful fake manner.

The crowd screamed in a frenzy. The flashing of cameras blinded Emilie as she approached the podium. Over a hundred media people were camped in front of her. For a second she felt a sense of vertigo and lost her balance. She corrected herself. *This is the hardest part of acting ... I'm going to do it perfectly.*

"And here she is! Emma Gallant!" The mayor motioned her forward, now more envious than ever of the crowd's adoration. Emilie reluctantly came to his side, walking past the mayor's wife, who gave her a haughty but awestruck look none-the-less. She leaned into the microphone and thanked the audience for attending. Her fans went into an electrical pandemonium as their Juliet from Hollywood, their princess from Egypt, their daughter of Isis, stood before them and smiled, so shyly.

~

As the Saturday sun streamed into his quiet study, Romeo finally made some tea and relaxed by the open windows of his house. For some reason, he couldn't stop looking at Emilie's posted schedule. She had a Wednesday appointment with David Letterman. Although he didn't want to stalk a famous movie star, he was glad to be free. He had been delivered from the hell of not knowing who Juliet was. *At least now,* he thought and smiled, *I can lose.*

He looked at her schedule again and knew what he had to do. He still felt that forces within Hollywood had destroyed their connection — social forces, just as in Verona, just as in Egypt, had separated them, probably forever. He had essentially two choices before him. He could send her fan mail into that same black hole of Hollywood that had taken her from him or he could try something else, a more direct way of contact. And that something else would be the Letterman Show at the Ed Sullivan Theater. He decided to attack into the heart of Hollywood's darkness with only flowers. He picked up his cell and eagerly began to dial.

~

"Hello," the black robed monk answered the phone.

"Roshi Jeff, this is Romeo."

"Romeo, it's good to hear from you! How are you doing?" Jeff Garrity exclaimed.

"I have a favor to ask of you, Jeff," Romeo began.

"Anything, after all we are brother monks."

"I need you to arrange delivery of flowers and a love letter to a movie star," he explained deadpan. "She will be at the Ed Sullivan Theater in New York City Wednesday."

Jeff was dumbfounded but smiled. "Are you kidding me?"

"No, I am not. I love this woman."

"Who is she?"

"Emma Gallant"

"Never heard of her," Jeff remarked. "Are you serious?" he couldn't contain a grin as he asked the question.

"Very serious, Roshi, what is there not to understand?" Romeo challenged his old teacher respectfully.

"I don't understand why you would be in love with a movie star, that's all. Does she even know who you are?" Jeff asked, exasperated.

"Yes"

"How did you meet her?" he was curious now.

"On the Internet," Romeo replied tentatively. Of course he knew he had met Emilie many times, in many lives prior to that.

"Oh Romeo!" Jeff sighed, as if Romeo had come down with a disease. "Are you sure it's even her?" he asked. "And how can you love a woman you've never met?"

Romeo decided to tell the truth. "Jeff, as you remember, Master Lee used to kid about my name Romeo — and about Juliet."

"Yes I do … Romeo." Now the name suddenly took on new and different power. He felt the conversation was about to get heavier.

Romeo continued seriously. "As you know, when I came to the Zen Center in New York City I had no identification papers."

"Yes … ." Jeff's voice tapered off. He gulped. Romeo continued dramatically:

"I am Romeo Montague, from Italy, and Emma Gallant, the movie star, is Juliet Capulet," he confessed earnestly. "She is my wife, reincarnated into this world," he announced almost joyously.

"Calm down," Jeff implored, in the most pleasant and tranquil Zen tone he could summon. "Did Master Lee tell you all of this?"

"Master Lee knew I was Romeo Montague … so yes." Romeo paused, uncertain for the first time of his own visions. "But I did not know Juliet … um … Emilie during Master Lee's life. When I tell you she is Juliet that is my seeing."

"I see," Jeff said tentatively. "Now what is it you want me to do for you?"

Romeo explained his plan. Jeff was to print out a love letter that Romeo would email. Romeo would find a florist that delivered flowers to the guests of David Letterman. Jeff would have the letter taped to the flowers. The plan seemed simple enough. Emma Gallant would receive a beautiful bouquet of flowers and a letter from Romeo, probably a goodbye — he sadly realized, as he mapped out his plan to Jeff.

"Romeo," Jeff interrupted. "How do you know this woman ... Emma ... has any feelings for you? You only chatted with her on the Internet."

"Jeff we were falling in love ... again," Romeo paused. "And then my account was hacked into by forces within Hollywood."

"How do you know all of this? Maybe she decided to break it off."

"I don't know anything. You may be correct. But I do feel with all my heart that she is my wife from Italy and that we will always love each other deep inside."

Jeff was speechless. His friend seemed to be on the verge of insanity. Romeo sensed Jeff's consternation and continued. "I don't expect you to believe any of this. But trust that I love this woman and need you to send her flowers and a letter. That is all I am asking of you, Roshi."

"You may read the letter first, if you wish," he offered.

"No thanks, Romeo. I think if I did ... I would go insane," Jeff half-joked. He paused and finally agreed to help his old friend.

~

E milie now lay in Paris' strong arms in a penthouse suite at the St. Martins Lane Hotel. The frenzied opening of *Mary Queen of Scots* had been a rousing success and a huge media event. Paris had made love to her when they returned.

"Darling," he began, affectionately.

"Yes dear," she asked lovingly. He was so good to her. He was sweet and sexy and had rescued her from the dark night of the soul that was Johnny Perfection. She stroked his hair gently and smiled.

Paris continued, "I'm going to miss you dear. Please don't fall in love while you are in America," he added playfully.

"Of course I won't, darling. I will be thinking of you the whole time."

Paris held her tighter and they kissed again. Little did Emilie know, as she held her lover that soon she would be thinking of another, a man she had never met in person, a man she had totally put out of her mind — yet someone she had known and loved for countless lives.

Juliet and Flowers

The orchid walls are high and hard to climb,
And the place death, considering who thou art,
If any of my kinsmen find thee here.

- Juliet

The black stretch limousine stopped smoothly alongside the curb of the Ed Sullivan theater amidst the hurried sounds of Broadway and 37th st. Emilie stepped out into the sunlight, prepared for the hot muggy summer day with a comfortable red blouse and loose fitting jeans. Her new white Jordan's glistened in the harsh noon sun, making her look very cute.

Her publicist Beth exited on the driver's side and followed Emilie around the car. Beth was dressed in a starched grey business suit and awkward high heels. She barked directions to the limo driver and followed Emilie to a side door of the Ed Sullivan Theater. A large, muscular black guard with arms folded stood by the entrance.

"Hello, Miss Gallant," he said charmingly.

He recognizes me, Emilie proudly realized. "Hello," she cheerfully replied to the huge guard as she began to walk up the steps toward the Theater.

Beth interrupted. "Hello, I'm Ms. Penhard, Emma Gallant's publicist.

Miss Gallant needs to be shown to her dressing room. I'm carrying a twelve thousand dollar dress and her hair has to be made up." The guards' eyes glazed over as Beth continued her sermon.

"Yes, ma'am," the guard said a few times. "Let me take Ms. Gallant to her dressing room. There was a flower delivery earlier today," he added cheerfully.

The guard opened the large doors of the theater, then carefully locked them with his heavy key chain. He led them down an old dark corridor with a shiny, but tacky, green rug. They stopped by a small beige dressing room door. From the other direction, Emilie saw one of Letterman's assistants scurrying toward them.

"Hello, I'm Gregory Richards," the well dressed man introduced himself. "Welcome Ms. Gallant." Gregory stopped and bowed ever so slightly, as if she were royalty. "Is there anything we can get you?" he inquired like a loyal servant, glancing wearily over at Beth.

"Could you get me some iced tea please," Emilie asked politely. She wanted to stay cool for her performance.

"Don't worry, Ms. Gallant, we have tea and coffee in the dressing room already," Gregory replied with a smile. Behind him, a young Indian assistant in a white coat opened the door of the room, revealing a sumptuous coffee and tea spread with assorted cookies.

"We've been in New York a few days, Gregory." Emilie stepped through the doorway. Beth went on, "I'd like to go over some of the questions Dave is going to ask her. Is that still your responsibility?"

"Well, yes, but as you know, Beth, Dave will ad-lib sometimes. We can't promise anything."

Suddenly Gregory's words became a distant echo and the lavish tea and coffee spread, a shadow. Emilie beheld the most breathtaking flower arrangement she had ever seen. The flowers seemed to glow in colors unimaginable, speaking to her of distant lands. Her heart told her they were from Romeo. She walked nervously over and opened the card:

From:	Romeo
To:	Emma Gallant
Message:	Aloha Beautiful

Emilie's face flushed crimson and her vision blurred slightly. She was in the dressing room of the Ed Sullivan Theater and about to go on national television, as close to those glaring lights of Hollywood as you could get. Now, in front of her was a beautiful memory that seemed to be from another world, another time.

Romeo in Hawaii, her mind echoed. The flowers exuded a sweet fragrance; their bright colors made the hues of New York City and the old dusty Ed Sullivan Theater lifeless and cardboard. The moment was something that couldn't be for her. She felt faint.

Emilie snapped out of her reverie and quickly closed the small note. She noticed a blue envelope taped to the base of the flowers and reached to pry the envelope free from the tape. She needed to hide the envelope in her purse before Beth came through the doors of the dressing room.

"Emilie, who are the flowers from?" Beth asked nosily, leaning through the doorway, still in the hall with Gregory Richards.

"Oh ... just a friend," she replied flustered, breathing quickly as she finally wrestled the envelope free. She felt both waves of excitement and anger toward Romeo, as she hid the letter in her purse.

"Emilie, those are lovely flowers! Are they from Paris?" Beth asked in a curious tone.

"No, just a friend," she repeated and turned from her publicist's peculiar stare. "I'm going into the changing room now Beth," Emilie announced as forcefully as she could, snapping shut her purse with the letter safely inside.

Captive in her purse, the letter made Emilie feel supercharged, like an exotic spy carrying secret codes that would save the free world, or maybe an Elvin queen bearing a ring of power. She quickly moved into the small changing room and closed the door.

"Emilie! Emilie! Are you all right?" Beth asked through the door, agitated. "You're hair isn't even done. Why are you changing so early?"

"Beth I just want to compose myself and freshen up," she explained, putting on her best well mannered tone, hoping her publicist would get the hint. She turned on the water loudly so she could have time to think.

At that moment, Emilie could have read the letter in her purse, but that would have been too much. After all, she was preparing for a huge moment on national television. She knew her limitations. Simply hearing from Romeo was already too much. *Maybe he is here in the audience,* she worried. *Maybe Romeo is a stalker.*

He is acting like an obsessed fan, she nervously chastised him, gazing into the small mirror above the sink. Romeo was as far outside the industry as one could be, yet had struck so exactingly close to the sacred center of her world. *Not even John would dare send flowers here!* her mind angrily flashed.

Is Romeo in the audience? she worried. *Is he in New York?* her thoughts spun faster. She was doing what she dreaded most, panicking before a live performance — so she decided to simply assume the letter was trivial.

"It can't be that important," she rationalized, brushing it off. She looked into the mirror and splashed water on her face. She was determined and would concentrate on all the little things she had to do to get ready for David Letterman. The letter was simply a mistake, trivial. When she arrived at her hotel, she would realize that and probably throw it away.

"Besides, I am dating Paris now," she reminded herself, massaging her eyelids with a towel. This was her moment and she was not going to let anyone, certainly not someone from the Internet, spoil it. Romeo had never responded to her email, she reminded herself, as she dabbed her face with the towel and opened the door.

"Emilie are you all right? You look pale," Beth remarked, genuinely concerned. "Is it something about the flowers?" she asked, suspiciously.

"No Beth, nothing is wrong with the flowers," Emilie calmly replied. "Let's get ready."

She dipped her delicate hands into a jar of Mario Badescu face cream and carefully rubbed the ointment on her intelligent forehead, hoping to appear calm. The rest of the afternoon went by as if she was in a dream. The letter from Romeo was more of a ring of power than she had anticipated. It seemed to radiate from her purse. She watched detached, while makeup people, camera operators, and Gregory Richards all prepared the star for her appearance.

As she waited behind the stage, listening to Dave Letterman stumble through his monologue, she noticed her usual stage fright had miraculously disappeared. Strangely enough, she was more focused on the future, the near future, when she could get back to her hotel and read the letter.

Surly this is a mistake, she reasoned again as they cut for a commercial break. *Why did he have to send this here! Doesn't he know I am with Paris?*

~

"**L**adies and Gentlemen our first guest — the young, beautiful, and very talented actress, Emma Gallant!"

Emilie sauntered onto the stage under the scorching lights of the Ed Sullivan Theater. *I'm not nervous!* she realized. *None of this matters! I need to find out what is in that letter.* She mindlessly crossed the smooth shiny floor toward her seat by Letterman's desk. Loud whistles and catcalls rose from the rambunctious audience. *I wonder if Romeo is watching this. Do I look good?*

She sat down and glanced at David Letterman as if he was a creature from Mars. She imagined Romeo watching later and wondered if she looked as pretty tonight as in the photo she sent him. *Probably not*, she pushed the thought out of her mind, and smiled at Dave.

"Wow, what a reception! Do you always get this reaction from men?" he asked.

"Well Dave, I try. Things would get terribly boring otherwise, don't you think?"

Letterman seemed surprised by her witty response and laughed nervously. "Well I can't imagine anyone ever getting bored with you," he said leeringly.

She heard more catcalls from the audience. A young man with a butch haircut stood up and whistled at her — he wasn't Romeo. Dave continued, "Emma Gallant, you're only eighteen and are the star of the new movie *Mary Queen of Scots*. How does it feel?"

"It feels great, Dave. The cast and I had so much fun making the movie," she remarked, recalling the talking points Beth had gone over with her this morning. The trick was to fill space and get people to love you. That was it.

Things are going fine, she assured herself. Stranger still, as she sat before millions of viewers, none of this mattered. It was much more important to get back to the hotel and read the letter. *I hope he isn't watching this*, she thought. *I wonder what is in the letter... .*

~

Wearily, she slipped the plastic key card into the hotel door at the Waldorf. Beth had dragged her to a "celebration" after her appearance on Letterman, proclaiming to everyone present how the Capulet Agency was going to milk Emilie's performance as news itself. The dinner had been at Tavern on the Green, looking out over the dazzling lights of Central Park. It had been very crowded and noisy, hosted by the head of her agency, Peter Segal. At one point, he offered Emilie a toast:

"Our Capulet Agency, named after Shakespeare's play, now has its own bona fide Juliet, Emma Gallant! I propose a toast to Emilie!"

Peter Segal tipped his glass with hers and smiled, an almost wolf-like grin. This was the man who had ordered Beth to put a stop to her online romance, Emilie reminded herself, realizing the head of her Agency had no respect for her. She had smiled back politely at the time.

"Thank God that is over," she sighed and opened the door of her suite.

"Ma'am where do you want me to put the flowers?" the bellman asked, following her.

"Oh just put them here," she motioned to an empty table near the window. The young man placed the flowers gently on the clean table and politely nodded.

"Thank you very much, Ma'am! Is there anything else I can get you?"

"No! No ... thank you." Emilie replied, trying not to be rude.

She slumped down on her bed and looked over at the bouquet. Their sweet fragrance reminded her of the Hawaiian beach she had once dreamed of walking arm and arm with Romeo on. She pulled out his letter. It felt so soft, Crane paper. Her hands trembled and her eyes watered. There was something about Romeo's love she couldn't deny. She realized how much she had missed him and knew in her heart she would never meet another man like him again.

Maybe Romeo is right, she admitted. Maybe they had been lovers in other lives — soulmates. Her body tingled and shuddered in agreement and her eyes became wet.

God, why did he have to do this now! Why did Romeo disappear and come back into my life, she lamented. A wave of resentment rose within her. After all, she had everything, fame, fortune, men who wanted her and Paris who loved her. Romeo now stood in magical opposition to all of that.

Why did he have to send flowers to the Letterman Show? she complained, upset that he had interfered with her work. She also felt something like guilt. Only a few months ago, she had told Romeo how much she loved him and that she wanted to be with him forever in Hawaii.

Yes, but that was the Internet! she scolded herself. *Oh God, what if people find out that I fell in love over the Internet! What if Paris finds out? What if the world finds out?*

Emilie sat with tears in her eyes. She looked at the spectacular flower arrangement again. The colorful smooth petals seemed to radiate a peace and warmth that contrasted with the hectic greyness of New York City. *Maybe it won't be that big a deal.* She decided to hold that thought in her head as she carefully held up the letter to read. The bright white sheet of paper seemed to radiate a golden light. She willed her eyes back into focus.

Dearest Emilie:

This is your friend Romeo in Hawaii. I have come in from a run on that beautiful beach we used to talk about.

She smiled, almost sadly. He still loved her. The letter wasn't going to clear anything up.

I hope this letter finds you well. I admit I was surprised when I found out, by chance, who my beloved Emilie was. I mysteriously lost my Yahoo account a few months ago and I felt I owed it to both of us to write you.

Emilie couldn't read any further. Tears were running and his remark about Yahoo frightened her. *Why did he have to do this now?* she asked again. Questions spun in her head faster than she could answer them. *What is he saying about Yahoo?* She suddenly thought of John, then focused again on the letter, regaining her place through her wet eyes:

It is my heart that compels me to seek you out.

Her hands quickly folded the paper. Just those few sentences were too much. She glanced over at the wonderful colors of the flowers. *That's Romeo's world*, she thought, *Hawaii.*

Doesn't he know I have a boyfriend? She asked again, exasperated. Emilie decided she couldn't read the letter now. She needed to take a shower first and relax. Today had all been a little too much for her.

The warm water of the shower shot across her face and relaxed her. She recalled how deeply she had loved Romeo, how she had dreamed of traveling to Hawaii this summer to meet him. She turned off the shower and dried herself with a large bath towel. The shower had heightened her senses and the fragrance of the tropical arrangement smelled even more intoxicating. Emilie abruptly sneezed and decided she had to read the letter now. She couldn't stand the curiosity:

Dearest Emilie:

This is your friend Romeo in Hawaii. I have come in from a run on that beautiful beach we used to talk about. I hope this letter finds you well. I admit I was surprised when I found out, by chance, who my beloved Emilie was. I mysteriously lost my Yahoo account a few months ago and I felt I owed it to both of us to write; it is my heart that compels me to seek you out.

I have missed our conversations and I have missed you. You are an irresistible woman. But that alone would not cause me to contact you as I have done. You must think me an impetuous fool — yet, we both know why I am writing, and the reasons are deep.

Emilie, trust me; you are my Juliet, my soulmate. Someday I will tell you how I know this. But I do know you are searching for true love just as I am. I have felt your heart and understand you. Our love is endless and love is the most powerful force in the universe — it can't be denied, compromised, or faked.

I admit, like most men, I was enchanted by your beauty when I first saw your picture. Yet what I found most striking was your balance, charm, and refinement in a world that seems to have lost these qualities. I love you deeply and want to be part of your life, maybe in a small way. I am sure you are busy as you climb the ladder of success. Where I live in Hawaii, everything is still and peaceful, the world moves around me quickly. Yet at the center of it all — I feel our hearts and our timeless love.

Well, I don't have much more to say. I hope you write me back or call. Please don't feel obligated, darling. Your Romeo is a kind man and understands your heart. I love you now and forever, my Juliet, regardless of our fates.

Love,

Romeo

Tears were flowing across her smooth cheeks. She put his letter down with shaking hands. She felt an overwhelming warmth surround her, a love she had been searching for and dreaming of since she was a child.

She wiped the wetness from her eyes. Emilie was an adult now and didn't need a prince charming. She felt a twinge of guilt again. When filming began in England, the dream of Hawaii faded fast amidst the bright lights and fancy dinner parties of London.

Still, her intoxicating love for Romeo, which had blossomed in Los Angeles, had returned full force. Emilie realized she still loved this man and knew his love for her was even stronger. She caressed his soft letter and was tempted to drop everything, to call her Romeo and fly to Hawaii. She would immerse herself in his world and escape her own hurried existence. She would follow his love forever and trust only him.

But of course she couldn't do that. Emilie hardly knew him. And the last time she had acted impulsively with an older man, she had been badly hurt. Johnny Perfection had not turned out as advertised. She didn't want to make the same mistake twice.

"Why did this have to happen to me now?" she asked her silent suite. Suddenly the phone rang, and her current life came crashing back.

"Hello, Emilie, this is your mother. I heard from Beth that your performance on Letterman was a smashing success!"

"Yes, mum, why are you calling me here?" she complained.

"Well, darling, I wanted to make sure you found yourself comfortable at the Waldorf." Emilie knew that wasn't true. Mum was simply checking up on her.

Her mother broke the silence. "I invited Paris over next week for dinner when you return."

"Mum, please don't do that!" Emilie snapped. "I don't know what my schedule will be. Stop prying into my life!"

"Emilie, what's come over you, dear?" her mother asked, taken aback. "Please tell me what's wrong."

"No, mother. I'm tired. I have to go." Emilie hung up, brooding.

~

The next day Emilie awoke with a knot in her stomach. She had been thinking of Romeo and his letter all night. When morning arrived, she tiredly showered and picked at a small fruit plate she ordered for breakfast. As she reached for a slice of peach, she noticed his letter sticking out of her purse. It was so sincere and romantic but she felt no urge to read it now. She needed to go outside and think. She had planned to go shopping today anyway.

Emilie finished her meal and left the Waldorf. She briskly walked up Park Avenue toward the fashion district, clutching her purse closely for safety. She felt the black smooth Prada leather, remembering Romeo's romantic letter was tucked inside. Her purse had become its unintentional home — for she had nowhere else to put it.

It was a clear bright morning in the City. The warm sun seemed to bathe everyone's smile as she started uptown. She passed couples arm in arm. *What a romantic day*, she thought and found herself wishing Paris had made the trip with her.

Then she thought of Romeo. A chill went through her. She realized she could never be with him. She stopped at a red light. Something made her pull out his letter, as if another part of her wanted him, regardless the cost. The light turned green and she stepped off the curb mindlessly, holding his letter in her trembling right hand, reading as she walked:

I hope this letter finds you well.

A huge wave of love for Romeo swept through her. The idea that she couldn't be with him became tragic. Tears began to flow. She couldn't control the deep passion she felt for this man. It blossomed in her like a magical but unwanted flower. Suddenly she tripped, while stepping onto the far side of the curb.

"Oh God," she said aloud as she awkwardly corrected her footing. She was wearing heels and had almost fallen. She began to walk again, still clutching his letter with tears in her eyes. A man wearing an impeccable grey three-piece suit and spectacles stared at her, concerned, rubbing his goatee nervously.

Emilie walked faster now. She didn't want anyone to recognize her. She stopped by a wastebasket, sobbing. *Oh, God I love Romeo*, she lamented. She felt so much passion for this mysterious man and didn't know why. She also felt his overwhelming love for her. Their special connection was so overpowering, it frightened her.

Another part of her, Emilie's more proper British side, wanted to drop Romeo's beautiful white letter in the trashcan. Maybe that would magically solve everything, she reasoned. She held his letter out, timidly, almost hoping the yellow basket would grab it for her, but no such luck. She wiped the tears from her eyes, folded the letter again, and returned it to her purse. She would shop now and, hopefully, that would cheer her up.

~

"I feel the portent of tragedy," Romeo intoned dreamily, staring out his living room window toward the bright blue ocean below. It was a perfect day and the sounds of it all, the wind, the waves, and the rustling of the palms made a mockery of his sadness. It was as is if the gods had placed him in paradise, but a paradise without Juliet. Now they were laughing at his suffering, his attachment, amidst the heavenly coastline of Hawaii.

He noticed a few people strolling below the cliffs on the bright sandy beach below. He decided to walk down the steep wooden stairs to the sea. Maybe he could clear his thoughts by the crashing waves. Waiting and hoping that Juliet would respond to his letter hurt too much, especially since he knew the chances were slight that his former wife from Italy would respond at all, would remember at all ... .

She is not my wife, he sternly reminded himself as he closed the front door of his house. *She is Emma Gallant, a famous movie star and doesn't know who I am,* his mind lectured as he thrust his keys into his pocket. He descended the narrow stairs to the beach and recalled, only just a few months ago, feeling Emilie and he would one day walk these sands, together hand-in-hand.

Romeo knew it was his misfortune that Juliet had attained fortune and fame at such a young age. In Verona it had been the walls of the Capulet mansion which symbolized the social barriers he had to overcome. Now these same walls seemed impossibly high, as he walked on a Hawaiian beach and dreamed of a film star he had never met. It was ludicrous indeed, he realized with a faint smile.

He relaxed by a rustling coconut tree on a dune above the sea. It was afternoon and gentle waves lapped up soothingly against the shore. The palm fronds shimmered and danced in the wind. He closed his eyes and fell into a deep sleep:

He was back at Master Lee's ranch, a teenager again. It was his first day wandering, helpless and hungry, out of the jungle. He held the warm wooden ax handle in his hands, about to chop wood for an evening meal.

"Wait!" Master Lee said from behind him, grasping his arm, stopping his swing.

"The time for chopping wood is over. You are in this world because of her. You must do more than send her flowers and sleep on the beach! She will not remember you. The Maya is thick. You must go to her now. Go East and experience your love — the Romeo I knew in Verona would not hesitate!"

Suddenly, instead of holding an ax, Romeo awakened clutching an old piece of driftwood, lying in the sand. The waves crashed in the distance and the wind ruffled his hair. He knew Master Lee was right. All his letter had done was upset a beautiful young lady who hardly knew him.

Still, she was his wife and although she would not remember that, he had to go to her. Romeo needed to tell Emilie the truth and hold Juliet in his arms once again. He stood determined, brushed off his sandy pants, flipped opened his cell phone and scrolled through the directory.

"Hello, United Airlines, how may I help you?"

"I'd like one first class ticket to New York City from Kona, leaving as soon as possible," he answered.

269

Tybalt and Juliet

Is there no pity sitting in the clouds,
That sees into the bottom of my grief?

- Juliet

The next evening, Emma Gallant could be found walking confidently above the cooling sidewalks of Manhattan wearing tight fitting jeans and a modest white blouse. It was early evening and the whole city reflected an orange glow as the summer sun inched toward the western horizon of New Jersey and beyond. She was leaving for home tomorrow. There in Cambridge, she would decide what to do with Romeo's letter.

As she passed the closed shops, the sun's last rays reflected against the large windows of the Chelsea district. She looked down at the glittering sidewalk and watched her white shiny sneakers trace energetic steps toward the apartment of Johnny Perfection.

John had invited her to dinner when he had called to compliment her on her Letterman performance. She was actually flattered. John seemed to be in a good mood, calm and relaxed on the phone. He was going to cook her one of his famous pastas tonight. He seemed genuinely contrite and apologized for their ugly breakup last spring.

Emilie wasn't stupid though, and knew John wanted to seduce her again. She had reminded him she was seeing Paris, but that had not dissuaded him in the least. He had already stolen her from Paris once and apparently was determined to do so again.

"How shallow," she remarked aloud, critically. John just assumed she would jump in bed with him tonight — like many women would. Yet he did hold a special power over her, being her first. She surprised herself with that revelation. *A few months ago, I would have been the sucker for John.*

It was funny, she reflected. The two older men in her thoughts now, Romeo and Johnny Perfection, acted like bigger children than her young boyfriend Paris did. Yet she adored that side of them both. She also felt a power and wisdom from both men, especially Romeo, something Paris seemed to lack. Since the arrival of the letter, Paris had begun to feel more like a big brother again and less a lover.

She walked up to the front steps of John's apartment building. The Manhattan skyline was overwhelming from her vantage point. Wisps of rosy red clouds glided over the spires of the Brooklyn Bridge. The setting sun bathed her smooth tan shoulders as she ascended the stairs.

The warmth of the day abruptly left as she entered the cold lobby. She could almost feel the chilling winter, seeping back into her bones. She recalled trudging up the same icy steps, knowing the man inside didn't love her, or that he was out drinking himself into misery, a misery that her love was not powerful enough to heal.

Emilie stepped into the small elevator, prepared to forgive John now. She arrived at his floor and gently tapped on his apartment door. The sound of his eager footsteps moved toward her and he opened the door. His hair was carefully combed and he wore a paisley vest over a white shirt, buttoned to the collar.

"Hello darling, would you like to have dinner with a lonely actor?" he asked in a debonair but campy tone.

"I'd love to!" she replied with a soft smile, offering him her hand. John had actually dressed up for the occasion and was already making her feel special again, as he had done last summer when their love affair had first blossomed.

He gallantly took her hand and led her to his small dining area. She quickly scanned their old love nest. The apartment hadn't changed much since she had last seen it, aside from the fact it had been recently cleaned, not the usual mess it was when they were a couple.

"Your apartment looks nice, John," she remarked with a smile.

John took hold of her shoulder and kissed her.

"John, you know I am seeing Paris now," she reminded him and backed off, flushed from one of his patented kisses.

"Yes I know." He straightened and held her hand, perturbed that she had backed away so fast. Not fazed, he continued, "You're dating Paris but…" He lowered his voice and whispered into her ear, "You will always be my angel." He kissed her neck. She grinned, genuinely glad to see the man she had once loved.

"John, you are in such a good mood tonight! I didn't expect this much affection," she remarked. She was lying, of course, since she had expected it.

"You didn't?" he asked, sounding somewhat hurt.

"Well," she admitted, "I guessed you probably did want to seduce me. I just didn't figure on you being so agreeable!"

"Well I am, darling," John announced, "and here's looking at you kid!"

She chuckled at his Bogart impression and sat down on a small chair by the nicely set dining table. He reached over and poured her a glass of Château Lafite Rothschild. She cautiously tasted it and remarked, "I hope you aren't trying to get me drunk, John. I would like to think you don't see me as that easy," she quipped and shot him a friendly smile. His good mood relaxed her.

For an instant, John looked offended and taken aback, as if she had exposed his secret plan of seduction. Just for a second, she noticed a hurt, surprised look on his face.

"No, no, Emilie, have some more wine," he encouraged her, taking a large gulp himself. "Anyway, I planned on seducing you with my good looks," he added jokingly.

"Well, John, you've already done that. I would think you would want new conquests," she remarked and lifted her glass to take another sip. She returned his smile with a nervous one of her own. John still wanted her, this she could tell. He refused to believe how serious things were with Paris, and of course, knew nothing of Romeo's letter.

"So, speaking of conquests, how is Paris?" he asked, breaking the silence.

"I wouldn't call him a conquest, John. Paris treats me well. I am happy with him," she confessed shyly.

"Happy?" John asked, visibly jealous. "Not in love?"

"Of course I love him," she corrected him.

"Oh yes, of course you do," he agreed and quickly finished his glass.

Emilie felt apprehensive whenever John drank fast. Their private dinner party seemed to have taken a turn for the worse in just a few minutes. But she had anticipated that they would have a lot of talking to do. The conversation still seemed healthy and she was flattered that one of the most handsome men alive still wanted her. John poured himself another glass and studied her with a serious gaze.

"I didn't question your love for Paris, Emilie," he began in a more ominous, deep voice, sounding like a concerned, but jealous father.

"I'm sure you love Paris," he agreed and took a large slurp of wine. Then he shot Emilie a cunning smile and threw his dagger:

"Just like you loved Romeo."

His smile grew large and he toasted her glass. Emilie gasped. She was shocked at the mention of Romeo's name. *Does he somehow know about the letter?* She looked down nervously, hoping beyond hope John would change the subject.

"You seem embarrassed, Emilie," he noted, not willing to let go of his advantage. Emilie said nothing.

"I forgive you," he said compassionately. "I fucked around also." The statement surprised her. Emilie had never considered cybersex "fucking around."

John put his hand on hers. He had forgotten how sensitive Emilie was. Apparently he had not anticipated the effects of his actions when he had hacked her account months ago. *Maybe that wasn't the best move after all.* For some reason he became nervous and wished he had never brought up Romeo's name.

"Let's both forget about the Romeo thing, OK? I think it's cool you had cybersex," he conceded, desperately trying to retreat. *Is this pervert still talking to Emilie somehow?* he angrily wondered.

Emilie sensed John was nervous. She was furious herself and hurt by his words. John had already told her about his philandering, why rub it in her face? And how dare he mention Romeo to her!

275

"That's funny you should mention Romeo," she began almost unconsciously in a soft proper tone. "He just sent me the most lovely bouquet of flowers the other day," she exclaimed, as if offering small talk at a tea party. She took a sip from her glass and noticed her hands were trembling. Suddenly, she did not want to look up at John and gage his reaction.

"What the fuck did you say?" John raised his voice menacingly. She gasped, startled, and spilled some wine on her blouse. John was glaring at her, expecting an answer. She was beginning to feel trapped. She decided to tell John about the letter and then leave his apartment.

"Romeo found out who I am," she confessed with her head down. "He sent flowers to my dressing room before the Letterman show."

"YOU STUPID FUCKING BITCH!" John screamed in astonishment. His strong hand flashed quickly, knocking his wine glass and shiny plate to the floor. She noticed steam from the kitchen; the pasta was boiling now.

"WHAT THE FUCK ARE YOU TELLING ME? HE KNOWS ABOUT US!"

"Oh God, John!" she began to tremble. She had never seen John this angry. Wine and bits of glass were dripping off the table. John sprung up from his chair and whirled toward her.

"THIS GUY IS A STALKER," he yelled a few inches from her face. She could smell his hot wino breath rush against her.

"John, don't!" she pleaded, turning away terrified. No man had ever yelled at her like this before. Instinctively she covered her face with her hands, afraid he was going hit her.

"YOU STUPID FUCKING BITCH," he screamed at point blank range, slamming his fist on the table.

He grabbed her wine glass and hurled it across the room. It shattered above his stereo and red wine trickled down the white wall. Everything seemed to move in slow motion for Emilie now.

"John, don't!" she yelled frightened.

"DON'T WHAT? YOU FUCKING BITCH," he screamed. "YOU'RE THE FUCKING BITCH WHO BLEW IT!" he continued to yell. "HOW IN THE FUCK DID HE FIND OUT ABOUT YOU?" he demanded.

"John, I don't know," she moaned and trembled, slumping off her chair and onto the floor in the corner. She instinctively curled up to protect herself. It felt like he wanted to kill her.

"YOU DUMB FUCKING CUNT! NOW THAT MOTHERFUCKER KNOWS WHO I AM ... YOU FUCKING WHORE!" he swore with his fist clinched.

"YOU HAVE A STALKER ON YOUR HANDS. YOU STUPID BITCH. HE KNOWS EVERYTHING!" he screamed from a more merciful distance.

"I'm ... sorry ... oh ... John ... I'm sorry. Please stop!" she pleaded, curling up in the corner for protection. *Maybe I deserve this*, Emilie surprised herself with the thought.

"YOU FUCKING WHORE!" he angrily repeated, as if she was a bad dog cowering in his dining room.

"YOU DON'T EVEN BELONG IN HOLLYWOOD, YOU STUPID FUCKING NEUROTIC BITCH. YOU FUCKING TOLD HIM EVERY-THING!

"AND NOW HE FUCKING KNOWS ABOUT ME!" he screamed to the ceiling and beyond — to whoever his gods were.

"NOW FUCKING DAVID LETTERMAN KNOWS ABOUT US!" John's chest was rising and falling fast to excited breaths. He took a swig from the bottle on the table to calm himself. He looked down at Emilie's cowering figure with disgust.

"You dumb fucking cunt. You led on some loser, middle-aged stalker and now he knows all about you ... why don't you just go to Hawaii and fuck him in his grass shack!" He glared at her but she wouldn't look back. She was sobbing and shaking. For some reason that made him angrier.

"I fucking taught you everything. You fucking bitch!" he growled and then paused to take another swig of wine. "I fucking taught you how to keep our shit private and now you FUCKING blow it with a pervert on the Internet. FUCK YOU BOTH!"

John straightened himself quickly and yelled over her. "HE IS PROBABLY FUCKING COMING HERE WITH A GUN T0 KILL ME. YOU DUMB FUCKING CUNT!"

Emilie was sobbing and shook uncontrollably. Strangely enough, as she trembled, something inside her felt free from John forever. She now was ashamed she had ever given herself to such a cruel man. She also felt she deserved whatever was coming next.

"WHY ARE YOU CRYING, YOU BITCH? YOU MISS YOUR FUCKING ROMEO. WELL GO AHEAD AND FUCK HIM!"

"Oh, God, John, no," Emilie replied sobbing, now a little less afraid, since John had backed away. She added, "I'm crying for us, John."

"YOU SHOULD BE FUCKING CRYING FOR US!" John exploded, furious she would talk back. "I BET THIS FUCKER IN HAWAII HAS TOLD EVERYONE!" he leaned into her face again.

"I hope he fucking goes on Letterman and tells everyone, you sick bitch!" he spitefully exclaimed and took another swig from the bottle he clutched. Her cowering sobs made him realize how spoiled and sheltered she was. *Why did I ever fuck this bitch*, he angrily asked himself.

He bent down and hissed into her wet face: "Upset that everyone has found out what a fucking pervert and hypocrite you are? Poor little slut!"

"John," she pleaded and looked up at him. He was still breathing hard. She continued. "I'm crying for us, John. We should never have gotten together. Oh God, I can't believe I was so … Oh God … I'm so sorry, John. It was my fault," she rationalized and buried her head in her hands, sobbing harder.

John's eyes glazed over as he took another gulp of wine. He hadn't expected such a response. "You fucking spoiled princess, You fucked me and loved it. You're just another groupie, bitch."

He leaned into her ear and screamed: "I'LL JUST FUCK JOHNNY PERFECTION, TO SEE WHAT IT IS FUCKING LIKE! YOU PLAYED THE GAME BITCH, AND NOW YOU HAVE TO PAY!"

She was moaning, but managed to speak: "Oh God John, I know … we both have to pay." Her body shook with fear.

He noticed she had skillfully turned the conversation away from Romeo again. He could have handled her crying for him, but she was actually crying for *them* in some sacrosanct pathetic way! *How dare she condescend to me like this!* he thought with disgust. *She doesn't know shit about love.* In his mind, she was just another teenage girl he had fucked.

"Yea, go ahead and cry bitch," he coldly began. "And by the way, I was the one who fucking hacked your Yahoo account."

"Oh my, God, John, what are you saying!" she exclaimed, looking up with wet puzzled eyes. "Please, John, don't say that!" she begged, covering her face ashamed — a part of her had known it all along.

"I WAS TRYING TO FUCKING PROTECT YOU, BITCH!" he began to explain in his fury. "WHAT? DO YOU THINK I AM GOING TO LET YOU FLY OFF TO HAWAII AND FUCK A PERVERT YOU MET ON THE INTERNET! HE WOULD PROBABLY HAVE FUCKING KILLED YOU, YOU DUMB CUNT!" he screamed. He wanted to kick her like a dog at that moment, but resisted the temptation.

"DO YOU THINK THE FUCKING CAPULET AGENCY OR YOUR FUCKING MOTHER WOULD LET YOU GO, BITCH?" he screamed his question into her covered face, shooting spit against her hands.

"Oh God, no, John ... No ... No John," she moaned, confused, wishing this was a bad dream. "Don't say that about Romeo!" she pleaded. "I don't believe you."

"BELIEVE IT, BITCH. YOU FUCKING MORON! YOU FELL IN LOVE WITH A PICTURE OF SOME PERVERT NAMED ROMEO ... YOU ARE SUCH A FUCKING WHORE!" John ached to hit her. Instead, he grabbed a candle from the dining table and hurled it against the stove. The red thick pasta sauce boiled over, and flowed onto the recently polished kitchen floor.

"Oh God, John, what's happened to you?" Emilie asked, almost unconscious of what she was saying.

John leaned into her ear and screamed. "WHAT HAPPENED TO ME? I WAS TRYING TO FUCKING PROTECT YOU, YOU STUPID FUCKING CUNT! I WAS TRYING TO FUCKING PROTECT YOU!"

"Oh god, John," she sobbed and continued. "No ... No ... you weren't." She furiously shook her head and then screamed: "OH GOD, JOHN ... please ... please, stop this!" She was incoherent and dizzy, as she pressed her hands against her ears.

"Stop what bitch?" John lowered his tone. He was disgusted with her now. He felt he had the moral high ground and continued, "You're the one who fucks perverts on the Internet. You fucking used Romeo also, bitch."

"Oh God, please, no John … don't say that," she muttered, crying. For some reason, his last accusation hurt, hurt more than anything he had said so far — maybe because there was some truth to it.

"YOU ARE A FUCKING USER, BITCH," he accused, seizing the moral high ground. "YOU AREN'T CAPABLE OF LOVING ANYONE. GET THE FUCK OUT OF MY APARTMENT!"

"No, John," Emilie refused weakly, cowering in the corner, unable to move. She didn't want to be thrown out like a piece of rubbish. That would be too much — maybe too real.

John walked up to her delicate face and screamed: "GET THE FUCK OUT OF MY HOUSE, YOU DUMB FUCKING CYBER-WHORE, BEFORE I TELL EVERYONE ABOUT THIS!

"GET THE FUCK OUT!" he commanded again.

Emilie somehow found the strength to get up. She was shaking and could barely walk straight. She felt powerless and frightened. Her stomach knotted in fear, making it harder to move.

John turned away as she slowly stood. He was afraid if he looked at her, he would strangle or punch Emilie. He knew he was out of control. She had been his woman, his responsibility, yet somehow he had lost her to a pervert on the Internet and a stupid rich kid named Paris.

"Get the fuck out," he muttered, weakly.

Emilie sobbed as she clutched her purse with trembling hands. John suddenly felt a deep raging sadness hit him as she moved for the door. It felt like the better part of himself was leaving, leaving forever. Yet that peculiar feeling only enraged him further. He threw a plate at her — It whizzed past her hair like a Frisbee and smashed into a movie poster on his wall. Emilie shuddered but continued to walk bravely to the door. John watched her shaking hand grasp the handle. Suddenly a wave of guilt hit him.

"Emilie," he called out.

She cried harder and leaned against the door It hurt to hear him speak her name.

"No, John ... Oh God ... No," she weakly cried. She turned the doorknob, opened the door, and left with her head down.

"I was just trying to fucking protect you," he whined. She closed the door as gently as a mouse.

"I WAS JUST FUCKING TRYING TO PROTECT YOU," he yelled through the wall.

Now tears welled up in his eyes. He grabbed his bottle of Château Lafite to throw against the door, but thought better of it. *Why waste a good year?* Instead he took a massive swig, laughed, and then began to sob. He knew he had blown it with Emma Gallant and would not see her again for a long time.

Romeo and Juliet

With love's light wings did I o'er-perch these walls;
For stony limits cannot hold love out,
And what love can do that dares love attempt.

- Romeo

While Emilie walked confidently toward John's apartment for dinner, Romeo approached the steps of the New York City Zen Center for the first time in many years. He had flown east overnight, first to Los Angeles, then nonstop to New York City.

It was sunset when his silhouette appeared at the front door of the Zen Center. He realized how much he had missed the place. Life had been simpler then. The practice of Zen had been the perfect haven from his painful memories of Italy.

As he entered the Zendo and bowed, he saw his friend, Roshi Jeff Garrity, teaching a class on the importance of mindfulness. Jeff, sensing someone at the door, immediately turned and did a double take. Of course, Romeo had been on his mind, along with the letter and flowers he sent to Emma Gallant.

Despite that, Jeff was surprised and happy when he saw Romeo leaning against the open doorway. As he surveyed his old friend, he could tell Romeo was different — stronger, wiser, and full of a power and purpose that was almost frightening. Usually, Romeo gave one the impression he was wandering aimlessly through life. But now Jeff could feel his strong aura by the door and the force of his determination.

"Excuse me, everyone," Roshi Jeff addressed his students and bowed. His students bowed back and glanced warily at Romeo. Jeff walked to the doorway to greet his fellow monk.

"Romeo, what are you doing here? It's so good to see you," Jeff said and held out a hand. Romeo's eyes stared back determined at him, almost like Master Lee's. He said nothing but bowed to Jeff. Jeff bowed back, according to etiquette, grinning, unable to contain his excitement.

"Judy and I have missed you. How are you doing?" he asked. It felt good to see one of Master Lee's direct monks returning to the Zendo.

"It's good to see you also, Jeff," Romeo replied. Jeff had been like a second father to him. If he had any friends in this new world, he knew he could always count Jeff among them.

"I need a favor from you, Roshi," Romeo continued and bowed again.

"I'm afraid to ask," Jeff commented with a sardonic smile, "considering what your last request was."

"And thank you for that, Jeff," Romeo began. "Yet I need your help again. I need you to create a distraction at the Waldorf Hotel."

"Is she staying there?"

"It would be better if you didn't know that, Roshi," Romeo remarked, looking curiously over Jeff's shoulder at the new crop of Zen students.

"Your students look good, Jeff. Maybe they can come along," Romeo thought aloud as he gazed at them. A plan was beginning to take shape in his mind.

"Come along?" Jeff asked puzzled.

"Yes Roshi, to the Waldorf, as is my request of you."

"Romeo," Jeff began exasperated, "You and I are both Zen monks. I cannot use my students for ..." he paused, searching for the right word, "for your Juliet."

"I will not beg you my friend. I respect your decision," Romeo assured him and bowed. He turned to leave, knowing he would find Juliet somehow.

At that instant, a flash of intuition hit Jeff Garrity. In his gut he knew what Romeo was asking — for some reason — was the correct thing to do. Romeo's request had everything to do with Buddhism and Zen. Something whispered to him that it was the dharma to help his old friend, as he had done years ago when Romeo first appeared penniless at his Zendo door.

"Romeo!" Jeff called to him.

"Yes, Roshi?" Romeo turned.

"For some crazy reason I want to help you," Jeff smiled, embarrassed. "What do you want us to do?" he asked and glanced back at his Zen students.

"I need you to distract the concierge at the Waldorf," Romeo stated, like a general preparing for battle.

"How do you know she is staying there?"

"I called around," he admitted.

Jeff turned to his students, now emboldened himself, feeling as if he was taking part in an historic event. After all, maybe his old friend was Romeo in Shakespeare's play. Jeff addressed his Zen class:

"Zen students, our plans have changed. We will be taking a field trip today with one of our senior monks!"

"Cool, man, where?" one of the newer students asked.

"Always address me as Roshi," Jeff instructed the young, wide-eyed student. He continued to look over his Zen initiates like an officer surveying troops before battle.

"We are going to the Waldorf Hotel to practice dharma," Jeff announced to his class.

~

And so, as Johnny Perfection frothed at the mouth, screaming at Emma Gallant, about two dozen individuals in black Zen robes and immaculate white socks began marching south to the Waldorf Astoria. As their queue moved downtown, fashionable women shopping for summer outfits, hesitated, gapping at the spectacle. Late commuters froze in their tracks and stared at the line of impassive monks making their way down Park Avenue.

In the lead, Romeo excitedly explained his plan to Jeff. Jeff then went back through the line of students, instructing each of them on what to do, making sure they were all comfortable with their role. To his surprise, they all were.

When the small Zen army arrived at the plush red carpet of the Waldorf entrance, Jeff turned to Romeo. The door attendant eyed the crowd of monks uncomfortably.

"Are you sure you want to do this?" Jeff asked.

"Yes Roshi," Romeo answered. He dramatically beckoned to the glass doors of the Waldorf and joked, "Shall we?"

Jeff and Romeo opened the large doors and walked through. Jeff motioned for his students to follow. As the Zen initiates entered, to his surprise, a guard smiled at him and one of the reservation clerks winked at Romeo.

It must be a convention of some sort, the female clerk reasoned, *more money for the Hotel.* Romeo smiled at her and angled toward the concierge desk. He winked at Jeff once he was behind the concierge; Jeff motioned with his hands and all of the Zen students abruptly sat in a perfect circle.

"Excuse me sir," the concierge began and looked accusingly at Jeff, "Are you people guests of the Hotel?"

"No, we are here to chant," Jeff said firmly and motioned again to his monks.

Suddenly, the lobby became full of the sounds of an ancient Zen mantra. The chants filled the marble expanse:

Gate' Gate' Para-gate' Para-sam-gate' Bodhi Svaha'

The concierge, alarmed, quickly dialed security, then left his chair to confront the leader of this strange cult. Hotel workers and guests all gawked in the direction of the foreign, yet soothing sounds. The concierge failed to notice Romeo moving toward his chair.

"Excuse me sir!" The concierge exclaimed again to get Jeff's attention.

Jeff remained calm as the concierge confronted him with a disapproving frown. Like many Zen teachers, Jeff was a black belt in karate. He simply bowed and continued chanting with his students:

Gate' Gate' Para-gate' Para-sam-gate' Bodhi Svaha'

The sounds of the mantra filled the Waldorf lobby with an unearthly vibration — *Going, going, going on beyond, always going on beyond, always becoming liberated* — Jeff began to chant louder with his monks, as he watched Romeo take a seat at the concierge's desk. Luckily, the concierge was glaring at Jeff and was turned completely away from Romeo.

"Sir, I am going to have to ask all of you to leave!" the concierge's voice rose shrilly.

Jeff bowed and smiled, out of the corner of his eye he could see Romeo, the math genius, typing furiously fast, desperately trying to find Emma Gallant's suite. He felt as if he was in a dream.

Suddenly, two security guards flanked him. The grey-uniformed men appeared nervous, outnumbered by the sea of chanting monks. "What seems to be the problem here, sir?" A tall, overweight guard asked Jeff. Jeff glanced again at Romeo, still frantically typing. No one seemed to notice though — all the attention was on him and his chanting students.

"This is the problem!" the concierge yelled at the guard, pointing to the perfectly motionless monks.

The guard tapped Jeff on the shoulder and began in a polite but menacing tone. "Excuse me, sir, your group must leave immediately, or I will have to call the police. We don't want any trouble," he added.

Jeff nervously glanced back at Romeo. To his relief, Romeo winked at him and rose from the desk. Jeff felt ecstatic and beamed a smile at the guard. They had succeeded. Romeo had found his Juliet!

"We were just about to leave sir," he assured the guard with genuine relief. He motioned to his students. The chanting stopped precisely on cue. He was proud of his new Zen initiates.

Before the amazed security team or the flustered concierge could say anything, the Zen monks rose in unison and started for the doorway. A crowd of guests and hotel employees had formed around them in a loose semi-circle, attracted to the chanting like bees to honey.

Jeff quickly headed for the doors, wanting to leave before the police came. His students followed silently. He looked back at Romeo who gently mouthed a "thank you" to him. As Jeff walked out the Waldorf Astoria, a strange sadness struck him — something told him he would never see his friend again.

~

E milie cried gently in the taxi taking her home from her terrible encounter with John. She was stopped at a light near her hotel and couldn't help but notice a long queue of men and woman dressed in black marching across Park Avenue. The strange out-of-place image made her smile for some reason.

"I guess it takes all kinds," the taxi driver complained sarcastically in a thick Brooklyn accent and waited for Jeff's small army to cross.

She looked at the monks again. It stirred something within her. They looked Buddhist. She thought of Romeo. *He is also a Buddhist.* The thought only made her shed another tear — for his letter and all the trouble it had already caused.

~

A *nd so it has come to this,* Romeo thought to himself confidently, standing in the dark alley. He looked up at the rusty old fire escape that led to the sky — to Juliet, his beautiful wife from Verona.

And so it has sweetly come to this, he thought with a smile. The clear moonlight streamed down and bathed the dark soot-covered fire escape in an ethereal light. He was calm and sure, for he knew it was the same moon that had shone above Juliet in Italy, the same moon that had hung over Egypt, as he and his ancient soulmate made love by the Nile. Then, a great river had separated them, now only a steep fire escape.

He smiled comically, knowing he was playing the fool again. *And so it has come to this*. He bent his legs like a tiger about to spring, gathering all his energy. He had to jump high to grab the first rung of the ladder. He sprang forth and his determined hands barely gripped the cold rusty iron that was the pathway to his beloved.

"Go for it, Romeo!" an old raspy voice below croaked, startling him. Romeo pulled himself up and noticed an unshaven man lying in newspapers below watching him.

"Go bang your Juliet," the old, haggard drunk added, and lifted his brown bag in a toast to their love. He flashed an innocent toothless smile. Romeo nodded and continued his climb. Ironically, he was more famous than Emma Gallant or Johnny Perfection would ever be. Romeo was a timeless legend — yet no one knew who he was. Not minding the paradox, he moved ever upward.

He knew Emilie's suite was on the southeastern side of the building. Once he approached the roof, he would have to shuffle dangerously sideways on the ledge toward her window. Romeo glanced back at the alley below. He was climbing fast. *Oh God, this is much higher than the Capulet's walls!* he complained fearfully and continued his ascent, trying not to look down.

When he reached the top of the fire escape, the glow of the moon seemed stronger. He carefully shuffled along the top ledge with only a few inches to spare. He almost slipped and glanced down at the cold asphalt far below. He realized he wasn't afraid of death. He had already cheated it once. No, he was afraid of losing Juliet again in this vast creation.

Finally, he came to the large window of her suite. There was a light on. *What if she is in bed with another man?* he worried. His whole life had lead up to this absurd moment. *What if she is not Juliet from Verona?* another voice in his head inquired, but his heart ignored it. All he could feel was their overwhelming love, blossoming again into a wonderful zenith.

He carefully turned toward the window, balancing his weight. Bracing himself, he slowly rotated the latch of the frame with his outstretched hand. Thankfully, It didn't resist his grip. He looked down again at the shadowed alley. He wanted to be inside now, inside the light and warmth of his wife's embrace.

Romeo leaned against the fluttering window curtains as a soft breeze blew past him and into the suite. And as it had been in Egypt, he heard a beautiful sound. He peeked further through the curtain and beheld the one he loved, sobbing gently on her bed. She was turned from him, but even that profile was the most fulfilling sight he had ever seen. Her long streaming hair flowed against her nightgown like a magical river. His heart was full of love. Now, nothing could stop him.

He slowly put one leg over the windowsill, then the other, and quietly landed on the carpet like a cat. She didn't hear anything. To her left on the nightstand, he noticed his letter and the beautiful flowers he had sent her. Romeo stood before his crying Juliet, feeling a little foolish; for he had not planned what he was going to say once he reached her.

"I love you," he uttered. He couldn't help himself.

Ah!" Emilie gasped and turned quickly to the foreign voice. Their eyes met, as she placed a startled hand on her chest. Her heart skipped a beat. *Am I hallucinating? Is there really a man standing in my room?* she asked herself in a detached manner.

She shot a glance toward the window and noticed it was ajar. Yes, there was a man standing before her and he was very real. For some reason, her heart told her he was Romeo. He smiled at her gently, but seemed nervous and awkward. Emilie was outraged that someone would intrude into her space and also terrified.

"Who are you? I'm going to scream if you don't leave immediately!" she threatened the stranger and leaned toward the lamp by her bed, possibly to use it as a weapon. She couldn't lift her gaze from the smiling man who wore an open leather jacket and a Hawaiian shirt, a shirt she could have sworn Romeo wore in the only photograph he had ever sent her.

"You know who I am, Emilie — I am Romeo," he revealed. His voice was pleasant and he was handsome, she had to admit, very handsome, just as she had imagined. He smiled at her; both were losing themselves quickly in each other's eyes.

"I'm sorry I had to do this," he broke the awkward silence. He bent his head, almost in shame. He wanted to calm his beloved wife and reassure her; after all, they had never met in this life.

"Oh my God!" she exclaimed, embarrassed, realizing she was wearing only a nightgown. "Everyone was right about you," she accused him, raising her voice, trying her best to sound angry. "You *are* a stalker, aren't you?"

"Emilie!" he implored.

"Don't Emilie me! You don't even know me," she said, indignantly. After all, she was a famous star.

"No, Emilie, you're wrong," he said firmly, staring into her eyes again. "I am Romeo Montague and you are Juliet, my wife."

Oh God, I wish he wouldn't look at me like that, she thought to herself, appreciating his handsome visage. His eyes shone with a force that warmed her heart. Then, she heard the sweetest sound ever to reach her ears:

"*Angelo luminoso, siete glorious a questa notte come messaggero alato di cielo.*

"I said that to you in a garden overlooking your father's orchards long ago, under the same full moon, darling. Tonight, as I stand before you, I mean that more than ever."

He approached her, admiring the beautiful light in her eyes, the same light that he had once loved in Italy so long ago, the light he had searched the world over and traveled beyond death for, just to behold again.

"Don't come any closer!" she commanded and wiped the wetness from her cheeks.

He stopped a few feet from her. He didn't want to startle her. He saw his letter on the nightstand and grinned. Emilie shot a glance at the letter, embarrassed. *I shouldn't have left it out like that!* she chastised herself.

"I love you, Emilie," he began again. "I want you to be my wife. We were robbed of that before. Don't let them do that to us again," he pleaded. He wasted no words now, sensing he didn't have much time. He was fighting against that unknown and awful star-crossed pattern they faced in every life.

"Don't be foolish. I don't even know you!" she shot back, blushing and trying to hide a smile. She certainly hadn't expected a marriage proposal this evening!

"Can you look into my eyes and tell me you don't feel the same, my love?" he asked sincerely, as he had months ago online.

She smiled, remembering that beautiful moment last winter, when she had to admit she was developing deep feelings for a man she had only chatted with on the Internet. She looked into his steady, strong brown Mediterranean eyes and knew she couldn't deny his love. She averted his gaze and said nothing.

"Why were you crying when I came in, my beloved?" he asked and moved closer.

"Why do you keep walking toward me?" she questioned, nervously, not because he threatened her. She felt helpless around him and overwhelmed by their crazy love.

"I'm sorry," he apologized and stopped again.

"You can sit in that chair," she offered, motioning him to a seat near her bed. She grabbed a tissue to wipe her wet cheeks. She sniffled and looked at him again. He was smiling and leaning toward her. John's tantrum had left her a trembling wreck, but now a magical calmness possessed her. For some reason, she felt relaxed and safe with this handsome intruder.

"May I hold your hand Emilie?" he longingly asked.

"I can't believe you would ask that, whoever you are. Of course you can't!" she chastised him.

"Yes, that was rude," he admitted. "You just offered me a seat. I should be more of a gentleman."

"I should think so," she remarked, in the same disapproving tone her mother always used.

"You were crying, Emilie. That is why I wished to hold your hands, dear," he explained.

"You certainly don't waste time," she replied, sarcastically, but with an appreciative smile.

"Well," Romeo began, "I love you, my angel, and I remember things about us that you probably have forgotten."

"I suppose you know who John is?" she cut in bitterly. Romeo was now another person who knew of her ill-fated affair with Johnny Perfection.

"I do, Emilie," he said kindly to comfort her. "He has opposed us in many lives," he explained, wanting more than anything to hold this woman in his arms, to wash away the pain in her life, a pain too deep for anyone to see but him.

"Well he has opposed us in this life," she admitted, sadly.

"I know, darling," he said softly. "The Yahoo accounts, he did it?"

"Yes," she confirmed sadly. "And I was stupid enough to tell him that you had contacted me. He is in New York now. I saw him tonight." She broke down and began to sob again.

Romeo rose from his seat and boldly sat next to her. He rested his hands gently on her shoulders. *How many centuries has she cried for me?* he wondered sadly. *How many lives has she been alone while I foolishly chased her through time?* He gently massaged his wife's shoulder and had no doubt she was Juliet. One beautiful, tender moment was enough, enough to remember. He realized how much he had missed his beloved. Whatever happened next would be worth it.

"So what are you going to do? Rape me?" she asked incredulously, with a slight smile. She was turned from him and his hands felt so good. Their love seemed to explode and fill the air with a sweet electrical charge.

"I would never hurt you, my wife, *Jule*. Why do you say such things dear?" he admonished, adding softly into her ear: "I know you love me also."

"You mean I loved you when I was Juliet?" she corrected him, and leaned away.

"Well … yes, my love, you are Juliet Capulet reincarnated," Romeo explained. "I know you don't remember me, darling. I understand you must think I am crazy."

"I don't think you are crazy, Romeo," she reassured him. His touch felt warm and healing. "But you know I have a boyfriend now," she added, reminding herself as much as him.

"Yes I do, the good Count Paris," he remarked casually.

Emilie nervously giggled. "And I suppose he is Paris from Shakespeare's play?" she deduced with a slightly ironic smile.

"He is from Verona and even looks the same," Romeo answered. "I'm sorry I didn't recognize you earlier, dear; but you are even more beautiful in this life than you were in Italy!" he bent toward her neck to smell her hair.

"That's good to know," she remarked and smiled appreciatively. She leaned away again. "You're quite the player, Romeo, aren't you?"

"No Emilie, I am not what you would call a *player*." He took her soft hands in his and gently lifted them, gazing into her eyes. Oh how both wished they could be together forever at that moment! A magical power coursed through their bodies, filling the famous star-crossed lovers with a warmth and love beyond human understanding.

"I love only you, Emilie. I am not embarrassed to say that," he declared, marveling at his wife's beauty.

"I like you also Romeo, but we cannot be together," she sadly explained and lowered her head in shame, realizing how much havoc this eccentric Italian man would cause within the gilded walls of Hollywood.

"I understand, my love." He let go of her hands.

"Oh Romeo!" she lamented, looking at his handsome face. "I wish things had worked out differently. I'm so sorry."

"I know," he agreed, resigned. He stood up and sighed. He had intruded into this sensitive young woman's life, a woman who didn't remember being his wife at all. If he did once have a chance to win her heart, it had been skillfully crushed because of who she was, and more specifically by his old nemesis, Cousin Tybalt.

Emilie remained seated at her bed with watery eyes, her charmed future felt cold and empty. Before her stood a person of great warmth, a man who loved her for who she was. All the answers to her questions seemed to lie in his stranger's arms and not in the plush, empty hotel suites that had become the backdrop to her success, a success that would only lead to more empty rooms, more lonely nights.

"Romeo?" she asked meekly, for the meek shall inherit the earth.

"What, my love, my Juliet?" he said, willing to do anything for his soulmate who had been cast in this cruel world as a movie star.

"Don't leave me," she uttered, looking at him shyly for comfort. Again, their eyes locked. Drawn to her as if in a trance, Romeo sat beside her and took her hands in his. He kissed her once delicately on the lips.

"I could never leave you, my Emilie, my Juliet. My heart sings the songs of your soul. I feel there is already a place, somewhere in infinity, where we are one," he declared, gazing into her soft eyes and touching her marvelously soft hair.

"I love you, Romeo, kiss me again," she said to him gently, craving another taste of this wonderful man's lips. He kissed her and she kissed him back, deeply, longingly — both were transported back to that balcony in Verona so long ago.

"I love you *Jule* ... I mean Emilie," he corrected himself and kissed her more passionately now.

"Oh, Romeo, call me what you will ... for what's in a name?" she replied, trying to impress her beloved Romeo. She was flushed, very aroused. It was hard to speak. No man had kissed her like this before.

"That which we call a rose, by any other name would smell as sweet," she moaned between their kisses. Romeo smiled at her remark, not knowing the reference, and kissed her slim neck. Then he gently lowered her down against the white silk sheets of her bed.

And so, as the warm evening air of Manhattan swirled through the open windows of the Waldorf Astoria, Emma Gallant, the famous and wholesome actress, was made love to by a man from Hawaii she had met on the Internet. As he filled her, Images of their many lives flashed through her mind. Each life was a glistening bead on an endless string of beads that wove its way through eternity. As she felt him inside her, she saw herself as an Egyptian Princess, an actress from lost Atlantis, a dancer from another world, and many other selves that she had assumed throughout the timeless eons.

Emilie lost herself to his adoring rhythms. Soon she became one with his thoughts, his love, and his soul. He filled her with a calm clear light. She had found what she had always been searching for. As she wildly gripped his strong back, she knew she was Juliet Capulet. Nothing could be more true as they merged into one being.

They continued to couple in passion, under the streaming moonlight, first on the bed and then on the thick white carpet of the suite. Emilie had found where home was — it was in Romeo's strong embrace. If she had to run away from Hollywood, she would. Finally, Emilie lay exhausted. They had slept together and then awoken again to make love. It was past midnight.

"I love you, Romeo," she intoned, resting against his shoulder, but now the dark silence of the Waldorf pressed in on her. What if someone caught them together? What if her phone rang? Mercifully, she was traveling early tomorrow and her people knew not to bother her.

"*Jule*, stay with me forever," he dreamily implored, falling asleep against his beloved's soft angelic form. Romeo had flown straight from Hawaii and needed rest. As he drifted off into his dreams, he could feel her long luminous hair stream down against his face. He became lost in its perfect curls, just as he once had been in a magical rain forest where he first begun his quest for this moment.

Emilie didn't say anything else as her Romeo drifted further into sleep. She kissed his forearms gently as he held her. There were tears in her eyes, now. She realized their love was too beautiful for this world and could never be. She kissed him again, almost sadly. Romeo felt her soft lips touch him for the last time in the perfect garden of their eternal love.

~

It was barely dawn when Emilie walked softly toward the bed where Romeo lay. Was he her soulmate? As to that question, she had no doubt, for she had never loved a man as she loved him now. And maybe it was because her love was so strong and so out of place — a love between a movie star and a Zen monk — that she now held a small blue sheet of paper. She gently folded it as a tear came to her eye.

She looked out at the pale grey horizon past the curtains of the open window. Everything was still in the windless sky. She was returning to England to continue filming and to promote further *Mary Queen of Scots*. Hundreds, no thousands of people depended on her. She knew she could not bring Romeo into her complex world, into those wonderfully bright lights that now beckoned her.

She folded her note and gently laid it next to her beloved's sleeping form. A single tear dropped on the fine blue paper. She knew they could not be together. She had to leave now. She wanted to cry but did not want to awaken her prince — for if he awoke, she would stay with him forever.

~

Hours passed as the summer sun rose above the New York City. Romeo smiled to its warming rays, knowing it was the same sun that had shone down through Juliet's bedroom in Verona after their wonderful wedding night, ages ago.

He turned and saw she was not there; and before he could glance with a smile toward the bathroom door, where he thought she might be, he noticed a small blue note, folded on the now wrinkled sheets next to him. His heart sank:

My Romeo:

I will always love you, my magical prince. But I ask that you do not follow me. Oh my love, if we were Romeo and Juliet, then you must know I was only in a deep sleep when you turned your dagger on yourself. Juliet awoke and killed herself to be with you. Please, my love, let us not repeat this tragedy. Trust me — we will be together someday, this I know.

Love always,

Emilie

Tears ran from his eyes as he held her note. He felt an uncanny wisdom to her words and more importantly, he felt her love for him, her pain, her sincerity. Perhaps that is why he did not fling himself out of the open window of the Waldorf after reading her goodbye. Instead, he sat upright on the plush bed, still wearing a faint smile from last night's magic, not yet lost amidst the tears.

He looked again at her beautiful handwriting. He noticed a teardrop on the edge of the note. She had been crying also, he realized. *Why does our love cause us so much pain?* he asked the silent room. Only horns from the river of taxis below answered him.

He rubbed his eyes and wondered if there had ever been a time when their love had not been star-crossed, had not been fated for tragedy. Did Romeo and Juliet ever have a place they could call their own? And if there had been such a wonderful world, where they could love each other freely, what deed originally caused the terrible change?

As Romeo sat on the bed he had just shared with his beloved wife Juliet, he remembered such a time, the age of Atlantis... .

Second Remembrance: Atlantis

These violent delights have violent ends,
And in their triumph die,
Like fire and powder,
Which, as they kiss, consume.

- Friar Laurence

The grasses of the Gin Shawl Hills are of a green that cannot be fathomed in this later earth. One would have to be dreaming to behold the pure colors of late Atlantis. Yet as Romeo sat high in the Waldorf, lost and forlorn, his awareness was suddenly transported to that magical green isle that existed on our earth so long ago. He beheld a deep blue sky, a blue that has not been seen in this world for over twelve thousand years. Romeo had been Hollen Cel Nar in Atlantis, composer, mathematician, and cousin to the Emperor himself.

Hollen Cel Nar walked confidently through the swaying grasses wearing his robe of plush blue silk, signifying his mastery of computer science and pure mathematics. Computers were composed of crystals in Atlantis, processing was done with light — electricity is much too slow. Across his chest was a golden sash to signify his study with the High Priest of Atlantis. He also wore a red band signifying his mastery of the musical arts. Hollen was one of the most respected men of the Atlantean subcontinent. He had lived for over four hundred years, yet was middle-aged for an Atlantean. More importantly, he was happy. He had found his soulmate and had made her his wife, a gifted young woman of only forty years.

He moved down the grassy slopes of the Gin Shawl Hills to meet his new bride for lunch. Below him, the western sea glistened frivolously blue with raging whitecaps, roaring beyond the sandy borders of late Atlantis. Even more spectacular than the coastline of Atlantis, was the sight of the Crystal Dome towering magnificently over the white beaches and turquoise lagoons. The Dome was the most celebrated place on the subcontinent. Under its magnificent crystal roof, musicians, actors, and holographic composers would present their art forms, always for no charge of course, to the inhabitants of the island.

Hollen smiled in anticipation of surprising his wife, Ashanti, for lunch. He reached out with his mind and felt her in the dome rehearsing for an upcoming performance. She was a skilled actress for her age, and her lovely aura always lit up the dome's intelligent crystals.

"I love her so," he remarked aloud in a language we will never know, shuffling carefully down the last steep slopes of the Gin Shawl hills. He had met Ashanti over the holographic crystals that connected Atlantis in much the same way the Internet now connects the world. One evening, he had put his palms on the crystal interface and found himself face to face with the most beautiful woman he had ever seen. She immediately recognized him as a musician and cousin to the Emperor.

After interfacing in the virtual worlds for a few weeks, Hollen and Ashanti realized they were falling deeply in love. Their physical meeting was only a formality — they were already planning an Atlantean marriage. When they did meet by the Gin Shawl rivers and kissed, their love was even more powerful than either had dared hope or imagine.

As Hollen recalled that first beautiful kiss by the river, he reached the bottom of the last grassy slope that lay by the side entrance of the Dome. He made his way for the doors as windswept grasses caressed his ankles. Once inside the great theater, he was greeted by the gay sounds of song and laughter. A synthesizer, at the far end of the vast circular space, sent musical notes high into the crystal rafters. Dancers whirled about him, laughing and leaping in unison without a care in the world. Beautiful light streamed down in rays from the crystal roof and bathed him in a bright rainbow. A petite female ballerina cartwheeled by him and then stood upright, smiling before him.

"Hollen Cel Nar, I believe. Your wife is over there eating lunch," the dancer bowed low and motioned with her hands in mock grandeur, as if Hollen was the emperor.

He politely thanked her and looked over the woman's slim shoulder searching for his wife. Performers pranced around him, juggling intelligent crystal formations that sang tunes in the air. Behind them was a man riding a circular wheel of magnetic energy, much like a unicycle.

Finally, he located his wife. She was sitting at a table with a few other actors. He waved and walked toward her, carefully avoiding three dancers sequentially throwing each other in the air and landing gracefully. The dancers were wearing purple outfits with strings of flowers flowing from them. A juggler caught a crystal balloon above his head. Hollen laughed and dodged him. The Crystal Dome during lunch break was both playtime and practice. You had to be on your toes here. Nowhere else in Atlantis, he realized, were people acting this crazy. He knew his powerful family looked down on the actors and musicians that now danced and sang below the Dome's high roof.

He saw his wife Ashanti turn to him, happily surprised. She wore a long white dress with a garland of flowers around her neck. She smiled with such love at him. *God, her blue eyes shine more each day,* he realized.

"Hollen Cel Nar," a voice suddenly bellowed to his left. A hand roughly patted him on the shoulder. He turned and saw it was the jovial and plump holographic composer, Seth.

"Seth, you surprised me," Hollen exclaimed happily. He had not seen him in ages.

"Oh Hollen! Oh Hollen! Wherefore art thou?" Seth asked and then bowed to him in jest, as the dancer had earlier, reminding Hollen that the acting guild didn't think much of his emperor cousin, and even less of the controversial anti-gravity experiments being conducted beneath the jagged eastern mountain ranges. The artists of late Atlantis were nonviolent, freewheeling, and politically radical.

"I've been busy, Seth," Hollen replied. "And to think my happiness is all due to an actress," he added playfully while his wife approached and put her arms around his waist.

"Thank you for the compliment, my dear husband," she said, kissing him deeply.

"You look more beautiful each day, my dear. I thought I would surprise you for lunch," he remarked, kissing her back.

"I love surprises," she replied seductively.

"Why thank you, my love," Hollen said, as he drew her closer for another passionate embrace.

"Hollen," Seth broke in, "why don't you act or play the synthesizer in the dome these days? You're such a good performer. We need you."

"I have too many projects as it is, maybe someday," he replied.

In his youth, Hollen had been a promising actor and was still considered a top mathematical composer of music. His family had been relieved when their eccentric son had given up the arts for computers and mathematics. It was probably why they hadn't given him a hard time when he married the daughter of a simple farmer.

Seth turned to Ashanti feigning insult. "Hollen is too good for us. After all, why would a famous mathematician want to be seen in the company of common actors!" he rolled his eyes dramatically, in mock indignation.

"That's not it at all," Hollen assured him, grinning embarrassed.

"Come eat with us," Seth offered and led him back to the table where Ashanti and a small group had been gathered.

"Hollen Cel Nar," a deep formal voice uttered as Hollen stopped by the table. It was Dexter Perfect, rising cautiously. Dexter was an actor who worked with his wife. He had been jealous of Hollen from the first day they met.

Hollen nodded to acknowledge Dexter as they awkwardly stood across the table from one another. Ashanti, sensing the tension between the two men, broke the silence. "Dexter, please be seated. My husband doesn't stand upon imperial etiquette. Remember that he is an actor like us." All of them sat.

Seth turned to Hollen and began eagerly, "I had a dream a few nights ago. In this dream, I was watching a play that occurred in the future. Do you believe that is possible?"

Hollen smiled and broke a piece of bread. "Of course I do, Seth. Do I not study in the mystery schools? A dream about a future play seems

307

strange, though. Who would care?"

Seth laughed. "I would care. I am always looking for good art. And who is to say art is not important?"

"Hear, hear," Dexter muttered.

"I never said art wasn't important," Hollen defended himself with a chuckle. "But to dream of a future play seems silly."

"Of course it is, Hollen," Seth agreed and smiled. "Artists are silly. But it was a beautiful dream." Everyone at the table looked at Seth, curious. Seth looked back at his small audience and dramatically began to speak:

"Well it wasn't that interesting," he began in protest. "It was about two star-crossed lovers who died in a tragic love affair. I was sitting in the audience in some barbaric land watching the play. The acting was atrocious!"

Hollen took a sip of juice and then remarked, "I don't like tragedy."

"He doesn't like tragedy," Seth replied, turning in mock disappointment to Dexter. He looked at Ashanti and hung his head low, as if Hollen's words had stung him. She laughed.

"I bet you don't even want to know the name of this play?" Seth cunningly asked him.

"The future play you mean?" Hollen corrected him with a skeptical smile.

"Yes, of course," Seth replied. "The name of the play is ..." he paused dramatically: "*Romeo and Juliet!*" He announced the title, with arms outstretched, as if it was the greatest story ever told.

"Ro-me-o," Ashanti pronounced slowly in her soft voice. "Romeo and Juliet ... how strange," she finished. A visible chill ran through her.

"Well Seth," Hollen smiled sarcastically, "It looks like you have the greatest performance the dome has ever seen."

"Well, no, I don't," Seth feigned sadness. "Alas, I had wanted Hollen Cel Nar, cousin of the Emperor, to be Romeo and his lovely wife Ashanti to be Juliet. Yet Hollen is too busy with his mathematics … so my fate is ruined." He put his hand on his forehead in mock distress. Everyone laughed but Dexter.

"Yes, I am busy," Hollen affirmed, "and to think that my mathematics will only be remembered for thwarting your great play." He shook his head in mock dejection.

"I think your mathematics will be remembered for more than that," Dexter broke in, cutting off everyone's laughter. Even among actors, Dexter was considered radical.

"I take it you refer to the anti-gravity experiments?" Hollen challenged. "How do you know my mathematics is being used on these projects?"

Dexter smirked. "I have my sources. After all, my family actually fights the wars your cousin emperor dreams up."

"Dexter!" Seth boomed in protest and quickly stood over him. "Hollen is a guest and fellow actor, have some manners!" Everyone at the table was nervous. In late Atlantis to speak against the royal family was dangerous.

"Dexter," Hollen addressed his rival, "I am a rebellious cousin of the imperial family. Yes, the scientists use my mathematical software, but they also play your holographic dramas and attend your performances in this very dome." He motioned with his hand to the center of the vast space.

"Yes, Hollen," Dexter replied coldly. "That is why I call for this place to be shut down!"

"And that is within your rights," Hollen retorted and paused. He didn't want to appear condescending. "Perhaps ..."

Suddenly, a deep, powerful rumble interrupted him. The ground shook violently beneath the dome. *This is an earthquake*, he realized and instinctively put his arm around Ashanti. He looked up and saw crystal tile crumbling. Gasps could be heard, as people dodged the failing shards. The synthesizer that had filled the air with its wonderful music was silent.

And then, as abruptly as it had started, the shaking stopped. Actors moved toward the fallen crystal shards, clearing the mess with ionic brooms and the music began again. Earthquakes had become routine for Atlanteans in the last few months.

"A message from the scientists, I think, Hollen — No offense," Seth said in a lower tone.

Hollen laughed. "You don't actually believe the recent earthquakes are from the experiments beneath the eastern ranges, do you?"

Seth laughed nervously. Dexter smiled cruelly.

"Of course we do, darling," Ashanti declared, surprising everyone.

"Dear, that's ridiculous!" Hollen protested, hurt that his wife would take the other side.

"No, my husband, it is not," she replied firmly. "Most people in Atlantis believe what we believe, darling. I have listened to the banished scientists in this dome. They tell us what is really happening in the eastern ranges." She put her hands on her husband's hand and continued, "Remember, dear, I almost joined the scientist caste myself. I understand what they are saying."

"Ashanti, don't waste your breath," Dexter cut in. "Hollen chooses to believe the official reports on these earthquakes." He shot Hollen a condescending grin.

Ashanti glared at Dexter. "This is not about my husband but the future of Atlantis!"

"Really, I thought it was about me," Hollen protested in a menacing tone, staring back at Dexter.

Seth decided to diffuse the situation. "Ladies and gentlemen, calm down ... we have just had an earthquake. I will need to check my equipment. Dexter will you come with me?" Seth asked disappointed, as if Dexter was his truculent son.

"Hollen, it was a pleasure," Seth said as he rose, visibly shaken by the earthquake and the argument. "Please visit more often and excuse any offenses. We are only foolish actors," he apologized, shooting Dexter a look of chastisement.

"Well thank you, Seth," Hollen rose and bowed to him.

"Seth, what was the name of that play you wanted me and my husband to act in?" Ashanti asked. She bit into an apple.

"Romeo and Juliet."

"Romeo ... and Juliet," Hollen repeated aloud, slowly and dreamily. He felt a chill run through him, just as his wife had earlier.

"I still want to play Juliet even if my husband doesn't want to be Romeo," she declared playfully. She turned to her husband seductively and winked.

"Well, Seth," Hollen began. "Maybe someday I will be Romeo, but for now ... parting is such sweet sorrow," he joked, thankful Seth had put an end to his argument with Dexter.

"Good luck, Hollen," the plump holographic director said and bowed back. He quickly walked away with Dexter, no doubt scolding him for his treatment of a royal.

"My dear husband," Ashanti said taking Hollen's hand. "You create controversy wherever you go."

"Darling, we both know the controversy is that Dexter loves you."

"I know he does, Hollen. But you just swooped down from the palace of Alta and married me. It upset quite a few men, not only Dexter," she said proudly and then laughed.

"I am sure it did," he agreed with a coy smile and kissed his wife on the cheek. After lunch they strolled arm in arm, out of the Crystal Dome, to make love on the green grasses of the Gin Shawl Hills. He would never see that wonderful place again.

~

It was late now and Hollen was admiring his beautiful wife. She stood by the window of their room, bathing her hair in the rising moonlight and gazing out over the imperial gardens. The party they had returned from, he knew, had upset her. There had been powerful members of the scientist caste in attendance, sporting their genetically engineered pets. The scientists were shunned by the common people of Atlantis but were of great value to the emperor, and thus tolerated in the capital city.

The Atlantean physicists had recently been denounced by the priest-hood for their anti-gravity experiments. The High Priest of the Temple of Light himself had warned that anti-gravity technology would bring doom to the Atlantean subcontinent.

A shadow loomed over Hollen's heart as he thought of the ominous warning. He looked at his beautiful wife, Ashanti. Was it possible Atlantis, once a small outpost in a long forgotten galactic empire, would fall after a hundred thousand years? he wondered as he unbuttoned the royal sash that he had worn to the party.

His wife turned quickly toward him from the open window, reading his mind. "Your friend Adam looked very friendly with his pet monkey. Does he have a wife?" she asked sarcastically.

He sensed her anger. *I shouldn't have taken her to the party*, he realized. She made him feel as if he had dragged a beautiful flower through a puddle of mud. She was skilled at triggering the emotion of guilt, he noted.

"I'm not trying to make you feel guilty," she assured him, showing off her uncanny ability to read minds, without the formal mind training he had received. That was one reason why he loved her so. She was simply the most remarkable woman he had ever met.

"Darling Ashanti," he began, approaching his wife to appreciate her beautiful blue eyes. He took her hand in his and spoke gently into her ear. "My love for you is infinite. Do not trouble yourself with rumors of what scientists do with their monkeys. I cry your pardon for bringing you to the party."

"Apology accepted, my love," she replied with a graceful smile.

He put his hands on her delicate shoulders and massaged them. He felt fear within her body, hiding behind her shy smile. He gazed into her soft eyes. *They are more beautiful than the Atlantean sky, how could she be wrong about anything?*

"It is my love for you that makes my heart ache so," Ashanti revealed, turning from him as he continued to rub her shoulders. "You assist these scientists with your knowledge when your own teacher, the High Priest, has condemned them."

"Darling you know I spoke to the High Priest personally about this. He felt my mathematics would increase the safety of the anti-gravity experiments," he gently explained.

"He was only coddling you!" she stated coldly, surprising him. He took his hands off her shoulders.

She turned to him and went on the offense. "You always have to be the exception," she began almost resentfully, lowering her head. "After all, you are from one of the ruling families. You are wealthy, intelligent, and a good man — and that means you really don't have to follow any rules; doesn't it, Hollen?"

"How dare you bring my family into this matter?" he protested, angry and shocked. His wife had never attacked him this harshly before.

"How dare I, Hollen?" she responded. "Do you know what it is like being married to you?" she paused, as if to gain the strength for what she needed to say next.

"Everyone tells me how lucky I am to have you. 'I am so lucky', people say, 'To think, only an actress, married to a famous mathematician,'" she explained, almost bitterly. Her words stung.

"And, of course, I am lucky," she admitted, in a tone of resignation. "After all, you are a mathematician, musician, and you could be a great actor any day of the week if you wanted." Hollen detected a touch of envy in her last remark.

"What are you trying to tell me, Ashanti?" he asked. *Does my wife still love me?*

"I am trying to tell you it is hard to love a star that shines so brightly," she answered and looked down again, embarrassed by what she was going to say next.

"I sometimes think you feel the way others do, Hollen — that you married beneath yourself. I sometimes think you don't respect my opinion."

He put his palms to hers. "If you were to leave I would be nothing," he said tenderly. "You have changed me more than anyone. You are a part of me now."

She smiled softly and sat down on their bed. "Oh Hollen, I love you. Don't worry about our love. It will always be strong dear, but I am afraid, afraid for both of us!"

He sat by his wife, who now had tears in her eyes. He put his arm around her. She broke their embrace, stood, and walked toward the light by their open window.

"What are you afraid of?" he asked.

"I am afraid of what the good people of Atlantis are afraid of, of what you in the ruling families can't see. I am afraid of the anti-gravity experiments," she finished, staring out their window

Hollen stood, taken aback but not surprised. He looked into his own heart and felt the same shadow. *Is my beautiful wife right?* he wondered.

She approached him again, seizing the advantage, and began to speak: "You know I am right, darling." She took hold of his hand. "You can't see it clearly because your family benefits from the genetically engineered ape slaves who harvest our crops and fight our wars. Oh, how could you see it, dear?" Ashanti lamented, almost in pity, as she delicately put her hand on her husband's cheek.

"Darling," he protested, gently removing her hand. "What would you have me do?"

"I don't know," she said with her head lowered. "At least you could stop helping the scientists with your mathematics."

"I can't do that, dear," he complained. "Everyone would think I was crazy for petitioning the High Priest and then doing the opposite!"

"Who cares what people will think, Hollen?" she grasped his hands and looked firmly in his eyes. "You would only be coming to your senses by doing this, my husband!"

He gazed again into her sky blue eyes. They were timeless, like a lake that you could swim in forever, happy and content. *How could they ever be wrong?* he asked again and gently kissed her forehead.

"Come to bed darling," she said softly, not wanting to argue with her husband further. "Let's make love."

~

Later that night, Ashanti awoke distressed. The old moon cast an unearthly white light on the marble floor. Its shine reminded her of death for some reason. She had drifted out of her sleep with a deep foreboding she would never see her husband again.

Is it because of the anti-gravity experiments I feel this? she wondered, turning to their large window. *I can't keep bothering him,* she admonished herself.

She rolled on her side to face her husband's sleeping form. He looked so peaceful. *What if we are separated forever?* something inside her asked. *What if we are separated for more than one lifetime?*

She wanted to wake Hollen but knew how tired he was. *He has worked so hard in the last few months on his mathematics,* she realized, recalling the earthquake at the dome today.

What if Atlantis is destroyed? What if Hollen and I are cast out, never to be husband and wife again? Fears like these whirled through her mind; although, his calm form steadied her. He was strong. He would never leave her. She knew he would do anything to find her again if they became separated. She rolled on her back and looked at the ceiling. Maybe she was being silly. She recalled the summer solstice festival. Newlyweds hand in hand, they had been presented to the emperor and then to the High Priest of Atlantis.

The emperor of Atlantis had been dressed in turquoise silk and sat on a throne of gold. Ashanti had been so frightened and nervous when he smiled at her and then startled when he winked at his cousin Hollen. Her husband had then led his star-struck wife through the royal court to the High Priest of the Temple of Light, the religious leader of Atlantis. The old wizard surprised everyone in the court by leaning forward on his meditation dais and whispering into her ear:

"I agree with you. The wealth and power thing doesn't go well with Hollen."

She had been too afraid and confused to reply. His voice made her tremble and he seemed to glow gold on his dais. Her parents, a simple farming family in southern Atlantis, had taught her well. *Emperors and kings will come and go darling,* her father had once remarked, *but the High Priest is the real power of Atlantis.*

The High Priest studied her for a moment and then spoke again, this time in a clear loud voice: "Hmm ... actually, the wealth and power thing works better with you."

Now everyone, even the emperor, turned toward them. Ashanti had never been so embarrassed in her life. The High Priest lifted his right hand and made a series of mystical motions with his fingers. Ashanti felt as if her whole being was magically adjusted, her fate modified for many lives. She recalled what her father had once uttered to her long ago:

Ashanti, my child, remember this: One moment with an enlightened priest is worth more than all the jewels of the island.

She smiled, recalling the event. Hollen stirred. Now, she could sleep. *The Temple of Light will protect Atlantis*, she reassured herself, lying next to her husband. She closed her eyes and cuddled up to his sleeping form. *I want to hold him forever. I want to give him my soul … .*

~

The last sun ever to rise over Atlantis shone through the large windows. It was the last morning of the golden age of humanity. Ashanti lay curled by her husband's sleeping form, smiling in a dream. It was a clear cool day. Birds sang in fountains outside their beautiful villa and a gentle autumn breeze swept through the spacious bedroom.

Suddenly, the communication crystals on the nightstand lit up and buzzed. Hollen stirred and looked over. It was red, he noted. *Who could be calling this early?*

He put his hand on the crystal and tiredly watched the image of Quirk Terrance, the administrative adjunct to the High Priest, appear above him in three-dimensional clarity.

"Hollen, the High Priest has called a mandatory meeting immediately. He wants all of his students to gather immediately at the Mermaid Temple. Do you understand?" Quirk Terrance asked, emotionless as a computer.

"Yes, I do. Thank you," Hollen replied, still half-asleep as he flipped off the communicator. He felt Ashanti stir next to him in their bed.

"Darling, who was that?" his wife sleepily asked.

"Quirk Terrance," he replied and quickly sat up. "I have to attend a meeting with the High Priest."

She smiled and looked over at him. "I hope you tell him that you won't help the physicist's, darling. Please talk to him about it."

"Darling, I don't know why we are meeting. I can't even promise that I will speak to the High Priest, as you know." He turned to his wife and kissed her forehead.

"Hollen, I don't care about anti-gravity. I will always love you," she proclaimed sleepily.

He leaned into her graceful form. *It feels like she is saying goodbye.* He pushed the thought out of his head and kissed her tender lips then rose to dress.

"I love you also, my wife," he declared and reached for his priestly gown. "I am going to consider your wise words, my love."

"May we not touch palms once more before you run off to your mystery school, my prince?" she asked and sat up in their bed.

He finished buttoning his temple robe, walked over to her, and knelt. *What could be more beautiful in all of Atlantis than my wife?* he wondered as he put his palms to hers. He felt their energies merging, like the excited union of two cascading rivers. Regardless of what happened, he knew their love was eternal.

"Ashanti, I am grateful everyday that I found you again — in this life.

319

I must leave now," he said, withdrawing his palms from hers.

"Be safe, dear husband," she called out, not knowing why. For some reason, her eyes were watering now. "Hollen, promise you will never leave me … never in any life."

"I do promise that, my beloved," he replied and walked out their bedroom forever.

~

Students were wailing; masters were crying; wizened sorcerers of the mystery schools wandered aimlessly like little children with tears in their eyes. The High Priest stood fiercely above them all on a granite slab by the sea. The priesthood of Atlantis had seen this day coming and had prepared twelve crystal ships, only twelve. Some wept because they knew they would die. The ships had room for only a few. Many were crying, like Hollen, because they knew they would live — and witness everything they love sink below the waves.

Like a scythe ripping through autumn corn, the High Priest had read off a list of names that were to be on the twelve boats. One enlightened master would command each ship, full of the knowledge of Atlantis and the best and brightest of the island. The boats would sail in twelve directions toward the barbaric continents of Earth to preserve the knowledge of Atlantis, now about to be lost under the waves forever. The four branches of Atlantean civilization: law, science, medicine, and art would soon only exist on these twelve ships.

Hollen shed bitter tears. Just a few hours ago he had promised his wife he would never leave her. He looked longingly northwards, past the docks. Up the coast, many miles, was the Crystal Dome. *Oh, how I have been so foolish. I should have listened to the one I loved,* he grieved.

320

He had been an arrogant fool, offering advice on the very anti-gravity project that now ran wild in a recursive loop below the mountains to the east. In a few hours, critical mass would be reached and Atlantis would sink below the waves forever. Hollen bent over in pain, knowing he had helped murder his wife. Surprised, he felt a hand on his shoulder.

"Be brave, Hollen. Board your ship now." It was the voice of the High Priest, kind but stern. Hollen straightened himself.

"Go to the Nile River." His teacher gestured to the crystal ship beyond. "Preserve our mathematics and hieroglyphics. Make up for what you have done."

"I want to die with my wife," he pleaded.

"No. You will be with her again," his teacher firmly replied.

"Yes, but in what kind of world?" Hollen asked, furious the old wizard would not let him die with his wife.

"That question," the High Priest considered for a moment, "is left for the enlightened to worry about."

"Now board your ship!" the High Priest commanded in a sterner tone. "We haven't much time."

His teacher abruptly walked away. Hollen, still in tears, made for the pier. Hours later, when they all saw the majestic blue wave, he wept harder, feeling his wife leave this world, knowing he could not follow.

~

Things are serious now. Yes they are, she realized. Ashanti had come to the Dome this morning to rehearse for her upcoming play. *Things are serious now indeed.* She had been frightened when her husband received the call from the Priesthood at dawn. However, that didn't matter much anymore — the earth shook violently beneath her and people were dying.

She gazed around in shock at the once beautiful Dome. Screams filled the huge space. A portion of the majestic roof had caved in. She pivoted in fear as the ground continued to shake and buckle under her. A flying glass slab cut the dancer in half who had, just yesterday, directed Hollen to her. As the dust rose and the shaking subsided, she looked down and noticed Seth, the great holographic composer, pinned under a huge chunk of marble.

"Seth!" she exclaimed, kneeling to grasp his free hand. Her father had taught Ashanti never to panic in a crisis. *Quick, think!* she forced herself. *Dexter is around.* She held Seth's hand tighter, as Blood trickled out of his mouth.

"Ah ... Ah ... Ash ... Ashanti ... No ... save ... yourself!" he struggled through a mouthful of blood.

She knew her great acting teacher was dying. Through the corner of her eye Dexter emerged from a cloud of dust, as the bright morning sun pounded against her back. Ashanti realized there was no more great dome to house her performances.

"Dexter!" she turned, pleading. He moved beside her and knelt mindlessly. She could tell he was also trembling and in shock.

"Run!" Seth admonished them both as he gurgled blood through his mouth. He looked into her eyes. "Get out of here!"

"Oh Seth!" she cried. Nothing could be done for him. The earth began to shake harder now.

"Goodbye ... Ashanti," Seth said, struggling. Suddenly his eyes took on an ecstatic glow, as he stared up into the blue sky beyond the cracked dome.

"Ju ... Ju ..." he struggled to speak.

"What is it?" She knew he was trying to tell her something. She held his trembling hand.

"Ashanti, We must leave now!" she heard Dexter's plea, as if from a great distance.

"Ju ... Ju ... " Seth chanted again. He gasped for his last breath.

"Juliet," he exhaled, smiling contently. Then he was gone.

Juliet? I can't think of that now! her mind angrily flashed. She didn't want to panic. She let go of Seth's hand and quickly stood, wheeling toward Dexter. *He looks like a frightened child*, she angrily thought. *I wish Hollen were here. He wouldn't panic.* She noticed blood on her arm. The rumbling beneath her made it hard to stand. She looked to her feet as huge cracks crisscrossed in random directions throughout the marble floor of the dome. She noticed an impossibly large shadow developing around her.

Dexter was turned, staring at awe into the West. His eyes were wide with both fear and marvel. She turned with dread and found herself face to face with a vertical ocean, the largest wave ever seen on earth. *Like a mountain towering over the world*, she calmly thought. As she looked into that blue raging wall rushing toward her, she knew Atlantis was over. She also felt Hollen on the other side of that impossible wave, which roared with an infinitely loud sound.

"Ashanti, may I put my arm around you?" Dexter yelled, pleading like a little boy.

"Of course you can," she bravely replied. A strong gust of wind hit her hair. She was mesmerized by the thundering blue ocean above her. She could hear the sounds of all of her future lives in its majestic roar. She felt Dexter put his arm around her, just for an instant — then both were swept violently away into the future.

Romeo Transcends Juliet
and Ed Sullivan

Can I go forward when my heart is here?
Turn back, dull earth, and find thy centre out.

- Romeo

It was late summer. Two months had passed since Romeo's magical night with Juliet. He had wept on his flight home to Hawaii — not in memory of brave Atlantis — No, he finally summoned the courage to read William Shakespeare's *Romeo & Juliet*.

Oh, the pain he felt when he read the truth! Years ago, he had not only murdered Tybalt and Paris, but had essentially killed his own wife. Juliet had not been dead when Romeo turned his poison dagger on himself. She was only fast asleep at the hands of a potion administered by Friar Laurence. He had not followed his wife into death as he wished, but instead died a fool, causing Juliet to follow him instead — causing his beloved soulmate to kill herself.

Romeo now understood why Master Lee had cautioned him about reading the play. If he had read the truth after struggling through the rain forest for his life, after following Juliet through time and space, he surely would have killed himself — again. The pain would have been too great, knowing his rash suicide only encouraged the same from his wife.

Fortunately in this new world, he had loved Juliet again. She was alive and well. No use lamenting over death, for life was eternal, as was their love. He understood Emilie's painful letter now. Even if she didn't remember her short life in Italy, her soul did. He remembered what Master Lee had told him the night before he had left for New York City:

At the moment of death, she let go as one should. But you clung to her and chased her through the void.

Romeo had lost almost eight hundred years in his chase for Juliet, years he could have spent with his beloved, lifetimes they could have been born into together. By cheating death and clinging to his wife, he had only grown more distant from her. He was not of this age. He didn't belong here. He came from another time. His old life was long gone and the young woman he had once kissed on that moonlit balcony in Italy was dust in the wind.

Romeo had one more task to complete before he could leave — so he wrote and wrote and wrote until one day he was finished with his story. He was ready. Sometimes he would gaze at the mists that shrouded the great Mauna Kea volcano where he first entered this world. He felt a longing, a longing for the other worlds. It was time to go home.

~

"Shoots, Romeo, I'm going to miss you," his neighbor, Uncle Ukali remarked sadly, holding out his hand.

"I will miss you also," Romeo replied and shook the Uncle's calloused palm. He had just sold his property to the Uncle, a local pig hunter.

"Are you sure you're going up there?" Uncle Ukali asked, tilting his head toward the great volcano.

"Yes I am," Romeo replied calmly.

"Pele' lives there and her sisters, be careful bra," he advised, patting Romeo on the shoulder.

"I know. I have one favor to ask you."

"Shoots, what?"

"Could you mail this for me?" Romeo held out a manila envelope containing his manuscript. It was addressed to a book agent, Tina Mansfield, of New York City.

"Sure thing, bra," the Uncle agreed. "I'm going into town today."

"Thank you again, Uncle," Romeo said and handed him the keys to the house.

"Aloha, Â Hui Hou," Uncle Ukali waved and turned to his old beat-up pickup truck.

Romeo watched his neighbor slowly back out of the driveway. He grabbed his backpack and began to walk up the gravel path. He crossed the highway beyond his house and began to stride purposefully up the same dirt road Judy Garrity had driven him down years before. He trudged up the steep uneven path toward Master Lee's old ranch under the hot cloudless sky. It would take three days, at least, to reach the place he knew he must go.

It was almost dark when Romeo, exhausted, finally came to the end of the long dirt road. He had walked miles and climbed thousands of feet in elevation. He wandered into the overgrown fields of Master Lee's ranch and collapsed into the cool tall grass. He stood and stretched, gazing out at the vast, dark ocean horizon far below, stretching out endlessly like a desert against the evening stars. He recalled the first time he beheld the Pacific. It was still as beautiful.

Master Lee's ranch was empty. It was formally owned by the New York City Zen Center, but had fallen into disrepair. Jeff Garrity had explained to Romeo, years ago, that he simply didn't have the money to maintain the ranch and keep up with the expenses of the Zen Center.

Romeo studied the old ranch house where he had first met Master Lee. The paint was peeling. Wood was still stacked perfectly in the same spot he once had chopped wood for dinner and shelter. Weeds had grown in between the rotten logs. He noticed a broken window and considered climbing through to spend the night. *No, that wouldn't be respectful. This was the home of a Zen Master,* he reminded himself. So instead, he slept in one of the empty stables where Master Lee had kept his horses.

When the cold morning came, Romeo used the old pump by Master Lee's bedroom window to fill his canteens. There would be no dirt road today, only that ancient broken trail through the jungle he had followed downward years ago. Romeo strode through the tall Eucalyptus trees where Master Lee's horses had once trotted in the shade. Beyond the field, he could still make out the narrow path leading upward.

He walked past the line of trees, and disappeared into the rain forest. He looked back one last time at the ranch, at civilization, and turned away forever, determined. Romeo made his way uphill in the humid jungle for hours, stopping once for a small lunch. It wasn't until nightfall that he reached the beautiful waterfall he had passed when he first entered this world. There, he set up camp to the melodious sounds of cascading water. The air was thin and cold. He started a fire for warmth and nibbled on beef jerky. As the fire grew dim in the dancing wind, Romeo fell into a peaceful sleep, imagining Juliet in his arms.

At dawn, he was awakened by melodious birdsong. He packed up his camp and continued uphill. He was apprehensive, knowing the trail led to the cottage of Leheau, the Hawaiian goddess who seduced him during his first night in this world. She was a guardian of the magical doorway that he now sought. As he climbed higher, he wondered if she would let him pass.

~

It was late afternoon when Romeo, sweating and breathing hard, reached the glade by Leheau's cottage. He noticed her immediately, leaning seductively against a large tree, wearing the same immaculate white gown. She smiled as if he had only been gone days.

"Romeo, so good to see you again," she said knowingly and began to walk toward him.

"You won't need this anymore," she remarked and gently took off his pack. He tiredly sat down on a log by her cabin. "I can tell you are still afraid of me, Romeo."

"Well I am, Leheau, although I am grateful for your help. You are a goddess and I am only a man. How could I not be afraid?" he asked.

"No, Romeo, it is you that are not of this world. This is my place," Leheau smiled and motioned to the majestic trees around her. "It is I who should be afraid of you," she corrected him.

"Of me?" he asked, surprised.

"Yes. It is humanity that is most dangerous — not the gods. You kill each other in wars and destroy the land for silly trinkets. Did I not see blood on your vest when you first came into this world?" she asked rhetorically. He lowered his head and said nothing.

"Romeo?" Leheau began.

"Yes?"

"Have you noticed how ugly and gnarled the Ohia tree is, yet how beautiful are its red flowers in the spring?"

"Yes, I have," he hesitated. *Is she testing me?*

"I once loved a man as you loved Juliet," Leheau confessed and folded her hands. "We played together as lovers do, endlessly on these islands ages ago, long before your *Atlantis* existed — when Hawai'i was truly a paradise. But my sister was jealous and turned him into an ugly tree with her magic." Tears poured down Leheau's cheeks, yet she was unashamed, maybe because of who Romeo was.

"I prayed to the gods as you have done, and trust me, they cannot alter the fate of two star-crossed lovers," she painfully stated, her voice cracking. "But the gods granted me one thing — that our love would forever blossom on that ugly tree." She gestured upward to the tall grove around them, red with stunning flowers. Romeo sensed an ancient tragedy within her words that paled his suffering.

"That is why I am *Leheau* and why the Ohia tree exists," she explained. "I am sentenced to roam these magical heights forever — to see my beloved's tortured form, everywhere, as the Ohia tree. Yet when the Ohia blossoms," she paused and smiled to the high trees, "I see our love." Her body shuddered.

"Romeo," she finally uttered with her head hung low, "consider yourself lucky and know that somewhere the flower of your love will always blossom."

Romeo said nothing and gulped.

"Don't tarry here long; the sun will be up only a few more hours. The high plateau awaits you!" She advised him, her face brightening with a smile, as if she had never told her tragic tale. The ancient goddess rose and proudly flung her long white hair backward.

"So you will let me pass? You will let me leave this world?" he asked. Leheau laughed heartily to the sky. The laugh didn't seem as threatening in the daylight as it had on that first dark night when Romeo had met her.

"You were never of this world," she corrected him. "You are a shadow from another age, a ghost that traveled through time for love. How could I let you leave, since you never were here?" she smiled cleverly.

"Hurry now, Romeo, you haven't much time," Leheau advised. She gestured with a motion to the rain forest rising steeply beyond her.

"Thank you," he replied tiredly. He stood and bowed to the Hawaiian goddess. She laughed at the gesture, making him feel like a small awkward boy. He turned uphill, toward the great volcano.

"Oh, Romeo!" Leheau dramatically called back to him, as he entered the thick foliage. "Don't forget to say hello to that *lolo* Zen Master of yours!"

He turned to say something, but Leheau had already vanished.

~

Romeo carefully made his way through the dense jungle, the same forest he had struggled through during his first night in this world. Now the ferns and glades were not ominous shadows, but radiated calmness and serenity as the low tropical sun bathed them in a golden light. There was no trail to follow — all he had to do was climb past the tree line.

The sky was a beautiful orange when Romeo reached the edge of the great rain forest. Beyond the ferns he saw the barren windswept volcanic plateau he had awoken on, years ago. He had tears in his eyes, as he walked past the last gnarled trees and onto the volcanic plain. His body told him it was time to leave this world forever.

The wind picked up and it grew cold, as it had years ago. Those same indifferent gusts that had once greeted him, now caressed his hair and whispered to him of endless journeys, as if Romeo had been gone only moments. He grew worried. He had left his backpack at Leheau's cottage. *What if I can't find the doorway? What if I am stuck here?*

"You are stuck in time," a voice calmly answered to his right. Romeo turned, startled. It was Master Lee, smiling at him.

"Desire creates time," his teacher explained cryptically, walking up to him. Romeo bowed low.

"Why are there tears in your eyes, Romeo?" Master Lee asked.

"The world," he explained and looked up to the beautiful orange-red clouds floating above him. "I will miss it. I wish you had stayed Master Lee — to help me with her. I made so many mistakes."

"I once tried to help you both," he confessed. "But things just didn't work out." he shrugged and smiled, almost apologetically. The Zen Master's form began to shift and shimmer. Romeo beheld the face of the High Priest of Atlantis, of Egypt, and then, finally, Friar Laurence from Verona.

"You're Friar Laurence!"

"Yes, that's why I decided not to get involved this time. I made a mess of things in Verona, didn't I?" he smiled sheepishly. "I was trying to make up for Egypt."

332

"So what happens now?" Romeo asked, feeling an exciting journey ahead of him. His body tingled.

"We walk forward. That is all anyone can do in this vast creation."

So Romeo and his Zen Master did walk forward across that cold high Hawaiian plateau. Their silhouettes wavered in the sunset and then dissolved into that eternal wind which blows endlessly between the worlds and dimensions. And if you believe in time, Romeo and his teacher left this dark world forever. But if you believe in love, Romeo never left his Juliet — his heart is still with her and will be forever.

Emilie and Juliet

Therefore love moderately; long love doth so;
Too swift arrives as tardy as too slow.

- Friar Laurence

The old woman tried to sit straight in her wheelchair as the well-dressed butler carefully rolled her across the cold marble floor. Emma Gallant, although sick and feeling very weak, had agreed to let her great nephew interview her today. He was an aspiring journalist, according to his mother, Rosaline. The last time she had seen her great nephew, he had been four.

That was back in 2061, she recalled, her butler, Raymond, wheeling her ever closer toward the lanky young man that stood nervously by the huge entrance doors of her mansion. He wore a shining white suit and held his hat low in respect for his great aunt, the movie legend.

2061, the year my dear husband Paris became sick. There were shortages that year. It was so hard to get him medicine, she remembered sadly. That was also the year Raymond began his employment. Her butler had really saved them both, waiting in long ration lines, fighting through food riots, and purchasing medicine on the black market. He had been a godsend when dear Paris fell ill. She felt weak and dizzy in her chair. She tried to straighten her posture to make a good impression as she wheeled closer to her great nephew. After all, Emma Gallant was never one to slouch. *I try never to do anything unladylike.* She had typed that long ago to a mysterious man on the Internet named Romeo. Romeo was to be the topic of conversation today, although her great nephew didn't know it — nor did her butler.

Raymond carefully parked her chair by the arched entrance of the mansion. She could feel the warm sunshine on her knee, streaming through the open doorway.

"Dear Aunt Emilie," Andrew greeted her kindly and bent to shake her hand. "So good to meet you. I hope I'm not disturbing you."

She smiled shyly. *My great nephew is gay,* she realized. Emilie's intuition seemed to grow stronger with age. *I wonder if Paris would approve,* she asked herself. *Probably not,* she guessed with a smirk.

"Andrew Beauregard," she remarked in her still beautiful voice, "we've met before. I saw you last throwing cake at a party when you were this small." She made a dramatic hand motion to the floor and grimaced. God, her arthritis hurt today. She looked the young lad over sternly. Emilie loved children, then reminded herself Andrew was twenty and not a child.

"I don't remember that, Ma'am. I can assure you it wasn't intentional." He smiled meekly at his famous aunt.

He rather reminds me of a gay Paris, Emilie thought playfully, while painfully wheeling her chair into the main receiving room of the mansion. After all, she didn't want her great nephew to remember Raymond pushing her around!

Emilie decided she liked Andrew. Her intuition had been correct. He was the right person to tell the story she had needed to tell for so long. It was time to tell her tale — for soon, it would be too late.

As they entered the spacious reception room, she shot a glance toward the huge cedar bookcase above the fireplace. She had memorized where the novel was. It was slightly to the left and above the now vigorous fire that kept the spacious room somewhat warm.

"Do sit down." She weakly motioned to the antique sofa that kings and noblemen had once sat on in Versailles. It had cost her three million euros in 2020. Today she was glad to have it. Her butler stiffly poured Andrew tea. She watched as Andrew sat awkwardly on the old dusty couch, awestruck by his great aunt, the Hollywood legend.

"So how is Rosaline?" she asked to break the ice. She wanted him to be comfortable. After all, he needed to comprehend what she was about to tell him.

"Mother is fine," he replied. "She still assists the refugees from Los Angeles. I keep trying to convince her to return to London, but she refuses." He lifted the china teacup to his lips.

Rosaline is like me, Emilie proudly reflected — her life had been one of charity also. She had traveled Africa, Asia, and Latin America giving millions to the poor children of the world, and later, hundreds of millions through the *Emma Gallant Foundation,* after the nuclear war had wreaked its havoc on the old civilization.

Emilie recalled the beautiful poetry, written long ago, in a different world, by her mysterious lover, Romeo:

> *Far from the wars my love,*
> *I will hold you in my arms.*
> *I will enfold you in these western jungles,*
> *And we will hold together and witness,*
> *The end of this age.*

And now I tell all, she nervously realized. She noticed Andrew was fidgeting with his teacup. He looked so adorable to her — it would make the telling of her tale easier.

"So, Andrew, why are you here?" she wanted to test him first.

"Well, of course I want to visit, since you are my great aunt," he replied endearingly.

Emilie looked at him sternly and tipped her spectacles down in the way Johnny Perfection used to do. She wanted Andrew to know she was too old for any bullshit. He got the message and continued nervously.

"Well, Aunt Emilie, I came across an old interview in Playboy by the actor Johnny Perfection. He claims the novel *Romeo and Juliet* is about an affair you had with him!" he remarked incredulously, then looked down, embarrassed.

"Well, of course, I know all about the article in Playboy. It made my husband very angry at the time," she casually began. "As you know, my agency denied both the affair and John's absurd claim about the novel *Romeo and Juliet*," she finished out of breath, yet managed to shoot him a cunning smile. She did miss acting — this was going to be fun.

"Yes, Aunt Emilie. I would never doubt your honesty. Of course, I can't imagine you, at the tender age of eighteen, having an affair with that legendary cad Johnny Perfection! He had a reputation, as I am sure you know."

"Yes, he did," she smiled mischievously, recalling how wild and exciting sex had been with John that first night above the Champs Elysee in his beautiful suite. The world seemed so perfect then and she had been so naive. *The affair was so silly*, she reflected, straightening her plaid dress in a dignified manner.

"Andrew, get your laser-pad out," she commanded daringly. "I've decided to tell the truth today. Who did you say you wrote for?"

"My college newspaper, Cambridge," he said, almost in defense. He fumbled for a laser pen in his backpack.

"Andrew are you nervous because I am famous or is this just how you are?" she asked. "I actually find it quite adorable."

"A little bit of both, Aunt Emilie," he stuttered. "I admit I am nervous because of who you are. I've always loved your movies and my friends adore your films too. We recently purchased an antique DVD system just to see them!" he proudly bragged.

"Well, Andrew, don't be nervous, please. I need you to pay attention to what I am about to say. Do you want the scoop or not?" she asked playfully, then coughed.

"Yes I do, Aunt Emilie." he finally answered.

"Andrew, I want you to know my first lover was indeed Johnny Perfection. He was telling the truth and the Capulet Agency was lying on my behalf." she dramatically paused after dropping the bombshell. Andrew began to write nervously with his head bent over his laser-pad.

"I look back on those days and find them clichéd and silly," she remarked and lowered her head.

"Aunt Emilie!" Andrew protested, "You're a Hollywood legend! I think everyone would want to hear about your affair. It would make a great article." He put on an endearing smile for the old matriarch of his family.

Emilie laughed weakly, causing her stomach to knot in pain. She reminded herself not to laugh anymore and instead feigned a smile in Andrew's direction and became dizzy.

"Andrew," she corrected him, "a young actress being seduced by an older married actor is hardly news. I find it silly, as I said before. I was naive and totally unaware of the dark side of Hollywood." She smiled and recalled what a man named Romeo had proclaimed to her ages ago:

I want to protect you from the negative energies of Hollywood.

Andrew looked dumbfounded at his great aunt and buried his head again, writing quickly with his laser pen.

"Andrew, I didn't invite you here to talk about my affair with Johnny Perfection. I wanted to speak to you about *Romeo and Juliet*." A chill went through her, as she uttered the two timeless names.

He looked up, "Oh yes, the novel." He fumbled through his college backpack and brought out a plastic laser-book undoubtedly loaded with *Romeo and Juliet* in flash memory.

"God, those laser books are so hideous," she remarked and unconsciously glanced toward the hardcover above her fireplace. "I preferred the original artwork of the first edition," she remarked dreamily, still turned from Andrew, gazing at Romeo's novel on her bookshelf. She had paid a thousand euros for the book almost fifteen years ago. Even though she had bought it after Paris' death, Emilie had felt guilty and had paid for it in cash, so no one could trace the purchase.

Andrew shot a glance toward the fireplace, probably wondering why his old Aunt Emilie was staring at a wall. She turned to him mindlessly and continued:

"I want to speak to you about *Romeo and Juliet* today, Andrew." she lowered her head and folded her hands. "John was telling the truth about that also," she confessed.

Emilie looked at her wrinkled soft hands. She felt embarrassed, like a teenager confessing a secret lover. Yet telling the truth about Romeo felt liberating.

"That's extraordinary!" Andrew exclaimed, popping his head up like an awkward bird then down again to take notes.

It was ironic, she realized, Romeo's mysterious tale had grown in popularity over the decades; whereas her old movies seemed to fade into the past. The new holographic videos were now the craze. *Flat screen movies* had long since gone the route of silent films.

"I must confess, Aunt Emilie, I read the novel when I was a teenager," Andrew started tentatively. "I couldn't help but think it was about you. But mother told me it wasn't!"

"Well, Andrew, you are very intuitive; it was about me. Of course, the novel wasn't accurate. Romeo and I … we never actually knew each other that well." She lowered her head and recalled that magical night at the Waldorf. They had indeed known each other very well. She could still feel his tender touch, his thick hair, and how it felt to be loved by a man who loved her infinitely. That one night had transformed her forever. Tears formed in her eyes.

She continued, "You see, Andrew, my affair with Johnny Perfection was silly; of course, he broke my heart. I needed someone after that. Both your great Uncle Paris and Romeo were there for me."

"I think I understand," Andrew said tenderly.

"Well," she started again in a deep voice, hoping to regain her composure, "You don't seem to be a very good reporter, young Andrew. I would think you had questions prepared for me. I'm not going to spoon-feed you the story!" She reached for a nearby tissue and dabbed her eyes.

"I ... I ... don't know where to start, Aunt Emilie. It seems your affair with Johnny Perfection and your revelation about the novel are two separate stories," he remarked, genuinely perplexed.

"There is only one story here, dear Andrew. I didn't invite you for tea so you could find out your great aunt fucked an alcoholic actor seventy-five years ago. I want to discuss Romeo and Juliet!"

"I ... I'm amazed no one found out about you and Johnny Perfection," Andrew muttered to himself aloud, embarrassed his old great aunt had used the word *fuck*.

Emilie laughed. "Well my dear great nephew, many people did find out. Most of my close friends knew, and of course Paris knew about John and found out soon enough that *Romeo and Juliet* was about me."

Emilie suddenly recalled that ancient picture of Romeo by the beach in Hawaii. God, she hadn't used a keyboard in ages. He had looked wonderfully tan in that photograph, and even more so on that moonlit night at the Waldorf.

She glanced down at her spotted hands and continued to speak. "Of course, Romeo changed everyone's name in the novel; but I was still furious with him at the time," she admitted.

"Later, when John bragged of our affair to Playboy, the Capulet Agency denied it ever happened. But anyone who understood how Hollywood worked, realized he was telling the truth. No one cared about his obsession with an obscure new-age romance novel — the big news was our alleged affair."

She paused to catch her breath and forced a smile. She continued again slowly. "After all, Andrew, your great aunt had already won her first

Oscar playing *Estella* when the article came out. I think that's why John told everyone. He became jealous of me as the years went by."

"Well, Aunt Emilie, I can't say I blame him; after all, you have won three Oscars."

She smiled knowingly, recalling the words Romeo had typed to a lonely young woman on a cold January night in New York City years ago, in a world that was no more:

I think you are destined to win three Oscars.

Why do you say that?

Because I meditate, dear. Your aura is so strong and you are far more beautiful and intelligent than any actress I have seen.

A single tear dropped from her eye. Andrew was scrolling through his notes, oblivious. He finally looked up at her and spoke.

"That's amazing, Aunt Emilie! You actually knew the author of *Romeo and Juliet*. No one ever found out who he really was."

"Yes I know," she agreed, with a touch of sadness. "The original publisher of the novel said that the manuscript was received by mail from Hawaii, only with instructions to send all royalties to a small Zen center in New York City." She instinctively turned toward the dining room where her butler Raymond waited.

"Aunt Emilie," Andrew said with pride. "This story of yours is of genuine academic value. Did you ever meet the author in person?"

"Yes I did, once," she confessed.

Emilie lowered her head, ashamed she had betrayed her future husband that night. Worse yet, for years she regretted not running away with Romeo. Lately though, she had come to realize it had been for the best. Their love had been so strong and so out of control and that type of love usually ends in tragedy. *Any Shakespearean actress could tell you that*, she joked to herself, smiling weakly. She had made the right choice years ago, by staying with Paris. But right choices, she now understood, were sometimes the most painful parts of life.

"In a perfect world, Andrew, I would've been with Romeo," she suddenly blurted out, surprising even herself. The tears were flowing now. She was old; it was time to let loose. She thought of how much that remark would have hurt her husband and felt ashamed.

"Why do you say that?" Andrew asked, glued to his aunt's every word, mindlessly sipping tea.

"God, I don't know why," she answered and then lowered her head to her hands and cried soft tears. She was grateful the tears came slowly. Her stomach hurt so. She didn't want to cry or laugh much more today. *The cancer must be spreading*, she realized.

Andrew sprung up and put his hand on his legendary aunt's shoulder. She felt frail to him, as if her brittle frame would blow away with the next autumn storm.

Emilie straightened dramatically. "Andrew, sit down." she command-ed. "I don't want my great nephew to remember me this way." She reached for a tissue.

"I loved your great uncle very much," she began. "But there was something between me and this man Romeo that was magical. It was a fantastic feeling, not practical, of course." She smiled painfully as her stomach knotted. "Being with him felt ancient and timeless."

"Aunt Emilie, I'm sorry if I've upset you. I don't need to write the article!" Andrew dutifully exclaimed. He leaned forward and held one of her soft trembling hands.

"It's all right. I'm just another old woman thinking about what could have been," she mindlessly straightened out her dress in the wheelchair again. She hadn't cried this hard since they had honored her at the Oscars when she was eighty years old.

"You see, my dear great nephew," she bravely started. "What you need to learn from this is that even Emma Gallant, the film legend, has regrets. Don't take this the wrong way. I was lucky to marry your great uncle. Yet in everyone's life there is that magical love that could have been. Do you understand?" she broke off and looked dreamily at the special book above her fireplace.

"I think so," Andrew answered with empathy.

"Do you have any other questions?" she asked, turning to him again. He was evidently shaken by her story. Romeo always had that affect on people she remembered, smiling knowingly.

~

Emma Gallant and her great nephew, the aspiring journalist, spoke for another ten minutes. Her butler now stood beside her chair. She knew Raymond didn't want her to have any long visits. She had heard her doctor speaking in low tones to him the other day. Did they both think she was stupid? Emilie knew she was dying.

Raymond, dressed in an impeccable black suit, politely reminded her it was time for her nap. Andrew rose, promising he would visit again and thanked his great aunt profusely for sharing her story.

Emilie let Raymond wheel her to the huge entrance of her mansion to see Andrew out. Telling her story to Andrew had exhausted her. The afternoon sky was white and bright as it glistened above the expansive front gardens. She squinted and asked Andrew if he was going to run with the scoop she had given him.

"I don't know, Aunt Emilie. I don't think the Beauregard line of our family will take it well," he replied with true consternation.

Aunt Emilie smiled. "Well your great uncle Paris, God rest his soul, didn't take it well either. It's your decision, Andrew." She nodded to him.

She watched her chauffeur escort Andrew to the classic 2025 Bentley that Paris had bought years ago. Her great nephew waved a final goodbye and then ducked into the glossy black vehicle. Emilie sat in her chair and watched the rounded automobile speed down her tree-lined driveway. Her part of the story now rode with Andrew. Emilie could relax.

~

Raymond slowly and carefully wheeled Emilie back to the main receiving room. The fireplace still roared. She reminded herself that Raymond was over seventy. Was it her imagination, or was he moving more slowly these days?

"Ms. Gallant, where would you like to have your nap?"

"Will you please call me Emilie, Raymond?" she asked, exasperated. He always refused to use her first name!

"Yes, Emilie, where would you like to have your nap?"

"In here, Raymond. I want to rest by the warm fire."

"Yes, Madam."

Why can't he call me by my name! her mind protested. *Does he do this on purpose?* He never called her Emilie — unless ordered to!

"Would you like more tea, Madam?" he asked.

346

He must be playing with me! Why doesn't he call me Emilie? she wondered again, nodding for him to fill her cup.

Raymond, unperturbed as usual, slowly poured the hot tea. She looked over at the novel again. Finally telling her story had given her the courage to ask her butler the one question she had been afraid to ask him since he started employment long ago:

"Raymond, didn't your father run a Zen center in New York City?" she inquired quickly, trembling as she lifted her teacup.

"Yes he did, Madam. I think we spoke of that during my job interview," he answered softly and then retreated to the door of the dining room.

"I know, Raymond ... that is why I hired you," she clearly said, making sure he heard her words. She calmly waited for his answer. It felt so good to be able to speak the truth — finally.

Raymond turned by the door and looked with admiration at Emilie.

"I know that also ... *Juliet.*"

~

Ray Garrity, son of Jeff and Judy Garrity, gently closed the dining room doors. Now he was the butler of the great film legend Emma Gallant; long ago, he had been the son of a Zen Roshi and his beautiful wife. His father had run a small Zen Center in New York City, which had come into millions of dollars from the royalties of a mysterious romance novel.

He sat at Emilie's huge mahogany dining table and recalled the tale his father told him as a boy of twelve while they fished the Adirondacks. The story was of a beautiful actress, a very important letter, and a march to the

Waldorf Hotel for a mysterious Zen monk named Romeo. Raymond sipped some tea, and could still hear his dad's voice above that shiny deep blue lake they had fished so long ago:

We take care of our own son, Zen Buddhists, his father had proudly explained. *After the Waldorf, I felt like a hero. I made love to your mother that night and we had you.* His dad patted him on the shoulder and winked. Young Raymond realized he was now part of a mysterious story, a family secret.

Emilie's coughing broke him out of his reverie. He could hear it clearly through the dining room doors. That is why Ray spent so much time near her, watching over her. She was sick, very sick. *Tomorrow,* he promised himself, *I will call the doctor ... Juliet is dying.*

~

Emilie's smile stretched larger than she could ever remember when her butler called her *Juliet.* And what was her true name, if not that? He had quickly retreated into the dining room after his confession. She realized, with quiet joy, Raymond Garrity had known all along about her and Romeo.

Emilie knew she had one last thing to do. She had finally told her story, now she had to let Romeo tell his. She glanced over at the fireplace, to the dusty novel resting above the mantle and gently smiled. She was old now — it was time. She rolled her wheelchair slowly toward the tall bookshelf.

Emilie had never been able to read Romeo's story. She remembered throwing his book against the wall and screaming when her friend Sarah had first shown it to her, years ago. She had been furious with Romeo at the time. Later in life, she tried to read his tale, but seeing his words made her tear up each time. It was simply too painful.

Now it was time. She parked her wheelchair by the roaring fireplace and looked up at the book. She was going to read Romeo's words and nothing was going to stop her. She would finally accept the gift he had left for her so long ago. She stretched painfully from her chair and clutched the spine, as her hands shook with anticipation.

Emilie, you're not going to cry now! she admonished the girl still within her. She straightened her posture and rested Romeo's faded novel in her lap, then proceeded to wheel herself back toward the mahogany end table by her Versailles sofa and reached for her reading glasses.

As Emilie opened the book, she realized there had never been a reason to be afraid. If she had to, she would laugh. Emilie knew she was going to make it through the story this time. She was finally going to be with her Romeo. After all these years, she was coming home. Emilie was Juliet, again, now and forever. Her trembling hands slowly turned the first pages and Juliet read the words of her beloved Romeo:

I awoke curled in a vast cold desert with harsh gusting winds dancing around me — and all I loved was Juliet ... .

The End.